Blood [illegible]

Chronicles of the Hunter

Created by J.A Bullen and KcLynne

Written by J.A. Bullen

Other works by J.A. Bullen

The Legends of Valoria Series

The Last Paladin of Highmoore: Enhanced

Rise of the Divine Knight

Coming soon...

The Legends of Valoria: The Shield of Aneira

Printed in the United States of America

First Printing, 2017

ISBN 978-1546523734

www.jabullen.com

I wish to give thanks to my Beta Readers, who continue to put up with my late night questions. I do not know as though I could have finished this, without your encouragement. This is a large step outside of what I have ever done.

To Juliet and Joe,

Thank you from the bottom of my heart, for your support. I deeply appreciate you both.

J. A. Bullen

I would like to thank Kristian and Ash, my keepers. May you always keep my heart safe, for it is with you two that it has been solely entrusted.

Table of Contents

Table of Contents cont.

Prologue

In six days, God made the world, and man, to walk upon it. On the seventh day, as God slumbered, creation rested within the clutches of evil. On this seventh day, the supernatural world was born, ripe with terrors, which mirrored the creations of God.

Too late to intervene, humankind was left defenseless, until thirteen angels, descended upon man. These angels, each selected a single disciple to create Hunter clans, and tasked them in God's name, to wage war against that which defied God's creation. The thirteen clans, for millennia, defended our world, until one day, when the threat of the darkness was to consume our world, no one was left to answer the call to arms. That day was known as 'The Fall'. Something else from that damned day was created, something too appauling for God and too terrible for the Devil, was born.

With a snap of a finger, man went from apex predator to cattle. Just as cattle, most humans are oblivious that they are raised for slaughter. To those that are aware, The Fall doesn't only refer to one specific day. Two hundred years ago, the last hunter's clan fell. In those days mankind's faith, their culture and all hope of escaping the eternal darkness, started to dwindle. Demons, monsters and unholy nightmare creatures began to crawl out of the shadows and dance in the sunlight of the human world.

These once believed 'imaginary terrors' raised themselves center stage integrating with our society. With the passing of time, and the advancement of civilization, the means of the sources of our terror, evolved. With the advent of politics, came elected officials, who served as thralls or slaves to the world of the supernatural. They were quickly swayed from their civil duty, by promises of longevity, wealth and influence. With manipulated lawmakers, creating an influx of power, the balance quickly shifted in favor of the immortal terrors, and life continued on.

Those few left who had fought against the forces of evil in secret became the target and the vengeance sought out upon them was swift, brutal and merciless.

It is now the year, two thousand twenty Anno Domini. Terror permeates the air and there is only one creature left that can bring fear and the scent of death to those who would use it against the humans. After centuries, the unknown masterminds behind The Fall, are still dormant. With the right players in the correct positions, the stakes are high for the masked architects of the world and the battle for humanity. A flicker of hope remains for those humans, which still exist as such. These are the chronicles, of the one immortal, which remains to defend God's creatures.

He is simply known as, The Hunter.

Chapter 1 – I am The Hunter

Panicked screams filled the blackened streets beneath the brilliant shine of the full moon. Six frightened persons ran in frenzied flight at the devilish beast that stalked them. Each has a mark upon their cheek with a moon tattoo with claw struck through it, a sign that each is owned by the werewolves.

The beast in pursuit of them could be heard from behind, roaring in rage, as it jumped from building to building, one bound closer every minute. One of the men looked back and vanished into the night. A blood-curdling scream, announced his departure, followed by the vomit inducing sound of teeth crunching through bone, confirmed to the group they now numbered five. Among the survivors, one man shed a tear, kinsmen to the recently deceased as he saw blood and limbs sprayed across two buildings.

The rest of the group kept running as the beast devoured the remains of their lost friend. As they ran, they heard the chewing echo down the alleyway. As a mob, they screamed in terror as they fled, after a single breath, again hearing the beast pursuing them.

Their lungs gasped for air, their legs cramped and giving out on them, they turned a corner and hid for a moment to catch their breath. Their hands lay on their knees, as they quickly caught their breath. Each shed an article of clothing in an attempt to throw off their pursuer. The men and women quickly removed their jackets, tossing them down the street before they ran in the opposite direction.

They neared the end of the next alleyway, before they heard the sounds of their pursuer. They had desperately hoped to have bought more time. The sound of the beast grew nearer as they come to realize, beyond a doubt, it was back on their scent. They ran for a few more minutes darting down no specific path to evade their pursuant.

Their leader motioned for them to duck for cover within a crevice too small for the werewolf to enter. Beneath the veil of shadow, he signaled for them to do their best to control their breathing. They each placed their bodies together, covering their hearts and one another's mouths to keep them perfectly silent. They sat still as statues for what seemed to last forever before they heard the monster.

They could make out its shadow pitched against the wall as if some phantom silhouette were stalking them. A moment passed and the dancing black shade vanished from sight. They listened closely as the sound of the monster trailed off into the distance.

They wait in silence. Their breathing slowed, their hearts began to normalize in pace.

They rose, as it was too late to run and a large clawed paw, the size of a catcher's mitt swooped down from above them, raking across the torso of one of the women, leaving only four suited to run. Three of the survivors took off running, while the youngest among them, a boy in his late teenage years, stayed behind to aid the injured woman.

First, the boy removed his over-shirt, wrapping it around the woman's torso and used his belt, to tighten it around her. Ever so gently, yet urgently, he helped lift her to her feet and placed his shoulder beneath her for support. They managed a few steps down the alley before she collapsed and blood seeped through her clothing.

The woman looked to the young boy and with a simple yet unmistakable message, shook her head, lightly pushed him away as she sat down to clutch her side. Their eyes met, she nodded her head again and as instructed, the boy ran to save his life. He sped off to rejoin the cowardly group within a brief moment of shock and panic.

The remaining thralls turned a corner in search of cover, somewhere to hide their scent from the bloodthirsty predator. The punishment for a thrall abandoning his master was a brutal death. The alleyway was poorly lit, water poured from atop the easels and rooftops.

Garbage littered the streets, a potentially perfect hideaway. The four of them stop, each doing their best to place their backs to a separate dumpster, assuming better two escape if one is found, then all of them slain in one stroke. They sat there in silence for what seemed to be hours, but in reality, was minutes.

In the distance, they heard the monster searching for them. Down the opposite side of the alleyway, they heard as another creature approached. Their hearts froze in their chest, as they realized there would be no escape for any of them now. If one was found the others would also die.

A deep, malicious growl pierced the silent air, one of the men hear it from behind, falling to the ground, as the dumpster flew across the alleyway. The man let out a scream before he was bitten into by the beast, and lifted into the air by the fangs in his ribs. The other wolf howls victoriously, summoning the other pack members to feast on the kill. The man watched through clouded vision, as his blood poured out onto the street, droplets of red rain decorating the face of the woman who had given them away. He looked down to his ruined torso as a jagged silver spear bursts through the werewolf's chest.

The man groaned as he fell to the ground, trying to stay conscious, and watched on in horror, as the massive werewolf once standing over seven feet tall, was dragged away into the engulfing darkness. Its nails tore away the flesh of the concrete jungle's floor, as it vanished from sight. The other werewolf reared its head and howled out another deep bellowing tone, different from before. This time the beast emits the call of panic. The dying man coughed, blood spattering the ground next to him, as the head of the beast who murdered him lands only a few feet away. His eyes strained to see what could possibly kill a werewolf and caught only a glimpse, as something shot past him.

Tall leather boots, trailed by a flowing leather trench coat, topped with a black hat, was all that he saw. He could hear the whistling melody of metal cutting through the air and the howling of the one receiving the blows. Dying, the man turned his head and watched the ensuing chaos, as the bloodied werewolf continuously lunged at the man in black. Each time the man in black dodged off to the side, a brief glimmer of brilliant light, flashed in the air, blinding the surveyor as he watched. The two tiptoe around one another attacking back and forth for a moment, when he hears a loud thud followed by an enraged wail, another of the pack had arrived.

Although his vision was blurred and his head pounded terribly, the faint light provided by the street lamps dimly lit the alleyway, he swore that he could see the black robed man smiling. A slight silhouette of the man's face shown in the moonlight, icy blue eyes with dark hair, a handsome face and matching frame, any woman could lust for. As the new arrival prepared to lunge, the black robed man spun around his bloodied foe and with a quick fleeting gleam, a spray of blood coated the brick walls. The wolf howled in pain as it collapsed upon its severed limb. A first glance of the man's weapon was given as one of two massive heads, of a double bladed crescent axe, smashed down upon the skull as if it were a jack o lantern.

For a brief moment, the fighting ceased as the hunters stared at one another, the larger of the two coming to terms with its likely demise. After a moment, the blood covered, unconscious woman came to and rose to her feet. The dying turned from her and watched on, as off to his right sprang the other thralls. The young man, kneeling beside him, began his attempt to impede the bleeding, while the others watch on in awe.

His nostrils were filled with the stench of bloody gore and fermented garbage. As he lie there, desperately clinging to life, he could not help but let out a brief smile as the last of the men in his group, the young boy, bent in half and vomited profusely. As the scent of bile began to add to the collective, another thrall contributed their own fragrances to the already pungent aroma.

Turning his attention back to the fight, he watched as the werewolf gripped the dumpster, tightly crouched down and lunged high into the air. The werewolf's body rose up above the man, digging its claws into the building's side and bounded back and forth, around the man who merely stood his ground. Hidden beneath his coat and the brim of his hat, he remained, seemingly uncaring of the wolf circling him.

The creature stopped its lunging for just a brief moment, long enough to line up its next attack and for the mysterious man to notice. As the wolf lunged, the man whipped around silently, flinging a long silver chain up into the air, piercing the beast in the chest. The man, using all of his weight and inhuman strength, pulled the beast to the ground where it landed on its head, cracking the pavement. It twitched and convulsed for several moments. The man approached his fallen adversary and with one quick, nimble twist shattered the werewolf's neck and spine.

"Thank you, sir." The bleeding man called out but all he heard were the sounds of the man's boots striking at the ground as he walked away, disappearing into the darkness from whence he came. The newly freed thralls stood in a circle examining the scene. Blood dripped from every conceivable surface and covered everyone. The stench of bile, wet hound and entrails mixed with the garbage and fuming manholes, causing everyone to vomit once more.

The blood soaked woman looking around to the remaining thralls, turned her head toward the darkness the man vanished into. Taking another moment to observe, she surveyed her surroundings and scoffs.

"It's not so bad. I've been through and seen worse." She turned and saw her remaining compatriots and then she herself sprayed excrement on and in front of herself. Between their separate pauses, two of the others looked to her and laughed.

"If it's not so bad, why are you vomiting, then?"

"It's your fault! If you two weren't barfing I would be just fine right now." She continued to yell at the other two when she heard a growling from behind her. Slowly she turned and her eyes met those of another massive wolf. Slowly, the woman backed away from the beast, as it bore into her with its evil green eyes.

She continued to shuffle backwards, until her hands touched the still gore covered wall that was opposite of her. The beast approached her until it was within range of her, so that she could smell its breath. Steaming, warm saliva dripped from its bared fangs, causing her to feel a strong urge rising from her stomach and she barfed yet again. The beast snarled as its fur was covered in the filth and raked its claws against the brick, peeling it away.

"Just in time!" The werewolf turned its head too late, as it was propelled backwards just off to the side of the woman who cowered and then crawled away from the thrashing monster. As her eyes reached up the creature's body, she saw a long two foot stake sticking out of its shoulder. She heard a loud thudding sound, as if a large amount of gas were escaping suddenly and another stake pierced the opposite shoulder. The beast screamed again, trying its best to reach for the metallic pins holding it to the wall. Two more shots fired, this time into each of the creature's legs, followed by the clanking of a weapon, dropping to the ground. The man in black resurfaced from the shadows and approached his helpless prey.

"I'm going to be very clear with you. This is how this is going to happen. I AM going to torture you but know this, your friends that held back waiting for me, are already dead. There is no one coming to rescue you, so I have all night to play operation, however you will find me to be merciful. I am going to ask you a series of questions and for every one you get right, I will let you keep a piece of yourself attached. Answer all of my questions and you get to go back to your master. Now, first question, where is the den?" He asked as he pulled a long knife and placed it by the monster's ear. The werewolf snarled and smiling, the man in black removed said ear. The beast howled in pain as it pulled against its restraints in an attempt to grasp the side of its skull.

"Wrong answer! Where is the den!?" In a voice too deep and dark to be human, the hellish creature boomed back at his captor.

"Your blood shall run through these streets once my brothers find you. It will take you weeks to die..." He was cut off, by the pain of having his other ear removed.

"I would be more concerned about how you are about to die, if I were you."

"Does it matter? Either way I am already dead. Whether I meet my end by you, or the pack makes little difference to me, son of Grey." The man stopped for a moment, grinding his teeth angrily and clenching his fists so tightly, the bones popped at the very mention of the name.

"Well that's a shame." The Hunter responded a bit disappointed as he slipped his hand into his pocket and brought it back out, massive metal rings covering his knuckles. "But at least we can have some fun." He spoke again with an excited maliciousness as he began beating the beast in the face, the first strike clearly shattering the bones in its snout. The wolf cried something terrible, in tongues both human and inhuman. Had the thralls not nearly been murdered, they would have shown sympathy.

They watched on in horror as the brass rings were exchanged for various other instruments as the man worked methodically from fingers and toes to femurs, patellae and tibias.

After nearly an hour of ceaseless, uninterrupted brutality, the wolf lacking an unbroken bone to support him, hung from the wall, nearly lifeless, blood pouring from it, staining its fur. The beast whimpered pitifully through its mangled features, convulsing and twitching, having sustained such immense amounts of pain.

"Kill me." It begged the man. "Kill me. Show mercy." The thralls all knew immediately, that the request would not be well received. As the lights in their posts flickered, the devilish man began to speak.

"Did you creatures show mercy to your victims!?" The air surrounding them became thick with a black aura that made it hard to breath. They at this very moment felt the presence of lord Death and they now knew what it was for demons to feel fear.

"Did your master show mercy to any of the lives he's destroyed?"

"But you are the son of Grey. You are the hero are you not?" The man tipped his head backward and laughed darkly pulling a container from within his jacket.

"Feel fortunate that you have not yet met Grey's son. As for your "hero," that I am not. I am nothing to you short of the devil, you unholy piece of shit!" He screamed with rage at the beast, as he splashed him repeatedly with the terrible smelling liquid from the canister. As he began to walk away, the wolf began to call out to his brothers, begging them, to avenge his death. The man stopped and slowly turned.

"You thought I was going to let you bleed to death? No, no, no, that just will not do. You see, I have an hour before sunrise, which means that you have plenty of time for your wounds to cauterize." Without prior warning, the man pulled a lighter from his pocket, clicking and tossing it at the beast. The screams the creature emitted, as it burst into flame, were indescribably horrific. It lashed about in anguish, wishing for something as sweet as death. Without a final word, the man turned and began to walk away as the dying, bloodied man on the ground, spoke up.

"We thank you for our lives stranger but what should we call you? Who do we offer our thanks to and tell our friends of your deeds?" The man turned his head to face the thralls, granting one final look at his face. His skin was milky, his eyes a piercing icy blue, his facial structure strong and bold looking, no older than his late twenties. The glance was enough to catch the attention of the women, as they stared into his luminous blue eyes, which glowed in the moonlight. He turned his head back around and as the man disappeared into the night, he spoke one last sentence.

"I am The Hunter."

Chapter 2 – The Devil Deals in Darkness

"It's going to be alright Cyrus." The young boy assured the dying man, as he tore off the man's belt and began fastening the wound, which was bleeding profusely, everywhere on the ground. Inwardly, the boy cringed at just how much blood Cyrus had lost. The smell alone was permeating through the garbage and stench of the city alleyway, they were crouched in.

"John..." Cyrus called to his helper desperately gasping for each breath. As John worked on tightening the belt, keeping pressure on the wound, he jerked his head up at hearing the injured's plea.

"Cyrus!" John chastised the dying man. "Save your strength. Don't talk."

Cyrus could see the glint in John's eyes that meant he was not joking around. Finally, he calmed down, whether it was due to the silence that filled the air or the loss of blood, he was unsure. Cyrus only knew that a sense of calm washed over him some time later, as John sat with him in the cold, steam filled air. The others stirred and shifted uncomfortably in the dark damp night.

The only source of light within the alleyway was the still burning werewolf, who whimpered helplessly awaiting for the remaining combustible fur and flesh to simmer out. They looked to one another as the woman who had previously cried, pulled a piece of cloth from within her pocket and began to dab away at her bloodied face.

"We need to get the hell out of here!" She grew frustrated, as she stamped back and forth across the pavement.

"Just calm down Carla, we can't just leave Cyrus like this." The other woman stepped forth and placed her hand on Carla's shoulder.

"The hell we can't!" She yelled as she flung back the woman's hand and stomped away. "We left Alice didn't we? Cyrus is worse off than she was. Why can't we just leave him too?" This time John turned around, carefully placing Cyrus's left hand over the makeshift tourniquet.

"Stop it! We need to stay calm. We have gotten this far. We can still make it the rest of the way. We can find someone in the resistance. They'll take us in." Carla sneered and laughed at John as she walked over to Cyrus.

"Your precious resistance doesn't exist, John. We have no hope now. You led us on this silly crusade of yours and now we are all dead. You hear me? They are dead now, because of you. Alice, Keagen, Cyrus and the rest of us."

"Carla stop, it isn't his fault. We all agreed."

"We all agreed to what? To run out here in the middle of the night, with no plan and no hope? Just to be slaughtered like animals." John spoke up still trying to hold onto Cyrus.

"Carla, no one is keeping you here. If you will not help me with Cyrus, please leave." Carla glared at John's back and fumed angrily before stomping away.

"Jocelyn, will you please help me? We need to move Cyrus away from here, before the others arrive for their friend." He spoke as he gestured towards the smoldering beast. Jocelyn trembled uncontrollably as she looked between John, Carla, the beast and the pool of blood that had formed around Cyrus.

"I...I..." She turned her head toward the werewolf again and then looked back at John. "I can't John. I'm so sorry, I can't." She ended as she ran down the alley and vanished in the night.

"Jocelyn, stop! Wait!" John attempted to call out to her as she ran off into the darkness with Carla, leaving him alone with Cyrus, desperately clinging to life.

"Don't worry Cyrus, I'll get you out of here, I promise." John placed Cyrus' left arm around his shoulder and slowly lifted him from the ground, carefully placing one foot in front of the other.

"Cyrus can you lift your feet for me?" No response came. "Cyrus?" John shook the man who twitched uncomfortably and then answered.

"Lift, feet?" Cyrus looked down at the foreign bodies dragging behind him and slowly, began to place one of them, in front of the other. Gradually, they began making progress down the alleyway. As they rounded the corner, the werewolf spoke.

"Let me free little thrall and my master shan't kill you upon our return to the ranch. Leave me and you and your "friends" shall be slaughtered as the cattle they are." John turned his head toward the beast.

"You listen to me beast. My friend and I are going to leave this place, we are going to find the resistance and then we shall be free." The werewolf did its best to let out an amused chuckle at John's back, who pretended not to notice.

"My brothers shall find you within the hour, there is nowhere you can hope to run, with your crippled friend here. As soon as they catch wind of the blood, you shall be finished. Why not take my offer, let me loose and at least you shall be spared?" John continued to walk as Cyrus squeezed his arm tightly and began to let out a light whimpering whisper. John leaned his head into Cyrus to hear.

"He's right John. I am done. All I am going to do is slow you down, get you killed as well. Leave me. Go find your resistance, please. My soul is already damned. Don't let your death rest on my conscience too." John gritted his teeth in aggravation and began to search around the alleyway for some sign of hope or direction. He looked Cyrus in the eye again and the man nodded to him.

"Alright Cyrus wait here, I'll be back shortly. I'm going to go and find some help but you have to hang on, alright?" Cyrus smiled weakly and did his best to let out a pitiful laugh. John rested Cyrus' back to a wall and taking care to cover him with various materials, so that he would not be spotted, took off at a full on sprint. He tore through the streets looking for any sign of people but even he knew how unlikely it was that he would find someone active, at this hour. He rounded corner after corner, running to every shop light that was still on but as he had assumed, all of the doors were still securely locked.

He tore through the streets, peering into each and every window. As he approached, he witnessed several dwellers hiding behind and beneath counter tops, dimming their lights. John grew furiously depressed. They knew why he ran. They all knew of what terror he must be facing and yet they were content to watch him die.

John gripped his fists angrily and began to pound on one of the doors. He would not let their cowardice be the end of Cyrus.

"My friend is wounded. I need some help, please help me." No answer came. John could feel the heat in his blood rising, causing his temples to pound.

"Open up, my friend is injured and needs help!"

"Hey kid. Come over here." A young brown haired woman, in a short skirt and a leather jacket walked up behind John, who turned quickly.

"Will you help me?" He asked. The woman nodded her head and motioned towards a mob of similarly dressed women. "Me and my girls will help you."

"Thank you, really, thank you." The woman waved him off and motioned toward the outskirts of town, which John had just arrived from.

"Cute but if you don't mind, save the gratitude for when we get back."

"Right of course, let's go." John began to run, the mysterious women riding his heels. He took them through the various twists and turns he had taken to find them. After several heart-pounding moments, he came upon the place where he had left Cyrus. He ran forward, pulling away the blanket of filth, beneath which, remained nothing but a pool of blood.

John whipped his head around, noticing a small trail of blood, then nothing. He ran to the spot and saw a splatter a few feet ahead, part of a hand not too much farther from that. It was then, that John truly took in his surroundings and noticed the one thing, which should have been most obvious. Although the smell of burning flesh and fur was still pungent in the air, the alleyway was no longer illuminated. Where once there had been a burning werewolf, there was now nothing.

"Where is your friend?" The woman in the leather jacket stepped forward.

"He's gone!"

"Your friend?"

"Not just him, the werewolf that was pinned to this wall." He said as he pointed to the four, blood covered, silver stakes that lay on the ground. It was not long until they heard a maniacal moaning screech, permeate the air. The other women began to search around the alley nervously.

"Ghouls! The boy has led us into a trap! Soon we will all either be dead or enslaved again!"

"You!" The woman in the jacket grabbed John by his collar and forced him against the wall.

"You led us into a trap? We will deal with you in a moment but first, Girls!" She yelled and not only did the screeches become more intense but each of the women pulled out their own individual weapons, preparing to fight. John sat on the ground, his back to the brick as first; his sense of smell was assaulted, by the scent of festering boils and rotted flesh. He was forced to recall a more pleasant time when he had smelt blood, guts, gore and vomit, now longing to be back, as his eyes burned, stomach churned. Next, he longed for blindness, as the source of the stench rounded the corner.

His assumption of festering boils and rotted flesh were dead on, as he witnessed the horrendous face of his soon to be assailant. The creature came into the dimly lit alley. He saw the pus green skin and long bony fingers with the extra lengthy nails, which were the color of dried blood. It walked awkwardly, as if with a hunch, dragging its feet behind it, the sound of chains around its shackled body, rattling, echoing eerily.

The leading lady lunged forth with chains in hand and thrashed down. The metal clanged as it struck its target, forcing the pus-filled head downwards. The other leather-clad women rushed forward and began lashing out, as more of the fetid feeders, reared the corner.

Watching the brawl, John stepped up and fetching one of the four silver stakes, charged into the fray. Taking care to step around the flailing, he struck downwards, planting the stake into the brittle skull of the nearest ghoul.

A shriek rang out, shrill and terrifying, the sound of something inhuman being wounded. Another scream followed, this one human. John turned his head to the sound and saw one of his saviors clutching her arm.

"Ahh! It burns!" John flinched at the hissing sound ensuing before him. Looking to his silver stake, which had begun to hiss, boil and melt, he threw it aside, noticing his sleeve hissing as well.

"They bleed acid!" He screamed as he tore away his burning sleeve and threw it to the ground. He turned his head again to watch the progress of the battle.

Two of the brawlers were sporting acid burns, yet continued on, while their leader and two others excelled while fighting from a distance. One brawler fell to ground dying, acid covering the side of her face. Four of the ghouls now lie in pools of acidic blood. From out of the alley, a loud growl permeated the darkness. They turned their attention expecting more ghouls only to see the distinct silver haired body of another werewolf.

"Everyone, run!" The leader called out to her comrades, as one of her girls, was torn into and left for the ghouls, her heart still fighting to beat on. The leader turned towards the wolf and placing herself between he and her friends, attempted her last desperate act of heroism.

The wolf lunged and John watched as if in slow motion, facial muscles twisted and contorted, just before bursting outward towards the street. John looked on as the remaining ghouls each fell, one after another, similarly wounded. He watched, as each time the forms fell to the ground, his ears were suddenly assailed, by the commanding cry of a high-powered weapon, echoing through the alleyway.

"What just happened?" John looked at the devastation, which had been rendered.

"Isn't it obvious? We've been saved."

"Yes but by whom?"

"My personal angel of death." The leader steered John in the proper direction and pointed to the skyline. John squinted his eyes, just barely making out the shape of a slender form, who signaled back to them with a series of flashes from a reflected surface.

"So what do we do with him?" One of the surviving brawlers tightened a tourniquet around the arm of a wounded friend, whilst attempting to keep her own blood from her eyes.

"I haven't yet decided."

"We should kill him for leading us into this trap! Three of our girls died on his foolish rescue mission, if this ever was such a thing."

"I shall be the one to decide his fate. I require some time to consider the matter."

"What do you mean that you need some time? Dahlia, three of our sisters are dead!"

"Listen! I said that I would think about it. Who calls the shots around here anyway?"

"Harlee would kill him."

"If that were the case then he would already be dead and we wouldn't be having this conversation, now would we? Now, get out of my face and help the other girls so we can get out of here before more of the familiars show up. We all knew that the streets had grown more dangerous, since the freaks started teaming up. Now, we have vampires and their ghoul pets to deal with. We do not have time to dawdle." The other girl turned away and left to tend to her friends, while Dahlia turned on John.

"You are coming with me."

"Do I have a choice?"

"Not if you don't want Harlee to put a bullet in your head."

"Who's Harlee? Is he the Hunter?" The woman turned her head back toward John, one eyebrow raised slightly.

"What do you mean by the Hunter?"

"You know, the one that has all of the ranch hands on full alert. The supernatural man with the moonlight blue eyes." Dahlia pressed her arm into John's chest, pinning him to the wall.

"You've seen him?" John nodded his head and attempted to swallow.

"He is the one who saved us initially. We were cornered by a..."

"Quiet for now boy, we need to get you back now and have ourselves a chat. Girls, do not take too long with cleanup. The streets will stew and fester with filth regardless. Only do enough to clear our trail. I'm taking the kid back with me."

None of the girls, as Dahlia referred to them, spoke but it was clear to John they all understood what was expected of them. Each looked to John as if knowing his fate. Reluctantly, John followed Dahlia through the winding back alleys of Sin City and watched, as the structures grew less and less habitable.

"Aren't you worried that we'll be spotted?"

"No, it will be light out soon and we are closer to the sex rentals, than the blood suckers or the flea bags."

"Well, what about the familiars?" Dahlia turned and looked at John as if about to say something but resisted.

"Trust me kid, its fine. Just follow my lead and we'll be safe in no time."

"It's John by the way."

"Yeah there's a bathroom there too."

"No my name is John, not kid."

"That's nice kiddo but I prefer to keep things less personal, less connected. More affiliations make life in Sin City tough you know. If you make it through the month, then maybe we can sit down and talk names but until then I prefer it this way."

"Where are you taking me?" John asked.

"A friend of mine. His name is Jeremiah. He helped Harlee and I out, awhile back. He is also an expert on everything related to the Hunter. He has been studying his movements for some time now. If there is anyone who can help us sort this all out, it's him."

They strode down the dark alley for several more awkward moments, before Dahlia stopped in front of a heavily dented metal door.

She rapped on the door and a slot slid open.

"Who is it?" A low growl emitted from the blackness within.

"It's Dahlia, I came to speak with Jeremiah."

"I don't know who you're talking about, go away!" The slot closed abruptly. Dahlia sighed and tapped on the door again. The slot opened as the man inside, grumbled angrily.

"I have information regarding the Hunter." Again the slot slammed shut but this time, John could hear the locks releasing followed by the opening of the door.

"Inside, quickly, quietly." The large man ushered them in impatiently and after a quick scan of the alleyway, slammed the door shut.

John felt the door lummox pressing firmly into his back, leading him through the hallways of the house, until they appeared in a large room. John looked around to see himself surrounded by dozens of armed men, wearing tactical assault gear. John was goaded into the center of the large room and forced into a metal chair, his hands and feet were clamped down, after he sat.

Up the stairs, leading to the balcony above his entrance, a man appeared from behind a set of heavy double doors. Beyond the man, appeared more armed guards, which flanked him on either side. John searched from left to right. Whoever this man was, he was guarded by nearly thirty heavily armed men, which meant John was in the presence of someone important.

"So this is the boy who had a run in with the infamous hunter and lived to tell about it." The man spoke as he clapped his hands.

"How do you know that?" John asked.

"You wouldn't be here otherwise. Needless to say boy, I have many questions for you. You answer them correctly, you live. Otherwise, we'll have to make it look as though you were turned into a late night snack." John swallowed hard but remained composed.

"First question, why are you here?" John scrunched his face confused by the over obvious nature of the question.

"Because she would have had Harlee shoot me if I didn't." He spoke as he pointed to Dahlia. Dahlia smiled though Jeremiah looked less than satisfied with his answer.

"I shall rephrase...what exactly happened with the Hunter?" John cleared his throat and began to deliver a full account of what had happened. Jeremiah, his guards and Dahlia all listened intently to what John had to say. Once John had finished his story, Jeremiah took a deep breath.

"That was the extent of your interaction with the Hunter? He showed up, saved you and your friends, then left?" Jeremiah's tone suggested that he was growing angry.

"Well as I said before sir...he tortured the werewolf, wanting to know where the den was."

"Ah yes, that is right and then after which, he simply just vanished."

"I wouldn't say vanished, I said he simply walked away and that his clothes made him appear to evaporate." Jeremiah was clearly unhappy with the information he was receiving. John watched as Dahlia shuffled uncomfortably and John knew that things were not looking up for him.

"Second question, are you a friend of the Hunter's?"

"I don't' see how I could be. He came, fought and then left shortly afterwards." The doors John had entered through suddenly burst open and in walked another leather-clad woman. She wore a rather bizarre, suggestive outfit. The look she bore to John as she looked at him, suggested that its design was more for combat than its appeal. She handed her sniper rifle over, unstrapped her weapon pouches, from her legs and handed her backpack to one of the guards, before taking up stance beside Dahlia.

"Third and final question." Jeremiah spoke as he placed both hands behind his back and puffed his chest out to John.

“Where is the Hunter now?” John looked up at Jeremiah whose expression was one filled with hatred.

“I don’t know.” Jeremiah slammed his hands down on the back of John’s chair.

“Lies! You are in league with him, aren’t you?”

“No,” John exclaimed. “He showed up in the middle of the night, saved myself and some other thralls, from a pack of wolves and then left. That was all. Honest, I am telling you the truth.”

“Guards!” Jeremiah turned, snapping his fingers, as he began to walk away. John suddenly realized, every gun holding guard in the room had cocked their weapons and were now pointing them at him. John struggled against his restraints but knew breaking free would not save him. Dahlia and the one John presumed was Harlee, stepped forward.

"Jeremiah, what is the meaning of this?" Jeremiah held his hand up to the women and Dahlia grew silent for a moment.

"Bring me the silver." Jeremiah spoke and from the back of the room, one of the many guards approached, carrying an old wooden box and presented it to his leader. Jeremiah opened the box and pulled from it, a single silver knife. John guessed he was not going to enjoy his captor's intent.

"We shall see if you are what you claim to be." He approached John and pressing the blade against his forearm, slowly drug the blade across his flesh. John flinched slightly, as the blade peeled away his flesh, causing for a stream of sanguine to run out onto the floor.

"Garlic." The man called and as before, a guard approached him with another item, which Jeremiah received, before displaying it to John. It was a small vial with a dropper top, which Jeremiah used to squirt several drops into John's wound. Again, John winced at the pain but did not elicit the response they were obviously looking for.

"Just a thrall, after all." Jeremiah spoke as he turned back to face his guards. He looked around the room before turning back to John.

"Fortunately, we have an answer for that as well." He spoke as he reached for his sidearm and began to pull it out on John.

"CRASH!" Everyone ducked as the glass above them shattered, covering all of them in a spray of transparent daggers. John ducked his head, the best he could, as he saw the man in black float down from up above, throwing several weapons into the air, as he descended. Jeremiah's gun was forced from his hand along with the weapons of many others, as the man in black's projectiles struck their designated targets. John watched as the black clothed man, landed in front of him, his coat stretched out as if a pair of wings.

"Good to see you again Jeremiah," The Hunter spoke as he reached inside his jacket, pulling another throwing knife and twirled it in his fingers. He smirked and then looked back at the man. "Goodbye Jeremiah." The Hunter spoke in his supernaturally deep voice as he launched another dagger across the room, which plunged its way into Jeremiah's chest.

"Almighty God, please shelter us from this demon!" One of the many guards stammered.

"Those who have love for God, have no place here. Your lord does not live nor see that which resides in this city. Here you shall find only devils." The Hunter responded to the guard's prayer.

As the guards began to recover, John, who had moved far from range of the impending crossfire, caught a glimpse of the hunter's eyes, which had become black.

"And the devil deals in darkness." The Hunter said, lifting his head into the air. John watched, as every light in the room burst. The room went dark and all that remained was the sound of thirty assault rifle armed men, going to war.

Chapter 3 – The House of Fallen Angels

"Dahlia, get down!" Harlee yelled, as she ran, grabbing her friend's shoulder and forcing her backwards, as the room exploded into a thundering torrent of lights and bullets. Harlee dropped down to the ground, as the first of the many screams rang out. She could hear as the guard nearest to her, fell to the ground.

Quickly, she turned and fumbled around in the dark, until her hands found what she was looking for, her rifle.

"Stay down Dahlia." She yelled over the sound of bullet fire and rolled onto her stomach, resting on her elbows as she backed away. Bringing the rifle to her shoulder, she peered through her scope, to see through the night vision lens.

The room had turned to bloody chaos. She could see already, several bodies lying on the ground. The firing stopped and she could see the guards had already placed their goggles on. She, the same as them, were now searching for the Hunter.

"Aaaah!" She heard, followed by the sound of someone's neck, snapping. She quickly turned her sights toward the sound and could see a body being dragged away. The guards yelled, firing again but the lights from their muzzles blinded them and they did not see the monster launch itself skyward. It landed on the ceiling and with unnatural speed, crawled across the ceiling, pouncing at another guard and began...she paused to examine, feeding on them.

"Vampire." She whispered to herself, as she reached down to the artillery belt strapped to her thigh and wriggled a sniper bullet free. She grabbed three more, as the beast lunged from one guard to the next, tearing into each as it went.

She had grown very accustomed to using her rifle, loading the round carefully, being sure to move as little and make as little noise as possible. She dropped the round into the loading chamber, and slowly slid it into place. Harlee carefully lifted the weapon, while the monster's attention was on the guards and slid her way back to Dahlia, until she could feel her friend's warm body against her own.

"Dahlia, get ready to move." She spoke as she held her breath and slid the firing pin into position. Dahlia placed her hand on Harlee's shoulder.

"We cannot leave John behind."

"What?"

"Harlee, we are not leaving him." Harlee gritted her teeth and placed the scope back up to her eye. There were now less than a dozen guards remaining. Blood decorated everything around but Harlee could not see the creature. She searched about and found John, still cowering at the far end of the room, in front of the window ledge.

"On my "go," ok?" Dahlia tapped her on the shoulder, signaling that she understood. Harlee grabbed her pack and the rest of her things from off the guard and began stealthily putting them on. Equipped, Harlee continued searching the room.

"Ready," still no sign of the beast, she turned her eyes toward the balcony. No sign of Jeremiah or his personal guard either.

"Set," she reached into her pack, grabbing a flare and handing a grenade to Dahlia.

"Go," a deep masculine voice spoke. Harlee and Dahlia lurched around, to see the monster was above them. Harlee pulled her trigger and the blast narrowly missed the man who launched himself sideways and struck at Harlee. Harlee ducked down striking the flare and placed it on him as she rolled sideways.

"Here!" She cried and the remaining nine men began unloading their weapons.

"RUN!" Harlee cried to Dahlia and the pair took off as Harlee struck more flares, throwing them across the room. As they neared John, Harlee grabbed an assault rifle off a dead guard, a spare clip and quickly turned in time to see the man flying towards her. She jumped backwards, pulling her trigger and unloaded her weapon into the creature.

She hit the floor and rolled as the man landed inches from where she had just been.

"Hyaah!" She kicked off from his chest, being sure to drop a grenade at his feet as she flew through the window, John and Dahlia jumping with her.

"BOOM!" The building lit up into a violent cacophony of exploding glass as the three of them, fell down towards the building below. Harlee landed hard, yelling out as she pulled another clip and reloaded the assault rifle.

"Keep moving!" She yelled to John and Dahlia, who struggled to get to their feet.

"I think my leg is broken." John moaned as he rose. Dahlia placed his arm over her shoulder and helped him run towards the other end of the roof. Harlee turned her eyes back to the blaze and saw a black silhouette, crouched in front of the inferno, staring down at her.

"Go, go, go!" She yelled as she opened fire. She watched as her bullets went on ignored for a moment but then the creature leapt from the building and landed where they had moments ago. She continued to fire, her bullets continuing to fly true but land just off their mark.

"Click, click, click," her rifle empty, she threw it aside and pulled a pistol from either leg. She turned her head momentarily, to see Dahlia beating on the door handle, trying to get inside the building they had

landed on. She snapped her head back in time, to see the darkness a few feet from her.

She threw out both arms and began unleashing her wrath. She could see the blood splatters from her shots but the beast would not stop. He ran up on her and she ducked to avoid the incoming swing. The punch narrowly missed her and she kicked out with a leg sweep, knocking her adversary's legs out from underneath him. Quickly, she reached out with her pistols again and pulled the triggers several times, unloading the rest of her bullets into the man's torso.

He pressed firmly off the ground and lunged out of eyesight as Harlee quickly rose to her feet, reloaded her weapons and shot the lock on the door. Dahlia opened the door and the three of them ran inside as Harlee searched for anything she could use to barricade the door. They sat in the hallway, panting heavily as they examined themselves for the first time since the firefight.

"Is anyone hit?" Dahlia asked. Harlee carefully looked herself over, several cuts, gouges and scrapes on her arms and torso, plus a split lip.

"Nothing life threatening."

"What do we do now?" John asked. Dahlia turned to look at him.

"Well if we don't decide to kill you, then we will take you somewhere safe." John smiled, realizing that he would have died in the building had they any intentions of killing him.

"You cannot escape, you know." Everyone jumped back, the best they could at the sound of the supernatural man's voice. "I have no intentions of hurting any of you. I just need the boy. Give him up and you can go." Dahlia looked at Harlee who smiled murderously as she pulled the pin of a grenade and threw it down the stairs.

"BOOM!" The hallway below exploded, shaking the building.

"That should have taken care of that damn vampire." Harlee let out a sigh and rested her head against the wall.

"I am not a vampire, by the way." Everyone snapped their attention back towards the hallway where the fire now provided ample lighting in the background for them to see the shadow of their pursuer.

"Now, if you please, the boy." The man spoke as the three looked to one another contemplating their next move.

"Will you let them go?" John spoke up. Dahlia shoved him down as he attempted to sit up and Harlee drew her rifle.

"I have no interest in the women. They will come to no harm." He spoke as Harlee's eyes spotted a piece of broken glass, allowing her to triangulate her shot.

"How can we trust you?" They could see the shadow lift up its hands.

"I suppose we will just have to go on faith." He spoke mockingly, as if the words bore him no meaning. "Listen if I had wanted any of you dead, you would be dead. I just need to ask the boy a few questions, go grab a cheeseburger, slice of pie, and that's that. Is it really worth all of this trouble?"

"What do you need to know?" There was a long pause with no sound but a crackling fire and approaching sirens.

"I don't exactly have time to divulge my plans. We have three minutes until the helicopter drops troops on the roof. They know this is no normal fire." John, Dahlia and Harlee sat in silence listening. All they could hear were the sirens.

"I don't hear a helicopter." Dahlia spoke.

"Well I wouldn't expect you to. You did not just drink half a gallon of werewolf's blood, now did you? Despite what you do or do not hear and what you do or do not think, I am taking the boy and leaving."

"BOOM!" John's ears began to ring as Harlee's rifle went off. The bullet, masterfully aimed, pierced the wall and came out on the other side, striking its intended target. There was a brief moment of silence, broken only by the man's voice.

"Ow...I may have to rescind my offer, to let you live! I said I drank werewolf blood, not that I am a werewolf. Damn, that stings." There followed a slight pause. Harlee smiled and readied another round. The door behind them flinging open, Dahlia and John were knocked down, as Harlee was lifted up by her throat.

She kicked and squirmed for a moment, against the powerful man, who lifted her off from the ground but she could not breathe.

"Now that wasn't very nice." The ominous man's deep voice dropped a full octave. Harlee continued to fight, dropping her elbow against the man's wrist and kicking at his chest.

"Now...for the last time. The boy, if you please." Dahlia lunged out at the man and stabbed him in the chest with a dagger.

"I would caution you not to press me...you just might let HIM out!" He grabbed onto Dahlia's wrist with his free hand and pulled against her with ease, removing the knife from his torso.

"Please! Don't hurt them, I will come with you." John did his best to rise, though his leg still tested him greatly. Harlee's eyes began to roll into the back of her skull, as she fought the urge to pass out from lack of oxygen. Her eyes glazing over, she glanced at her wrists and reaching out with one finger flipped the small switch, located just below her wrist bone.

"Aaahh!" The man yelled as electricity flowed through Harlee's hands and jolted him, causing him to lose his grasp on both women.

"Run!" Harlee yelled as she reached out, grabbing the man's face with both hands, shocking him, before placing her feet into his chest and kicked off from him. She landed gracefully at the bottom of the stairs, as Dahlia and John stumbled down them.

As they ran, they could hear the sound of several fully automatic weapons, sounding off in unison. They turned from the sounds of gunfire and ran down a smoky hallway, to be met in the face by several bright beams with accompanying red laser dots.

"Down!" Dahlia shoved Harlee and John as they heard the first round, fire. Harlee and John landed several feet away but watched as Dahlia took three more blasts, before crumbling to the floor.

"Dahlia!" Harlee yelled as she ducked and quickly reaching out, dragged Dahlia to cover. Harlee pressed her back against the wall and pulled a pistol from her hip.

"Try to get the bleeding to stop. I'm going to try and find a way out of here!" Harlee commanded. John began tending to Dahlia, as Harlee searched for an exit. The only way they could escape would be to cross in front of the firing squad. The hall they were in was partially collapsed and flames behind the rubble reached out to them, daring them to come in closer.

Harlee tipped her head to see around the corner and let off a round from her pistol into the direction of the lights.

"One of them is armed, FIRE!" Harlee dropped down lower to the floor and shielded herself as the bullet spray tore apart the walls around, launching splinters of wood and glass into the air, as an erupting cloud of ash. John laid his body over top of Dahlia and ducked his head down beside her. They waited for the torrent of bullets to stop for countless moments.

Once they finally subsided, Harlee tried to listen for movement, though her ears had gone silent and her head spun from the noise. Instead, she rolled out slightly and began to fire her weapon into the thick cloud blocking her vision until she rolled into something hard. She looked to her side, her weapon empty and met a pair of tall, black, combat boots.

"Put this on." The supernatural man with the blue eyes spoke and she lurched, as he dropped a bloody tactical vest on her.

"Get the boy and your friend out of here, I will buy you time." Harlee looked up at the man who held two more gore covered vests, which obviously once belonged to a trio of the engaging law enforcers. Harlee grabbed the vests from the man as he reached into his coat and pulled from it a large, gleaming, double bladed axe.

"Why are you helping us?"

"I told you, I need the boy."

"I'm not leaving him with you."

"I'm convinced that you won't get far. Your friend needs help and I assume that you will not be visiting the hospital anytime soon. If you trust me..."

"Which I don't," Harlee interrupted. "You killed Jeremiah."

"That man was no friend to mankind." The man spoke to her, his voice so deep, it reminded of a ghoulish moan, though possessing a commanding, ominous and alluring power.

"He was our leader."

"The only thing that man wanted, was to militarize your kind for his own agenda."

"What agenda?" Harlee asked.

"We do not have time for this. Take her to The House of Fallen Angels, ask for father Matthew."

"The priest working on all of the community projects?" She asked.

"A friend of man. Now go!" The man held out his arm, turning it over so that his axe blade was sticking out and then ran into the fog. Harlee could hear the sounds of fighting and snapped to. She ran over to John and Dahlia, placing her hands under Dahlia's arms.

"You're going to have to carry yourself John." John nodded, doing his best to lift himself from the ground and hobbled along behind Harlee. They could hear the screams of the men, down the hall, as the three of them slowly made their way through the smoke filled hall.

They each remained as close to the ground as possible, to avoid stray gunfire. As they crept, they could hear the sounds of the supernatural man slaying his adversaries. The men he hunted were numerous and their automatic weapons were deadly, though Harlee could hear as one after another, they fell to the horror that was her savior. They continued making their way down the hall as the violence lead away from them. They managed to pass the plume of smoke and came out to the clear hallway of what appeared to be an apartment building.

"Stairs," John pointed toward the sign of the stick man and Harlee kicked the door open as they began their descent. Before they even reached the first landing, firefighters began pouring up the stairs.

"I have three here!" One called as he and his friends ran to their side and began helping them down the steps. They halted as they noticed Harlee was still carrying her small arsenal of weaponry.

"Are you from special division?" The first in line spoke as he slowly stepped backward. Harlee nodded her head as she looked back up the stairs.

"We need to move these people out of here, now. There's a war up there right now." The firefighters nodded their heads.

"Don't worry everyone, we've got you." John could not help but worry as they were escorted down, while a war was being waged up above. Having arrived on ground level, Harlee turned her head skyward and witnessed the weak rays of moonlight, piercing the veil of smoke rising from the inferno above. Paramedics rushed to their side, quickly pulling Dahlia and John away as another approached Harlee.

"You from special division?" The female paramedic spoke as she nudged towards Harlee's weaponry.

"Yes, in fact if you could help me. It is probably for the best that I not been seen by civilians." The paramedic agreed as she turned towards the man tending to Dahlia's wounds. Harlee was not sure if she saw it or not but she noticed a quick glint in the man's eyes, as if his pupils had suddenly enlarged for a brief moment.

"I need these two for questioning. They were close to the target."

"Understood! We will give you a lift then." The man strapped Dahlia to a stretcher and though he lacked in size, hoisted her and John up inside the ambulance with ease. Harlee did her best to breathe slowly, as to not elevate her own heart rate in the presence of werewolves. Harlee climbed into the ambulance, as the female paramedic followed and closed the doors. Harlee sat down next to John, whose leg was in a splint. Harlee heard the roar of the engine and felt as the vehicle pulled away.

The paramedic continued to look over Dahlia as she ensured that her condition was stable.

"Where is this one's mark?" It took Harlee a moment before she caught on to what she meant.

"Free range. Caught her snooping at the sight. Figured she was with him." The paramedic's outstretched fingernails began to lengthen into a claw as she brought it close to Dahlia's eyes, which had glazed over from the pain medications.

"I had intended on delivering her intact." Harlee spoke calmly, still focusing on controlling her heart rate. John must have caught on to her deception, as he made no attempts to stop the paramedic nor seemed to be particularly uncomfortable. The werewolf turned back and eyed Harlee for a moment before withdrawing.

"We will have you back at the den shortly. The elders will want your full report." There was a loud thud on the roof of the ambulance. Everyone tilted his or her heads skyward, as the vehicle swerved slightly from the impact. Harlee gripped her rifle tightly as John pressed himself in the corner.

"I can smell you, son of Grey!" The woman growled deeply, as her voice dropped below human level, while she began to grow and turn to her true form. Her skull elongated, as her body grew shaggy and grey. The driver swerved once more, as the beast's arms spread out to the length of the cab. Harlee held on for dear life as she, John and Dahlia, bobbed about helplessly. Harlee was thrown backwards, hitting her head on a container housing various medical supplies. She could feel as the back of her head grew warm and she knew that her time was limited.

After a moment, the cab leveled out and the crescent shaped blade of an axe pierced through the roof. The medic growled as she raked her claws against the ceiling, peeling away at its cover. As if sensing, she were his objective, the wolf leaned in towards Dahlia and grabbed her around the throat.

"I will kill her, son of Grey. Is that what you want? I will devour her flesh and bathe in her blood as it paints these walls!" The axe blade desisted it's tearing as Harlee slowly moved her rifle into position. The wolf began to sniff the air for a moment and looked down toward Harlee.

"The scent of your blood..." she took another deep sniff. "You're human!" Next, she looked down to Harlee's flak jacket, decorated with the blood of the wolf. "You're with the Hunter!" The wolf screamed as she lifted her arm into the air. Harlee quickly tried to place the rifle in between herself and the wolf, as she heard the sounds of bursting tires. The entire ambulance lurched towards the driver's side, launching Harlee up as she heard the sounds of the metal rims grinding the road.

Harlee squeezed the trigger as the beast swung wide at her. The wolf howled in anger as the round scraped its flesh and Harlee was propelled across the vehicle where she hit hard and fell. The vehicle lurched again as the ambulance ceiling was torn away by a silver axe. Harlee tried to lift herself up but felt the immense pain in her torso, from where she had been struck. Unable to move, she looked up and watched as the lady wolf reached upward and grabbed onto the Hunter's arm and dragged him down into the cab. As the Hunter landed, he struck with his opposite hand and stabbed the beast in the chest with a dagger. Again, she howled with pain and threw him backward, opening the doors.

The vehicle veered again as the blow caused the already unstable ambulance to shake and all attention reverted back to Harlee. The wolf began to walk towards her as Harlee saw the door of the cab swing back, revealing the Hunter hanging from it as he launched his silver chain towards the wolf. As the spear on the end of the chain permeated the lycanthrope's shoulder, he wrenched backwards against it, pulling him back into the cab. As he released his grip on the door, he slammed forward into the lycanthrope, pushing them both towards the front of the cab and out the window.

The vehicle began to slow and Harlee could see from behind the ambulance, the road was being torn apart from ahead.

"John! We have to jump out now!" John looked at her, shocked as she unlocked the girdie from the floor of the ambulance and pushed. With little warning, the man in the leather duster, launched himself over top of the trio and wrapped his body around the girdie, toppling sideways, protecting Dahlia, as he slowly rolled them to a stop. John and Harlee, followed just behind them and groaned, as they rose to their feet.

"You need to get out of here!" The Hunter told them as he snapped his right arm back into place and ripped the straps from Dahlia's stretcher. Dahlia groaned, unable to move well from the drugs as John and Harlee ran to her side.

"The House of Fallen Angels." The man mumbled to them, under his breath as he charged after the ambulance to conclude his confrontation.

Harlee, John and Dahlia moved as quickly as they were able, through the darkened back alleys. They moved as silently as possible, hoping to avoid detection. Several blocks down from where they had been thrown from the ambulance, Harlee saw an old, abandoned looking cathedral ahead. The three of them hobbled along and scaling the front steps, quickly walked inside.

The inside of the building was much the same as Harlee imagined, although nothing occupying the room appeared to have been created within the past fifty years. The sole sources of light in the room, shone in through the windows and flickered off from the many, strewn candles. Each stained glass window was complete with various depictions from the bible. An older man, in his sixties, ran from the far back of the room.

"John, welcome back." He said. John stared at him curiously, as he helped Harlee with Dahlia.

"Quickly, we have to get her to the back, so I can help her." The man said as he guided them back.

"How do you know John?" Harlee asked.

"It is a long story. I am not surprised that he does not remember me but let us worry about your friend, first. My name is Father Matthew. Through here." He said as they passed through the doors, leading to the back of the church. Through the doors, was a sitting area, with a kitchen just beyond. Matthew lead them to the right, down a narrow hall with several doors on either side.

"Ma'am, would you please make sure that the doors are locked? We do not want anyone barging in just now, do we?" Harlee stared suspiciously but Dahlia waved her off. Harlee quickly ran to the front of the cathedral and secured the door. Being sure that it was locked, she ran into the back of the cathedral. Down the hall, the second door on the left, was ajar. Harlee ran to it and peered inside.

Father Matthew was leaning over top of Dahlia, who lay on the bed. Harlee came up on his side as John left the room. Father Matthew's hands worked with great dexterity and speed, as he tended to Dahlia's various wounds and turned to Harlee.

"We are going to need to remove her clothes. Otherwise, I cannot address the gunshot wounds. There are some towels over there, we can cover her with." He pointed to the end table, where in fact, several towels sat in a stack. Harlee nodded her head and began stripping Dahlia down, while Matthew grabbed a pair of pointed clamps.

"You may wish to hold her hand. This is not going to feel good." Matthew warned as he reached into Dahlia's shoulder and grabbing onto the bullet, began pulling it out. Dahlia cried out in pain, squeezing Harlee's hand, tightly enough to nearly break it. Matthew removed the bullet and setting it aside, began cleaning the wound.

"It's alright, Dahlia. I'm here." Harlee told her as she stroked the trembling woman's hair. Matthew moved on to the next few bullet holes but determined them to be clear. Harlee worked alongside Father Matthew, to patch her friend back together.

Over an hour later, both of them sat, breathing heavily, wiping sweat from their brows. Matthew looked down at his bloodstained hands and turned to Harlee. Harlee's eyes locked on Dahlia, who was still breathing rather aggressively.

"Why don't you go ahead and get in the shower. I will begin cleaning up here." Father Matthew suggested. Harlee shook her head.

"I appreciate your help but I am not leaving her side." Matthew nodded as someone knocked on the door.

"Is she alright?" John asked as he poked his head inside.

"I believe that we have made it through the worst."

"It was a close call." Harlee muttered. "But she is resting, now." John looked over Harlee, who was staring out blankly, covered in her friend's blood.

"You look as though you could use a shower and some rest." He told her. Harlee snapped out of her trance for a moment, looking at them both.

"Do you suppose she will be alright?" Harlee asked.

She will be, alright, now." Matthew said. "John, we could use your help, cleaning up and then I will show both of you to your rooms. Harlee, if you decide not to, I understand but you could really use the rest. You won't be able to help Dahlia if you do not take care of yourself." Matthew said as he began picking up the soiled linens and wiped up the blood on the floor. After observing for a moment, Harlee and John, helped him. Afterwards, when everyone and everything, had been cleaned, they were shown to their rooms.

"Have a good night, God bless, you both." Father Matthew said as Harlee and John entered their respective rooms.

"Thank you, Father." John said as Harlee nodded her head, utterly exhausted.

“Thank you, so much for everything.” She said. Matthew smiled.

“It is the Lord’s will. Now, if you would both excuse me, I have some matters to attend to. I am expected to meet with some friends from the police station.” He told them as he moved to leave. Harlee closed her door after he left and moved into the dark bedroom, charting a straight course to the bed. Undressing, Harlee dropped face first onto the bed and barely crawled beneath the blankets, before falling asleep.

Chapter 4 – I Can Still Hear Their Screams

Harlee awoke abruptly, drenched in sweat, her heart racing from her nightmare. Her blonde hair, clung to the side of her face. She sat upright in the bed and swung her bare legs over the side, her bare feet touching the cold, wooden floor. Rubbing her eyes, she searched about the empty bedchamber, Father Matthew had prepared for her. Harlee placed her hand against her bare chest and willed her heart rate to slow.

"In the great, green room, there was a telephone, and a red balloon." She whispered to herself as she focused on her hastened heart rate.

As both the beating of her heart and her breathing, normalized, Harlee listened intently and heard the repetitious beating of a drum. Curious, Harlee rose from the bed and walked to the bedside wardrobe. Grasping the hand carved handles of the antique, she pulled the doors open and peered inside. It was immediately apparent to her, that only men lived at the cathedral as she plucked a tuxedo shirt from within and fastened the two-centermost buttons.

Her modesty defended, Harlee moved to the doorway and carefully opened it. Entranced by the rhythmic beating of the ominous drum, she followed the sound. One foot planted directly in front of the other, creeping about as if escaping from a bad one-night stand. Harlee traversed the dimly lit halls, until she came to a lone metal door, camouflaged into the wall. Her hand shook and her heart began to pound with tremendous force as she felt a foreboding presence beyond, the narrowly opened door.

Again, she reached beneath her shirt, placing her hand over her thundering bosom. Closing her eyes, Harlee focused on her beating heart. A cold sweat decorated her skin, while she focused harder, repeating the passage.

"In the great, green room, there was a telephone and a red balloon." She whispered to herself as she drew a deep breath. Her heart eased though she was still perfectly synchronized to the phantom drum. Confidently, she reached out for the door and turned the knob. She cringed as the door creaked slightly. The door, ajar enough for her to peek her head through, revealed a set of stone steps. Peering around, she did not see any sign of people near her, and slowly crept down the stairs.

The passageway beneath was poorly lit, a few candles here and there, leaving a haunting silhouette of light, which danced across the uneven face of the stone walls. Harlee carefully removed a sconce from the wall, guiding her footsteps with the shallow light as she walked nearer to the source of her obsession.

The end of the hall opened up into a larger room. Old fashioned, red carpet, had been restored and laid out in various places. The thudding grew louder, from her heart or the instrument, she could no longer tell.

The pulsing, having grown so deeply engrained within her soul, it no longer possessed a distinguishable origin.

Harlee, stepping into the center of the room, stopped before the lone altar, a blade of untold origin, the only thing upon it. Harlee examined the twelve-inch dagger, its serrated edges, blade black, with a dark red, glassy handle. Looking away, Harlee noticed a shelf, across from her, a collection of tokens upon it. Photographs of young children, dressed in various fashions, a single object, toy or book, rested beside each. Slowly, Harlee began to spin as she noticed the methodically organized collection, ran the entire circumference of the room.

Harlee jolted, at the sound of a man's anguished cry from far down the next hall.

"It is not safe for you here." Harlee spun on a heel, hands ready to strike as Father Matthew came into sight. "There is no need for that, my dear." He spoke calmly, hands raised. "I apologize for frightening you but you should not be down here. Please follow me. I will prepare fresh clothes and a hot meal for you." Harlee turned to follow Father Matthew, glancing back at the room.

"What was that back there? It looked like a shrine of some sort." Harlee asked.

Father Matthew sighed at Harlee's question.

"You could say that, I suppose. More accurately, you could call it a memorial." He answered.

"Are those children all..?"

"Yes. All of them have since passed."

"I am sorry for your loss." Harlee spoke, letting the brevity of the subject matter seep in.

A stagnant pause hung heavily in the air as they stood for a moment before Father Matthew spoke again.

"Come, let us go back upstairs. I am sure that you wish to see your friend." He held his hand out to help lead her away.

"I would, thank you." As Harlee and Father Matthew reached the top of the stairs, Father Matthew, closed the door behind them, hoping that she would never again venture down there. Harlee watched in wonder as a bookcase slid in front of the camouflaged, metal door. Father Matthew nodded his head and turned to Harlee.

"There, now that should resolve that. Please, make yourself comfortable. I will have breakfast ready, shortly." Harlee moved into the next room and took up a seat at the table in the dining room. As she moved toward the table, she noticed a number of pictures and medals, displayed. Looking at them, she was drawn to the portrait of the handsome young man, in officer's uniform, who could only have been a much younger Matthew.

As she sat, she carefully tucked the shirt in between her legs and closed them. Harlee sat, waiting patiently as Father Matthew came back, carrying two steaming pans of food. He sat them on the table, the powerful aroma of omelets and breakfast potatoes assailed Harlee's nostrils. Her mouth watered as the priest pulled a glass pitcher, filled with milk, from the fridge and sat it at the table as well.

Harlee did not budge a muscle, fearing that any of the table's offerings might be poisoned. After a moment, Father Matthew returned, coffee pot in hand. Looking at Harlee, he sat three glasses on the table.

"Forgive me, miss but do you drink coffee?"

"When can I see Dahlia?" Harlee asked a suspicious tone to her voice.

"Ah, forgive me, my apologies. Your friend is still just down the hall, second door on the left." Father Matthew pointed behind Harlee, who rose.

"Thank you, and I take my coffee black." She spoke as she walked down the hall, opened the second door on the left and walked inside. The room was dark, the curtains closed. Harlee walked to the bed across from her and stared down at Dahlia. Harlee placed two fingers beneath Dahlia's nose and felt the steady release of warm air.

"Rest well, Dahlia." Harlee spoke as she stroked the woman's hair and looked around the room. The room was nearly identical to the one she had woken up in.

She heard voices coming from down the hall and made her way back out to investigate. Harlee moved out into the hallway and could hear the soft, silky tone of another woman. Harlee slowly peeked around the corner and saw Father Matthew, John and a woman, sitting at the table, staring at the small tv.

Harlee stared at the woman, who was obviously of Mediterranean descent. She had beautifully bronzed skin, long, raven black hair and elegant features that would render her irresistible to most men and women. She wore thigh high boots, fish net stockings, a mini skirt and a see through belly shirt, which left little to the imagination. The woman slowly turned her head to face Harlee and glared at her with eyes the color of milk and honey.

"Ah, this must be Maxwell's new girl?" She spoke with an obvious tone, ripe with jealously and dejection. "Priest, you were cross with me, about the way I dress and you allow this to traipse about that way?" She motioned with her hand, a disgusted look on her face. Harlee began eying the room in search of a weapon, finding a knife on the counter behind John.

"I only made such a request, on behalf of young John here." Father Matthew answered. Harlee and the other woman turned toward

John, who was visibly trembling as he was caught between the incredibly attractive, provocatively dressed women. "Your attire is your business and I would expect John to treat you with respect, regardless. However, if I do recall, the request was made while you were dressed in less, Miss Almalexia." The Greek woman rolled her eyes as she turned her honey eyes on Father Matthew.

"Please, Matthew. There is no need to address me so formally. I have known you since you were a young boy." Almalexia spoke. "Where is Maxwell, anyway? I have a bone to pick with him about his new pet?" Harlee slammed her fist against the wall, capturing the attention of everyone present.

"That is enough!" Harlee yelled at Almalexia. "I do not know who Maxwell is, let alone sleep with him. Who are you to call me out, on my apparel, when you, yourself, are dressed as a dolled up whore?" Harlee yelled as Almalexia smiled and stood.

"Well honey," she began in a tone as smooth as her flawless skin but as deadly as an angered viper. "Dressing this way, keeps the customers coming and my girls have to eat."

"You have daughters and you present yourself to men, dressed as a leather handbag?" Harlee spoke. With supernatural speed, Almalexia dashed around the table and grabbing Harlee by the throat, lifted her from the ground.

"Let me be clear with you, wench!" Almalexia seethed, her honey colored eyes, now glowing red. "In this city, you do what you need to get by and when you are the madam to a coven of succubae, you tend to make compromises, for their sake! You ever had to make sacrifices, so others could make a living?" Harlee held onto the powerful woman's wrist, supporting her own weight but still prey to her incredible grip.

"What the hell is going on out here!?" A deep masculine voice yelled. Almalexia immediately released her grip on Harlee's throat, letting her drop to the floor.

"Maxwell!" Almalexia spoke excitedly as a man, wearing cowboy boots, jeans, vest and hat, all black, entered. Beneath it all, he wore a white tuxedo shirt, nearly identical to the one Harlee wore. The only thing he had on, that off set his outfit, from that of a classic western gunman, were the sunglasses he wore. He also carried a bottle full of dark liquid.

Harlee rubbed her throat as she stood beside John. John continued to stare back and forth between everyone as Father Matthew and Almalexia approached Maxwell. The man lifted his bottle into the air, taking a long, uninterrupted draw from it. Harlee leaned against the counter and watched as Maxwell wiped a red substance off from his face with a dishtowel.

"I am sorry, father." The priest spoke, confusing Harlee. "I was hoping not to wake you." The cowboy gently pat Father Matthew on the shoulder.

"Might as well get this over with." He mumbled as he took another long draw from the bottle and massaged the edges of his eyes, beneath the shades. "This shit is already giving me a hangover." He spoke as he moved passed the priest and Almalexia, approaching Harlee and John. As he neared, Harlee placed herself in between Maxwell and John.

"I am not in the mood. Move." He commanded though Harlee did not budge.

"I was already trying to get rid of her, Maxwell. I must say, I am hurt that you would downgrade to her, after having me." Almalexia scoffed, causing Harlee's blood to boil over more.

"Give your relentless vanity and unfounded jealousy a rest, Almalexia. You and I, are hardly a couple, nor is she anyone's replacement." The Greek woman glared at Harlee, who smiled.

"At any rate, Maxwell." Almalexia began. "I rushed over as soon as I saw the news." At that precise moment, the news report flashed up, detailing the night's events.

"In recent events, terrorists strike once again as the local Tri Corps, pharmaceutical building, comes under attack by an as of yet unknown, criminal element. S.W.A.T. responded to the distress call and were met with heavy fire as the terrorists set fire to an apartment building, in Green Meadows.

Three suspects were injured and transported via ambulance, to Sin City hospital, only to come under attack by what we believe to be other members of their organization. With the help from their friends, the suspects escaped custody.

When police responded to the secondary attack, they were met with extreme hostility. With several confirmed dead and two buildings leveled, police are asking civilians, to stay in their homes, while authorities hunt down these violent elements.

Police did release, that they believe this to be the work of the infamous Hunter, a known killer, one of the FBI's, number one, most wanted. At this time, no further information is available."

Everyone turned to look at Maxwell, who had not even bothered to watch the broadcast.

"It was a rough night." He spoke as he continued to approach Harlee, still holding his head. "Allow me to try again. Please move." He spoke as he gently pressed against her. Harlee shoved Maxwell in the chest as she defended John.

"You are going to piss me off!" Maxwell growled as Harlee backed up against John, eyes glancing across the room.

"Please, he will not harm the boy. I swear to God, himself. My father means him no harm."

"BULLSHIT! I suppose that he 'did not harm' those children, whose pictures are in the basement!" Harlee yelled as she grabbed a knife off from the counter beside John and slashed at Maxwell, narrowly missing. Father Matthew's expression, suddenly sunk down as Maxwell tore off his glasses.

"BE QUIET! STAND THERE! DO NOT EVEN BREATHE!" He yelled, eyes glowing a deep maroon. Instantly, Harlee felt her entire body freeze as even her lungs seized. She began to panic, though she could not even force herself to blink.

"MOVE!" Maxwell commanded again and without her consent, Harlee took one-step away from John.

"Father. Please do not hurt the girl. She's only protecting young John." Father Matthew pleaded.

"I don't know. She is not so bad, in this state." Almalexia joked, feeling victorious until Maxwell shot her an angered glance and she too, bit her tongue. John squirmed uncomfortably in his chair as the massive, supernatural man approached. Maxwell stopped in front of John and stared deep into his eyes.

"I grant you release!" Maxwell spoke in the same deep voice he had used to paralyze Harlee. John suddenly jolted upright and looked around the room, panicking.

"It's alright, John. You are home." Father Matthew spoke as Maxwell turned his gaze on Harlee. She stared at him, her eyes preparing to roll into the back of her skull, as she felt herself losing consciousness. Maxwell leaned in close to her and stared into her eyes.

"You are released." The moment the words left his lips, Harlee collapsed to her knees as the hold on her body, vanished and she gasped desperately for air. John too, blinked his eyes rapidly before looking up at Maxwell. He smiled as he recognized everyone in the room.

"Are you alright, John?" Almalexia asked in a kind, motherly tone, her honey eyes filled with concern. John nodded his head as he looked away from her.

"Yes ma'am. Thank you." John answered, to which Almalexia smiled lovingly. She turned her eyes back to Harlee and her cruel, disapproving expression returned as Maxwell put his sunglasses back on.

"You would be wise to mind your own business and your manners, within these walls. And better yet, to use that brain of yours, before opening your damn mouth!" Maxwell growled as he walked away, his boots tapping behind him. Father Matthew turned his head to Almalexia, who nodded.

"Yes, I will make sure that he is alright." She said as she followed him.

"What...the hell...was that?" Harlee panted, savoring each breath as she drew one in after another. Father Matthew held out his hand to help her. Harlee glared at the priest and stood on her own, pushing his hand away as she leaned against the counter.

"I am sorry you had to experience that." Father Matthew began. "What my father did, just now, is a technique called, 'compulsion'. It is an ability used by..."

"Pure blood vampires." Harlee finished. "I shot and stabbed him with silver weapons. How is he still alive?"

"Simply put, my father is not a vampire." Harlee stared at the priest, confused as John piped up.

"Harlee...Maxwell is not one of them. He saves people." Harlee turned to John, shock on her face.

"Why in the hell does Father Matthew, keep calling him father and how come, you suddenly remember who these people are?" Father Matthew pulled out a chair and sat. Taking a sip of his coffee, he looked up at Harlee.

"Because, the man you just met, adopted both John and myself, while we were young." Harlee looked at John, barely an adult and Matthew, a man well into his sixties.

"That seems highly impossible." She spoke. Matthew and John both smiled.

"Maxwell is immortal, you ditz." Almalexia spoke as she came back from around the corner. Harlee could feel herself growing angry again, but this time, her curiosity kept her in check. "Those pictures you saw, in the basement. They are the pictures of the children Maxwell has rescued and raised, over the past two hundred years." Harlee's eyes grew wide as both Matthew and John nodded their heads.

"He is sleeping off the vampirism, now. Come tonight, he should be through the worst of it." Almalexia spoke as she brushed passed Harlee, heading towards the door.

"Thank you, Miss Almalexia." John spoke. The succubus sighed as she stopped.

"No need to thank me. Maxwell is my friend, too. I was worried about him, so I came to see you all. I do have to go back to work, though. The girls will be worried if I am gone too long, during a state of emergency. You know where to find me." She spoke as she left the room. Moments later, Harlee heard the cathedral door shut. Harlee placed her hand on her throat, which still burned from Almalexia's grip.

"I hate that bitch." She mumbled as she moved back towards Dahlia's room.

"I am sorry for the delay on your clothes, miss. It took me some time to clean them but they are hanging up to dry, now. I can pick you up something to wear around here, if you wish?"

"I appreciate the offer, Father, but I do not intend to stay."

"But do you intend to wander about, in your current attire, until your friend has recovered?" Harlee stopped, placing her forehead against the wall as she rubbed her right calf with her left foot.

"Size four hips, small shirt." She answered.

"I shall head out after breakfast, miss..."

"Harlee." She answered as she moved back to the table.

"Alright then, miss Harlee."

"Just Harlee, if you please." She interrupted.

"Alright then, Harlee. I will bring you some different clothes, when I come back. I have to drop off some things from the charity fundraiser and deliver some food to the shelter. I will be back before evening."

"Thank you, Father." Harlee spoke as she, John and Father Matthew ate breakfast.

"What was that woman's deal, anyway?" Harlee asked, breaking the silence at the table. John and Matthew eyed one another, waiting for the other to respond.

"Almalexia, has been a confidante of our father's for a long time. She has been established in this city, for quite some time and helps us."

"Why does she act that way?" Harlee asked. John turned his eyes to Father Matthew, who smiled.

"I suppose that you could say our father and Miss Almalexia were an item, a long time ago. They have been a reoccurring element for the past fifty years."

"How long have they been in this city?"

"We have only been here for a couple of years." Father Matthew answered.

"What are you doing here?" Harlee asked.

"Much the same as you are, I suppose." He told her. "We are attempting to save this city." Harlee snorted at Father Matthew's response.

"We should clear a couple of details before you make any more assumptions about me. I do not give a shit, about this filth-infested city, or anything in it. I am here for one thing and one thing alone."

"And what might that be?" Father Matthew asked. Harlee's jaw dropped as she turned her head away.

"That is none of your concern." She snapped at him. Father Matthew leaned back in his chair, as he eyed Harlee curiously. They sat in silence, for some time before John resumed eating.

"Were you a police officer?" Harlee asked, nodding her head towards the photos and medals, on display.

"I was." Father Matthew said, sipping at his coffee.

"Why did you become a priest?" She asked.

"My heart was no longer in it, I suppose." He began. "I followed in the footsteps of my father and became a priest." He said. Harlee nodded her head, shrugging off his reasoning, as she continued eating. After a few more minutes, Harlee began sipping on her coffee, as Father Matthew placed his hands on the table and stood.

"Well then, if you will all excuse me. I have some errands to attend to, in town." Father Matthew turned to leave as Harlee and John continued eating. A short few minutes later, Harlee heard the cathedral doors close.

"John." Harlee began, speaking out of the corner of her mouth. "I can get you out of here, someplace safe. Somewhere far away from this supernatural nightmare. Just give me a sign, anything and I promise you, that I will get you out." Harlee stared at John, out of the corner of her eye, waiting for his sign.

"Harlee, I appreciate your concern but I am quite safe here. Maxwell protects me." Harlee shook her head.

"John, please trust me. You cannot trust any of their kind. We are nothing but their playthings and their food. They do not possess feelings, you mean nothing to him." Harlee was beginning to grow angry until John, set down his fork, wiped his mouth and stared back at her.

"Nine years." He told Harlee, who squinted at him. "Nine years, I have lived with Maxwell and Father Matthew. Never once, in that time, have they harmed me."

"That does not mean they never will. You can never trust their kind."

"What I do not trust, are my own kind!" John's tone changed to a low growl. Before I moved in with Father Matthew and Maxwell, I lived in a remote village, in the mountains. They had these strange beliefs, they did. The kind you read about in books, or see in movies.

One year, there was a bad crop. Our local priest believed that an offering had to be made, in order to appease the harvest god. Funny thing about that town, was there was this drawing. The winner got to be the one to save the town, although in order to save the town, you gotta die.

The whole town was gathered for the drawing. Turns out, my father and the mayor had something of a nasty rivalry. The mayor lost his boy one year, to the lottery and tensions between he and my father, had gone south, ever since. The day of the drawing, I, the youngest, sat in between my father and mother. My two sisters sat beside them, as we all waited to see who would save the crop.

My father was so angry, when my name was drawn. In fact, he was so angry, he confronted the mayor personally, in front of the entire town. Turns out, the drawing had been rigged from the start." Harlee stared at John, gripping the handles of her chair as she leaned forward, waiting to hear more.

"What happened, John?" She asked as John stared off into space, eyes already growing red, as his body trembled.

"I can still hear their screams." His voice trembled. "Almost every time I close my eyes, I hear them. They came to our house, killed my father, as he answered the door. My mother took care of the one that killed my father. Paring knife through the eye. The villagers grabbed all of us, my mother, sisters and myself, drug all of us to the fields. The priest was there, to perform the ritual." John had begun to cry. Harlee could see the anger in his eyes.

"John, I think I understand. You do not have to tell me anymore." Harlee cut him off as his anger made him shake.

"I watched as they cut my mother and my sisters', throats. One by one, their blood spilled out onto the fields. Although, once it was my turn, it was not my blood, which was spilt." Harlee listened in horror as John continued his story.

"When my binds were cut, I looked up to see Maxwell beside me, the priest and several of the villagers were slain."

"So Maxwell saved you?" Harlee asked. John nodded his head.

"He placed me in Father Matthew's care. I have been with them ever since."

"Maxwell just happened to be there, when this calamity struck your town?"

"Not exactly." Harlee and John turned to see Maxwell, standing in the doorway.

"I am sorry, Maxwell." John spoke as he stood. "Did we wake you?" Maxwell shook his head as he stumbled into the kitchen, still wearing his hat and sunglasses.

"No harm done, John." Maxwell waved as he opened the cabinet, grabbing a plate. "And it was a Pesta, by the way." He informed them as he grabbed a fork out of the drawer and moved to the table.

"Good. It is just unusual to see you at breakfast." John commented, though Harlee was still locked on Maxwell's words.

"Pesta?" She asked.

"Well, it seems that there is still some dog left." Maxwell spoke to John, ignoring Harlee. "It's currently duking it out with that elder liquor from earlier. I am hoping that some food will help with the nausea." He spoke as he filled his plate.

"What's a Pesta?" Harlee asked again.

"There is a raw steak in the fridge." John pointed. "Father Matthew picked it up last night, before the hunt," he said. Harlee was beginning to grow impatient from being ignored. Maxwell scraped his plate back into the appropriate pans and placed his dishes in the sink, before opening the fridge door.

"Thank you." Maxwell said as he pulled a glass plate with a raw steak and to Harlee's horror, began eating the raw meat.

"A Pesta is a type of vengeful spirit. They are difficult to track, even harder to kill and bring about widespread plague and famine. You see, it had been a Pesta, born into our village, which had caused the harvest to fail. Maxwell had heard rumors of our troubles and had accepted a bounty, to deal with the problem." John stopped as Harlee began to speak.

"Thanks for explaining but what is his problem?" She asked, pointing toward the room Maxwell had left through.

"He always gets that way when he has to feed. It is better just to let it take its course. He is not so bad, otherwise." John answered.

"He feeds!? As in on people!?" Harlee spoke as she rose from the table.

"No, no, no. It is not like that. Maxwell does not feed on people. He only feeds on them."

"Them?" Harlee asked. When it finally dawned on her, what John meant, her eyes opened wide. John nodded his head.

"Exactly. Maxwell only feeds on the creatures that hunt us." Harlee sat back for a moment, processing what John had just revealed to her.

After breakfast, Harlee walked into Dahlia's bedroom and sat on the bed, beside her injured friend. She carefully examined Dahlia's shallow breathing, while looking upon the many bandages on her body. After staying by her side for several hours, Harlee turned her head at the sound of a gentle knock.

"Come in." She spoke as she turned her head away. She heard the door creak as light seeped into the room, casting a gallant shadow across the bed. She listened as she heard the subtle taps of her visitor's approach. Harlee felt a fluttering in her chest and placed her hand over her heart, to feel the altered rhythm. Harlee was distracted by the phenomena, until she turned to see Maxwell, looming over her.

"How is she?" He whispered, though Harlee had immediately grown on edge and angry. She tensed, ready for an altercation, though Maxwell paid no interest as he leaned forward.

"Relax, Harlee. I am not in harm's way." Dahlia mumbled. Harlee snapped her head back to see her friend, eying her.

"Dahlia, you miserable bitch. You had me worried." Harlee spoke as she hugged her friend.

"I am alright. Believe it or not, I've been worse." Dahlia answered, patting Harlee on the back.

"I will leave you two alone, then." Maxwell spoke just above a whisper as he backed away from the two.

"Thank you, Hunter." Dahlia spoke as Maxwell left the room. Harlee continued to glare over her right shoulder as the door closed behind the mysterious man. Now alone, Dalia stared eye to eye with Harlee.

"He does not seem so bad." Dahlia muttered.

"Dahlia!" Harlee jolted back with shock. "You must still be delirious! He is one of them! A freak! A monster! Their kind are responsible for our world's current state! You saw what he did to everyone at headquarters!" Harlee continued until Dahlia stopped her.

"Are we so perfect, ourselves?" She asked. Harlee immediately thought of John's story.

"I am still convinced that it is us, or them." Harlee stated, matter of factly. Dahlia closed her eyes.

"Perhaps. I am sorry, Harlee but I can barely keep my eyes open. Look out for the boy for me, would you?"

"I will. Now rest. As soon as you are well, we can leave this place." Harlee spoke as she rose from the bedside and left the room.

"How is she?" John asked as Harlee closed the door behind her.

"She pulled through. Now we just wait for her to recover." Harlee answered.

"I am glad." John said as he smiled at her. "Are you sure that you cannot stay with us?"

"Absolutely not. In fact, the moment Father Matthew returns, I will head out to plan our next course and find our new hideout." As the words left Harlee's lips, the fluttering in her chest returned. Harlee placed her hand over her heart and felt the rhythm.

"John. Can you please come help me with these?" Harlee heard Father Matthew's voice from the sanctuary.

"I will be right back." John said as he trotted off. Harlee looked down at her tuxedo shirt and was ready to be rid of it.

"It even smells like him!" She said with disgust, as she smelled the intoxicating scent of Maxwell's, natural, masculine musk. Harlee rose from her seat as Father Matthew and John entered the room, carrying several bags. He smiled as he entered the room, while John, fully loaded with bags, looked rather unhappy. Father Matthew set a bag on the table in front of Harlee, still grinning ear to ear.

"I do believe, that you will be most pleased." Father Matthew said, proud of himself as he motioned for John to set the remaining bags down.

"Thank you, Father. You really shouldn't have." Harlee said gratefully.

"It was my pleasure. Now please, have a look. I had the clerk assist me, in finding clothes for both you and Miss Dahlia. She assured me that you would both be happy." Harlee looked down at the package in front of her and slowly opened it.

"Oh my!" She spoke as she looked inside and closed it.

"Please, feel free." Matthew spoke excitedly. "Go on, step into the next room and try it on." Harlee stared again at the packages and taking a deep breath, grabbed one. "And the shoes." Father Matthew started. "I grabbed you some shoes, too." Harlee looked back and attempted to fake a smile, before grabbing a large bag of boxes and went into the next room, shutting the door.

"You are really into this makeover bit, aren't you?" John asked Father Matthew, who was still beaming.

"You know just as well as I do, that she did not wander into the catacombs, last night, by accident. There has never been a female keeper before.

Chapter 5 – No. We Did This To Each Other.

"It isn't that I am ungrateful, I am. This just is not what I am use to wearing." Harlee spoke as she modeled off her multicolored, flower patterned sundress.

"I see. Well then, how are the shoes?" Father Matthew asked, gesturing towards the silver clasped heels, the clerk had recommended. Harlee looked down the dress, which accented her body wonderfully and passed her long, smooth legs, to the shoes.

"Well they are beautiful, as well but as I said, I am just not accustomed to wearing such things." She spoke as she continued to stare at the two gawking men.

"Shouldn't a woman possess things, which accent her God given radiance?" Father Matthew asked. Harlee stared at Father Matthew blankly.

"Think of it as a disguise." John suggested. "Just while you are lying low, waiting for Dahlia to recover. This way, you will attract less attention if you need to go out." Harlee stopped to consider his proposal.

"This is true. It will be easier to move about if I blend in." She said as she watched herself in the mirror.

"That's the spirit!" Father Matthew spoke joyously as John continued to eye her.

"What is your first move?" Harlee thought to herself, as Maxwell entered the room. In his hands, he carried his axes, which she had only briefly seen, the night they arrived at the cathedral. He sat them down on the table, along with his sliver chain, which she also recognized. Everyone watched as Maxwell came back into the room, sliding into his leather duster, his hat and boots, already on.

"Another hunt, tonight?" Father Matthew asked.

"Yep." He grunted. "John, we will have to talk when I get back. Take your time. Write down what you remember. I need to know everything that happened." John nodded his head and turned to look at Harlee, who realized that Maxwell was not going to notice her change of clothes. She turned to leave the room and change back into her hunting gear, as Maxwell stopped what he was doing.

"You look nice." He grumbled under his breath, taking her by surprise.

"You think so?" She asked as John and Matthew both observed the exchange.

"Wouldn't have said it if I didn't." He resumed what he was doing as she took the compliment and moved back to prepare herself. Once she had left the room, Maxwell eyed Matthew.

"I know what you are trying to do. It won't work." He scolded. Father Matthew smiled as he scratched the back of his head.

"I have no idea what you're talking about." He told him. Maxwell nodded his head irritably as Harlee came back into the room, wearing her tactical pants and a sports bra, her other gear in her hands. John's eyes grew fixated momentarily, until Father Matthew turned him away and Harlee finished dressing.

"What do you think you're doing?" Maxwell asked as Harlee began putting on socks and her combat boots.

"You're going on a hunt, right?"

"That's what I do." He grumbled.

"Well, that happens to be what I do, too. We might as well work together." She responded, pulling on her second sock and boot, tying it.

"I work alone." He growled. Harlee stood up, chest to chest with Maxwell as she stared up into his eyes.

"Suit yourself. You would probably slow me down anyway. All of that talking and Batman bullshit, you pull, beforehand." She said as she picked up her lightweight, long sleeved shirt and tactical vest.

"Fine." He growled.

"Fine." She replied back, snapping the buckles on her vest and then sliding her weapons into their appropriate slots.

"Are you finished yet?" Maxwell asked, several minutes later, holding out Harlee's jacket to her.

"As a matter of fact, I am. Thank you." She said as she slid her jacket on, slung her sniper rifle over her shoulder and walked toward the front door.

"Not that way." Maxwell said. "Follow me." He turned and walked toward the hall where Harlee had discovered the doorway, leading to the room with the children's pictures.

"Stay close. Don't wander." He spoke gruffly with her as he pushed the bookshelf out of the way and opened the metal door leading below. As they walked down the stairs, Maxwell entered the permeating dark, veiling him from sight. Harlee clicked the light on her vest, allowing her to see where she was going.

At the bottom of the stairs, they took a left. Harlee stared off to the right as she felt the beating of her heart, shift to match that of the beating drum she heard beyond. Harlee continued to slow her pace as she waited for something to appear.

"Keep moving or I'll leave you behind." Maxwell grouched. Harlee turned her head towards him and scowled.

"You know, this is going to be a long night, with that attitude of yours." Harlee told him.

"I'm immortal. You'd be surprised how quickly time flies."

"I'm mortal, I don't enjoy wasting my time, with assholes with crappy attitudes." Though Harlee could not see it, Maxwell smirked.

"I had forgotten, how obnoxious keeping women around could be." He muttered, to which Harlee responded with offense.

"Freak like you, I can only imagine the women in your life." Before long, Maxwell stopped just in front of a ladder, which led to a manhole cover.

"This way." He said as he began to climb up above, sliding the cover out of his way, before rising to the street above. Harlee quickly followed him, wondering how this night was going to progress.

"So what's the plan?" She asked him as she slid the manhole cover back into place.

"Go out. Find things, which need killing. Kill said things." Maxwell spoke sarcastically. Harlee eyeballed him, in disbelief.

"That's your entire plan? You don't have any leads, no additional information, or informants. Nothing?" She asked, following him through the alley

"I do have a lead, as a matter of fact." He said to her as he climbed up a ladder. Harlee followed behind him and at the top of the roof, she looked around.

"Well? What are we doing up here?" She asked. Without a word, Maxwell walked to the edge of the roof and jumped over to the next building. "Hey! Where are you going?" She asked.

"I told you that I have a lead." He barked back as he slowly walked away from her.

"Asshat!" She yelled as she turned toward the ladder. As she reached the ladder, she turned back and saw Maxwell, still walking down the length of the rooftop, which connected to several buildings beyond it. Harlee glared at the man's back, impatiently and making up her mind, shook her head.

"This is not a good idea, Harlee." She said as she secured her rifle and ran. As she neared the edge of the building, she tried to push herself for more speed. She leapt as she grew close to the edge, landing upon it and used all of her acquired momentum, to launch herself forward.

Harlee's feet touched down on the next building, all of her momentum, dragging her forward. Harlee dropped to the ground, landing hard on her shoulder as she rolled several feet and came to a stop. Rising to her feet, she dusted herself off, with her cut up hands and bruised body, then ran after Maxwell.

The man had not traveled far, by the time Harlee caught up to him. He looked back over his shoulder at her, noticing her angered glare as she walked towards him. She adjusted her rifle on her shoulder, as she attempted to burn a hole through his soul, with her eyes.

"Took you long enough." He commented as he turned away and walked towards the far end of the next building and sat, waiting patiently.

"Asshat!" She mumbled to herself as she passed by. Maxwell smiled as he walked just behind her. Side by side, they walked to the far end of the building, where Maxwell perched at the edge. Harlee sat on the edge of the building beside him and stared at him.

"So...what's our play?" She asked.

"Play?" He asked her without taking his eyes off what he was staring at.

"You know...the plan. What is our plan? Why are we out here? Who, what are we looking for?"

"Our play," he said mockingly, "is three men, chasing a woman this way."

"Where?" Harlee asked.

"Give it a moment." He said. Harlee waited on edge, as a few seconds later, she heard the screams of a woman. A split second later, she saw as the woman ran into sight, three attackers pursuing her, weapons in hand.

"Give us your purse, lady?" One of the men yelled as Maxwell shook his head.

"Humans." He said shaking his head as he stood.

"What do we do?" Harlee asked.

"You can watch." He said as he dropped twenty feet down, landing in between the woman and the men. As he fell, he spread out his coat, wrapping around the first, who he punched once in the face. Allowing the attacker to fall to the ground, bloody, Maxwell turned toward the woman.

"Go home." He growled as he turned away and approached the frightened men.

"I'm going to count to three. Be gone or become a lawn ornament, such as your friend." Maxwell warned them. "I have no interest in humans."

"You better beat it, freak! We have heard all about you, Hunter! We're gonna fuck you up!" The first yelled as he charged Maxwell with an aluminum bat in hand.

"One..." He counted as he stepped sideways, avoiding the attack. He easily dodged the second, stepping backwards as the man swung horizontally.

"Two..." He sighed with irritation as the man charged forward, bat held high.

"THREE!" Maxwell yelled and pressing his hand forward, shoved the bat against his attacker's face, breaking his nose and knocking him unconscious.

"Oh ho!" The third man laughed as he pulled a gun from the back of his pants. "Now, you've gone and pissed me off. Hope they got a box ready for you, old man." He said as he pointed his gun at Maxwell.

"LOOK OUT!" Harlee yelled, catching the gunmen's attention. The gun went off, in the man's shock and Maxwell took the bullet in the chest, at point blank range.

"You know, these shirts are difficult to come by." With inhuman speed, Maxwell lunged forward, avoiding the next two shots as he grabbed the man's wrist and shattered it.

The man howled in pain as Maxwell tipped his arm behind his head. Grabbing onto the man's index finger, he jerked violently, snapping the bone. The man continued to howl in pain as spectators began to accumulate.

"Hey! Let's get out of here!" Harlee yelled down to Maxwell below, who waved her off irritably.

"Scum." He growled at the whimpering man. "If I find you out here again, harming the innocent, I will kill you, slowly." Maxwell moved down the dark alleyway, out of sight as Harlee ran back towards the alleys exit. As she neared the edge, she looked down.

"What are you looking for?" Maxwell asked, standing beside her. Harlee whipped around quickly, drawing her pistol and moving to aim it. Maxwell placed his hand on the back of her pistol and pushing the slide toward Harlee, took it off.

"There is no need for that." He growled at her. "Put it away." He said, handing the slide back to her.

"You shouldn't sneak up on people." She complained.

"You should be more alert. You're not going to last long in this city, if you don't keep both eyes open." He said as he looked around and grabbing Harlee, jumped sideways.

"What's the big..." She started as she heard a gunshot, followed by the sound of an impact, where they had just been.

"Stay down!" Maxwell yelled as he peeked around the corner and saw four men approaching.

"Dammit! I should have known." He grumbled to himself.

"Should have known what!?" Harlee yelled over the gunfire as she readied her rifle.

"That woman, down there, smelled of blood but had no injuries. It's not entirely uncommon but she's one of them."

"A vampire?" Harlee asked. Maxwell dipped his head back out and quickly moved back as another gun fired.

"Are you ready?" He asked her. Harlee smiled, Beretta in one hand, rifle propped against her hip and held in the opposite hand.

"Always."

"I'll draw their fire. They have each fired at least three shots. Wait for the reload and take your shot." He said as he ran out from cover. Harlee listened as several gunshots, broke the otherwise silent night. Harlee slid into position, counting the shots as she heard them. She listened carefully, waiting for her signal. At the sound of clicking, she smiled and rolled out from cover.

As her targets, ejected their clips and reached for another, Harlee lined up her rifle and fired. Her first target looked up, just in time to take a bullet in the chest, as she pointed her Beretta and opened fire. Almost as quickly as Maxwell had moved, the remaining two vampires began moving around her bullets, as they tried moving toward her.

Harlee readied herself, pulling her second Beretta and readying the blade on her thigh. As her enemy approached, he pulled back his hand to strike. Harlee slowly sank on her knees and flailed out with her knife, while firing. As the vampire dodged, a large, streak of silver, sliced into his head, horizontally, above the bridge of his nose.

Blood sprayed out, splashing Harlee dead in the face, as Maxwell jumped onto the scene and launched his silver chain out towards the last. As the chain secured its target, he pulled back against it and readied to swing. Harlee, scowling, lifted her gun and shot, bursting the monster's head, just as Maxwell leaned in for the swing.

As the body fell to the ground, Maxwell whipped his chain, flinging the blood from it. Next, he turned toward Harlee, face dripping. Wiping his face with one hand, he flicked the blood off and glared.

"Now we're even. What's next?" She said as she began reloading her weapons and slid her spare clips into their slots.

"Search for clues, grab anything valuable." Maxwell said as he searched through the pockets of the nearest corpse.

"Seriously? You rob them after you've killed them?"

"I'm sure he doesn't mind." He said as he pulled a wad of cash and a watch off from the body and moved to the next.

"What about the cops? Aren't they going to show up soon?" Harlee asked. Maxwell lifted his head to the sky and listened.

"You have four minutes. Then we will move to the ground and head back to the manhole. We will be on our way back, before they catch us but you have to hurry." He said as he searched the next body. Harlee shook her head as she moved to the third body and began helping Maxwell. As she searched the final body, she looked over to see Maxwell, kneeling head down, eyes closed.

She saw something in his hand, which he held close to his lips as he prayed. Harlee stared in wonder as she watched the man. After a moment, Maxwell ceased his recitation, opening his eyes and placing the objects in his hand, back in his pockets, before standing. Moments later, they had moved back to the street level and underground, as Harlee heard the sirens above.

"I cannot believe you had me do that." She mumbled to herself as they walked back toward the cathedral.

"Cannot be taking on freeloaders. You want to eat, you've got to pay your way." He answered to her. "I killed three of them. I'll give you a quarter of the take." He told her as they walked.

"Where in the hell did you learn to count? I killed two of them and you killed two of them." She told him. Maxwell was silent for a moment.

"Fine. Have it your way. You're going to need the money anyway." Maxwell said.

"What makes you say that?" Harlee asked.

"I'm sure that you have noticed but we are not exactly equipped, to have female guests. I am sure there are certain amenities that you will require." He said as they neared the gate, leading to the cathedral.

Unlocking the gate, Maxwell opened it, allowing Harlee to walk ahead of him. As they approached the stairs, Harlee could not help but lock eyes again, on the room beyond. She held her gaze to her left as she ascended the stairs. She turned the door handle and gently pressed against the metal door.

"Harlee! Father! Welcome back!" Father Matthew spoke cheerfully as he rose from the lounge chair in the sitting room and moved to see them. Harlee still bore an angry expression, her face, clothes and hair, all covered in blood. Maxwell maintained his usual expression, likewise coated.

"Was it that bad, tonight?" Matthew asked.

"No. We did this to each other." Maxwell grunted as he moved out towards his room, dropping wads of cash and watches on the kitchen table, as he passed. Harlee looked at Father Matthew, arms out, body covered in bodily fluid.

"It's alright, dear. Just set your things anywhere and go clean up. John and I are used to this sort of thing." He said.

"Thank you." She said as she began removing her gear and sat it on the floor gently.

"Umm..." Harlee started after she removed her boots. "Do you mind going into the other room for a minute?" She asked as she unclipped her gun belts.

"Ah yes, my apologies." Father Matthew said, holding his hands in the air as he left the room. Harlee shook her head and smirked as she undressed to her underwear and walking around the bloody mess, headed for the bathroom. Closing the door behind her, she turned the hot water on and stripped down the rest of the way.

Stepping beneath the steaming spray, Harlee tipped back her head and allowed the water to wash over her, washing away the blood. She remained under the water, until she could feel the steam, cleansing her soul. She took in a deep breath, before scrubbing her hair intensely.

Once she was finished, Harlee exited the bathroom, wrapped in a fresh towel. As she walked out, she stopped before John, who was innocently walking through. He stopped, frozen in fear as she stared at him, barely covered.

"Sorry John." She said as she scurried away, concealing herself within her room. Shutting the door, she threw the towel aside and opened her wardrobe, removing a pair of pajama bottoms and a tank top. After a brief visit with Dahlia, Harlee decided to turn in.

Flopping herself down onto the bed, Harlee sprawled out and stared at the ceiling. She stared at the wooden beams above her, as she heard the others, quietly tiptoeing about the cathedral. As she listened, she heard Almalexia enter and sit down with John, who was talking with Maxwell.

Chapter 6 – Wash It All Away, As Blood in the Rain

That following morning, Harlee rose from her bed and stretched her sore body. She had been kept awake, by the sound of the phantom drum again, as she had most nights since arriving. Rousing herself from her sleepy state, Harlee rose from the bed and walked out into the hall. After a brief stay in the restroom, she peeked again on Dahlia, checking and caring for her personal needs.

She was glad to see that her wounds had already healed quite well but still worried. Dahlia slept most of the day, though Matthew assured her, she had awoken and eaten a small amount each day, before returning to sleep. Harlee kissed her friend on the forehead and left the room.

Back out in the hallway, she heard the sounds of Father Matthew, moving about in the kitchen and followed them. The elderly man smiled and nodded his head to her, as he went to work, mixing ingredients. Looking into the sitting room, Harlee saw that John had fallen asleep on the couch, mouth wide open.

"He had a rough night, I suspect." Father Matthew said. "It was tough but he could recall a great number of details, for Maxwell to gather a lead from." Father Matthew leaned in close, being sure to look around before speaking.

"If you're up for another hunt tonight, I'd suggest staying close to my father." He said. Harlee nodded her head, as she took a sip from the cup of coffee, Matthew had already prepared for her.

Sitting in one of the chairs, Harlee laid back as she saw Almalexia walk out of Maxwell's room, wearing practically nothing. Having caught her attention, Harlee kept watching as Almalexia, turned and leaned against the bedroom wall as Maxwell, in only his boxer briefs, stepped into the doorway. Almalexia draped herself over his shoulders, kissing on his neck, as he attempted to dress. Noticing Harlee, Maxwell shut the door.

Harlee looked down, suddenly interested in the contents of her cup as she blushed, a slight smile on her face. A moment later, Almalexia entered the kitchen, fully dressed, eyes filled with the promise of death as she glared at Harlee.

"You'd think a creature in heat, such as yourself, would find its own kind to pant and beg at." She scoffed as she went by.

"I would have thought freaks, such as you, with no feelings, souls or hearts, would be used to being on display." Harlee replied.

Almalexia ignored Harlee, entirely. She gently touched Matthew on the shoulder and said goodbye before leaving. A moment thereafter, Maxwell exited his room, suited in his regular attire, fixing the cuffs on his shirt.

"Will you be heading out again, tonight?" Harlee asked. Maxwell stopped and slowly rolled his gaze over to Matthew, who averted his.

"That's the plan." He growled.

"I want to come with you again." Harlee said.

"I'm not going to save you, if you are caught in the line of fire again." He warned.

"I understand." Harlee nodded. "Where and when do we go?" Maxwell sighed as he sat down at the table, massaging the corners of his eyes.

"Tonight, after nightfall. There is an abandoned warehouse, in the old business district. It seems many of the slaves, were held there. They have likely been moved at this point but perhaps we will find something of interest. I will suspect that a number of wolves are still active in the area. It is a popular place for people to frequent, or go missing from." He said. Harlee nodded her head as she thought on the mission.

"Do you wish for me to provide back up, or would you rather I go in beside you?" She asked.

"What does it matter?" He asked.

"Clearly, I would bring different weapons, based upon our circumstances. If you wish for someone to cover you, I will bring the fifty cal. If you need me to charge in with you, I'll bring appropriate equipment." She said.

"Makes no difference to me. Bring a damn pizza and a beer, for all I care. I don't anticipate needing help." He said as he walked away from her. Harlee clenched her fists, angrily as she shook slightly, imagining that Maxwell's throat was in her hands.

"Asshat!" She grumbled to herself as she rose from the table, downed the last of her coffee and began to walk away.

"Breakfast?" Father Matthew asked as he entered the kitchen, bacon, eggs and sausages on three plates. Harlee turned and narrowed her eyes at Father Matthew.

"I know what you're trying to do." She said, plucking a piece of bacon from the plate. "It isn't going to work." She said, grabbing three more slices and walking away. Father Matthew shrugged his shoulders as he sat the plates down.

"Apparently, I'm more devious than I thought." He smiled and shook his head as he walked away.

Harlee spent the majority of her day, exerting her body. It had long been her daily ritual, to continue pushing herself to her physical peak. Every day, filled with thoughts of why she had come to the city, reminding her why she could not afford to idle.

Preparing for the day's hunt, she instead stretched her body. Moving through various forms, she could feel her body perspire. John, having returned from his daily routines, walked in on Harlee, during her routine. Harlee, limber body twisted into a complex pose, happened to notice the young man, as he froze.

"Can I help you with something, John?" She asked.

"I..uh...nope. I will be on my way, now." He said, walking away. Harlee smiled, as she returned to her poses, waiting for evening.

Later that night, Harlee stood in the kitchen, checking her Berettas, spare clips, knife and wrist stingers. She tightened her boots, strapped her tactical vest securely and put everything in its proper place. The entire time, Maxwell stood impatiently, tapping his boot.

"Are you ready, yet?" He asked.

"YES!" She yelled, irritated after his sixth time asking.

"Follow me, then." He said as he walked towards the front of the cathedral.

"We aren't going to use the catacombs?" She asked.

"Can't." He said.

"Why not?" Harlee asked him.

"You're too damn slow. I would have to spend all night, waiting for you to walk to the docks." He grumbled. "Better we take the car." Harlee grinded her teeth slightly, growing ever more agitated with Maxwell, before the night had begun. She followed him out the front door and turning to the right, began walking down the sidewalk.

"How far away is the car?" Harlee asked, following behind Maxwell.

"Not far." He muttered under his breath. They walked for a few more minutes as he pulled a keyring from his pocket and began flipping through them, as he turned and walked towards one of many storage containers. He stopped and grabbing the appropriate key, opened the container.

"Oh, wow!" Harlee said as she saw two things that caught her eye. The first, a black, nineteen seventy, dodge charger. Harlee marveled at the vehicle for a moment, as her eyes turned to her other fascination, a custom black motorcycle, which was fully upgraded. She approached it, running her hand down the slick leather seat, while admiring the majestic beauty of both vehicles.

"Are you coming?" Maxwell asked.

"Practically," she whispered under her breath, tracing her fingers across the handlebars before moving to Maxwell, who was standing by the passenger door.

"You're going to let me drive?" She asked, excitedly.

"No, but there are rules to consider." He said as he opened the door for her. She eyed him carefully for a moment, as he took her equipment and she climbed into the car. Leaning back against the comfortable seat, she heard the smooth leather rustle beneath her. After placing Harlee's things in the back seat, Maxwell climbed into the driver seat and inserting the key, brought the car to life with a roar.

"Yes!" Harlee cheered to herself at the sound as Maxwell shifted the car into gear and pulled out from the container. He stepped out long enough to close the storage container and climbed back into the car, before pulling out onto the road.

They sat in silence for several minutes. Harlee watching out the window, took occasional breaks to stare back at Maxwell, before returning to the scenery. She repeated this process several times, while tapping on her thighs, before mustering her courage.

"Mind if I turn on the radio?"

"Fine." He said. Harlee pressed the radio button and immediately reached for the volume dial, as hard rock music, blared in her face.

"It's fine." He told her as she turned the dial back. "I enjoy this music." He said. Harlee looked at Maxwell, surprised and sat back, enjoying the ride. As they drove, Harlee leaned her head back and fell asleep, the blaring sound of drums and guitar riffs, drowning out the many torments of her mind.

"We're there." Maxwell whispered, waking her. The music was off, the car was parked across the street from the old pier and it was pouring rain. "You may want this. If you're in trouble, figure it out." He spoke as he handed her an earpiece. Harlee stirred, rubbing her eyes, as she accepted the earpiece and Maxwell got out of the car. Harlee unbuckled herself and turned to open the door, as it opened for her.

"I told you. There are rules." Maxwell said as he held out his hand, to her. Harlee accepted it, awkwardly and stepped out of the car, as Maxwell closed it behind her.

"You are going to want to take point up there." He said, pointing toward the work crane. "Should offer you little accessibility but a full visual."

"And also no way to escape if needs be." She muttered, looking for a better spot. "I am going to set up there." She said, pointing towards the crate hanging from the crane.

"It's not too far, I can jump onto the roof or to the ground below, without injury. That will offer me the most options." She said as Maxwell shrugged, opening the back door for her. Harlee pulled her fifty-caliber rifle from the seat and slung it over her shoulder.

"Suit yourself." He said as he crossed the barren road, Harlee just behind him. They moved quickly, using the rain to cover their scent and sound, as they moved in on the potential den. Harlee tapped Maxwell on the shoulder as she broke off from him, moving towards her sniping spot.

Climbing up the side of the crane, proved difficult, with the rain and additional weight but Harlee managed, reaching one hand over the other. As she came upon the top of the arm, she moved towards the cable and slid down it, reaching her destination. She laid, in prone, mounting her rifle at the edge of the suspended container and adjusted her scope as she peered within the building.

Maxwell, had already neared the front doors and was carefully eyeing inside before entering. Harlee kept her breathing calm as she waited. The rain continued pouring down on her, ticking against her leather pants, vest and boots, as it clanked against the container. Harlee quickly put her earpiece in place, as she took in a deep breath and sighed.

"In the great green room, there was a telephone and a red balloon." She whispered to herself as she visually followed Maxwell inside the building.

"Reading stories?" Maxwell whispered into her ear through the communicator.

"Shut up." She whispered back. "See anything?"

"No. Not yet but they're here." He said. "Keep your eyes open and watch your ass, if you don't want it to be a steak."

"Best rump roast they'd ever have." She commented, as she followed his every move.

"I'll take your word on it." He said as she watched him move around the corner, into the next room, pulling out his axes. He reached out gently, pressing against a broken wooden door, with the tip of his axe. Harlee could hear the wood creak as he pressed against it.

"What do you see?" She whispered to him.

"They were definitely here. This place reeks of them. Fur all over the floor, claw marks on the walls...ah, damn!" Harlee snapped to attention as a massive figure, launched itself across the room, tackling Maxwell.

"Hang on! I'm on my way!" She yelled as she stood atop the container.

"No! Stay put! There are too many of them!" She could hear Maxwell yell, through the sounds of multiple, large beasts, growling, snapping their jaws and tearing everything apart. Harlee stopped and laid back down, in position as she tried to find a shot.

Looking through her scope, Harlee watched as pieces of the room, collapsed from above, while the container beneath her began to shift. Pulling her head from the scope, she moved up on her elbows and turned her head, eying the empty crane controls. She could still hear Maxwell's battle through her earpiece and quickly glanced back into her scope.

Maxwell stood in the center of the main room, arms wide, mouth open as he roared at his attackers. Four werewolves and a number of people holding knives and bats, glared at him as they slowly approached.

Harlee focused her vision, taking a deep breath as the container continued to sway slightly.

"Over your right shoulder, stay left." Harlee whispered into the earpiece as she lined up her shot and fired. The werewolf, nearest to Maxwell dropped, its head having burst. The others all jumped, staring outside as Maxwell charged. Harlee quickly ejected the blank cartridge as she slid in another bullet and loaded it in place. Lining up her shot, she whispered.

"On your left hip, stay right." She said as she pulled the trigger, shredding the torso of one of the thralls. Maxwell sliced through another, blood painting the walls. Harlee ejected and prepared to load again, as the container shook violently, spinning nearly ninety degrees, before the cable snagged, wrenching it back.

Harlee was thrown sideways, losing her rifle, which fell to the ground below. Grabbing onto one of the crane cables, Harlee rolled over the edge, narrowly holding on as she saw what awaited her below. As Maxwell continued to battle with those inside, two more had found their way to her.

As Harlee hang precariously over the edge, of the still spinning container, the two beasts beneath her launched themselves, trying to catch her. Harlee flailed her feet, kicking as they continued to grow close to her. As the container began to stabilize, she lifted her body up and over the side, twisting her wrist slightly in the process.

She growled with irritation as she held herself in place, while reaching to her left thigh, pulling her Beretta. As the first of the two, launched itself at her, Harlee squeezed the trigger. The beast tipped off course as the bullet struck it in the side of the face. As its body struck the container, Harlee's platform, again, was sent on a wild ride.

Her body was thrown backwards, forcing her to hit her head against the metal. As she slid backwards, head spinning, Harlee reached out, gripping onto the crane cable, in the center of the shipping crate. Harlee groaned through the pain in her arm, as she climbed up onto the cable and pointed her Beretta between her feet. The noise in her earpiece was excruciating as she heard the chaos unfolding within.

"Piss OFF!" She yelled as she fired the rest of her clip into the cable, severing the attached head from the rest of the cable. Harlee's feet dangled in the air as the container fell onto the wolves below. Harlee slid her pistol into her thigh strap as she maintained her height.

Several lengthy seconds passed, without the slightest trace of movement. Harlee dropped down onto the container and reloading her weapon, allowed her injured, bleeding arm, to hang at her side as she moved in on Maxwell's position.

"I am blind, no visual. I am on my way in. Breaching now." She continued to whisper as she kicked against the door, pointing her gun forward. Moving her body in line with her sights, Harlee crept through the building, the wooden boards creaking beneath her feet as she stepped.

Up ahead, she saw where a massive hole had been torn through the floor. Examining the shattered planks, the upward facing breaks, indicated the force came from below.

"They were waiting beneath for us." Harlee concluded as she continued to creep forward, noticing the horrific amount of blood, guts and bile, dripping from every surface.

"Maxwell?" Harlee whispered as she heard a noise up ahead of her. "Maxwell, are you there?" She spoke again, edging around the corner, aiming her gun towards the sound of a board creaking. Harlee stepped, the board beneath her cracked. As Harlee slipped, one last man rounded the corner, knife already soaring for Harlee's ribs.

In midair, Harlee twisted her body, catching the blade in her shoulder but allowing her to pry her leg sideways in the hole, propping her up enough to spin the man over her hip. As the man fell to the ground, breaking the rest of the floor, Harlee fired three rounds into his chest, killing him.

As they neared the floor below, Harlee held the man's belt as she pulled herself, over top of him. They both hit the ground with a heavy thud. Harlee groaned from the shock of the fall and out of anger, shot the corpse once more before attempting to rise.

"Maxwell?" She groaned again as she reached her feet. "I'm in the basement, on my way up." She said, holding her side as she limped to the nearby stairs. Climbing the staircase, she began searching for Maxwell but heard a noise outside, followed by another wolf corpse, toppling over the roof outside, dropping onto the ground ahead of her.

Harlee limped over to the backdoor, to investigate. Training her gun, she stepped outside and felt the rain, pouring down over her, washing away the blood, which had coated her. She tipped her head back for a moment and sighed before slowly moving towards the outside staircase. Reaching the top, she crouched down and peered around the corner but saw only Maxwell, kneeling in the rain, surrounded by bodies.

She moved towards him slowly, seeing his axes lying on the ground beside him, hunks of his foes, spread out in unimaginable formations. The man stared skyward, eyes closed as he whispered.

"Maxwell? Are you alright?" She asked as she saw that none of the enemy remained and holstered her weapon. Maxwell continued to mumble and so Harlee rested her back against the wall and extending her hurt left leg, slid her back down the wall, resting her head.

She continued to watch Maxwell as he pulled something from his pocket, which he brought to his lips and kissed. Harlee tilted her head to the side, seeing that the objects were a torn piece of an old blanket and a bejeweled rosary. Head still raised to the sky, eyes closed, kneeling in a flowing stream of rainwater, he prayed.

"Please, lord God, I, your servant, ask of thee." Maxwell said. "I ask of thee now, in the name of your children and your son. Wash away their sins, wash away their pain. Wash it all away, as blood in the rain." He concluded, kissing his blanket and rosary once more, before placing them back into his pocket. Harlee watched, as the blood continued to slowly drip from his coat and dissipate in the rain. After a moment, he slowly rolled his head towards her.

"Are you alright?" He asked, a low growl to his voice.

"You weren't talking through the communicator. I came to back you up." She said, tilting her head back. Maxwell tipped his head, showing Harlee where his ear and side of his face had been torn, three large claws, having cleaved through his flesh.

"Jesus! Are you alright!?" Harlee yelled as she attempted to stand too quickly and sank back down, holding her head. Pulling her hand away, she saw that she was bleeding.

"I will heal." Maxwell said. "Let me look at you." He rose to his feet, leaving his axes behind as he approached. Harlee leaned forward, hand still on her head as Maxwell knelt down beside her. Gently touching her wrist, Maxwell pushed her hand away and examined the back of her head.

"Doesn't appear to be serious. All the same, do try to stay awake, on our way back." He said.

"Thank you." Harlee said, eying the unnatural kindness, Maxwell had offered.

"It would be a pain in the ass, to take you to the hospital. Would rather just let Matthew deal with you." Harlee scowled as Maxwell walked passed.

"And there he is, the asshat, himself." She mumbled to herself.

"Come again." He said, pointing to his ruined ear. "Might bit deaf on this side." He grumbled as he jumped from the roof and walked back towards the car. Harlee slowly rose from her seated position and began limping towards the stairs. As she reached the steps, Maxwell began walking her way, her rifle in his hand.

"Thanks." She grumbled as he offered her his hand. "I think I'll manage." She said grumpily as she limped down the last two steps and moved toward the car.

"By all means." He said as he moved ahead of her, still carrying the rifle. By the time Harlee had managed to limp across the street,

Maxwell was closing the trunk of the car. She leaned against the hood of the car, as she hobbled around to her seat and saw that inside; the entire front of the car was covered, in plastic.

"Seriously?" She asked. Maxwell eyed her and nodded his head.

"Even I don't want to scrub blood stains out of the leather. I'm immortal, I don't have time for that shit." He said, opening her door for her. Harlee climbed in, rustling the plastic as she sat. Dragging her leg in after her, Maxwell closed the door and moved to the driver side. As he sat, the plastic he had laid for himself rustled and Harlee caught a better look at his ripped face.

Three slash marks, ran from the corner of his forehead and the width of his head, his ear partially missing. She saw that the bleeding had already ceased, and what could easily kill a normal man, barely phased Maxwell. As Maxwell drove, he turned the volume on the radio low. The steady rumble of the engine, sound of the rock and comfortable leather seats, began to lull Harlee to sleep.

"Stay awake." Maxwell spoke in a kind voice, as he tapped her arm gently.

"I'm sorry." She said, trying to shake herself from the sensation. "It's just so hard to keep my eyes open." She said as she tipped to the side and began falling asleep again.

"No. We aren't having any of that, right now." He said as he gently braced the back of her head and gently stroked the base of her skull.

"Uh, that feels good." She said as she tipped her head forward.

"So long as you stay awake, I won't stop." He said as he maintained constant pressure, holding her head up. As they reached the cathedral, Maxwell stopped in front of the door and quickly moved to open Harlee's door. Helping her, he walked with her to the front doors and opened them.

"What happened?" Father Matthew asked as he and John ran to Harlee's side.

"We ran into some trouble at the den." Maxwell said. "She may have a dislocated shoulder and a concussion, amongst other things." He said as John placed his shoulder under Harlee's outstretched arm and helped her limp towards the back of the cathedral.

"How is Dahlia?" Harlee mumbled.

"Fairing much better than you, at the moment. I suspect she will be up and about, shortly. Come now, let us tend to your injuries, before you take her place."

Chapter 7 – The Woman in Black

The following morning, Harlee awoke, lying in her bed, her head throbbing. She rolled her eyes around the room and felt something tugging on her outstretched toes. She looked towards her feet and saw Dahlia, sitting at the end of the bed.

"Good evening, Harleequinn." Dahlia joked as she patted Harlee on her uninjured leg.

"Hey, you beautiful bitch." Harlee replied back. "You're not dead." She smiled. Dahlia shared her smile as she moved towards Harlee's right side and brushed her hair to the side.

"You rest up, alright? I have some business to take care of in town. Check in on the girls, so on. I also want to check home." Harlee reached out, grabbing Dahlia's hand as she moved to leave.

"We can't stay here." Harlee said.

"Harlee, listen. Home is probably gone, now. Let's stay here, as long as we might. Make the best of it. Get along with everyone. If they ask us to leave or we feel threatened, we leave. Until then, this is a good thing. Let's do what we can to help out. I have to go. It may take me a few days, to track everyone down. Try not to hurt yourself, too badly before I get back." Dahlia told her as she rose from the bed and left the room. Harlee, laid her head back against the pillow and closed her eyes.

Harlee awoke again, the next morning, feeling much better but insatiably hungry. Carefully, she swung her legs over the bed and slowly applying pressure to both feet, rose from it. She stretched her body and ran her limbs through their full range of motion, confirming her recovery. Smiling to herself, Harlee drank the glass of water by the bed and walked out into the hall.

Upon entering the hallway, her nostrils were assailed by the smell of pancakes. Harlee's feet marched of their own accord and sat herself silently at the table. As John turned from the stove, he jolted at the sight of her and smiled.

"How are you feeling?" He asked, setting down a plate, which was fully stacked.

"Starving." She said as she eyed the food, the way a lioness watches a young gazelle.

"By all means, dig in." John said. "I can make more." Before he turned away, Harlee was already attacking the plate, transporting food from John's plate to her own, adding strips of bacon and syrup to the bundle. John stared in awe, as Harlee annihilated her food. He slowly crept forward, setting a glass of milk beside her and the entire pot of coffee, as without missing a single beat, Harlee continued to feed, while simultaneously pouring her coffee.

Twenty minutes later, Harlee's pace slowed and she began to taste her food. She could feel as a hard lump formed in the pit of her stomach and she smiled. Pushing her cleaned plate away, Harlee looked up at John, who was still staring.

"Thank you, John. That was delicious." She said. "I don't normally see you cook, though. Is Father Matthew away?"

"He is out front, meeting with the daily parishioners. He had a light breakfast but I assumed he would be hungry once he was finished. Also, Maxwell enjoys pancakes." No sooner had John said the words, he turned and jumped again as Maxwell stood at the end of the hallway. Harlee jolted, as well, having not noticed his approach.

"Good morning." Maxwell said as he walked into the kitchen and sat opposite of Harlee.

"Good morning, Maxwell." John said as he sat more pancakes on the table. "I can make more. Just give me a minute." He turned to the counter.

"No need, John." Maxwell said. "I will make my own. This was quite thoughtful of you. Eat. I know you're hungry." He said, gesturing towards the open chair. John sat and began eating as well. Maxwell leaned back in his chair and tipped his hat down over his eyes as he stretched out and sank slightly.

"How are you feeling?" He asked, a genuine, caring tone to his voice.

"Much better, thank you." Harlee said. "Another day and I am sure I'll be back in shape for another patrol."

"You may want to take it easy." Maxwell said. "You don't heal, the way I do." He said.

"Is your ear alright?" She asked, curious to see. Maxwell tipped his hat to the side, revealing not only had the scratch marks vanished, but also the ear had recovered completely, with no signs of damage.

"I wish I could heal, the way you do." She said.

"Things aren't too exciting right now anyway." He said, tipping his hat back down over his eyes. "Best we relax while we can. Not long from now, there will be a plethora of excitement."

"The Feast?" Harlee asked. Maxwell nodded his head.

"Good to know you're well informed."

"Seven days, celebrating seven sins, might as well hang out a supernatural welcome matt." Harlee said.

"I don't disagree." He told her. Harlee sat back, crossing her legs and stretching out, as she sipped her coffee. As John finished, he pushed his plate away and rested his hands on his stomach.

Harlee spent the majority of her day, relaxing around the sitting area, doing her best to rest up. She made sure to exercise her body, isolating her leg the best she could but being sure to work through the stiffness in her shoulder. By the end of the day, Harlee had found herself growing increasingly bored.

She sat at the small table in her bedroom, cleaning her equipment, which had not been maintained since her hunt and was in desperate need, of her attention. She made sure her sights were aligned properly and took an exorbitant amount of time, looking over every detail of her fifty cal. She looked at the clock and seeing that it was already nearing one, decided to head to bed.

That night, Harlee awoke, to the sound of the catacombs drum. She was unsure as to why she heard it but knew only, that it threatened to drive her mad. Rising from the bed, Harlee walked to her door and peeked outside.

Stepping out into the hallway, Harlee crept through it with silent steps. As she reached the bookshelf, which concealed the camouflaged door, she saw that it had been shut. Harlee carefully slid the bookshelf away; far enough for her to squeeze her body behind and begin feeling along the wall for the latch.

Her hands ran down the length of the door and eventually grazed something, which felt out of place. Giving it a gentle pull, the door opened. Harlee pushed it open enough, so she could squeeze inside and continued sneaking down the stairs, turning right, at the bottom.

Her heart, pounded in her chest, urging her to walk forward. She held her hand to her breast, trying to will the beating to slow. One-step after another, she came upon the altar room, with its many pictures and ancient dagger, resting at the center.

Harlee, driven by sheer instinct, stood within the center of the room, hands resting on the altar. She searched around, feeling the phantom pulse, coursing through her entire body, more powerfully than ever before. She knelt down, beside the altar and closing her eyes, could feel through the ground at her feet, the source of her obsession.

She heard a pair of boots, up above her and jerked upright, accidentally bumping the altar with her shoulder. She heard the dagger fall to the floor as she held her sore arm and closed her eyes tightly. As the pain subsided, Harlee reached for the dagger and picked it up. Rising to her feet, she looked at the dagger as she heard boots, stomping towards her.

"WHAT ARE YOU DOING DOWN HERE!?" Maxwell roared, his voice echoing dangerously off from the walls. The lights in the tunnel flickered, going out as he neared.

"I am sorry. I bumped the altar on accident." She began to explain but saw the fire in his eyes.

"YOU ARE NOT ALLOWED DOWN HERE! GET OUT!" He yelled, moving dangerously close to her, causing her to panic. The shadows cast by the flickering lights, caused Maxwell's presence to grow more menacing, more unpredictable than ususal. Harlee pressed against Maxwell's chest, in an attempt to keep him at arm's reach. Maxwell continued to press against her, causing Harlee to grow ever more uneasy as she shoved off from him.

"GO! SWEAR TO ME THAT YOU'LL NEVER COME DOWN HERE, AGAIN!" He yelled.

"MAXWELL!" Harlee screamed back in his face. "CALM DOWN AND LET ME EXPLAIN!" Maxwell stopped, the look in his eyes fading back, as the lights stabilized, no longer flickering. He stared at Harlee, as if awakening from a trance, seeing the panic in her eyes. Slowly, non-threateningly, he raised his hands, and took a step back from her.

"I am sorry," he seethed. "You must never come down here."

"I'm sorry." She said. "I couldn't sleep and all I could hear was this damn drum, pounding in my brain. I honestly thought I was going insane. I don't know why I came down here, I don't." She said, still staring at him. Maxwell stood between her and the altar.

"This place is sacred to me." He said. "This is the one place, I ask for you to stay away from. Not even Almalexia comes down here. Promise me, you'll never come down here again."

"I won't." She told him. "I promise."

"Just go." He waved her off, not looking her in the eye as he said it. "Go." Harlee turned, sped down the hall, moving back up the stairs and running straight to her room as she did her best to fall back asleep.

"That was a bad idea, Harlee." Father Matthew scorned, after Harlee finally came out of her bedroom, that evening. John sat across the room from them, minding his own business. "I thought that I made it clear, you shouldn't be down there?"

"I am sorry, Father. I could not help it. I heard that noise again. I could not sleep and it started driving me insane. I had to go down, just one more time, to find out what it was."

"Had you thought to ask Maxwell? Ask him, if you could see what was down there?" Matthew asked her. Harlee hung her head low.

"What can I do, to make it up to you?" She asked.

"I'm not mad at you, Harlee. He'll come back around, in time. He isn't as angry with you as you might think." Without saying a word, Maxwell walked by, leather trench draped over his arm and a large duffel bag in the other.

"Are you heading out tonight, Maxwell?" John asked.

"Yes." Maxwell answered as he continued to move back and forth.

"Has something happened?" Father Matthew asked.

"Full moon tonight. The wolves will be on the move, preparing for the feast." Maxwell spoke bluntly, as he began unloading the bags onto the table. Harlee stared at the various weapons and a thought struck her.

"I am going with you." Harlee said.

"I work alone." Maxwell grunted.

"Me too. I will go on patrol, separately, if that is how you want it. I know you're pissed at me, already, so I suppose it doesn't matter." She spoke, holding her ground against the much larger man.

"This is no game. I am hunting something much bigger than low class wolves in an abandoned warehouse." He growled angrily.

"Have you found him?" John asked. "Have you found Balthazar?" Harlee stared, unsure of who the man was, as Maxwell shook his head.

"No, not necessarily but the feast will be held on the next full moon. Surely, some of the big players will be coming to town. Almalexia and her coven have also been asked to entertain for a party of bloodsuckers." Maxwell told them.

"And you expect me to stay behind? I have been waiting for such an opportunity, ever since I arrived in this shitty town." Harlee stated as she turned to Father Matthew. "Father, are my things still in the back?" Father Matthew handed a keyring to John, who took Harlee into the back.

"I do not want her going, this time." Maxwell continued to growl as Matthew stared at him.

"You could use the extra set of eyes out there. This is far larger than what you have faced in the past."

"That's precisely why I want to go alone. I can't waste time babysitting." Maxwell argued.

"Last I checked, I held my own against you." Harlee commented, already fully geared up. Father Matthew chuckled as Harlee passed by, grinning.

"Only because I was trying not to kill you." He snarled as he stared at the back of her head. Harlee moved to the catacombs entrance and waited by the door. Maxwell stomped his boots as he walked down the hall and pushed the bookshelf out of the way. Harlee opened the door to the catacombs and they both descended into the dark halls below. Using the sewers entrance, they quickly made their way out into the back alleys and ascended to the rooftops.

"Where do you suspect the meeting point to be?" Harlee asked Maxwell. The hunter turned his body to the south, staring at the tallest skyscraper in the entire city.

"I believe that to be where Balthazar has built his throne." Maxwell said. "The wolf's den has moved time and time again and he rarely frequents this city but if Almalexia's lead is good, this is where they will be."

"You trust her?" Harlee asked.

"More than I do, you." He replied.

"Good enough for me," she said as she looked over the large gap between buildings. Harlee shifted her rifle across her back and began pumping her legs, preparing for the jump.

"Stop. You'll only hurt yourself." Maxwell spoke as he walked beside her.

"You better not have brought me up here to leave me behind." Harlee grumbled.

"Sounds like a good idea, to me." He said as Harlee glared at him. "Get on." He spoke as he bore his back to her and squatted down.

"What?"

"Did I stutter? Get on. You're only going to slow me down, otherwise."

"We could have taken the car." Harlee suggested.

"We would have been stuck in traffic and there is too much surveillance where we are going. If we are spotted, it would be far too easy for the enemy to track the car."

"Dammit." She grumbled as she grabbed onto Maxwell's shoulders and climbed onto his back. Maxwell gently wrapped his arms beneath Harlee's legs and firmly gripped her hamstrings. Harlee could feel her excitement swell as Maxwell stood and her feet lifted from the ground.

"If you try anything, I'll stab you." Harlee threatened as she squeezed her body tightly against his.

"It wouldn't surprise me if you did anyway." He remarked as he ran to the edge of the roof and jumped. Harlee buried her head into Maxwell's shoulder blades as they grew airborne and sailed over the street below. Maxwell's boots touched down on the next rooftop and he continued to run at full speed. Harlee opened her eyes, long enough to watch Maxwell leap over to the next building.

Harlee shielded her eyes once more, gripping onto Maxwell's chest, even tighter. Harlee felt the steady beat of Maxwell's pulse and it calmed her. As she relaxed, she felt the combination of fear, excitement, mix in an odd adrenal formulation, resulting in an increase in arousal. Her thighs began to quiver and her nostrils became saturated in Maxwell's melodious scent as various glands, throughout her body, swelled. Harlee's thighs gripped Maxwell for something other than a sense of danger, desire.

"We are nearly there. You can get down, now." Maxwell whispered as he tapped on Harlee's thigh. Harlee snapped from her distraction.

"What?" She asked him.

"We can walk from here." He told her. Harlee looked around, while slowly climbing down from his back.

"Are you alright?" He asked. Harlee wanted to answer with a resounding "no," having grown so deeply aroused by someone, she resented so vehemently.

"Fine." She replied sharply. "I just need a moment to recompose myself, is all." Maxwell pointed to the water tower at the far end of the building.

"That should provide us with a decent vantage and cover. That is where I will be." He said as he walked to the tower. Harlee closed her eyes and took several deep breaths, in order to ease herself.

"In the great green room, there was a telephone and a red balloon." She whispered to herself and exhaled, releasing her tension. Harlee held her rifle in place as she jogged after Maxwell and began climbing the water tower. Once there, she saw Maxwell, already perched, looking down below.

"Do you see anything?" Harlee whispered as she dropped to her stomach and crawled towards him.

"Guards." Maxwell replied.

"How many?"

"Enough." Maxwell said. Harlee narrowed her eyes as she glared at him. Once she had reached the edge, however, she understood why he had made the comment. At first glance, Harlee counted near fifty armed guards, all standing by awaiting something.

"With this many guards, we must be in the right place." Harlee stated.

"I am inclined to agree with you." Maxwell added. "Just remember, not everyone down there is human. Be careful with how much noise you make and how badly you perspire. If something is even slightly out of the ordinary, they will open fire on us." Harlee nodded her head, to confirm that she understood.

Together, they remained in prone, for over an hour waiting, until a number of headlights reared from down the road. Several armed escorts on motorcycle, swarmed around a stretch limo, which parked in front of the guards. Two guards approached the vehicle and opened the first set of doors.

Several characters, each dressed in lavish outfits, exited the limo. Some carried silver platters, while another carried bottles of wine. Each of the troupe, formed ranks on either side of the red carpet as one lone figure, dressed as a renaissance era nobleman, approached the limo.

"That is Balthazar." Maxwell whispered.

"You keep saying his name but who is Balthazar?"

"He is among the oldest of the Lycanthropes. He is the head of one of the original clans, a pureblood. If he is here, whoever is in the limo is extremely important." Harlee stared at the man, Maxwell identified. As he neared the limo, he reached out and opened the final set of doors.

A pale arm, attached to an elegant, red-gloved hand, reached out as a pair of long silky, legs, stretched out. Accepting Balthazar's hand, a gorgeous, auburn haired woman, wearing a blood red gown, fit for a queen, stepped out.

"That is Auriel." Maxwell whispered. "Queen of all vampires. The first of her kind." Harlee looked back through her scope and watched as arm in arm, Auriel and Balthazar walked down the red carpet and stopped to watch the limo. Another woman, brown haired, tall, athletic build; dressed in typical business attire, exited next. Harlee's heart burst from her chest as she stared.

"That's my sister!" Maxwell, we have to go down there!"

"Don't move!" He growled. "If you go down there, you're food!"

"But I have to help her. She's my sister." Harlee argued, growing desperate as her sister walked to Auriel's side and stood off the red carpet.

"There's not a damn thing you can do, if you get her or yourself killed, now is there?" Maxwell pointed out to her. Harlee froze. Maxwell nodded his head as they both resumed their surveillance.

Another man, massive in stature, rose from the limousine, immediately turned, kneeled and lifted out his hand. Another feminine hand, this one, gloved in black, reached out, the entire congregation prostrating themselves, Auriel included. Harlee, upon noticing this, turned to Maxwell, who appeared equally confused.

"Who is that woman?" Harlee asked. The woman stepped out of the limo, black stiletto heels, black, bare backed gown and hair, darker than darkness itself. The woman herself, radiated an aura, which sent terror into Harlee's heart. The woman stopped, turning her head towards their vantage long enough to smile. Harlee turned her head again towards Maxwell, to ask who she was but saw that Maxwell was doubled over in pain, gripping his sides.

"Maxwell! What's wrong?" Harlee moved to his side as he turned to face her.

"Run!" He groaned, looking to her with blood red eyes, vertical slits for pupils. Harlee stopped as she stared at him.

"Maxwell? What is happening to you?" Harlee spoke as she heard shouting from below, followed by gunfire. Harlee barely dropped to the water tower roof, in time to avoid evisceration.

"RUN!" Maxwell yelled but his naturally deep voice was accompanied by something else, as if the devil himself had borrowed the man's vocal chords. Harlee rose to move as a fully transformed werewolf jumped up beside her and slashed. Harlee narrowly rolled away from the slash and moved to train her gun as Maxwell, with blinding speed, jumped onto the creature's back.

Harlee watched in horror, unable to move as she bore witness to a scene, more horrific than anything she had yet seen. She watched as Maxwell, now possessing claws liking to a werewolf, gripped through the fur and flesh of the creature's face. The lycanthrope raged out in pain as Maxwell pulled its face away, exposing its neck, as the werewolf tried to fight off its quarry.

Next, the corners of Maxwell's mouth receded passed where his cheekbones should have been, revealing an extended mandible with an extra six inches of bite radius and several razor sharp teeth. Harlee shielded herself as Maxwell's dagger filled mouth, tore through the flesh of the creature's throat.

Blood sprayed everywhere, covering the entire water tower, as if a sudden rainstorm had blown through. As Harlee was drenched in the hot, sticky fluid, she noticed several other lycanthropes had approached but froze at what they saw. As Maxwell's prey grew limp and dropped, Harlee noticed the nearly twelve inch gash, missing from its neck.

Maxwell stood over top of it, head tipped back as he swallowed the entire hunk of flesh, without chewing. His black hair and entire face were painted sanguine, as he smiled with the jaws of a shark. He stared at Harlee with his deranged smile and she watched it slowly return to normal.

Maxwell's eyes flitted to the right and he dashed towards her. Before Harlee could fire her gun, Maxwell had wrapped his body around her. Harlee caught a slight glance at a number of assault weapons from across the street, trained on them as Auriel, Harlee's sister and the mysterious woman, casually walked inside.

Maxwell took off at a run and dove from the tower roof as the gunners opened fire. He roared with a tone fitting for a beast as several rounds struck him. Maxwell's boots struck the ground and he continued to run as two regular white and grey werewolves, plus one that was silver and massive, ran up on them.

"I SAID RUN!" Maxwell howled as he launched Harlee to the adjacent roof. Harlee hit the rooftop hard and felt her left arm go completely numb, after a sharp pain. Harlee groaned as she rose to her feet and saw Maxwell, combating the three werewolves. Remembering what Maxwell had told her, Harlee took off at a run, leaving Maxwell behind. She moved to the nearby fire escape and scaled it to the street below. Without any care to the make, Harlee broke the window of the first car she encountered and began hotwiring it.

Once the vehicle, came to life, Harlee shifted the car into reverse and pressed her foot to the pedal. She reached the edge of the alleyway and prayed no one got in the way as she whipped the car. She yelled at the sound of a large thud above her.

"DRIVE!" She heard Maxwell yell and Harlee pressed the pedal all the way to the floor. She tore through the streets as quickly as she could, not once looking back. As she neared the manhole they used to leave the cathedral, she whipped the car down the alleyway, propelling Maxwell from the hood. Harlee slammed on the brakes and jumping out of the car, ran to his aid.

"Maxwell! I am so sorry! I thought you could hold on!" She yelled as Maxwell rose from the ground.

"My God! Maxwell, look at you!" Harlee yelled as she noticed Maxwell's wounds.

"DON"T STOP! RUN! BACK TO THE HIDEOUT!" Maxwell growled, holding onto his torso, which had been nearly bitten in half. He stumbled as he walked, blood pouring out of his closed right eye and five large, one inch wide holes, pierced through his left shoulder.

"But your wounds!" Harlee said, pointing as a black substance, thicker than blood, seeped out from each wound.

"There is no time! It has already begun! RUN!" He yelled again as Harlee moved the manhole cover and descended. Maxwell, followed behind her and sliding the lid back in place, fell to the cement below.

"Maxwell!" Harlee yelled again as she turned to help.

"Get Matthew! Tell him to have it ready!" He yelled. Harlee hesitated for a brief second, then turned and bolted down the dark tunnels. Harlee ran through the passages, remembering by second nature, where to turn and when to go straight.

"MATTHEW!" She screamed as she came near the gate. "MATTHEW! COME QUICK!" She saw Father Matthew, running to the gate, unlocking it.

"What is it? What has happened?" Matthew asked as he flung the gate open, John just behind him.

"It's Maxwell!" She yelled, tears in her eyes. "He is hurt really bad! He told me to have you get it ready!" John's and Father Matthew's eyes, both grew wide as Matthew turned back towards John.

"John! Grab the cask!" He yelled and turned back to Harlee. "Follow me! I will need your help!" Harlee nodded and followed Father Matthew down through the tunnels. Harlee knew that should she keep to the forward path that she would arrive at Maxwell's shrine. Father Matthew took the first left as John ran forward with a sledgehammer in hand.

"What's going on!?" Harlee yelled as Father Matthew took two paths forward before turning right.

"You only take the paths, which have a light directly before them." He spoke as they walked through the next fork.

"That's not what I'm talking about! Maxwell needs our help!" She yelled. At the next fork, Father Matthew bent down to grab something.

"We are going to help him." Matthew answered as he lifted Maxwell's bloodstained duster from the ground. "But in order to help him, we might have to be prepared to kill him." John came running up on them, carrying an old-fashioned cask. As Harlee's eyes graced the box, she instinctively reached out to it, drawn by a mystic force.

"No, Harlee! Don't!" Father Matthew yelled as Harlee touched the box with her right hand. Immediately, she stumbled backwards, clenching her heart with her functioning hand and dropped to her knees.

"It will pass, Harlee. Just stay calm." Father Matthew spoke as he helped Harlee to her feet while she clenched her heart.

"It burns!" Harlee cried out as Father Matthew drug her behind him. "I can feel my heart shattering into millions of pieces!"

"You will pull through. You will not die." The priest yelled. Harlee squeezed her heart as her head pounded, as if she had been trapped within a massive drum. Every sense of her body, burned with anguish, pain and desperation, as the cask's presence began to break her mind.

"IT"S ALL TOO MUCH! TOO MUCH PAIN! TOO MUCH SORROW! MAKE IT STOP, PLEASE! MAKE IT STOP!" She screamed as before her waking eyes, she witnessed the damnation of several hundred souls.

"HARLEE! STAY WITH US!" Father Matthew yelled out, holding Harlee's arms down as she thrashed violently.

"LET ME DIE! I WANT TO DIE!" She sobbed.

"JOHN, RUN AHEAD! WE WON'T BE FAR!" Without complaint, John dashed ahead. Once the cask and John vanished beyond, Harlee collapsed to the ground and shook violently. The pain and the phantoms had passed, though she felt she may die from fright at any moment.

"What was that?" She asked.

"I don't have time to explain, now. I have to go help John or else he, Maxwell and God only knows how many more will perish, tonight. You can stay here. I will come back for you." He spoke as he dropped Maxwell's coat and ran faster than any sixty some-year-old man should be able.

Harlee held Maxwell's coat on her lap and stared at it. She looked at the places where he had been impaled, nearly ripped in half and saw the twelve bullet holes, from where he had shielded her. From further down the tunnel, Harlee shuddered as she heard piercing screams of anguish. She gripped Maxwell's coat, knowing the screams to be his, as she tossed the duster aside and rose to her feet.

"I'm coming to help!" She yelled as she gave chase, following Matthew's careful instructions.

"Hurry John! We have to finish chaining him down!" Father Matthew yelled as he held the ceremonial black dagger, Harlee had seen on the altar. As Harlee approached, she saw John, looking into a room, still holding the cask as Father Matthew charged inside. Harlee sprinted by John and the cask, sharply turning the corner to see Father Matthew battling Maxwell.

Maxwell was bereft of clothing, save his briefs, bearing the same face she had seen, when he slayed the wolf. His bones and muscles had nearly doubled in density and spines had begun forming on the ends of his joints. Harlee noticed that Maxwell's legs and ankles had been firmly shackled, but both hands remained free.

Maxwell swiped at Father Matthew, who dodged to his left and raked the black dagger across Maxwell's ribs. Maxwell howled in pain as the dagger cleaved through his flesh, as if made from obsidian. Maxwell staggered for mere seconds as the wound stitched itself back together.

"GRAB IT JOHN! WE WILL USE IT TO BACK HIM IN!" Matthew yelled as Maxwell backhanded him. John opening the box, yelled in pain as he plunged his hand inside, and pulling from it, an indistinguishable mass, ran forward with it enshrined within his arms.

Father Matthew hit the wall, as Maxwell's eyes locked on John's cradling arms. He slashed at Harlee, who leapt to Father Matthew's side and grabbed the dagger. Maxwell reached out for her, and without thinking, she stabbed through his hand. Maxwell lurched back in pain, cutting Harlee's face in the process. As Harlee stumbled backwards, John called to her.

"HARLEE! CATCH!" He yelled, throwing the mass into the air. Harlee caught the mass between her dislocated arm and hip, without looking away from the beast before her. She felt as the mass vibrated warmly but did not dare to look at it. Maxwell stood in front of her, glaring angrily at the blade in her hand.

"BACK!" She yelled, thrusting the blade forward as the lump in her arms, continued radiating warmth, as it vibrated and hummed. Maxwell continued to glare at her, as John ran up on his side and bashed him in the face with the chest. As Maxwell's head reared, Father Matthew hooked a collar around his throat. Maxwell wrenched angrily against the chain, trying to lash out at Harlee.

"Be careful you don't harm the heart!" Matthew yelled as John hit Maxwell again. Confused, Harlee stared down at her hands. First, she looked to the hand holding the blade. Next, she looked over to her other arm, which was slung across her hips, cradling a severely scarred, still beating heart.

Harlee immediately felt all of the blood in her body, drain out and turn to ice as she stared at the heart. John, Father Matthew and Maxwell, all became nothing more than background noise as Harlee's head began to swim from the sound of the heart's beating. She felt herself being drawn into it, and the dagger being pulled from her hand. As her eyes rolled into the back of her head, she cradled the heart to her own, as if her child, and lost consciousness.

Chapter 8 – Believe it or Not, I Was Human Once To

Harlee awoke with a start, nearly jumping from the bed. She looked down and saw she had been undressed and clothed in a wife beater and pajama bottoms. Harlee looked around the room she had slept in, the past several weeks and thought aloud.

"What the hell happened?" Harlee asked.

"I will begin by assuring you, it was not the boys who dressed you." Harlee snapped around and saw Almalexia, sitting in the corner.

"What are you doing here?" Harlee asked, a feline snarl to her voice.

"There is no need to get into all of that. I told your friend that I would look after you, while she got some rest. I am not here to cause you trouble." Almalexia spoke with an unnatural calm. Harlee sat back on the bed and tried to recall what happened.

"Are John and Father Matthew alright?" She asked.

"A little beaten and shaken is all. They are both up and about already. What do you remember?" The succubus asked. Harlee began to think, trying to reach back as far into that night as she could.

"Maxwell and I were following your tip. We..." She began to focus harder. "We saw some freaks...Maxwell said their names...Balthazar, Auriel. Then there was...Cilia!" Harlee jumped from the bed again, hurting her wounded arm.

"Harlee, please talk to me." Almalexia pleaded. Harlee could now sense that the woman was genuinely worried.

"You're right." Harlee said. "Maxwell told me I can't help her now, anyways." She spoke as she sat back and thought more.

"There was another woman. She looked at us and smiled."

"Did Maxwell say who she was?"

"No. He said he did not know. As soon as she smiled at him though, he began to double over, in crippling pain. After that, we were attacked and Maxwell...He turned into that...thing!" Harlee could already feel the terror swelling inside her.

"It's alright now, Harlee. That part is all over. Tell me what happened next."

"I don't even want to think about what I saw but after he started changing, we were shot at. He protected me and we ended up racing back here, through the sewers. That's when Father Matthew had me help, John grabbed a box and..." Harlee suddenly remembered what had happened as it rushed back, all at once.

"I grabbed Maxwell's heart!" She blurted out, feeling herself grow nauseous. Without hesitation, Almalexia handed Harlee a wastebasket, which she immediately began to fill with stomach bile. Harlee panted aggressively as she vomited several more times. Almalexia sat beside her and held back her hair, rubbing her back.

"There, there..." Almalexia cooed. "Just take it slow." Harlee breathed slowly and pulled her head from the wastebasket. "Here," the succubus said as she took the wastebasket from Harlee and set it aside. She next pointed to the glass of water on the bedside, which Harlee used to wash the taste from her mouth.

"Sorry," Harlee spoke as she used her shirt to dab her eyes.

"Think nothing of it. Matthew and John were the same way at first. Come to think of it, the only exception I know of was Kiefer."

"Who's Kiefer?" Harlee asked. Almalexia shook her head.

"I am sorry, forgive me. I should not have even mentioned the name. It is not my place, to speak on Maxwell's affairs."

"You said it is like this for everyone. Was it like this for you?"

"In all of the years, I have known Maxwell, it is safe to say that his heart is something, I have never possessed." Almalexia spoke in a tone filled with heartbreak. "I have never even seen his heart. I must admit, I am jealous, despite the consequences."

"I thought you hated me? Why help me and be nice to me?"

"I told you to think nothing of it. While hate is a bit harsh, I do not like you." Almalexia paused briefly and sighed. "I suppose jealous is more appropriate but you helped Maxwell, and for that, you have my sincere gratitude."

"You must truly care for him, don't you?" Harlee asked.

"I thought freaks, such as myself, had no feelings, souls or hearts?" Almalexia repeated Harlee's careless words, while boring into her with her amber eyes.

"I was wrong to have said that. Please, forgive me." Harlee spoke. Almalexia waved her off.

"I've been told worse. To answer your question, yes, I do care for him. I'm not sure if it is the same for us as it is for you humans but I can say with confidence, I'll never be able to repay the kindness he has shown me."

"Have you considered telling Maxwell how you feel?" Harlee asked.

"He knows. I suspect he knew, long before I did. Trouble is, I also know that he can never look at me that way."

"Don't say that, Almalexia. You never know." Harlee said without thinking, finding it strange that the Greek woman was speaking in such a fashion. Almalexia smiled at Harlee.

"That's sweet of you to say, but you obviously know nothing about Maxwell. Do you even know why he prays? Don't you find it strange, that someone such as he, prays to a being, meant for the souls of man?"

"I had not found it strange until now." Harlee spoke, befuddled.

"Ask him some time. If you can hold his heart, surely he will tell you." Almalexia spoke, rising from the bed and making for the door.

"Before you go, I do have one last question." Harlee said. Almalexia stopped and turned to listen.

"When I grew near and touched the cask, holding Maxwell's heart, I felt such agony that I cannot describe it. I wanted nothing more, in that moment, than to just die. Then, when I touched the heart, I felt warmth and immense power. It was as if I held an enormous flame in the palm of my hand but it could not burn me. Do you have any idea why?" Almalexia thought for a long while, before answering.

"As to your second question, I haven't the slightest idea. The first, however, is much simpler. When Maxwell is wounded, he channels the power of the sins he has absorbed. What you experienced, was the source of Maxwell's power, their pain, his pain." Harlee placed her hand over her heart at the mere thought of it.

"That is what Maxwell feels?" She asked. Almalexia shrugged.

"As I said earlier, I have never held Maxwell's heart. I would not know. When you think that you are ready, ask him."

"I will, thanks." Harlee spoke. As Almalexia opened the door to leave, she looked over her shoulder.

"Please keep him safe for me? His greatest fear is becoming one of them out there. Don't let that happen to him."

"I won't but why ask me?"

"Matthew, John and I, all have a deep love for Maxwell. I do not trust any of us, to do what is necessary, if the time comes. As you said, however, you hate Maxwell. Once he has helped you save your sister, you will no longer have any use for him."

"I don't think that he will help me save Cilia." Harlee commented.

"You truly don't know anything about him." Almalexia commented as she closed the door behind her. Harlee sat in the dark room, alone for a moment, collecting her thoughts. Harlee took a deep breath, before touching her feet to the floor, rising from the bed and walked out into the hall.

As Harlee slowly walked out toward the kitchen, she could smell the heavenly aroma of Father Matthew's cooking. She entered the kitchen, seeing John and the priest both sitting in silence. Harlee could see on both of their faces, just how hard on them, Maxwell's condition was. They both half smiled at her, as she sat down and began filling her plate with pot roast. None of them shared a word, until after Harlee had pushed away the emptied dish.

"Are you alright, Harlee?" Father Matthew asked. Harlee looked from John, who was still staring at the table, to Matthew.

"A little shaken but yes. How are the two of you?" Father Matthew smiled.

"Much the same, though we have been through this before. I thank you, for your help."

"It was the least I could do, after everything you have done for Dahlia and me."

"That was our pleasure. You have been a rare treat." The priest smiled. John slammed his hands on the table, angrily as he grimaced, still staring down.

"Maxwell still hasn't come out of his depression, yet!" He yelled, capturing the room's attention.

"How long has it been?" Harlee asked.

"Three days." Father Matthew spoke with a somber tone.

"What!?" Harlee jumped from the table. "He's still in the dungeon!?" Matthew shook his head.

"No. He came out from there, the morning after...you know. He's been up in the bell tower for three days. Just sitting. He normally becomes quite depressed after he changes but usually, after a day, he is right as rain. No, this is something different. Whatever happened must have troubled him, deeply. Of that, I am certain." Matthew informed her.

"Harlee, can you please go and talk to him?" John asked. Harlee put her hands up and shook her head.

"Woah now. If Almalexia couldn't get him to come down, what makes you think I can?"

"Things are different with you." Matthew answered. "I have never seen anyone with an effect on him, such as you have. Not even Almalexia, stands up to him, the way you do, backing him into a corner. Had John or I tried going with him four days ago, he would have found some way of keeping us away."

"He sent John to the wolves, literally." Harlee pointed out.

"That was actually my idea." John admitted. "He was pissed."

"What!?" Harlee let the shock roll out of her mouth with ease.

"Maxwell had been trying for a long time, to gain information on the wolves and their whereabouts. After over a year, he had still gotten nowhere. He needed a way to gain an informant within the wolf's den. He was not having any luck and so Father Matthew and I, came up with a clever plan. We convinced him, to compel me and allow me to become a thrall to the wolves. They enslaved me and you pretty much know the rest." John regaled the story.

"That explains his attitude, that day he released your compulsion." Harlee concluded. "Are you sure that it has to be me, that goes?"

"We understand if you are too scared to do it." John goaded her.

"I am not afraid of Maxwell." Harlee spoke assuredly. "I just don't know what good it will do."

"Please just try?" John asked. "The worst that would come from it, is him not talking to you."

"Now that would be a blessing." Harlee commented. "Fine. I'll talk to him."

"We appreciate anything you can do." Matthew said. "Thank you, Harlee."

"And I want to be transparent with you both. I am not doing this for Maxwell. I am doing this, because you two have helped me out and because I want to start looking for my sister. I require Maxwell's cooperation and am merely using him, until my sister is safe, understood?"

"Yes, ma'am." Both John and Matthew spoke as Harlee rose from the table and sighed. She began to cross the room and moved towards the back, where the stairs were. As she walked out of the kitchen, she turned back to see John and Matthew, still staring at her. Harlee shook her head as she continued moving forward.

One foot in front of the other, Harlee slowly climbed the stairs, which led toward the loft and beyond the roof. Harlee walked across the small loft to the next set of stairs. Opening the balcony door, atop the stairs, she looked outside, into the dull afternoon light and the pouring rain.

Harlee stepped out, the chilled rain an unwelcome invader against her lightly clothed body and bare feet. Shuddering and instantly drenched, Harlee ran across the terrace, to the bell tower and took up shelter beneath its roof.

"Maxwell?" She spoke into the darkness through chattering teeth. "Maxwell, are you here?" She continued to search around for any sign of the man but saw no one.

"Did I do that, to you?" Maxwell's voice asked but she still saw nobody. Harlee shielded her eyes from the rain and strained to see better.

"Maxwell! Where are you?" Harlee cried out against the rage of the storm.

"Step forward." She heard the man say and so she did. Moving around the old bell, Harlee moved to the other edge of the roof and looked out into the storm. Her body was completely chilled, the rain having iced through her soul. Harlee stepped back out and looked over the edge of the roof.

"It feels purifying, does it not?" Maxwell spoke as he dropped down behind her. Harlee, startled, jumped backwards quickly and slipped over the edge. Maxwell leapt forward and catching her uninjured hand, pulled her back from the edge. Harlee stumbled forward and Maxwell caught her in his arms. Harlee shivered feverishly as she laid her head on Maxwell's chest.

Maxwell, without saying a word, wrapped his duster around her shoulders. She looked up at him, eyes wide, lips slightly pursed and watched him place his hat on her head. Harlee smiled as she laid her head back on his chest and listened to his strong heartbeat.

"I don't believe that I have ever seen you smile before." He commented. Harlee shrugged her shoulders.

"It's a rare occurrence, anymore." She replied as she thought to the sound by her ear. "Maxwell, how can I still hear your heartbeat?" She asked.

"Because, hopefully, my heart is still beating." He said bluntly.

"You know what I'm talking about." She contorted angrily.

"It is part of the ritual that made me the Sin Eater. The heart can only endure so much pain. In order to keep our hearts safe and make ourselves a better conduit between the dead and the living, our hearts are removed. At least that is what my master taught me." Maxwell answered to which Harlee laughed uncharacteristically.

"What do you find so funny?" He asked her.

"I just can't imagine you having a mentor, is all. I suppose, I just assumed that you were always this way." She spoke as she sat down on the ledge inside the tower.

"Dashing and handsome?" He joked.

"Moody, brooding and stoic, was my thinking." She laughed again and noticing herself, was sure to quickly wipe the bliss away.

"Believe it or not, I was human once, too." He said as he stared at his hands. "Or at least, I once pretended to be." Harlee noticed Maxwell placing his fingers in his right side, vest pocket. The place where she knew, he kept his rosary and cloth square.

"Maxwell?" Harlee asked.

"Yes."

"Why do you carry that rosary in your pocket? Did you use to be a priest?"

"Of sorts." He answered taking his hand from his pocket. "Before I became...this," he held out his hands again. "I had a wife, Victoria. The rosary was hers, before she died."

"I am sorry, Maxwell. I did not know."

"You might as well hear it from me. Matthew is bound to tell you, sooner or later. His version is much more dramatic than mine. I keep the rosary to remind me of her and the blanket to remember my son, Connor. It also helps me, to remember my life before."

"I didn't know." Harlee whispered, tears in her eyes at the man's sorrowful expression.

"It's alright, though I would prefer not to say more, if you don't mind."

"I don't. Thank you for sharing something so personal with me."

"I am sorry about your arm."

"It's fine. It doesn't hurt or anything." She lied.

"Your heart is racing. You should head inside before you are chilled for the rest of the day. I will be down shortly. I just have one last thing to take care of, before we discuss out next move." Harlee noticed Maxwell, patting his right pocket.

"I'll go wait with John and Matthew. See you soon." Harlee said as upon Maxwell's insistence, she held onto his hat and coat, while she walked inside.

The entire walk back, Maxwell's words chewed at her heart, as she considered the extreme prejudice she had judged he and Almalexia by. Comparing it to her own life experience, Harlee realized the three of them were more alike, her thoughts conflicted and confused. Once inside the cathedral, she curled into a corner and released the tears and sobs, she had held back.

A short few minutes later, Harlee dried her eyes and moved back towards the main floor. She rounded the corner, walking back into the kitchen, where Matthew and John were still waiting. They both turned to see her, instantly noticing Maxwell's hat and duster, on her person.

"I assume you spoke with him." Father Matthew said.

"I did. He says he will be down momentarily." She answered.

"Thank you, Harlee." John said as he and Father Matthew both smiled.

"You are welcome. As I said, I need Maxwell's help to save my sister." Harlee replied. She moved to hang up Maxwell's hat and coat, then remembering her clothes were entirely soaked through, revealing everything beneath them, only gave up the hat."

"Will you both excuse me for a moment? I need to change." She said while motioning to the small puddle she had already formed.

"By all means. We don't want you coming down with something." Matthew added as John sat quietly, pretending not to notice.

"I'll be right back." She told them as she walked back to the bedroom, grabbed some fresh clothes and moved to the bathroom, to freshen up. Moments later, Harlee stepped into the shower and let the hot water pour down over her. She closed her eyes and turned her face skyward as the sprayer released a wave of refreshment upon her. She began to consider everything that had transpired the past few weeks and debated what she would do, once Cilia was safe.

"Father Matthew said we might stay here." She whispered to herself. "Although, I want nothing more than to take Cilia, far away from all of this. Here however, I know I can keep her safe." Harlee thought for a moment, realizing she had been assuming she would stay, in the city. "Do I want to stay?" She asked herself. A knock at the door interrupted her thoughts.

"Harlee, it's Dahlia. Are you alright?"

"I'm fine, Dahlia. I'll be out in just a minute." Harlee called back as she began washing her hair. A few minutes passed and Harlee exited the bathroom, seeing Dahlia and Maxwell, sitting in the kitchen.

"Good to see you up and about." Harlee said.

"Likewise." Dahlia replied. Harlee walked into the room and had a seat on the counter, opposite from Maxwell.

"Are we ready to begin?" Matthew asked. Everyone in the room confirmed they were. "Excellent." He continued. "We all know already, that this year's Feast, will soon be upon us. We discovered that unlike previous Feasts, this one will be overseen by Auriel, herself." John and Dahlia both jolted at the mention of the name.

"The vampire queen, herself." Almalexia mused as she entered the room. "Sorry I'm late. Girl's gotta eat." She smiled. Harlee and the others nodded their heads, knowing exactly what that meant for a succubus.

"There is someone else," Maxwell interrupted as Almalexia walked to his side and sat beside him. "There is another big player in Sin City. Someone even Auriel answers to. Lexi, do you know anything that might help us?" Harlee could tell the woman was thinking, by the way she scrunched her face.

"I do not. I will put my feelers out and keep my ears open, though. Someone is bound to know something and I hate to say it, priest, but in this city, people are more apt to confess to a whore than to a priest."

"The times have truly changed." Matthew commented.

"Depends on the view." Maxwell grunted. "People are more open about it, is all that has changed." Maxwell sighed as Harlee chimed in.

"What will we do about the Feast?" She asked.

"The Feast should begin the week leading up to the full moon. Auriel and Balthazar will be looking to recruit new thralls and those already in service, will fight to prove they are worthy."

"Worthy of what, exactly?" Dahlia asked.

"Worthy of being turned."

"Pardon?" Dahlia asked.

"Typically, after five or so years of service, thralls who have proven themselves, are given their master's gift." Almalexia clarified.

"And how do they prove their worth?" Harlee asked letting her curiosity get the better of her.

"I would imagine it depends on the master. Humans copy the same system to form their corporate hierarchy. The thralls kiss enough asses or prove themselves and are then brought up in the ranks. The same is true with them, except instead of becoming their bosses, they become longevities."

"So they help raise their master's bottom line or something?" John asked.

"Listen, I am a succubus. My kind are born, not turned. I have never fully asked the particulars, not that I'd expect them to tell me."

"What about all of those confessions to a whore?" Harlee teased.

"It didn't seem to be important information! Priorities!" Almalexia shrieked.

"Back to the topic at hand." Maxwell interrupted. "We will have to attend the Feast, make everyone else think we are thralls. Almalexia already has an open invitation. She will have no trouble getting in."

"What about you?" Almalexia asked.

"I will remain behind. I will observe from a distance and not jump in unless it is absolutely necessary."

"You want us to go into the monster's den, totally alone?" Harlee asked.

"We won't be alone," Dahlia interjected. "We'll have each other. Maxwell will watch out for us."

"Maxwell can't go inside, without blowing the entire operation." Almalexia stated. "He doesn't smell remotely human."

"I'll try and pretend that was a compliment." Maxwell grumbled.

"Of course it was." Almalexia chirped.

"Alright, so then." Matthew moved back to task. "In three weeks, the Feast begins. We are all attending but what is our objective?"

"Learn as much as we can. We need to each prepare separate back-stories. We also need to ascertain our targets and prioritize sources of information. I will go out, later tonight and steal blueprints of the grounds. That should give us more to work with. I also suspect that much of the Feast, at least the pieces we need, will be inside the tower." Maxwell finished.

"Alright, then. Who should each of us target?" Harlee asked.

"The werewolves already think that John is a thrall. John, you know best how to work around them. Avoid the slave pits and you should blend in just fine." Maxwell said. John nodded his head in agreement. "Matthew, it makes more sense, that an aging man, be looking to cheat the reapers their due. I need you to investigate the bloodsuckers. Dahlia, I would like you to go with him. Pretend to be his daughter or whatever you have to do."

"Done." Dahlia confirmed.

"Lexi, I need you to be my eyes on the ground. Work the room and help keep track of anything that strikes you as suspicious."

"Such as, I don't know, a bunch of freaks, feeding and fornicating on their victims?" Harlee butt in.

"I was going to say, ways to penetrate the enemy's defenses but that word choice hardly seems appropriate now."

"Regardless, I can manage." Almalexia smiled.

"Where am I going? I can help Dahlia and Father Matthew or I can go where John cannot?" Harlee spoke.

"I need you to stay back, with me. Be our eyes abroad. Help Almalexia find points of entry.

"What the hell is that!?" Harlee pounded her fist on the counter angrily. "My sister is in there! You can't expect me to sit this one out!" Harlee continued to yell. Almalexia stood, staring at Harlee angrily. She made to say something until Maxwell addressed Harlee.

"Balthazar not only knows your scent, he has seen your face. His men will specifically be looking for us. Your sister, compelled or otherwise, is an unknown element and we cannot afford for you to bump into her."

"How can you expect me to..." Harlee began to argue.

"Can you not see, he is doing what he can?" Almalexia interrupted. "Harlee, if our cover is blown, we will die." She continued. "Maxwell is putting you in a position, to spot the safest route to your sister, so that you, Maxwell and myself, can save her. Put the macho act to rest and think." Harlee squeezed her fists tightly but otherwise allowed Maxwell to resume.

"Right. We will have to be sure to find a path that does not attract attention. Or one that does not give away our intentions. I would suggest in the meantime, work on your covers. I will be back in the morning, with the blueprints." Maxwell said as he began to leave the room.

"Maxwell, it's midday and pouring rain. Where are you going?" Harlee asked. "Aren't you worried about being seen?" Maxwell shook his head.

"No. Should I be?" He asked, as he left the room, Almalexia followed him, quietly.

"It's better this way, Harlee. Maxwell will be fine. He just has a lot on his mind, is all." John spoke.

"Then why does she need to go with him?" Harlee asked.

"That's Almalexia for you." John threw in.

"Don't worry, Harlee. We'll find Cilia." Dahlia assured her. "Besides, what he does in his spare time has no bearing on us. Find out what you need to do until it's time."

"I'm going to go check my equipment." Harlee growled as she got up and stomped out of the kitchen.

“That’s my girl!” Dahlia cheered, as Harlee left.

Chapter 9 - Jules

"I hardly feel, I need help, Lexi." Maxwell spoke as he stood, completely free of his wet clothing.

"You've never complained about me watching before." She replied as she sat in a nearby lounge chair, crossed her legs and stared at the naked man.

"What do you want?" He asked. Almalexia cocked her head sideways as she stared at Maxwell ravenously.

"Oh, just feeling especially hungry, I guess. I am a stress eater, I am told." She answered.

"Didn't you just tell everyone that you just ate?" Maxwell spoke as he began laying out fresh clothes. "Aren't you worried about over indulgence?" Almalexia kicked out her legs and stood, marching her way over to Maxwell.

"Come on, Maxwell, don't make a girl beg." She spoke seductively dropping her dress and draping herself over his naked body. As she pressed her bare breasts against his back, she began rubbing her hands across his chest, working her way down. "You know that you're the only man who can satisfy me." She spoke, placing wet, hot kisses on his back and nape of his neck as she grabbed his hands.

Maxwell closed his eyes as she ran his hands down the length of her body, stopping them on her trembling thighs and making him unhook her garters. The room was filled with her intoxication, as the succubus doused the room in her pheromones and scented aphrodisiac. Maxwell could feel her heart pounding, he could smell how badly she wanted him.

Maxwell stepped away as she forced his hands into her panties and he turned to stare at her. Almalexia's eyes grew, as she batted her eyelashes and slowly dropped to all fours. Spreading out her body like a cat's, she bore herself to him. Biting her bottom lip, she stared into his eyes.

"Please." She whispered.

"You're really that hungry, aren't you?" Maxwell asked. Almalexia continued staring at him.

"Starving." She replied with a devilish smile.

Almalexia crawled up to Maxwell, eyes mad with hunger, as she stopped in front of him and rose to her knees. She kissed the head of his member, while gripping onto his glutes and outer thighs. Maxwell reached down to the back of her head, gripping a handful of her hair, tightly in his hand.

Almalexia groaned as she took in the entirety of his man hood and began massaging it with long strokes of her throat. As the man grew fully erect in her mouth, she looked up at him and pulled away, as she tickled the boys. Gently tugging at them with her lips, she felt as Maxwell pulled on his hair woven handle.

Rising to her feet, already dripping, Almalexia kissed her way up his shaggy, black haired torso, his spare hand, running down her body. She could feel his fingertips, pressing into her flesh as they worked their way across her body. Maxwell pulled her head back, as he squeezed her buttocks, while sensually kissing the underside of her neck.

Almalexia could feel his hot breath on her neck, as her own breathing grew more labored. Maxwell kissed his way down Almalexia's neck and she quivered at the exchange. Her fingers dug deep into his back, causing a noticeable groan to escape him.

"Harder!" She whispered into his ear as she reached down with her right hand and gripped onto all of him, aggressively. Maxwell's whole body tensed from the strength of her grip, as he opened his mouth wide and bit into her shoulder.

"HARDER!" She groaned out again, dipping her head all the way back, smiling, mouth wide open. Maxwell's hand left her hair as both hands dug deeply into her rear, bruising the flesh with his fingertips as he lifted her from the floor.

Almalexia wrapped her legs around his waist, as he released his bite on her and slammed her against the wall. She grunted, as the wind was partially knocked from her lungs. Maxwell, lifting her up in his strong arms, tossed her up on his shoulders, pinning her against the wall as he began eating her.

Almalexia's eyes, locked shut, as she gripped his dark hair, thighs wrapped around Maxwell's face, thrusting against it, as the man devoured her. She nearly wept; the delicate strokes of his rough tongue painting her canvas, making her lose all control.

As one tantric orgasm after another, flowed through her legs, as ocean waves on the bay, Almalexia tensed her thighs around his head and patted the back of it. Maxwell growled slightly, arousing her more as she continued to fight back against the forces stealing her will. She tapped him on the head again, all the while, her radical breathing and seismic convulsions, causing her to grow faint and weak.

"That's enough." She panted. "Fuckin stick it in me already." She begged as she pushed against his forehead.

"GRRR!" Maxwell growled, the voice of the beast, arising deep from within his throat as he slammed her against the wall, harder than before, resulting in another orgasm. Almalexia continued to press against his head as her eyes dared to permanently recede into the back of her skull. Her muscles grew lethargic as Maxwell licked away, all of her essence and consumed her soul.

Head, arms and body, too heavy to lift, they dropped to her sides. Her thighs' grip on his head loosened as she fell back to the wall, depleted, her palette licked clean. Maxwell gently gripped onto her buttocks again as he turned towards the bed and lowered her to it.

Almalexia groaned as he pressed himself on top of her, rolling her onto her stomach as he latched onto her opposite shoulder with his teeth. Her pheromones doused the entire room as she clenched her toes and gripped the headboard of the bed. Her legs dancing about, she slowly brought her knees to her chest, arching her back, positioning her rear for him.

Closing her eyes, Almalexia bit onto the sheets as she felt his strong rough hands, gripping her inner hips. Using his knees, he spread her legs wide, as he dominated her, taking full control of her every whim, every inch of her body, every sensation of her being, now his possession.

She moaned loudly into the mouthful of sheet as she felt his phallus, filling her. From the angle of the penetration, she felt the rough skin of his shaft, applying a vice of pressure against the back of her pelvic bone. The pleasure so intense, she felt tears form in her eyes, as she cried out for more.

"HARDER!" She screamed into the bed, her voice muffled but her desires conveyed.

She felt Maxwell's fingertips dig into her shoulder as he thrusted against her, with all the strength the supernatural man possessed. She felt as his cock, threatened to tear her in half, with every rapid thrust. The oaken framed bed groaned and shook from his sheer, savage intensity.

She could hear him growling in his throat, his inner beast, having come to play. She screamed out as her bay was overrun, monsoon season having suddenly arrived, leaving behind no possible hope for survivors, as wave after wave, tore away her every conscious thought.

"HARDER!" She managed to cry out, through long periods of holding her breath. She felt as with a thunderous hand, he slapped her ass, leaving behind a print. Any moisture, which was left in her body, poured out of her, onto his pelvis as she came her last.

His hands worked her body, claiming that which his penis had not, firmly gripping her breasts in his hands, and squeezing them in rhythm with his thrusts. As he slapped Almalexia's raw backside once more, the last of the strength her body possessed, left her and she felt him release inside of her as they climaxed in unison.

Drenched in sweat, the room reeking of Jasmine, Cinnamon and Lavender, Almalexia's personal aroma, Maxwell released her. She fell, lifeless to the bed, her body having long since gone numb. Gently, Maxwell rolled her onto her side, taking care to spread her paralyzed limbs as he sat at the foot of the bed.

"I have nothing left." She groaned, unable to move away.

"Was the meal satisfactory?" Maxwell teased, as he turned his head to her naked body.

"I feasted." She replied weakly as she closed her eyes.

Maxwell stared down at Almalexia, who had already fallen asleep. Maxwell placed his face into his palms and pressed his long, black hair back.

"No longer a man, yet still subject to their vices." He mumbled as he rose from the bed and walked to his wardrobe. Upon it, he stared at his wife's rosary and child's blanket, picking them up.

"But what causes it? The part of me, I pretend is a man, the sins I've taken in, or the piece of me conceived by Grey?" Almalexia mumbled in her sleep and Maxwell began to dress silently. He dressed in a nice, black silken shirt, well-fitting denim jeans, his black boots and a black baseball cap.

Wanting to remain disguised, he also forewent his duster in exchange for a more modern biker jacket. Maxwell took one last look at the beautiful woman in his bed, before grabbing his cloth and rosary, stuffing them in his jacket. Maxwell walked back through the kitchen and found everyone seated in the sanctuary, minus Harlee.

"Come to confess your sins, my son?" Matthew joked as everyone turned to look at him.

"You haven't got enough years left to hear them, old man." He grumbled.

"What's with the get up, Maxwell? You're not going out as a cowboy, today? There's bound to be a bachelorette party around here, somewhere." Dahlia teased. John and Matthew both turned to look at her and laughed at the unexpected jab.

"I thought that it would be wise to go in disguise." Maxwell growled.

"Hey, are you heading out to Jules'?" John asked.

"It had crossed my mind."

"Do you mind brining something back?" Matthew asked.

"Fine." Maxwell grunted. Dahlia looked back and forth, between the three men.

"Jules'?" She asked. John and Matthew both shot her a surprised look.

"You've never heard of Jules' before?" John asked. Dahlia shook her head.

"Can't say as though I have. What is it?" She asked.

"It's an old school, classy diner, with the best burgers, milkshakes and homemade pie you've ever had in your entire life!" John ranted excitedly. Dahlia's eye lit up.

"You mean there is a place, so close to heaven, in this God forsaken city? Can I go?" She said ecstatically, jumping from the pews. Maxwell sighed deeply.

"If you must." He mumbled.

"Yes! Thanks. Let me go grab my coat and tell Harlee." She said and then stopped herself. "On second thought, just let me grab my coat." She said as she trotted off. As Dahlia left the room, Father Matthew began to chuckle.

"What?" Maxwell's growl held a more dangerous tone.

"It just seems as though you've developed quite a weakness for those two, that's all."

"I'm done with this conversation." Maxwell continued to grumble as he walked away. Matthew and John, howled with laughter as Dahlia came back out.

"Did I miss anything?" Dahlia smiled as she put her jacket on.

"I'm leaving!" Maxwell yelled from the front of the room. Dahlia ran to catch him, as Father Matthew yelled.

"Don't forget an umbrella!" He bellowed. Maxwell grabbed an umbrella from the pot by the door and waiting for Dahlia, pushed the door and opened the umbrella. As he and Dahlia walked outside, Maxwell shielded her under the umbrella as they walked down the street.

"Is Jules' close by?" She asked as the rain crashed down around them.

"No but my car is." He spoke, holding the umbrella out for her to huddle beneath.

"You're rather chivalrous, aren't you?" She spoke as she huddled under his shoulder.

"I was raised by my mother, in a time complete with entirely different views. Chivalry had not yet reached its decline." As they walked, Maxwell pulled out his keyring and flipped to the key of his storage unit. They stopped in front of the container and Maxwell handed off the umbrella. Next, he knelt down, unlocked the door and opened it.

"Oh wow!" Dahlia said excitedly as she laid eyes on the classic charger and motorcycle.

"That was what Harlee said." He commented as he unlocked the car and opened the passenger door. Dahlia climbed in and he shut it behind her, before getting in himself. They buckled themselves in as Maxwell stuck the key in the ignition and turned it, bringing the car to life. Dahlia cheered to the sound of the engine's roar and Maxwell pulled ahead, stopping long enough to relock his storage. Getting back in the car, Maxwell and Dahlia, went out on the open road.

"Thank you for letting me come with you." Dahlia said.

"You're welcome." He said.

"Say, Maxwell." Dahlia started.

"Yes?"

"Do you not like having Harlee and I around?" She asked.

"No. It is not that. Having the two of you is an adjustment. It is good for John. I apologize for flying off the handle, at times. I suppose, we all have room to learn and grow."

"I just wanted to make sure, we weren't a burden is all."

"Harlee pisses me off but you are both welcome."

"Thank you. If something comes up, I have found another place. No hard feelings."

"I'll keep that in mind. We are nearly there." He spoke as he continued driving down the nearly barren road.

"Tell me about yourself, Dahlia?" Maxwell asked.

"What do you want to know?" She asked him.

"Harlee obviously hates the supernatural but then you, her closest friend, seem to accept what I am." He pointed out to her. Dahlia shrugged her shoulders as she considered the question.

"Well, I suppose I did not grow up in the slave camps as she did. I had a life before, friends before. Where I came from, we judged people by their actions, not their race. I suppose with Harlee, it is different, because of her experiences but for me, I see you for who you are. I cannot see the beast in your eyes, when I look at you. I am sorry if that doesn't make sense."

"No. It does. Thank you." He grumbled. "I have not been human, a long while. There are things I once knew, which I can no longer understand."

"Well, as far as I am concerned, you act human." She smiled as he pulled off from the freeway and traveled back on the main road. Dahlia watched out the window, all of the scenery they passed, foreign to her. Another ten minutes and Maxwell slowed to a stop in front of a small diner, which had its lights off.

"Damn! We didn't make it in time." Dahlia said looking at her watch. "It's not even that late, though. Do they have bizarre ours? I'll go check." She said as she reached for the door handle.

"Wait." Maxwell said kindly. Dahlia stopped and stared at Maxwell, who stepped out. She watched as he opened the umbrella and rounded the car. Dahlia smiled as Maxwell opened her door and placed the umbrella above the opening as he held out his hand.

"Thank you, kind sir." She spoke as she accepted his hand and climbed out of the car. Side by side, they walked around the back of the building, where a small duplex sat. Maxwell approached the one on the left and knocked three times.

"Who is it?" They heard a young woman speak.

"Sorry to call unexpectedly, Jules. Is it too late, to swing by for a bite?" The door flung open and a brunette woman in her mid twenties rushed out to hug Maxwell.

"Never for you, my friend. It is good to see you again." She said as she noticed Dahlia, who was staring awkwardly. "Oh, where are my manners? My name is Julia. I'm one of Maxwell's kids but you can call me Jules."

"Dahlia. It's a pleasure to meet you, Jules." Dahlia said, shaking the young woman's hand.

"Are you two hungry? Of course you are, follow me." She said as she stepped out of her house, locking the door behind her. Opening her umbrella, she led them to the restaurant and unlocked the backdoor.

"I hope you don't mind sitting in the back. My boyfriend is getting ready to open for our dinner customers."

"That would be great. Thank you, Jules." Maxwell said, an agitated look on his face. "What is this about a boyfriend?"

"My pleasure and don't worry about Michael. He treats me quite well."

"He better." Maxwell growled as Jules led them into the back room, which still resembled a classy diner, complete with chessboard tile squares and a classy booth. Jules sat down a single menu, in front of Dahlia and took a seat beside Maxwell.

"Just interrupt me whenever you are ready." She told Dahlia as she turned to talk to Maxwell.

"So, how is everyone? Father Matthew, John and Alma, still putting up with you?" Jules asked him, prompting Dahlia to laugh from shock. Both Jules and Maxwell stared at her briefly. Jules was smiling brightly, while Maxwell maintained his scowl.

"Yes, though I always imagined I tolerated them." Maxwell grumbled as Dahlia decided on what she wanted. Dahlia looked up at them, setting her menu down.

"Ah, you've decided?" Jules asked, eying her.

"Yes. I would like the Verne's cowboy burger with olives, a strawberry milkshake and a slice of Jules' famous apple, please." Jules smiled as she took Dahlia's order.

"Alright then. I will be right back with both of your orders." Jules said merrily as she stood and walked out.

"You're not ordering anything?" Dahlia asked.

"I am...Jules knows what I want, is all." He said, sitting back in the booth and relaxing. Dahlia did the same as she stared at the elusive man, hundreds of questions burning in her mind.

"Maxwell?" Dahlia asked.

"Yes?"

"Have you been alone this whole time?" She asked. Maxwell was surprised by her question and stared at her.

"Of course not. I have had Matthew, John and Lexi by my side for some time now."

"That's not what I am talking about. I am perfectly content, without a companion. I am able to come and go as I please and that is how I like things. To be immortal, without someone to share your life with must be horrible." Maxwell remained silent for a moment as Jules came back into the room.

"I feel as though I missed something." Jules commented as she walked back into the room and sat beside Maxwell.

"I was just asking Maxwell about his past lovers." Dahlia said. Jules looked at Maxwell and then to Dahlia, hopefully.

"We are not lovers, Jules." Maxwell told her. Jules' smile faded, for the first time since Dahlia had met her. Jules noticed Maxwell's hand in his right pocket and sighed.

"I had hoped, you bringing her here, had meant that you'd finally moved on. You haven't brought many friends by before."

"Sorry to disappoint but it seems I've been doing much, which is out of the usual for me."

"Did you tell her?" Jules asked.

"No." Maxwell grumbled.

"Tell me what?" Dahlia asked as Maxwell narrowed his eyes.

"Nothing." He continued to grouch as Jules laid her head on his shoulder.

"If you don't tell her, I will. You and I both know that my version will be much more tragic and romantic." She fluttered her eyelashes up at him. Maxwell sighed with irritation as Jules cheered with excitement and stood.

"Don't start without me. I'm going to grab the tissues." Jules quickly sprang into action and ran around the corner. Maxwell shook his head as he stared down at his lap.

"Sometimes I swear, that girl is as looney as her brother." Maxwell muttered to himself as Jules returned, carrying two trays, covered in food. As she sat them down, Dahlia had to check herself for drool.

"Dig in!" Jules spoke as she sat the food on the table and removed the trays. Next, she squinted her eyes at Maxwell, leering at him threateningly as she slammed a box of tissues on the table.

"Don't think you've escaped story time, Maxwell." She whispered. Dahlia took a sip of her milkshake and immediately sank into bliss.

"Ok! This is delicious! Thank you, Jules." Dahlia cheered as she tore into her food. Jules looked from her to Maxwell, who casually bit into his double bacon cheeseburger.

"You do still feed the people who live with you, don't you?" Jules teased, watching Dahlia ravage her food.

"Matthew does all the cooking now that you're on your own."

"Oh my." She exclaimed. "Has he improved?"

"He still does well with main things you've taught him. It will be a long time before he can spoil us, the way you used to." Jules smiled, blushing slightly.

"You make it sound as though you miss me?"

"You know I do. You had to go, however. It was for your own good. I did not want you to live that life. I didn't want that for any of you." Maxwell spoke in his normal tone but Dahlia could hear grief within it.

"If you're talking about Kiefer, don't blame yourself. My brother made his own choice, for better or worse." Maxwell nodded his head.

"I suppose." He took another bite.

"So how about that story?" Jules asked happily, as she pat Maxwell on the knee. "The pie will cheer us up after we're done crying." She continued to smile as Dahlia finished her milkshake, her straw buzzing at the bottom of the glass.

"I am curious to hear this story." Dahlia said. "It would be nice to know more about you. If you'd share with me, I'd be willing to share my story, as well." Jules' expression grew more and more excitable as Maxwell rubbed the corners of his eyes, irritably.

"And I'll even share my story." Jules added in.

"Let's just get this over with." Maxwell suggested.

"Dahlia, do you mind going first?" Jules asked. "I am curious to learn more about you and besides, Maxwell's story is worth the finale." Dahlia smiled as Jules sat another strawberry milkshake in front of her.

"Well, I suppose the best place to start would be when I was four years old. I lived in the city, with my parents. We use to go to this park by our house, every day, after my mom came home from work. Dad stayed home, something with computers, I cannot really remember.

At any rate, we would go to this park and we would spend the entire afternoon together. One day, when we were playing, some people approached my parents. Mom and dad did what they could but the men beat them down and took me. They dropped me off at a work camp, which is where I met Harlee and Cilia.

We were in the camp for several years, doing whatever work they brought us. After a few of us became close, I formed the band and Harlee and I began strategizing a means of escape. Most made it out but Cilia was one of the ones who got left behind. I've been helping Harlee search for her, ever since." Dahlia finished. Jules blew her nose, after dabbing her eyes, passing the box of tissues to Dahlia, who did much the same.

"Thank you for sharing with us." Jules began. "I'm afraid that my story is not so eventful."

"I would like to hear it." Dahlia prodded.

"Okay, if you insist." She said as her smile came back on. "The gist of my story, mom worked two jobs, trying to support my brother and. I was six at the time and my brother was ten years older. She was rarely home, so my brother, Kiefer, took care of me, while she was at work. Now there were other people, who checked in on us but Kiefer was there the most. Mom was not always the best at picking out men but that did not matter. We always came first and her dates were always made aware of that. Unfortunately, she did not always see what went on in the house, while she was gone. Her boyfriend at the time, Greg, little did she know, had a thing for little girls.

I remember it so vividly. He came into my room, one night, said he wanted to play a game." Jules covered her mouth as tears formed in her eyes. Maxwell placed his arm around her as Dahlia reached for her hand.

"You don't have to say anymore? I am sorry that I made you relive such an awful memory."

"Oh, but I've only just started. It gets much better, I promise." Jules assured Dahlia, who sat back in the booth.

"Alright, if you wish." She said. Jules wiped her eyes once more and smiling, continued.

"As I said, Kiefer always watched out for me. The moment he sensed something was wrong, he was there, at my side. He had sensed something had gone wrong, that night but I was too afraid to say anything. Afterwards, he made certain he was ready, if something happened again.

He warned me, should anything happen, to close my eyes. He told me, he needed me to close my eyes, as tightly as I could and to run from the room, if he told me to. He told me to make sure I hid somewhere and not to come out until he said so. I always listened to my brother, just as my mom told me.

That night, when Greg was watching us, my brother hid inside my closet. He waited for Greg, to come into my room. I closed my eyes and held them tightly shut. I felt Greg being pulled from me and heard my brother, yelling for me to run, so I ran.

I was still hiding under the kitchen sink, when my mother got home. She saw what Kiefer had done, having arrived just long enough before the police, to realize what had happened from our faces. Like I said, with my mother, we always came first. She grabbed the scissors Kiefer had used and told us to do everything she said. When the police arrived, they took our mother away. Even though they did not believe her, she cried and cried, told us how much she loved us and confessed to having killed Greg, having stabbed him forty seven times, in a heat of rage.

Kiefer was never quite the same after that night but he always kept me safe, like momma had said. The foster care system was kind to us, never separating us but we never found a home that stuck. Not until we bumped into Father Matthew, who through Maxwell, convinced the system to let us stay." Jules hugged Maxwell again as Dahlia thought.

"What happened to Kiefer?" Dahlia asked. Jules raised her hands and shook her head.

"No, no, no. My turn for stories is done. Maxwell?" Maxwell grumbled under his breath.

"If I'm going to do this, at least tell me how your mom is?" He requested.

"Oh, yeah, mom's doing just fine now. She has a nice little house, a few neighborhoods down. I call her almost every day and visit her on the weekends. I feel bad for her though. She never could bring herself to look for love again, after she was released. She gets lonely. I had actually considered asking you to meet with her, sometime." Jules said, looking at Maxwell.

"Jules, you know that I am not interested in looking for anyone either."

"Eww, you weirdo!" Jules teased. "I don't want you hooking up with my mom! I want you to meet her, because of what you do."

"Kill things?" Maxwell asked. Jules pushed him.

"No, Maxwell! That is not what you really do! You find broken people and you fix them! You make them whole again! Just like you did for Kiefer and I. You took two broken kids, with no hope, no future and taught them how to dream again. You helped me get an education and secured my first job at Verne's and now I'm the owner. Kiefer may no longer be with us but you gave him purpose again. You made him feel whole again. This man, is by far, the most broken soul I know and all he does is fix others. He is more worthy of being made whole again, than anyone I know!" Jules was clearly crying now.

"Jules, please stop." Maxwell spoke calmly.

"He raised Matthew from a baby," Jules continued as Maxwell asked her to stop, more aggressively. "Gave John a home and literally tore out his own heart, to save his wife."

"I SAID ENOUGH!" Maxwell roared as he rose from the table. He looked around, seeing Jules and Dahlia both looking to him, nervously.

"I'm sorry...I'm sorry." He said placing several bills and his car keys on the table. "I...I just can't. It was good to see you, Jules. You look good." He turned and moved to leave.

"Maxwell, wait!" Jules turned to stop him as he ran out. Sitting back down, across from Dahlia, she looked back at her.

"I am sorry about that." She said. "Do you know how to get back?" Dahlia nodded her head.

"What did I just witness?" Dahlia asked.

"I've never seen him so upset. Not that I blame him but listen to me, please. Despite what you may have seen, think or believe, Maxwell is a good person and he is in so much pain. He needs someone, to help HIM for a change." Dahlia nodded her head at Jules as she began telling the bubbly young woman more about herself.

Dahlia returned to the cathedral, that evening, bearing offerings of pie. She had the entirety of the drive back to the storage container and the remaining walk, thereafter, to think upon what Jules had told her and Maxwell's reaction to it. As Dahlia entered the cathedral, she was met with the crazed faces of several hungry people. Dahlia held up two bags of food as she put the umbrella away and smiled.

"Jules sends her love." Dahlia spoke as Matthew and John rushed her.

"PIE!" They cheered as they took the bags and ran back to the kitchen. As Dahlia took off her jacket, Almalexia approached.

Where is Maxwell?" She asked.

"We were telling stories, Jules was telling me about herself and her brother. Then, she told me a bit about Maxwell and he got upset. He paid for the food, sat his keys down and then left." Almalexia nodded her head.

"Jules has always been a bit of a hopeless romantic and she absolutely cherishes Maxwell. It wasn't her place to press Maxwell on telling his story, however."

"She told me," Dahlia leaned in to whisper. "She told me that Maxwell, ripped out his own heart, to save his wife."

"That explains why he is upset. Please do not repeat that to anyone. It was wrong of her to tell you that without Maxwell's consent."

"She said that too. She stopped talking about it, after Maxwell left but asked me to deliver a letter to him, when he came back. She also told me to tell you, that she found a boy." As Dahlia said the words, Almalexia's eyes lit up.

"Now that is something we must discuss. What is his name?"

"Michael."

"Good name, tell me about him. Did you meet him?" Dahlia nodded her head and smiling, began to tell the succubus about Jules' boyfriend.

Harlee sat on her knees, in front of the small coffee table in her room, dismantling and cleaning her various weapons. Everything was laid out, perfectly composed in front of her as she cleaned the many different pieces of her Berettas, with cotton swabs and alcohol, as Father Matthew and John, burst into the kitchen, startling her.

Curious, Harlee uncrossed her legs and walked into the kitchen. Walking out, she saw Matthew and John, hovering over several cardboard boxes, the plastic bags lying on the floor.

What are you two, up to?" She asked as she reached the kitchen and caught the powerful aroma. Both John and Matthew jumped as Harlee walked in silently, startling them.

"Excuse us, Harlee. We did not know you were there." Father Matthew apologized. "Would you care for a slice of pie? Our dear friend, Jules, has sent us several kinds but I highly recommend the pecan."

"Don't listen to him. The apple is by far the best. He just doesn't want to share it." Almalexia smiled. Father Matthew and John both glared at Almalexia.

"The strawberry rhubarb is also quite excellent." John grunted.

"That, I can attest to." Dahlia said as she joined the others. "But Almalexia's right, the apple is by far the best." She said at the cost of more dagger eyes.

"Jules'?" Harlee asked. "I've never heard of it."

"I hadn't either, until tonight but it is now my new favorite place." Dahlia said excitedly. "I'll have to take you there, some time. You'll love it." She assured Harlee, who stared.

"How did you find out about it?" She asked.

"Father Matthew, John and Maxwell were talking about it. I asked if I could tag along, so Maxwell took me out and bought me dinner. It felt good to get out." Dahlia answered. "I brought you back some food, too. Just in case." Dahlia pointed to the sole unopened box and foam cup on the table, which clearly had "HARLEE," written on it. Harlee could feel herself growing angry, though she did not understand why. Her heart pounded aggressively in her chest and she felt the urge to yell at Dahlia, in anger.

"Thank you but I'm not hungry. You go ahead." She looked at John as she turned away and locked herself back in her room. Without hesitating, John and Matthew, began divvying out pie as Almalexia and Dahlia stared curiously. As Dahlia continued to wonder, Almalexia turned her attention to John and Matthew, who were stacking multiple slices on their plates.

"Hey, you two. Make sure you save some for Maxwell. You know that apple is his favorite." She said as they attempted to run, as she made sure there was still some left.

Harlee sat in her room, back to the wall, hugging her knees. As she sat, studying the wall décor, she attempted to collect her thoughts.

Noticing her Berettas still gutted on the table, Harlee rose from the bed and sat in front of the coffee table.

"What the hell am I worrying about?" She said aloud. "I still have all of this work to do." She said as she began reassembling her weapons.

Chapter 10 – Maxwell's Heart

"Alright everyone, these are the blueprints, Maxwell stole for us." Matthew spoke as he unfurled them.

"How did he get these?" Harlee asked, looking over the elaborate designs.

"Maxwell has his methods, I am sure." Dahlia spoke.

"I would imagine, they are similar to my own methods." Almalexia commented.

"Have sex with random strangers, until you happen upon someone, who has them on their person?" Harlee teased.

"I was going to suggest, he put on a nice suit and used some old fashioned charm, although seduction is also rather effective. Believe me, Maxwell excels at getting what he wants, using such methods. You should try it some time. You're bound to eventually find someone who is into effeminate men." Almalexia smiled. Harlee smiled back at her and shook her head.

"You caddy bitch." She said, to which the succubus laughed.

"Likewise. Maybe that is why we get along so well." They both laughed, while everyone else stared in confusion.

"At any rate," Matthew continued. "If we continue to study these, we will be able to predetermine our points of entry. Now I believe," he spoke as he flipped to the pages, detailing the basement floors and the other buildings on the grounds. "The fighters' pit, located on floor B2, of this building, is where I suspect they will have the live fights. It is connected to the main building, through a lone access point, so it is worth considering as an access point. Any questions?" Matthew asked. Nobody spoke up, prompting Matthew to continue showing points of interest on the map.

Nearly an hour later, Matthew moved on, to tend to the morning worship. Leaving the blueprints out for the others, they continued to pour over them in study as John remained on standby, eating leftover pie he had hoarded. Harlee and Dahlia made notes, regarding the blueprints, as John stood behind them.

"Is there any pie left?" Harlee asked, having taken notice to his constant chewing. John shook his head, "no," but his eyes betrayed him.

"John?" Harlee said. "Are you not being honest with me?" As she asked, she heard a slight commotion from down the hall.

"Lexi, I've told you before. That is none of your concern." Maxwell grumbled as they walked down the hall, leading from his bedroom. "It is nothing against you, nothing against her or anyone else. It is a topic, which I simply do not wish to discuss." He continued as he opened the refrigerator and looked inside. Almalexia turned, noticing Harlee.

"What about her?" She asked, pointing towards Harlee. "You let her see your heart. You told her about the rosary. Why not tell her?"

Harlee and Dahlia both began to grow nervous, unsure of what they were witnessing.

"I didn't show her my heart. She was simply in the wrong place at the wrong time. I am not debating this anymore." He began to walk away.

"Maxwell. I have been by your side for how many decades? How much more, will it take for you to move on?" Almalexia asked.

"I can't." Maxwell yelled. "Not while Grey still has them! Not even for a second, can I escape the thought of what he is doing to them! Even after they are free, maybe never!"

"Is there no room in your heart for another?" Almalexia asked.

"You cannot have her place!" He growled and walked away, leaving her. She turned, seeing Harlee and Dahlia, averted her gaze.

"Almalexia, are you alright?" Harlee asked as the tearing woman walked by.

"It's that woman, again." She spoke firmly. "She's been gone, nearly two hundred years and yet she still haunts him."

"Who's haunting him?" Harlee asked.

"Victoria," Dahlia answered. Almalexia nodded.

"I'll be back, tomorrow. Please just look out for him, for me?" She asked the room as she walked away. Harlee and Dahlia both looked towards Maxwell's room and approached. As they neared the door, Dahlia reached out and gently knocked.

"Maxwell, are you alright?" She asked.

"I am fine. I merely wish to be left alone." He answered calmly.

"If you need anything, just ask. We care about you." Dahlia said again. Harlee stared at Dahlia, at a loss.

"Your concern is noted, thank you." Was the last thing he said. Harlee and Dahlia eyed one another, shrugged their shoulders and carried on with their day. Both of them spent the majority of their days, exercising, playing one of Father Matthew's various board games or staring at the television, as they waited for the coming days of the feast.

"We wish to remind everyone, with this year's upcoming Feast, seven days of seven sins, it is important to remember the upcoming Hell Night. Take care to lock your doors, never travel alone. Last year's lootings, were at an all-time high and this year's riots could shape up to be worse, yet. This has been your friendly, neighborhood, broadcast. Good evening and good night."

Harlee turned off the television as she and Dahlia looked to one another.

"As if we didn't have enough problems, with all of the freaks running around this city." Harlee said. "Now, we have to worry about the people as well?"

"Like I've said before, Harlee, people terrify me. The monsters have clear, distinct motives. People, well with people, you just never know what they will do."

The next several days progressed as usual. More and more people, began visiting the cathedral, now that Hell Night had neared. One afternoon, the night of the event, Father Matthew and John returned late from the daily parishioners. They sat for a quiet meal together, with no one exchanging more than a few words. After they had finished, Harlee collected the plates and began helping John wash them.

"Harlee?" Father Matthew asked. Harlee turned to look at him.

"Yes, Father?" Harlee asked. Father Matthew bore a troubled expression on his face.

"There is something I must tell you, and something else entirely, which I must show you. Do you trust me?" He asked her. Harlee thought the question over for a moment, then nodded.

"I do, Father. What do you need to tell me?" Harlee asked, growing ever more curious and concerned. Father Matthew looked around the room and locking eyes with John, the young boy nodded.

"Please follow me." He said as he rose from the table and began moving down the hall. Harlee followed him and grew curious as he pulled away the bookshelf and opened the catacombs door. Harlee watched Father Matthew descend the staircase and swallowed hard, as he turned to the right. Harlee's curiosity overwhelming her, she took a deep breath and followed.

"What you are about to learn, I am not sure Maxwell would approve." He warned her.

"Then why teach me?" Harlee asked.

"Because it is important that someone know what I am telling you and you are the only one who can utilize the information." Matthew said.

"Someone know what? Why?" She asked.

"In a week's time, the feast will begin. It will run for the expanse of a week and end on the night of the harvest moon, a blood moon."

"We've already gone over this, Father..." Harlee stopped mid-sentence as the room with the altar, came into view. Immediately, Harlee felt the rhythm of her heartbeat change and she began to panic.

"It is alright, Harlee." Father Matthew assured her as they entered the room and the cask came into view.

"Please have a seat and I will explain." Matthew said placing his hand on the box. Harlee cringed, having remembered her experience with the cask before. Patting the box gently, Father Matthew turned to look at Harlee.

"As you well know, my father was once a man." Matthew began. "Before becoming the Sin Eater, he lived a human life, fell in love, got married and started a family."

"Yes, I am already aware."

"Before my father, became all of those things, he was a part of an old priesthood, formed in secret by the Vatican, to keep God's children safe from the other realms."

"What other realms?" Harlee asked.

"The realms I speak of are Heaven, Hell and..."

"Earth?" Harlee suggested.

"More or less, however, there is one more, Purgatory." He told her. Harlee stared in wonder as Matthew continued.

"The group Maxwell was part of, has long since been eradicated. They were all lost, during the Fall, Maxwell being the only exception. One person, in every generation, was chosen to fulfill the role of the Sin Eater, so if any of the righteous were to fall, before they could be forgiven of their sins, they would not be denied passage into Heaven." As Harlee processed Matthew's words, a question came to mind.

"But Maxwell is immortal. Are not all Sin Eaters such? Why would there need to be one per generation?" Matthew carefully glanced around and pointed straight back to the room beyond.

"Back there," he pointed. "There is a room even I am not allowed to go into. When I was John's age, I use to sneak into a similar room, at the insistence of my predecessor. Inside, was a collection of journals, written by my father, detailing his life. Almost everything I know of my father, before he adopted me, came from those pages.

Sadly, I did not learn as much as I wished but everything I have just told, is a part of what I learned. I know from what I have read, that becoming the Sin Eater, is excruciatingly painful but is far from the most difficult part.

We are taught as children, our souls are pure but that they can grow tainted, as we give in to the temptations of sin. I wonder however, how much sin a single, human soul can endure before it is ruled by it. My theory, if you will bear with me, is that the reason a new Sin Eater was chosen, was to prevent the current incarnation from becoming overwhelmed." Harlee's eyes grew wide as Matthew's words sunk in.

"If Maxwell has been the Sin Eater for two hundred years...?" Harlee began. Father Matthew waved his hands to stop her.

"I believe it weighs on him, heavily as it were but I do not believe he has reached his limit. In my father's journals, he makes mention of his father, Lucien Grey. My father suspects that through this man, he was born something beyond just human."

"How can you be certain?" Harlee asked.

"My father, in his journals, references feats beyond human ability, on more than one occasion but also mentions a conversation, he overheard from his mentor, Samuel and his mother, Emilia. Their conversation, in some way validated his thinking, which is why he was chosen to begin with."

"Oh, okay." Harlee interrupted, waving her hands about. "Assuming that I believe everything you are telling me and I am not saying I do, but if I did, why entrust me with all of this?"

"That is actually the simplest part, to explain. You were drawn to Maxwell's heart." He said, placing the cask on his lap.

"I was what?" She said in disbelief.

"My father has a belief that all children of God, deserve to be loved as they are, with few exceptions. He also believes, while all of us possess the spirit of our maker, within us, we also all possess the spirit of the devil. It is for this reason, he believes, while all are deserving of love, only a select few are worthy to carry the heart of another and fewer still, possess it.

It seems too coincidental to me, while anyone might perceive what it is, that is in this container, it is rare to find one who can hear it and rarer still, one whose heart can synchronize with it." Harlee clasped her bosom tightly as she realized Matthew knew.

"Harlee, I know you don't enjoy my father's company and wish for nothing more than his help, finding your sister. I am not telling you these things, because I know you well. I am telling you these things, because Maxwell's own heart, has determined you are worthy of protecting it." Harlee remained in shock. As she sat trembling, Father Matthew began to open the box.

"I am not asking you to do as John or I have. That must be your decision. I am asking that should John or I perish, while searching for your sister, that you keep my father safe." Harlee's mind, screamed for her to get up and run away but something even more deeply engrained within her, begged her to remain. She could feel her chest burn to see what was in that box. She tried to overpower her legs, through force of will but only managed to move nearer.

"As you will see, Maxwell's heart is imperfect. It has been wounded many times over the years and for a time, has barely held itself together." He spoke as Harlee leaned down to see what he was staring at. Harlee peered over the edge of the box and stared at the red, pulsating mass.

Upon it, she could see all of the distinguished features she knew from her studies of anatomy. What struck out at her, however, were the innumerable tiny cuts and scratches, as if the heart had been wounded repeatedly. The various scratches upon it, merely peppered the area, which most distinguished itself. One massive crack, which branched off into two unique sutures, nearly split the heart in half. Harlee's eyes became fixated upon the heart and she forgot her urge to resist it.

"Harlee, there is one last thing I must tell you before we leave this place." Father Matthew interrupted Harlee's trance, snapping her back to him.

"What is that?" She asked.

"In order to protect my father, you must be prepared, at any moment, to kill him. He cannot help what he becomes, and it wounds him terribly, when he harms others. On the night of the blood moon, he will again transform." Harlee nodded her head, terrified by the thought of seeing that creature again.

"Does he change every blood moon?" She asked, to which Father Matthew nodded.

"Before we leave, I have one request." He added.

"What is it?"

"In all of my time, I have known of only five, excluding you, who could hear my father's heart. You, Harlee, are the very first I know of, who was able to touch it, without succumbing to extreme pain. What I am wondering, Harlee, if you would. Will you show me, one more time?" Harlee stared at Father Matthew, secretly wondering the same as him. Harlee nodded her head and with a touch as soft and as gentle as she could manage, she reached out for the heart.

"WHAT ARE YOU DOING!?" Maxwell burst onto the scene, startling both Father Matthew and Harlee.

"FATHER!" Matthew said as he jumped up from surprise. "I was merely..."

"I TOLD YOU NEVER TO COME HERE!" He raged and Harlee's heart filled instantly with fear and dread, as the lights around Maxwell began to fade as they had the night of his transformation. Maxwell's shadow began to stretch out beyond him.

"I'm sorry, Maxwell," she pleaded. "I just wanted to..."

"DO YOU HAVE ANY IDEA WHAT YOU COULD HAVE DONE!?" He continued to bellow with deafening volume as his voice echoed through the tunnels.

"Harlee, be ready to run." Father Matthew whispered. "Don't worry, I'll be alright. Maxwell may be unstable but he would never hurt one of his own." He spoke with confidence as Maxwell walked forward.

"YOU ARE NO LONGER WELCOME HERE!" He yelled to Harlee. "I WANT YOU OUT!" He bellowed. Harlee's body quickly sprang into action. Sprinting straight at Maxwell, she shot passed him and charged up the stairs, slamming the door behind her.

"What happened!?" Both John and Dahlia yelled as Harlee tore passed them.

"I have to get out of here!" She yelled as she ran, not stopping until she had left the cathedral several blocks behind. Harlee dipped into a nearby alley and placed her back to the wall, trying to still her beating heart.

"In the...in the great green room." She stuttered uncontrollably as she tried to calm herself. After several failed attempts at her recitation, Harlee sunk down the wall and buried her head into her knees.

"Stupid, Harlee, stupid." She yelled at herself as tears poured from her eyes. "Why did you go down there? You promised you wouldn't." She yelled at herself, unsure of why she was even upset. Harlee sat cold, afraid and alone for some time before she saw a flashlight, accompanied by a familiar voice.

"Harlee? Are you down here?" She could hear John's voice. Harlee looked up at John as he ran up close. John quickly took off his coat and draped it over her shoulders as he knelt down beside her.

"Harlee, are you alright?" He asked as he gently rubbed her back.

"I shouldn't have gone down there. Is Matthew alright?" She asked. John nodded his head.

"Yeah, Matthew is fine. Maxwell was still angry but he did not harm anyone. I feel bad for whomever he meets during his hunt tonight. Come on, it is not safe to be out tonight and Dahlia is out looking for you as well. We can meet her back at the cathedral. Maxwell won't be back until tomorrow." Harlee pulled John's hand away.

"I am never going back there! Not to him! Let him rot in hell or purgatory or wherever the hell his kind go! Let him take all of his souls and burn with them!" She yelled causing John to back away slightly.

"Do not be ridiculous. It is not just Maxwell's home. It is Matthew's and my home, as well. Give it a couple of days. It is still your home, too. If you want it to be." John told her.

"I don't ever want to share an address with that man again." She said.

"Well then at least come back with me to get your things. You don't want me cleaning out your underwear drawer, do you?" Harlee could feel her face growing hot with embarrassment and eyed John with shock. In the dim light, she could tell his face was red, also.

"I suppose that I can't leave my guns behind, either." She mumbled as she rose to her feet.

"That's the spirit." John said as he walked her back to the cathedral.

Harlee and John went back inside the cathedral. Father Matthew greeted them with a weak smile and a hot cup of tea. Harlee gratefully accepted the cup, as she sat and waited for Dahlia to return. Almost an hour later, both Dahlia and Almalexia returned. Dahlia ran to Harlee and hugged her as Almalexia approached Matthew.

"What did you do?" She asked. Her voice filled with concern. Matthew sat down on the pews.

"I took Harlee to see Maxwell's heart."

"What!?" Almalexia sounded a combination of angry and shocked. "What possessed you to do such a thing!?" She asked.

"I just wanted someone to know, in case something happens to John or I. I wanted to make sure that there was someone left behind, to protect my father from himself." Almalexia's face softened and she sat beside Matthew.

"You did the right thing. Maxwell will see, eventually." She said as she held the priest as if he were her own child. Turning from Matthew, Almalexia looked to Harlee and Dahlia.

"Almalexia, I'm..." The succubus raised her hand, interrupting Harlee.

"I understand. I am no stranger to being curious about that man. Are you alright?" Harlee nodded her head. "I agree with Matthew. If something happens, friends are in short supply these days. Do you two have somewhere to go for a few days, until things settle down?" Dahlia nodded her head.

"Yes. Jules said if we needed, we could stay with her for a few days." Almalexia smiled.

"I always loved that girl. Matthew, can you or John help them?"

"Yes."

"Good. Be careful out there. The riots have already started and Maxwell is not helping. It is a bloodbath out there. He is going after wolves, vampires, anything non-human he can find. I haven't seen him rampage this badly since John disappeared."

"We will be careful, I promise." Matthew told her.

"Please do." Almalexia spoke as she walked away. "It's going to be one hell of a night." She said as she left the cathedral. Father Matthew turned to Harlee and Dahlia.

"We should probably get your things around." He told them as they moved towards the back of the building, As Harlee and Dahlia gathered their things, Matthew rounded up boxes and bags, while John carried everything up front.

"Are you sure that you won't just be a few days?" Matthew asked. Harlee shook her head.

"I appreciate everything that you have done for us, Father. I really do. I think that everyone realized from the beginning that this would never be a permanent thing. It's probably better this way." Harlee said as she brought out another box.

"Would you prefer to store your hardware here for now?" Father Matthew asked. "If S.W.A.T. and the police are out, they will be searching vehicles."

"Thank you." Harlee said as she grabbed her gun bag, removing her thigh strap, a single Beretta and spare clip. "Just in case." She said as she grabbed the gun bags and carried them over to the staircase. Within the hour, Harlee and Dahlia had packed their things as John loaded everything into the car.

"Is it alright if I go with them?" John asked.

"Is it?" Father Matthew asked, staring at Harlee and Dahlia.

"Certainly." Harlee smiled, giving John a gentle hug before climbing into the car. Harlee and Dahlia waved to Father Matthew as they pulled away, John in the back seat.

After he watched the car pull away down the street, Father Matthew turned and walked back inside. Locking the large double doors behind him, he loosened his collar as he walked down the aisle towards the crucifix of the savior. Father Matthew kneeled before the altar to offer his evening prayer, as he heard loud banging outside the cathedral doors.

Father Matthew rose from his knees and walked towards the doors. Before Father Matthew had passed the first row of pews, the doors burst open and seven men, six of which, were dressed in camo cargo pants, combat boots and hooded sweatshirts. The leader of the group, a white male with slicked back black hair, who wore designer jeans, silk shirt, blazer and silver tipped shoes.

"I am afraid we are closed for the evening." Father Matthew began as the men, armed with pistols and assault munitions, spread out, moving towards the back. "If you would please leave, there will be no need to involve the police." Father Matthew spoke, as the leader of the group walked straight towards him, his arms open wide.

"But I've come to confess my sins, Father." The man smiled as he rotated his wrist, revealing the back of his hand. Father Matthew's eyes grew wide as he recognized the tattoo on it, a thorn covered heart with a crucifix handled sword, plunged through it. As the man reached behind his back, using his right hand, Matthew sprang into action.

As the man pulled a pistol from the back of his pants and fired, Matthew dove between the first and second row of pews. Matthew groaned in pain as the round struck his shoulder and he quickly scurried down the row, as he heard the guns of the six other men, cock.

"Kill him!" The leader ordered. "We were told to leave Maxwell a message!" With his many years of training under Maxwell, Father Matthew breathed slowly as he thought of a plan and immediately began implementing it.

He watched beneath the pews, following the feet of his nearest assailant, closer. He untied the lace of his right show as he watched. Wrapping the lace tightly around his fists, he crouched down as the first gunmen approached. The moment their eyes met, Matthew kicked off from the ground, flipping the pew up into the man's face. The gunmen shielded himself as Matthew ran up on him, wrapped the shoelace around his throat and dropped all of his body weight, flipping the man.

The gunman landed on a bench, breaking it as Matthew quickly snatched the dropped pistol, firing two blind shots behind him, as he ran towards the confessional. Keeping his head down as the other intruders opened fire, Matthew slid behind the confessional for cover. Matthew sat, facing towards his attackers, gun at the ready.

"All mighty Father, please forgive me, for my transgressions..." Matthew began to pray.

"Saying your last rites, priest?" One of the men yelled, giving away his position. Matthew listened as he heard a clip eject. Quickly he leaned to the side and took aim.

"Blam...blam..."He fired two rounds into a shinbone and a femur, on two separate targets. The men screamed in pain as they dropped to the ground. Matthew ducked back behind cover as the remaining four standing, opened fire. Matthew quickly checked his magazine, counting out his remaining four rounds, plus the one he had in the chamber.

"You two. Flush him out. We will cover you." Matthew heard the leader speak. He quickly pulled off his robe and after positioning himself, threw it away as he dropped down. The moment's distraction, as all guns turned on his robes, was all he needed to drop down and shoot the two approaching on his opposite side. Both men went down from gunshot wounds to the stomach. Matthew made sure to knock their weapons away.

"I've got plenty left for the both of you." He yelled. "Who wants the next one?" He yelled as he heard something metal sling against the tile. Matthew turned his head in time to see a grenade drop near to him. Without taking the time to think, he sprang passed and rolled the nearest downed man onto his side, as a shield.

The grenade went off, eviscerating the two gunmen and causing Matthew's eardrums to rupture as his entire body went numb. Severely shell shocked, Matthew trying to make some sense of where he was, crawled toward the altar bearing the crucifix. As Matthew crawled, he felt an immense pressure on his leg.

"Where is your father now?" The man with the silver tipped shoes said, as he stepped in between Father Matthew's shoulder blades, pointed his gun and pulled the trigger.

Chapter 11 – I, the Sin Eater, Maxwell Grey

Maxwell sat perched on a rooftop, holding his chest, as he surveyed the city. Phantom pains had stricken him, during his latest engagement, nearly subjecting him to his attackers' whims. Below him, lie his latest victims, a pack of ghouls, which had wandered from the nearby cemetery. Beside them, their vampire masters, also lay shredded. Hearing the sound of police sirens, Maxwell turned and began following the source back into the city.

As he neared, he noticed a S.W.A.T. car had arrived on the scene and a news helicopter, hovered nearby. Maxwell moved in closer and listened carefully. He only listened long enough to catch that the perpetrators had looted a building.

"Human problem." He growled as he turned and moved back towards home. Running across the rooftops, Maxwell made quick progress through the city and noticed several police vehicles parked outside, lights on.

"What the hell?" Maxwell said aloud as he leapt across the street and made his way to the cathedral roof. Carefully, Maxwell worked his way passed the bell tower and to the balcony door. Slipping inside, Maxwell could hear the police. He listened intently as they communicated on their radios but he could not quite make sense of the chatter. Maxwell crept to the balcony's edge and felt as another crack appeared in his heart.

Beneath him, he saw three bodies lying on the ground, two in pieces and the one, which was intact, surrounded by police and a coroner, was Matthew's. Maxwell gripped at his chest as he saw the bullet hole in the back of his adoptive son's skull and looked to the tumbled over crucifix. Upon the wall, where the savior once rested, painted in blood, was a thorn covered heart, pierced by a crucifix-handled sword.

Rage began to swell within Maxwell as he stared upon the message left to him. Blackness began to seethe from his being as his shadow stretched out beyond him. The coroner and the police officers, looked around as the lights in the room flickered from Maxwell's aura. Maxwell watched as all but one officer, moved from the room. As Maxwell's aura dimmed the lights further, he silently dropped to the ground floor. He walked to Matthew's side and rolled his son over. Matthew's eyes were still open, his hand outstretched towards the wall. Maxwell closed his eyes as he clenched his teeth angrily. He removed Matthew's rosary, closed his son's eyes and turning around, crept behind the officer.

"Where are they?" He asked, placing his hand over the officer's mouth. The officer struggled against the enraged man, who whispered again.

"I will not harm you. Tell me where they have gone and I will leave." As Maxwell began to remove his hand, the officer's radio came on.

"S.W.A.T. has been met with heavy fire. All officers are asked to report to the scene and set up a perimeter." As the crackle faded, the officer pointed to his radio and nodded his head. Maxwell recalled the scene he had passed on his route and growled. Maxwell turned his eyes back to Matthew's body.

"I am sorry, my son." He whispered, releasing the police officer and vanishing into the dark. The shroud of darkness vanished and the lights came on, as Maxwell left in pursuit of those who killed his son.

Across the city, beneath the spotlights of the news helicopters, several men, armed with assault munitions paced. Unbeknownst to the men above, Maxwell, filled with grief and rage, silently entered the building through a window. With the eyes of a nocturnal predator, he stalked through the halls, searching for prey.

The sound of the men's footsteps, though quiet from human standards, proved deafening, in Maxwell's current state. He heard every breath, every word, of every person around them. He slowed his approach, as he heard the sound of a heart, beating.

Maxwell smiled, his fangs baring, as he stared at the pacing man, who nervously patrolled the hallways. Muttering to himself, the assault rifle holding man, every so often, casually pulled back on the curtains, to examine the scene outside.

"Oh, I don't like this. Derek better figure out what we are doing." He spoke.

"Don't worry so much. The boss will figure something out." Another masculine voice assured. Looking down at his hands, Maxwell focused on his fingertips, which slowly grew claws. Pulling his silver chain from within his duster, Maxwell crept up on the first man.

Barely peeking out at him from beyond the corner, he watched as the nearest guard, approached. Just as the man came up on the corner, Maxwell sprang into action, jabbing his claws through the man's throat, and gripping onto his vocal chords, squeezed.

"Hey, what was that?" The second guard asked, turning towards them. Fear filled the first man's eyes, as he remained upright, held up by Maxwell's hand, as though he had been hung up to dry. Staring back at him, were eyes of pure evil.

"Hey, is everything all right?" The second guard asked again, walking closer. Silver chain in hand, Maxwell relied upon the cover of darkness, to conceal the chain as he began to whirl it.

"Hey, are you..." The man was cut off, the moment the chain pierced through his body. He slowly lowered his gaze, seeing the silver spearhead, pierced through his heart. As the man slowly dropped to his knees, Maxwell lowered the first guard to the floor, and removed his chain from the chest of the second.

Turning his head skyward, Maxwell could hear footsteps of several more men, pacing from one wall to the next, waiting. Though the men had blackened all of the rooms, to defend themselves from sniper fire, they could not hope to hide from both, Maxwell's, supernatural senses of sight and smell. Quickly, finding the staircase, he slowly made his way up, sensing several men up ahead.

"What do we do?" One of the men atop the rooftop yelled to his fellow.

"Our orders were to sit and wait." One of the other men on the roof responded. The rooftop door burst open as six more armed men, ran out onto it, screaming.

"What the hell was that, Derek!?" One of the men yelled to the man with the slicked back hair, as he pulled the pin from one of the grenades on his belt and threw the entire ensemble down the stairwell.

The following blast, launched dust and debris back up the stairs and out the door. All of the men present, trained their weapons on the cloud that formed. The spotlight of the news chopper, still hovering overhead and the lights of the cars below, continued to churn. The screams of one of their own broke the calm, as a silver chain pierced one of the men's chests, and drug him into the darkness beyond.

The remaining men, simultaneously opened fire into the doorway. As the gunmen's clips emptied, they continued pulling their triggers from panic. As Derek emptied his clip, he turned to look at his men.

"Reload you idiots! This is Grey's son!" He yelled. As his men ejected their clips, Derek opened fire at something, which flew at him from the doorway.

"Did you get my message?" He laughed as he unloaded his clip but was still knocked down with tremendous force. Noticing the body of his slain man, had fallen on him, he gasped as another figure pounced on top of him.

"I did!" A mouthful of canine fangs grinned at him as Maxwell spoke, his face only an inch from Derek's. Maxwell quickly, kicked off from the ground and dashed towards the others. Derek struggled to move as he heard the screams of his men but found himself encumbered from the one that Maxwell had taken first. As he shoved his deceased comrade aside, he rose to his feet and readied his weapon.

Maxwell, noticing this, launched himself backward and grabbing Derek's wrist, forced his arm behind his back. Derek cried in pain as he felt his elbow shatter followed by his knee as Maxwell kicked it out to the side. Maxwell launched himself to his next victim, as Derek rolled his eyes to bear witness and watch, as Maxwell tore the throat out of one of his men. As the man crumbled to the ground, Maxwell emptied his hand and pummeled the face of another, until nothing remained but bits. Once finished, Maxwell turned his gaze on Derek and slowly walked towards him.

"The Grey Brides will come for you, next! Lucien will rise and there is nothing you can do to stop him!" Maxwell slashed Derek's wrists, causing the man to writhe again. Maxwell pulled out his chain and tossing one end over some metal beams, stabbed Derek through the thigh and hoisted him up in the air. The man whimpered in pain and fear as he dangled, helplessly. Maxwell dabbed his fingers in Derek's blood as he drew ancient symbols on Derek's body.

"Are the Grey Brides watching now?" Maxwell asked, in a tone befitting of a devil.

"Of course they are! We have already infiltrated every level of this city! They know everything and see everything! Soon we will be more powerful than the freaks who pretend to rule this realm!" As the man spoke, Maxwell took a small metal container from his pocket and from it, pulled a single piece of bread, which he dabbed against Derek's chest. The man's body convulsed violently as a black, ethereal substance, seeped from the left side of his chest and was absorbed into the bread.

"What did you just do?" He asked after catching his breath.

"I've prepared something for you to take to Grey." Maxwell told him, sinister smile on his face as he bent down by the man's. Shoving the bread into Derek's mouth, he clapped his hand down over top of it and held it shut.

"I the Sin Eater, Maxwell Grey, have found the weight of your sins, too great to bear. I condemn your soul, to hellfire and damnation, to pay for the innocent blood you have shed." Derek began screaming into Maxwell's hand as steam rose from his body and his skin boiled. Maxwell released the man and walked from the news crew's spotlight as the hanged man, burst into intensely bright flames.

Chapter 12 – It Seems Only Yesterday

"Good morning, everyone!" Jules said with a bright smile, filled with cheer as Harlee and Dahlia walked out into Jules' kitchen, still wearing their pajamas. Jules, who was already fully dressed, stood at the stove, preparing fresh waffles, potatoes and sausages.

"Good morning, Jules." Harlee and Dahlia both mumbled as they sat down.

"Jules, is there anything we can do to help you?" Harlee asked. "We really appreciate everything and don't want to be freeloaders." Jules turned to Harlee and smiled brightly.

"Actually yes, there is something you can do." Jules began. "I asked John to fetch milk from the store. That gives us about twenty minutes of girls' time. With that being said, will one of you please explain to me what happened?" Dahlia turned to stare at Harlee, who tried to find the words. As Harlee opened her mouth to explain, the door was quickly knocked on three times, followed by John flinging the door open in a panic as he ran into the living room.

"John! What in the world?" Jules paused as a woman, dressed in a skin tight, motorcyclist's leather jumpsuit, walked in, removing her helmet.

"Alma! What a pleasant surprise!" Jules said as Almalexia removed her sunglasses as well, to reveal that she had been crying excessively of late.

"What happened!?" Jules, Harlee and Dahlia all asked. Almalexia shook her head and pointed to the living room, tears still flowing from her eyes. John sat, remote control in his hand as he turned on the television, flipping over to the news. He wiped the tears out of his eyes, as he sat on the couch, joined quickly by the three women.

"We now bring you reports from last night's Hell Night riots. Troves of looters and rioters came out in force, during the late hours of the night. While the riots were mainly contained to the downtown area, there was one attack in particular, that stands out above the rest.

Father Cornelius Matthew, a well-known, respected and beloved priest in the uptown area, was attacked last night, a few hours after evening mass. Though police have not confirmed the identities or whereabouts of Father Matthew's attackers, it was confirmed, the priest was fatally shot. Funeral services will be announced once any next of kin can be contacted.

In other news related to Hell Night, a standoff between vigilante, the Hunter and several heavily armed gunmen, results in a bloodbath on the city rooftops."

John, Harlee, Dahlia, Jules and Almalexia, all wept uncontrollably, unable to believe their dear friend was gone. The newsreel continued to roll and they quickly found themselves, transitioning from grief, to horror. Each of them froze in silent trepidation.

"Now, we would like to warn everyone that the following footage is rather graphic and may contain disturbing images. Viewer discretion is advised."

The news footage came back on and everyone cringed in horror at the war zone on tv. Explosions and several hundreds of rounds of ammunition being fired. Next, they saw a body fly through the air, followed by a quickly moving dark image, which could have only been Maxwell.

Though the cloud of smoke was thick, they could make out the burst of light from the firing weapons, worst of all, were the screams of pain and cowardice, accompanied by Maxwell's savage roar, all of which, perfectly captured on camera. When the screams faded and the dust settled, they saw Maxwell pummeling what appeared to be a puddle of crimson. Maxwell stood and walked towards the last man, who attempted to crawl away.

John, Dahlia and Jules looked away as Maxwell impaled the man, hanging him in the air. Harlee and Almalexia continued to watch as Maxwell spoke to the man. Harlee squinted her eyes, trying to figure out what he was doing with his hands.

"Almalexia? Do you have any idea?" Harlee asked.

"It looks like what he does before a sin eating but I can't..." As she spoke, the man burst into a plume of hellishly bright flames. Everyone gathered, burrowed into the couch as they heard the reporter, scream deliriously.

"Oh my god! The Hunter has just set that man on fire! The flames are so hot and bright, it is affecting us up here! He has gone too far this time, Jared!"

The footage continued to roll, the hanged man's screams, ringing out for all to hear, When the footage flipped back, those on the screen looked to still be in shock. Once the anchor realized he was back on, he shuffled his papers and continued with his report.

"You've seen it yourselves, folks. Has the Hunter, finally gone too far? Is the city, truly safe, with such a madman on the loose? Stay tuned!"

Everyone sat, stunned by what they had seen. Harlee and Almalexia turned and stared at one another for a moment. The others slowly came out of their trauma as Jules dialed her phone and waited.

"Hey babe, it's Jules. I am sorry to ask but can you cover the diner for me, today? My adoptive father...yes, the priest. He was killed last night and I need to go." Jules said, voice still trembling from crying. "Yes, I'll be alright. Thanks, babe, you're the best." Jules hung up the phone, wiped her eyes and stood.

"I would suggest you two get around, quickly." Jules said straight faced as she gathered her things. "Alma. Do you have any leads on Maxwell's whereabouts?" Almalexia shook her head.

"No. I had hoped that he would come here." She replied.

"Alright then. All we can do is go back then. If Maxwell cannot be found, he will come to us, hopefully. In the meantime, I can at least grant Matthew a proper send off." She spoke as she continued to compose herself. Harlee and Dahlia were both in awe. John rose and followed Jules' lead.

"How are you so well composed?" Dahlia asked. As Jules placed a magnum revolver and several six-shooter instant reloads on the counter.

"What is there to tell? I'm daddy's little girl." She smiled through her grief. Harlee and Dahlia both rose from the couch and began to grab their things.

"We leave in forty five minutes!" Jules said. "John, please help me in the kitchen while they are getting around. Alma, are there any safe places to stay?" Almalexia thought briefly as Harlee and Dahlia hustled.

"I can keep everyone safe in my district but I will have to check beyond that. A week before the Feast, about anything is possible." Almalexia warned her.

"Whatever you feel is best, will be fine, I am sure." Jules told her as she examined the revolver.

"Is that Kiefer's?" Almalexia asked. Jules flicked her wrist, snapping the chamber back in place.

"Was his. It's mine now." She stated as she turned to John. "I need you to help me prepare lunches for the day. It is going to be a long day. Start by packing up breakfast. We will have to eat it on the road."

Within the given time, they all left Jules' house and made their way back to Sin City. As she had suggested, the day was excruciatingly long as they each worked to deal with their grief. As John and Jules left to begin Father Matthew's funeral arrangements, Harlee, Dahlia and Almalexia returned to the cathedral.

They stood just outside the polices' caution taped area and stared as officers moved back and forth through the scene. Several of Father Matthew's regular parishioners, were also on site, waiting just beyond the barrier. Recognizing Dahlia, several paid their condolences and asked they be extended to John.

"Should we go through the catacombs?" Harlee whispered to Almalexia.

"We can wait until nightfall, when fewer people are present." She suggested. Harlee and Dahlia nodded their heads.

"Then what should we do in the meantime?" Dahlia asked.

"I suppose we should find a new place to stay?" Harlee suggested. Almalexia smiled.

"I can assume that you'd rather not stay with the girls and I, in the brothel?" She asked.

"You may." Harlee said bluntly.

"That is probably for the best. I'm not sure poor John would be safe." Almalexia joked.

"Would they go after him?" Harlee asked.

"Not if I told them not to, but that's not the trouble. The girls and I secrete pheromones, and put off a type of scented aphrodisiac when we are hungry, overly excited, or aroused. It can be difficult to control and I am afraid that poor John would be left, unable to function outside of a primal level. Not that you two would be safe, either." Harlee and Dahlia both eyed the succubus.

"You think that John would go that berserk?" Harlee asked.

"No. Our pheromones, act similar to a dangerously high dose of ecstasy, though without the dying part. I only meant our influence affects woman, as well." She said. "If ever you are present when I attempt to seduce someone, stay upwind, though having sex while under the effects, would prove most euphoric." Harlee and Dahlia continued to stare at her in disbelief.

"Whatever you say, I suppose." Harlee said. The three of them moved away from the crime scene and followed Almalexia to the nearest hotel.

"I am sorry, ma'am. We just do not have any vacancies, right now. With the upcoming festival, we are booked solid." The man behind the desk continued to tell Almalexia, who simply removed her shades and smiled. A few feet away, Harlee and Dahlia stood waiting. Harlee tossed her head from side to side and rubbed her neck, wiping off the perspiration.

"Dahlia? Am I going nuts, or is it fricking hot in here?" Harlee asked.

"No, it's hot as hell. Why do they keep it this way?" She said as Harlee's nostrils flared.

"And do you see any flowers? I swear, all I can smell are flowers and cinnamon." As she began to look around, she could feel her body trembling all over.

"Hey, you want to get out of here?" Harlee looked across the room and saw Dahlia, hanging on the arm of some handsome young guy.

"I have a room upstairs, if you'd like to join me?" The man spoke, placing his hand around Dahlia's waist. Harlee stared at her friend with confused jealousy, as the two approached the elevator. She watched Dahlia enter the elevator with the stranger. Harlee watched as the two began kissing and disrobing before the doors had closed. Harlee gripped her fists angrily, as it occurred to her, exactly what and why she was feeling the way she was.

"Your room key, ma'am." Almalexia said as she tossed a card key into Harlee's lap. "I'll give you about thirty minutes, to do what you need to do. Use the express elevator, top floor." She told her as she walked away. Harlee, still in a hormone-induced state of carnal hunger, began searching about for either a victim or an escape route. She rose and felt a draft blow through the open door and up her dress. Harlee about toppled over as her eyes rolled into the back of her skull. Her heart raced, every texture and fragrance sent her into a new state of shock.

Harlee stumbled to the elevator and pressed the button frantically, as she tried to remain composed. As she waited, she saw Almalexia kissing the desk clerk and pulling on his tie, coercing him from the seat. As the two of them worked their way over, the elevator doors opened, allowing Harlee in.

She quickly scurried in, and fumbled with her key card, before managing to insert her room key into the slot. Harlee hit the button for the top floor and pressed herself against the far back wall, as Almalexia entered with her new toy. The fragrance and effect of the succubus' toxin only intensified as the elevator doors closed.

The moment the doors shut, the aggressive woman forced the desk clerk against the opposite corner and began kissing him, as she tore his shirt open. The man began unzipping Almalexia's jumpsuit as his lips traced down the side of her neck and down to her exposed breasts. Thighs trembling, Harlee collapsed to the floor and continued to watch as the man kissed and groped on her exposed, honey colored breasts, manipulating her nipples as she groaned.

Harlee's hands worked furiously, fighting against her will, her body aching for release. Her legs danced across the floor as she dug her heels into the floor, severely aroused beyond description, by the scene playing out not more than three feet from her. Harlee began reaching down, her fingers trembling, ready to provide herself with the release, she desperately craved.

"You could join us, you know? I don't mind..." Almalexia sighed with excitement as the man plunged his hand deep into her panties. "And besides, he is rather excellent with his hands. At least let us take the pressure off for you." Almalexia offered, head back eyes closed, mouth half open as she moaned with pleasure. Harlee continued to watch the man ravage the woman as if the primal beast within him, broke loose and took control.

Harlee, hand grasping her pelvis already, knew she could no longer resist Almalexia's toxin. She feared the surmounting anxiety would soon kill her, should she not find some way to release it. Slowly, she began hiking up her dress until she reached her long since soaked through panties. Harlee began to pull them down her legs, longing to be made to feel, the way Almalexia did now. Almalexia, seeing this, pulled her man towards Harlee.

The man began running his hands through Harlee's hair as Almalexia began kissing up the insides of Harlee's thighs, removing Harlee's panties for her. Harlee's thighs spread wide, baring herself entirely to the two pleasuring her flesh. Harlee swore she was ready to climax there at that moment, already crying out with euphoria. Just as Almalexia grew close to Harlee's anxiously awaiting pelvis and the man neared her pleading breasts, Harlee closed her eyes and opened herself to what she was about to experience.

"DING!" The elevator bell rang as they reached the penthouse level.

"No thank you!" Harlee yelled as she ran, leaving her panties behind. Almalexia lowered the clerk to the floor as the elevator doors closed. Harlee ran straight for the shower, turned on the cold water and threw herself in, clothing and all.

As promised, nearly half an hour later, Almalexia returned, smile on her face. She walked into the main room and saw Harlee, sitting alone, wrapped only in a blanket, in total silence. Once she noticed Almalexia, Harlee rose to leave.

"You are quite safe." Almalexia said, taking a seat opposite of Harlee and placing her underwear on the table. "I apologize. Things got a little out of control but I am no longer secreting the pheromones."

"You should have warned us." Harlee grumbled.

"I did but I also thought that it might help us deal with our grief. I did not expect things to take quite the turn they did." She said softly.

"The only help I need is getting my sister back!" She growled angrily as Almalexia eyed her.

"I am sorry...I thought..." Almalexia reached for the nearby pillow and cradled it in her arms. "I thought that you shared our grief." She said, holding the pillow to her chest as if a child.

"Almalexia, are you alright?" Harlee asked, realizing she was not.

"It seems only yesterday, I was rocking him in my arms, feeding him, or laying him to sleep. The time went so fast and now he's already gone." Almalexia began to sob as Harlee felt guilty. "I wasn't actually his mother, nor was Maxwell technically his father but it felt real, you know. Not always between Maxwell and I but with Matthew it was real...and now he is gone and not even Maxwell's vengeance or love, can fill in the void left behind." Almalexia cried, unable to form further sentences.

Harlee rose from her seat and sat beside the heartbroken woman, cradling her in her arms. Almalexia leaned into Harlee, who began to stroke the succubus' head. They hugged for several minutes, allowing their respective tears to shed.

"Please don't tell Jules or John, you saw me this way?" Almalexia asked.

"Alright but why?"

"I want to remain strong for them. No matter what the cost. They need someone to help hold them up. Matthew was that cornerstone for us and they will need someone to remain strong for their sake."

"We should remain strong for each other." Harlee said. Moments later, after Almalexia had settled and Harlee was winding down to go to bed, watching a movie on the television, reciting her favorite quotes.

"Why do they always paint hallways that color?" She started as she heard the elevator doors ding again and Dahlia stepped in, carrying her shoes. She bore the look of extreme euphoria on her face, as she walked into the sitting room and flopped down beside Harlee, who muted the tv.

"Walk of shame?" Harlee asked as Dahlia rolled her eyes over to her.

"Hell...shame, anger, hatred...fucking euphoria. It was all of it. I tell you, I have never cum so hard or so much, my entire life. I've got nothing left." She sighed as she laid her head back.

"You realize that you were drugged by Almalexia's pheromones?"

"Hell if I care. Have to bottle her sweat or something. That shit is amazing." Harlee shook her head as Dahlia sighed again, already about to fall asleep.

"Did you take care of business?" Dahlia asked sheepishly.

"I managed the situation." Harlee replied. Dahlia sighed again as she rolled onto her stomach to stare at her friend.

"Harlee, I may just be the only person on this earth, who knows what you're dealing with and I understand. Allowing every positive experience in life, to fester and die within you is not going to help you or Cilia."

"You think I don't know that!?" Harlee snapped at Dahlia. A long pause followed the outburst until Dahlia began laughing to herself.

"What!?" Harlee grouched, causing Dahlia to laugh more aggressively. Harlee crossed her arms and remained still, maintaining an agitated expression. After a short while, Dahlia's laughter came to an end and she began trying to catch her breath.

"I'm sorry. I just find it so ironic." Dahlia said, gasping for air.

"You find what, ironic!?"

"The fact you and Maxwell don't get along but are so similar." She stated. Harlee's jaw dropped. She stared at her friend angrily but was at a loss of a retort.

"I'm going to bed. Try not to catch any STD's while I'm asleep, alright?" Harlee jabbed, only making Dahlia laugh again. Harlee walked into her room, laid her head down and fell asleep immediately.

The following morning, Harlee rose, irritated by the plethora of erotic dreams, she had all evening. She rose from the bed and wrapped a robe around her naked form before walking out onto the balcony from her room.

Out on the balcony, she stared over most of the city, noticing right away that she held a fair vantage over the cathedral. She eyed the bell tower and still could not believe Matthew was gone. There was a gentle knock at the door.

"Harlee, breakfast is ready." She heard Dahlia's voice. Harlee looked down at her stomach, which gurgled at her. Harlee took a deep breath and after a quick trip to the bathroom, walked out of her room. Once she reached the kitchen, she saw not just Dahlia but John and Jules as well.

"Good morning." Everyone exchanged as she walked out. Harlee sat in between Dahlia and John, to a table filled with eggs, sausages and bacon.

"I'm sorry it's not real extravagant." Jules said as she sat opposite of Harlee.

"Stop it, Jules. This looks fantastic." Dahlia said, still beaming from last night.

"Well, thank you, Dahlia. What, may I ask, has you in such a cheerful mood, this morning?" Jules asked.

"Just had an incredible night, last night. It really helped me work off some steam and get through...everything." She said, trying to be sensitive to John and Jules. John remained quiet as Jules stared at Dahlia.

"Almalexia hit us both with her toxin, yesterday." Harlee spoke. Jules smiled as she looked at Dahlia, who blushed.

"Good for you, Dahlia. Well then, Harlee. Did you have a good night as well?" Jules asked. Harlee thought of what almost happened in the elevator before replying.

"My night was fine, nothing like Dahlia's." She answered.

"I remember the first time Almalexia accidentally doused me. I about lost control, too. I didn't and managed on my own but I had the absolutely most amazing sex dreams the following two nights." She sighed as Harlee jolted.

"Two nights?" Harlee gasped.

"Oh, Harlee..."Jules smiled brightly, causing Harlee to squirm.

"You were watching that casino heist movie when I came in, last night. Was it Brad?" Dahlia asked. Harlee shook her head, though her cheeks darkened.

"Oh, George!" Jules exclaimed, excitedly as John cleared his throat loudly.

"Can we discuss the funeral arrangements, please?" He asked. The demeanor of the room, changed as they were forced to face reality.

"You're right." Jules spoke in a solemn voice as her smile evaporated.

"We saw to it that Father Matthew's body was cremated and talked it over with the police, afterwards. We have made some decisions. Obviously, having the service at the House of Fallen Angels is not an option but we are free to bury him within the cemetery on the grounds. We had him cremated, per his wishes but the public also wants to honor him with a memorial service. He will be given a funeral plot, first thing tomorrow afternoon. Jules said. "One of Father Matthew's closest friends will be sending him off and Friday was the day, which worked best for him."

Harlee and Dahlia, nodded their heads as they committed the details to memory. They sat in the remote silence while they ate breakfast. Afterwards, John rose and carrying an armload of dirty dishes to the sink, sat them down and stared at the floor. As they all sat, the elevator chimed, capturing everyone's attention.

"Good morning, Alma." Jules greeted as the succubus entered.

"Good morning." She greeted back as she joined them at the table and relaxed.

"How did everyone sleep?" She asked.

"Like a baby." Dahlia sighed.

"Just fine." Harlee grumbled.

"We haven't yet but thank you, for setting this up for us, Alma." Jules said.

"Despite our lack of blood relation, you're both my kids, too." She said. "Is everything arranged?" Jules relayed the information again as John moved into one of the bedrooms and closed the door.

"I wondered how hard this would be on him." Almalexia said, staring at the closed door.

"Of course he's taken it hard. Matthew and Maxwell have been the only family he has had for nine years. Not to mention, with Matthew gone, John will be the new keeper." Jules said.

"He will not be alone." Harlee spoke up. "Matthew's last request to me, was to help keep Maxwell safe, should something happen to he or John. I cannot ignore the final request of one, who has given so much." She said, in disbelief. The other three women in the room stared at her with an equal amount of astonishment, as what she felt. Almalexia smiled as she nodded her head.

"That sounds like Matthew." She said. "He always saw the good in everyone. I sometimes had to remind myself that he was not actually Maxwell's son. Let us all relax, recharge our batteries. Let us get through the memorial service and move from there." She suggested.

"A fine idea, Alma." Jules said as she rose from the table. "If you will all excuse me, however. I need to go lie down for a while."

"Of course, Jules. Thank you again, for being here." Almalexia spoke as Jules walked into another bedroom, in the massive suite. Almalexia, Harlee and Dahlia, all relaxed the majority of the day.

Harlee and Dahlia, proceeded with their typical routines, while Almalexia studied the room service menu. After their muscles burned and they had worked up a sufficient sweat, Harlee and Dahlia, showered and joined Almalexia, in the sitting room.

"We will have to rethink our strategy for the Feast." Dahlia said.

"Let us save that for after the service." Almalexia suggested.

"I have to agree." Harlee said. By midafternoon, Dahlia had left to check up on the other girls. After Jules and John awoke, they readied themselves and left the hotel. All alone, with little to be done, Almalexia turned to face Harlee.

"Are you still feeling the effects of my toxin?" She asked. Harlee considered the question for a moment.

"I am alright. I would prefer to not have that happen again, however." She replied.

"Noted. Again, I did not intend to cause you any grief."

"I know you meant well. Dahlia's happy about it. She wants to bottle your sweat for future use."

I would be more than happy to douse her and that young man again, if she'd like." Almalexia said. Harlee placed her hands out in front of her and pushed them out towards the elevator.

"I will allow you to take that up with her. I want no part of that." She said. Almalexia looked at Harlee curiously.

"Do you carry so much guilt, that you prohibit yourself from all pleasures?" Harlee shook her head "no" reflexively but after a moment's thought, could not dispute such a claim.

"I suppose, I can't forgive myself for what my sister has gone through." She reasoned. "Whenever I feel a moment of happiness, I suppose I am forced to remember that it's my fault Cilia can't experience this."

"I believe I understand then, why you can hear Maxwell's heart." Almalexia commented.

"You do?"

"You think a lot the way he does." She said. Harlee scoffed, losing interest.

"Please allow me to finish. You both deal with your problems in solitude and shoulder the entirety of your burdens. You have both lost much and will not stop until you have both gained recompense. Would you allow me to share something with you that Maxwell taught me?"

"What?" Harlee asked.

"Never lose sight of what drives you. Sometimes, the pain in our lives will become too much to bear. It is all right to find something to ease it. If you have to, numb it until you can regain your strength to face it. Whatever you do, do not forget it. In time, it will grow to become an essential part of you and take the form you give it. The same pain, which might destroy one person, defines another, giving them immeasurable strength. Do not ever forget yourself, Harlee. Once you do, you lose control over who you become."

"Words to consider, thank you." Harlee said.

"Harlee?" Almalexia spoke.

"Yes?"

"Would you like to learn more about Maxwell, as I know him?" Almalexia asked. Harlee stared over at her and nodded.

"I would."

"Then, my dear girl." Almalexia began. "You shall join me, in a small amount of indulgence." She said as she picked up the phone and dialed.

"What are you...?"

"Hello, room service, yes this is the penthouse suite. I need a bottle of your finest champagne and some desserts, decadently sinful, they make the devil blush. This is for two." Almalexia said before hanging up the phone. Harlee looked at Almalexia, who leaned back in her chair and smiled.

"Now then, while we wait for that to arrive, what would you like to ask me?" Harlee thought for a moment.

"How long have you and Maxwell known one another?" She asked.

"I would say nearly one hundred and fifty years." She answered. Harlee allowed herself a moment to process, before continuing.

"Has it really been that long? How long have you been by his side?" She asked.

"Not half as long and consistently as you may believe. I've joined Maxwell on a few of his more dangerous, fabled hunts and was even his prey at one time."

"What!?" Harlee said as the elevator dinged.

"Excellent timing." Almalexia said as the room service cart appeared. The man, dressed all in white, pushed the cart between the two women and began displaying their options.

"Torta Barozzi with raspberry drizzle and cream, gelato di riso cioccolato and tiramisu." The waiter spoke as Almalexia smiled and looked to Harlee.

"Looking to have a little fun?" She winked as the waiter began pouring the champagne. Harlee eyed her once she realized her intentions and frantically shook her head. Almalexia laughed to herself as she placed her hand on the waiter's.

"We are all set from here, thank you. Has this been billed to the room?" The man set the bottle of champagne in a bucket of ice and sat it on the table between Harlee and Almalexia as he turned his attention to her.

"Yes, ma'am," he replied as Almalexia handed the man some money, how much Harlee could not tell.

"Much obliged, ma'am, thank you." He bowed before leaving with the empty cart.

"Have at." Almalexia said as she raised her glass. "To overdue indulgence and the promise, to never lose sight of where we've come from nor forget who we've lost, yamas!" She finished.

"Toast." Harlee said as she clinked her glass to Almalexia's and took a drink. They sat together, celebrating as they both partook in the selection of desserts. Harlee's taste buds were in a cavalcade of delight as each bite complemented and exceeded the one, which preceded it.

"Thank you, for this, Almalexia." She said, unsure of what else to do or say.

"My pleasure. Times such as these, it is good to remember the world is not entirely evil. Just remember your promise to Matthew, is all I ask."

"I won't." She said as she took another sip of champagne and thought. As the question came to her mind, she turned her attention back to her hostess.

"What was Maxwell like, when you first met him?"

"Well to begin with, when we met, he had accepted a contract to kill me." She laughed as she stared at her glass, swirling its contents. Harlee remained silent as Almalexia recalled.

"He was fierce, to say the least, not so much as he is now, however. That aspect of his personality has aged as wine." She paused again. "He was kind. I believe that was what first garnished my attention. We were on the field of battle, preparing to kill one another and he acted with honor, kindness and chivalry. By your years, I was already old at the time and here before me, was the first taste of kindness I had ever received from a human. He wanted nothing from me, took no joy in what he had been sent to do."

"So, what happened next?"

"Well, we fought. That much was unavoidable. I may not look it but I am not unfamiliar with combat." Almalexia said.

"You would have to be proficient if Maxwell has allowed you on his hunts. He is hesitant to take me." She commented.

"You are rather confident in yourself, for a human." Almalexia stated.

"Since I lost Cilia, I have spent every day, honing my skills, to prepare myself to save her." Harlee looked to her feet as she began to feel her guilt sink in.

"Don't you start that, now." Almalexia chided. "The truest statement, I can make in regards to Maxwell, is that he always keeps his word. Never once, has he failed to honor something he has told me. He will help you find your sister, Harlee. He gave you his word."

"You are right, please, tell me more. Why are you so drawn to him?" She asked. Almalexia began telling Harlee about the elusive Maxwell, details both informative and intimate.

After a few hours had passed, Almalexia rose and made her way home. Dahlia returned early that night, as well, long enough to share a meal with a briefly stirring Jules and John, who both returned to bed shortly after. As Harlee and Dahlia, stretched out, they shared a brief few words.

"How are the girls?" Harlee asked.

"They're alright; I believe it is safe to say that our little group has disbanded."

"Well, we knew that was inevitable, from the start." Harlee commented.

"True. I am just glad they chose to quit and did not end up like some of the others. This shit runs much deeper than we ever imagined." Dahlia said.

"At least we made a difference, even if it was only a small one."

"Did we, though?" Dahlia asked. "Did we make a difference?" Harlee turned to her friend.

"You know for a fact we did. Not one of those girls would have been alive to retire, had we not helped. Sure, we could not save everyone but many escaped the slave pits, because of what we did?"

"Yes but how many were recaptured?"

"We protected John." Harlee pointed out.

"Maxwell protected John." Dahlia corrected. Harlee placed her hand on Dahlia's shoulder.

"Maxwell, himself, thanked us for saving John." Harlee corrected Dahlia, who paused for a moment and smiled.

"I suppose you're right. On the topic of Maxwell, what is with you all of a sudden?"

"What do you mean?" Harlee asked.

"First, you hate the guy and now you're volunteering to be his protector or something? What's up with that?" Dahlia asked curiously. Harlee rose and began moving towards her room.

"I do not have feelings for Maxwell." She stated. "Goodnight." She said as she closed the door, disrobed and went to bed. Outside, Dahlia smiled.

"I never asked if you did." She continued to smile as she readied herself for bed.

Harlee lay sprawled out on her bed, wearing nothing but her see-through negligée and lacey, black panties. She watched as her bedroom door opened slightly and a dark silhouette appeared in the doorframe. Harlee smiled as her legs slowly danced across the sheets.

"I was hoping you were coming to visit, tonight." She said as the dark figure entered the room and closed the door. The room, nearly pitch black, Harlee closed her eyes, as she felt the presence of the man at her feet, sweetly kissing their tops as he worked his way up her legs.

Her smile only grew, as she felt a pair of teeth, gripping onto the strap of her panties and began pulling them off from her body. Her legs continued to waltz on the bed, elegantly sliding herself out of her undergarments as a pair of rough, strong hands, gripped at her hips.

The anticipation nearly too much to bear, Harlee closed her eyes as a strip of cloth was placed over her eyes and secured. Her heart raced uncontrollably, from the excitement, her entire body trembled as she felt her top removed. As her bare breasts, were exposed to the slightly warm, night breeze, she felt as the hand rubbed across her erect nipples, gently massaging them as she quivered.

Next, she felt as both her wrists and ankles were tied to the frame of the bed, each new sensation traced by the hot, moist breath of her defiler. Firmly tied in place, Harlee pulled against her restraints as she felt a soft, strong pair of lips, pressing against her own.

She embraced the lips, biting and suckling on them, as her tongue was massaged by another. The lips traveled away from her own, tongue and lips of her lover, tracing down to her chin and running around the underside of her jaw line. She shivered with delight as she felt warm breath in her ear, as her earlobe was lightly nibbled on and her left breast was tightly squeezed.

The electricity in her body surged, following the hot, wet kisses down to her chest. She arched her back as she felt aggressive suckling on her right nipple and a tickling tongue, swirling circles around her areola, as the left side was repeatedly squeezed, fondled and massaged.

"I want you to violate me." She moaned out into the darkness, as the lips continued their conquistador styled dominance over her body. She whimpered, feeling the lips grace her stomach and moving to her inner hips, where they suckled indecently, leaving behind a large love bite.

Her legs fought against her restraints and her hands reached out, trying to claim that which was beyond her grasp as she felt wet, hot breath, gently blowing inside her poised vagina. She groaned out with ecstasy as she felt the man's beard, tickling her inner thighs as a long, papilla studded tongue, ran itself across the entirety of her clitoris.

The headboard of the bed groaned as Harlee pulled with all of her might against it, fighting to grip the head responsible for her euphoric pleasure. She felt an intense pressure upon the head of her clitoris as the man sucked on it, while placing two fingers inside of her at the height of her climatic climb.

Harlee opened her mouth wide, balancing on her forehead as if being exorcised of some demon, as she forgot how to breathe. She felt as a massive tsunamic force, swelled within her stomach and pelvis. Despite her best efforts to dam the raging current, she felt as the floodgates released and she came with such intensity, all feeling left her limbs.

She rolled her eyes down to her throbbing pelvis and saw as the dark figure, wiped his face and began slowly retracing his steps, all of the way back to her throat as he pressed his hard penis into her, stabbing all the way into her stomach. As Harlee cried out with ecstasy, she felt as another burst of ballast water, escaped her body, as the man thrusted in sync with her, his pelvis grinding perfectly against her inflamed genitals.

Harlee moaned out, with every orgasm the man wrenched from her, no longer in control of when or how she came. Too limp to thrust back, she felt as the pressure subsided and the man exited her and changed positions. She giggled in excitement as she felt a thin strip of cloth, fall across her open mouth and secure behind her head as, one of her feet was untied and she was rolled onto her stomach.

She bit down onto the cloth, lying flat on her stomach as her ankle was secured once more. She felt as the man kissed up the back of her calves, up to her thighs and groaned as she felt a thumb insert into her from behind as her left glute was firmly bitten.

She orgasmed again, from sheer built up tension as she was kissed on her hips and up the center of her back. She felt the lips, travel up her spine as strong hands gripped the inside of her hipbones, fingers firmly locking in place, activating her pelvic muscles. As she felt the phallus sliding into her once more, without the slightest effort, she used all her remaining strength, to clench onto it.

Again, her lungs were reeved of oxygen, as her mind was forced into a blank state, too overloaded by the deadly intoxication of lust, she now felt. She screamed against the gag, feeling her consciousness fading. As she felt the largest of her orgasms, swelling inside her, she clenched onto the man behind her, even harder, as he groaned from the strength of her grip.

Harlee felt her swirling typhoon, unleash with godly wrath as she was filled from within, with the warmth of her partner. As the man's sweat covered body, fell atop of hers, Harlee panted heavily, afraid she may be experiencing an asthma attack.

"There...are...no words." She managed out as she rolled her eyes over to the side and saw Maxwell, smiling at her.

"AH!" Harlee yelled as she jolted upright in her bed, heart racing fast, bed clearly soaked from the intensity of her nocturnal emissions.

"Holy shit!" Harlee said as she rose from her bed and stared at herself in the bathroom mirror. She looked at herself in disgust, at what had just transpired. "There is no fucking way, I want Maxwell." She confirmed to herself, as she feared returning to her bed.

Chapter 13 - Usque Ad Finem, Caecus Amor Prolis

No one spoke much that following morning. They each rose, long before the sun and readied themselves in silence. After they piled into the car, Dahlia turned the key and drove, heading towards the funeral home, which under the circumstances, was chosen to perform the service, on the cemetery grounds. They were not the first ones to arrive but as they pulled in, they quickly saw the place reserved for them. As they climbed out of the car, a man, slightly younger than Matthew, approached.

"God be with you, this morning. My name is Father Raziel, you may call me Father Raz. I was a friend of Father Matthew's and will be helping him along his final transition, today." The handsome, middle-aged man spoke with a bold smile.

"Thank you, Father Raz." Jules said, shaking the man's hand. "This is my adoptive brother, John and our dear friends, Harlee, Dahlia and Alma."

"I have heard much of you all. It is a pleasure to finally make your acquaintance." He said as he led them inside.

As they entered the large funeral home, Father Raz, took each of their coats. They all wore black, Harlee and Dahlia, were both certain to wear the finest of the dresses Father Matthew had given them. Father Raz guided them to a small seating area, where sat a few of Father Matthew's closest friends, two of which, arrived in their blues. As they sat, Father Raz stood in front of them, to relay the intentions of the day.

"Soon, a caravan of limousines, will line up outside. They will be transporting us to the burial site. I will need for John and Jules, Matthew's adoptive children, to travel in the lead car along with their friends, Harlee, Dahlia and Alma.

The limousines will take us as close to the memorial as possible. They will take us passed the news crews and the spectators, while our honorable civil servants, shall provide us with as much peace as they can. Let us not forget, Father Matthew once served as an officer of the law, as well. While we are here, to honor our beloved Father Matthew, please also keep all of them and their families, in your prayers. To these men and women, who continue to lay down their lives, in our defense, we are forever grateful."

Everyone took a moment, to bow their heads in respect to the men and women on the blue line and the other emergency service providers, offering their silent prayer. Their silence was disturbed, as a man in a driver's uniform, walked in and whispered into Father Raz's ear. The priest nodded his head with a kind smile, placed his hand on the man's shoulder and thanked him.

"That was our cue, everyone." Father Raz began. "If you would all be so kind as to follow me, we will keep moving ahead of schedule." He said as he strode outside. "Don't forget your umbrellas. I suspect even the Lord cries, this day."

As predicted, shortly after the driver closed the door behind Harlee, the rain came into sight, panning across her field of vision as if a flowing wall of descending water. Their driver nodded his head respectfully to them before climbing into the car and bringing it to life. Harlee and Dahlia sat facing across to where the others sat. Almalexia stared forward, chin up, head high as she rested one hand on John's knee and the other, held Jules' right hand.

John sat, staring at his feet and Jules, out the window as their car led the way. Harlee watched out the window, noticing the buildings, with their boarded windows and newly replaced doors. Looking upon the wreckage from Hell Night, she could not help but wonder which posed the greater threat to the human realm, the supernatural world or the humans themselves.

It did not take long for the scenery to change and she saw as the limo pulled into the cemetery gates, rows of camera crews, news vans and police vehicles. While the media teams did their job, standing just outside the line of officers, who stood at attention, saluting the limos.

Everyone's attention turned to the windows, to witness the show of support, while they traveled through the cemetery gates. It was not long after, the car came to a full stop and the driver turned off the ignition. First opening an umbrella, he walked to the side door, opened it and looked at Harlee.

"Ma'am." He spoke as he extended his empty hand to Harlee.

"Thank you." She said, accepting his hand and gracefully stepped out of the car, under the cover of the umbrella. One by one, the driver opened an umbrella to hand to each of them as he followed suit and guided them to a canopied area, where Father Raz already stood waiting. Harlee, Dahlia and Almalexia were guided to their seats, as John and Jules were escorted to the Hurst, where officers in uniform stood at attention. Once all of the limos had been cleared and their passengers, assembled on site, Father Raz began his speech.

"We have all gathered here today, to say farewell to a great man and a dear friend, to all. Father Cornelius Matthew, devoted his entire life, to the people, serving as not only a priest but at one point, an officer of the law.

No matter where, Father Matthew went, his heart remained with the flock, as it does now. Even now, I am certain, he watches down on us all, smiling. If I may be so bold, I dare to guess, while he is happy to see us all gathered, and honored at how beloved he is, he would be remiss to see so many sad faces.

In fact, speaking with many of his longtime parishioners, those he aided in his various community events and those whom he called family, I have gathered Matthew was always one to brighten the mood. I knew him well, and I can confirm this, as well. He always sought to see people at their best, often times proving guilty of meddlesome behavior, simply to see another smile. I would argue this to be among his finer qualities."

Harlee turned, along with everyone else seated, to watch as the pallbearers marched with Father Matthew's casket. Everyone rose to their feet as they neared, Jules' holding the umbrella for her and John, who was holding one of the handles on the coffin. Harlee felt the tears rolling down her cheeks, as she noticed something else that struck her as odd.

One hundred yards away, atop the roof of the cathedral, perched beneath the crucifix, she could make out a figure, which did not belong. Realizing what and who it was, she gently nudged Dahlia and Almalexia.

"On the roof, beneath the cross." She whispered.

"I see him." Almalexia whispered as Dahlia squinted her eyes. "He told Matthew, until the end. They swore it to one another. Maxwell never forgets a promise." Touching as the moment was, the moment Father Raz continued his speech, no one maintained their composure.

"We are joined here today, by two of Matthew's adoptive children, John and Jules. I would ask we keep them in our prayers, during this troubling time. Would either John or Jules, like to say something?" Father Raziel asked, staring at them. Jules looked to John, who stared down at his feet. Rising to hers, Jules approached the podium, tears in her eyes as she stared at the humble crowd.

"Hello, everyone. On behalf of John and myself, I wish to thank all of you, for being here today, on behalf of our father. While Father Matthew, may not have been our birth father, I believe he was our God given one. For both John and myself, Father Matthew came to us, during a time which, neither of us, had a future.

To us, Father Matthew was more than a father. He was our friend and our mentor. He gave both of us a future, taught us who we were and who we wanted to become. He nourished our desires, gave us dreams and helped us to achieve them. John and myself, will live the rest of our lives, honoring our father, by becoming as he intended. Thank you again." Jules finished as she walked from the stage. Father Raziel hugged Jules as she returned to her seat.

"Would anyone else care to share a few words?" He asked, opening the mic to several more individuals, who after sharing a few words, returned to their seats. After everyone had said his or her peace, Father Raziel, once again assumed his position at the podium.

I wish to recite a passage, from Corinthians, chapter ten, verse thirteen.

No temptation has overtaken you except what is common to mankind. And God is faithful; he will not let you be tempted beyond what you can bear. But when you are tempted, he will also provide a way out so that you can endure it.

This was among Father Matthew's favorite passages." Father Raziel spoke, as his eyes glanced up towards the one perched atop the cathedral. "With the coming of this year's Feast, I advise everyone to consider these words. May God be with you all." Father Raziel concluded as he among others, began tossing handfuls of dirt onto Father Matthew's coffin, before departing. After everyone began to walk away from the memorial, Father Raziel remained, as well as the last limo driver, who waited patiently in the car.

"Thank you for your words, Father." Jules said.

"It was my pleasure." Father Raz replied as the last of the news vans pulled away. Harlee turned her gaze back to the figure beneath the cross. She watched as it rose to its full height, before dropping off the edge of the roof. Landing on both feet, Harlee watched as Maxwell walked towards them.

Everyone turned their heads, as they noticed Maxwell nearing them and stepped aside, as he entered the canopied section. Maxwell walked to the edge of Matthew's grave and stared down at it. Harlee could not tell what he was thinking and simply watched from behind as Maxwell, holding Matthew's rosary in his left hand, reached out to the dirt pile with his right and held a fistful in his palm.

"I know you asked me to avoid killing humans, if possible, and I am sorry for going against that wish. The ones who put you here, I assure you, had long since forfeited that which made them human. I hope you forgive me." He spoke in his unearthly low growl, which gave near everyone present the chills. Not even Almalexia approached him as he said his farewells.

"Goodbye, my son. I am sorry. Usque ad finem, caecus amor prolis. " He whispered.

"Until the very end, the love of children is blind." Almalexia translated as Maxwell tossed his fistful of dirt on the pile and turned to Father Raz.

"I should have expected to see you here, Raziel." Maxwell began. "Did he?" Father Raz raised his hands.

"I saw to the details myself. Father Matthew is in heaven, with his father."

"Good." Maxwell turned, walking back out into the rain.

"What will you do now, Maxwell?" Father Raz asked.

"Continue the mission. I have a lead, a target and a hell of a lot of wrath to exercise." Maxwell said as he walked away. Harlee was not sure what possessed her but her body, as if of its own mind, pressed after him. As she chased him down, her heels began to sink into the ground and her umbrella was blown from her hands. As she felt the chill of the rain upon her skin, she called out to the man.

"Maxwell!" She yelled without knowing why. Maxwell slowed and turned his head as she moved in close to him. She stood toe to toe with him and looked straight up into his eyes.

"I am sorry about Matthew." She said as she threw her arms around him. She pressed her head to his chest, though Maxwell did not return the embrace.

"It wasn't your fault, Harlee. It was mine." He spoke as she shook her head.

"If I hadn't broken my promise, Dahlia, John and I would have been there with him."

"No. I drove you out and asked Matthew to send them after you. I know why you went down there, I overreacted. I am sorry." Maxwell said as he wrapped his coat around Harlee and walked away in the pouring rain.

"I promised Matthew, I would." She yelled against the torrential rain. "I told him I would become the next keeper! It was his dying wish!" She continued to yell out, unsure why. Maxwell stopped and stood with his back to her.

"Meet me in the catacombs, tonight. All of you." He called back as he walked away. Harlee stood still as John handed her an umbrella.

"Come on, everyone is waiting." He spoke. Harlee turned and walked with him back to the car. As they neared, the driver stood and waited, opening the door for them as they arrived.

"What did he say?" Jules asked as Harlee took her seat. Harlee turned her head and saw that everyone was waiting for her answer.

"He wants all of us to meet him, in the catacombs beneath the church, tonight."

Chapter 14 – Sword of Damocles

They waited back at the hotel, for nightfall to arrive. Once it had, they quickly moved out and parked a few blocks from the manhole. Lowering themselves into the sewers below, they walked towards Maxwell's sanctuary. As they came to the gate, Harlee reached out and pushed against it to find it already unlocked.

A little ways down, Harlee saw Maxwell, kneeling before the photos of his children. Harlee could already feel her heartbeat shifting, from being near Maxwell's and clenched her bosom gently. They all stood in silence, waiting for Maxwell to finish his prayer. Harlee immediately noticed Matthew's rosary, resting beside an old picture of a baby boy.

"Thank you, for your patience." Maxwell said as he rose from his knees. "I have asked you all here, so we might rework our strategy for the Feast, which begins two days from tonight. Without Father Matthew, we are now short a set of eyes on the inside. I propose that we..."

"I can do it." Jules spoke up. Everyone turned to stare at her as she continued. "I can fill in for Matthew." She clarified.

"No." Maxwell growled.

"Maxwell, I can do it!" Jules argued.

"Absolutely not."

"I am combat proficient. I am an excellent marksman. There was a time I was better than Kiefer."

"I said no!" Maxwell spoke with more aggression. "Think about your mother. What would happen to her, if she lost you too?" Maxwell asked as Jules turned her head, wiping away a single tear before crossing her arms.

"Then let Harlee do it." Almalexia suggested, causing an upset in the room.

"What?" Harlee asked, the most surprised of the group.

"Almalexia, we've covered this." Maxwell began.

"Don't interrupt me and I will explain." She demanded. "You and I, have the most experience of anyone here. After which, is clearly Harlee. She is trained, quick on her feet and has been hiding in plain sight for years. She may not be the ideal choice for this mission but she can do it. Jules is an excellent shot. She can easily fulfill Harlee's role." The room grew silent again as Maxwell contemplated Alma's suggestion, tapping his boot irritably as he considered it. Maxwell pointed at a spot on the blueprints.

"Jules, I want you to take point here. This vantage should offer the widest view range. I will need you to wait patiently, for everyone to come back out. You and I are merely back up, in case something goes wrong. We do not engage otherwise, understood?" He asked.

"Yes." Jules answered.

"Alright, then." Maxwell said leaning over the blueprints and relaying information, while Almalexia, Harlee and Dahlia, contributed their own. A few hours went by, as they ran through all of the ins and outs of their plan. Finally, they had ironed out all of the details.

"I don't believe there is much more to discuss at the moment." Maxwell said. "You should all head back and ready yourselves for tomorrow night's preparations."

"You could come with us." Jules suggested. Maxwell shook his head.

"Perhaps, once this is all settled. Harlee, I need you to stay behind. I need to speak with you." All eyes moved from Maxwell to Harlee and back. "I will drop her off, once we are done. I just need to speak with her." He assured them.

"It's all right, everyone. I will see you all, shortly." She told them.

"Alright then. We will see you back at the room." Dahlia said as she and the others walked away. Harlee turned around, watching as Maxwell slid down the wall, resting his head against it, as he stretched out his legs. He took in a deep breath and sighed as Harlee stood, waiting.

"Can you hear it, now?" Maxwell asked. Harlee turned her head to the cask and nodded as she listened to its strong, steady beat.

"I can, can't you?" She asked. Maxwell smiled before answering.

"I stopped listening to it so long ago, it no longer speaks to me." He laughed. Harlee approached the cask and looked from it to Maxwell.

"May I?" She asked.

"Just don't take it out. Being near it hurts. The cask helps."

"Alright, I won't take it out." She said as she slowly reached for the container. She tapped it gently, still wary from her first exposure. Harlee took a deep breath and slowly lifted the cask. Carefully, she moved towards the adjacent wall from Maxwell and sat. Resting the box carefully on her lap, she unclipped the locks and opened it.

Harlee looked down at Maxwell's beating heart with an odd sense of excitement. She remembered the last time she gazed upon it and grew curious. Her fingers twitched anxiously, as she turned her head to Maxwell, whose eyes were closed.

"Are you alright?" She asked.

"You're fine." He assured her. Harlee was unhappy with the answer, as she kept looking from the heart to Maxwell.

"Will it hurt you if I touch it?" She asked.

"Not if you're gentle." He whispered.

"May I?" She asked, her hand trembling from anticipation.

"You may." He replied. Harlee swallowed hard as she slowly lowered her hand into the cask and with one finger, gently caressed its surface.

"Ahh!" Harlee squealed, pulling her hand away as Maxwell suddenly twitched violently. "Are you alright?" She asked nervously.

"You're still fine." He assured her.

"I did not ask if I was fine!" She yelled at him. "I asked if YOU were!"

"Nothing you have done has hurt me. You may proceed. The sensation merely took me by surprise."

"You felt me, touching your heart?" She asked.

"Yes."

"How did it make you feel?" She asked, hand already poised to touch it again.

"Violated." He replied as Harlee glared at him. "Go ahead. It'll be alright." He told her. Easing back into her spot, Harlee slowly reached out and gently traced her finger across the heart. Maxwell stirred but was otherwise relaxed as Harlee continued to look upon the many wounds it had suffered over the years.

"What does it look like?" Maxwell asked. Harlee looked up at him in surprise.

"You've never looked at your own heart before?" She asked.

"Have you ever looked at yours?" He asked her.

"That's a little bit different. Yours is right here, in my lap."

"Do you want the truth?" He asked her.

"More than you know." She answered.

"The truth is, it terrifies me." He said. Harlee was unsure how she should react and instead grew more curious.

"Why?" She asked.

"Have you ever heard of the tale of Damocles?" He asked her.

"The Greek king, who sought out the power of Dionysus?" She asked.

"The one and the same." Maxwell responded, a mournful tone to his voice. Harlee snickered at his answer.

"I am sorry," said Harlee, shaking her head and waving her hands in front of her face. "I do not understand. What does an old legend have to do with your heart?"

"My heart is my sword. Or perhaps it is my strand of horsehair. Either way, all of my fears, reside within it."

"Maxwell?" Harlee's voice reflected a glimmer of pain. "Do you wish me to leave your heart alone?"

"Squeeze it gently." He spoke calmly. "But do not take it out of the chest." Harlee's face filled with concern.

"Are you sure?" She asked.

"Just do it. This is important." He said as he rose to his feet and moved away from her slightly. Harlee continued to stare at Maxwell's back, fearfully as she placed her entire palm over the warm heart and gently applied pressure. She saw Maxwell twitch.

"Harder." He said and so Harlee squeezed harder.

"HARDER!" He yelled and Harlee squeezed as tightly as she could.

"ARGH!" Maxwell groaned, as he collapsed to the ground, hand clenching where his heart should be.

"MAXWELL!" Harlee panicked as she closed the cask and set it aside. Rising to her feet, she ran over to him, wrapping her arms around him.

"Oh my god! Are you alright!?" She asked desperately, trying to help him up. Maxwell laughed halfheartedly, as she leaned him back against the wall.

"You should see your face." He laughed. Beads of sweat poured down the side of his face. His hand still firmly clenched his chest.

"You ASSHAT!" She yelled, punching him in the shoulder.

"Hey, I'm wounded, remember?" He slowly stopped laughing. Harlee settled down beside him, resting her head on his shoulder. "I can be killed, Harlee. By numerous methods, I can die. What you just witnessed is the simplest."

"Do you still wish to know what it looks like?" She asked him. Maxwell nodded his head. Harlee slowly rose and took up her seat by the cask. Gently placing it on her lap once more, she opened the box and peered inside.

"Its general shape and structure, is much the same of every human heart. It has all the same features to it, yet yours is covered in scars." She said as she ran her finger along several of them, noticing one such mark had not yet scarred over.

"There is a fresh scar here that hasn't scabbed over yet. Was it from me squeezing your heart?"

"No, it's not from you. It's from Matthew." He spoke. Harlee turned her eyes back to the heart.

"Does that mean the large ones are from you son and Victoria?"

"Yes." He answered. Harlee looked and examined how massive the scar was, in comparison to the others.

"I can tell you loved them greatly. Their loss nearly tore your heart in half." She told him.

"I did. I may be a dispassionate man, but to those I love, they know naught but undying adoration." He answered.

"Thank you for telling me."

"You are welcome." He whispered as Harlee turned her eyes toward his heart. She bore a smile on her face, as they sat in relative silence, Harlee tracing her finger gently across Maxwell's heart.

"Does my heart interest you?" He asked.

"It does." She replied.

"Despite its flaws?" He asked.

"Yes."

"Are you certain it is a heart, you could protect?"

"It is a heart, which I wish to protect, Maxwell. Whether I can or cannot, I desire to defend it." She said. Maxwell smirked slightly as he sighed.

"There is one more thing I must tell you, before you make your decision." He said.

"What is that?" She asked him.

"Every blood moon, I will change. Into what, you already know." Harlee remembered all too well, the horrors she had seen that night and wished to forget them. "You need to know, I cannot help but turn. If my body is too badly damaged, I will turn. I have taken in too much darkness, too much sin and cannot control it. I will need to be chained, in a prison before every Hunter's moon and you must be willing to slay me, if I ever get loose."

"Don't you think that's a little extreme?" She asked.

"No exceptions." He told her. "The only way you can save me, Harlee, is if you are willing to kill me. Do not give your answer now. Think it over. If you cannot fulfill this one wish, then I will not blame you. The last thing I wanted to do was kill my master. However, I will not ask you to take my place. Should you need kill me, I would gladly die the last of my kind." He slowly rose to his feet. Harlee looked up at him, eyes searching for some sign he was joking. He smiled weakly to her and she knew at once, he lamented the request.

"It is time. Are you ready to head back?" He asked. Harlee did not answer for a moment and shook herself free from her thoughts, as she closed the cask and accepted his outstretched hand. She tucked the box under her arm as Maxwell helped her up and leaving it on the altar, turned to walk with him.

"You go ahead and put my coat back on. It will be chilly on the way." He said as they walked down the tunnels and after a couple of turns, came upon a ladder they had never used before. Maxwell began climbing, as Harlee carefully followed, still wearing her heels.

Up on the street level, Maxwell held out his hand, helping Harlee climb out of the manhole. She thanked him, smoothing out her dress as he resealed the hole. He waited for her, holding out his arm to her as she finished.

"Thank you," she said as she accepted his arm and walked with him, to the sidewalk. They walked in silence, down the familiar walkway, as they neared Maxwell's storage container. Unlocking it, Maxwell opened the latch, revealing his motorcycle, the car still in Dahlia's possession.

"There is a compartment beneath the seat, where you can store your shoes." He said as he began walking the bike out of the container. Harlee took off her shoes and placed them into the aforementioned compartment, as he closed the container. Maxwell began to swing his leg over and stopped mid lift, as he eyed Harlee.

"Would you rather, or may I?" He asked. Harlee walked behind him and hiking her dress slightly, swung her leg over, just behind him.

"You're fine. I'll take the next round." She said as Maxwell sat down and she pressed her body up against his, hands wrapped firmly around his waist. Maxwell kicked the stand back and started the motorcycle. He handed his helmet back to her.

"Thanks," said Harlee as she secured it. She held on tightly as Maxwell started down the road, heading towards the hotel. As he drove, through the eerily vacant streets, Harlee relayed where they were staying. It did not take them long, with the lack of traffic, to arrive at the hotel. As Maxwell brought the bike to a stop, he flicked the kickstand down and helped Harlee down.

"Where are you staying tonight, Maxwell?" Harlee asked as she handed over the helmet, pulled her hair out of her mouth and tucked it back. Gently, Maxwell reached forward and brushed her cheek softly, as he tucked back a loose few strands behind her ear.

"I'll head back to the catacombs." He told her. Harlee reached forward and grabbed his hand in hers.

"Don't be alone, tonight. Stay with us. Jules, John, they need you right now. Just stay the night." She tried to convince him. "It would mean the world to them, to have you close and know you are alright." She urged. Maxwell thought about her offer, for a moment, as he turned his head towards the sky.

"I'm not so sure." He told her. "I don't know as though I am ready." He told her, handing Harlee's shoes to her.

"If you're uncomfortable, then leave. At least come up and have a drink with me, please?" She asked. "I must admit that I also wish for you to stay. No one should be alone, after what has happened." Maxwell sighed, setting his helmet down and adjusting his hat.

"Does that mean yes?" She whispered to him, tilting her head slightly to the side.

"Yes." He whispered back to her. Harlee smiled as she walked side by side with the devilishly handsome, dark haired man.

"Ah, Miss Harlee." The clerk said as she entered. "Good to see you again. You just missed Miss Almalexia." The man said, wide smile on his face.

"Goodnight." She said. As she and Maxwell walked to the elevator, the clerk watching Maxwell as they called the elevator.

"Friend of yours?" Maxwell whispered to her, playing with the chain on his pocket watch.

"Long story, to say the least." She shook her head as she said it. As the elevator dinged, the doors opened and they entered.

"I see. So you had a run in with Almalexia's toxin." He suggested, causing Harlee to drop her keycard as she tried to insert it.

"How did you know?" She asked, picking up the card and sliding it into the slot.

"Lucky guess, though you just told me. You and Lexi suddenly coexisting, tipped me off." He smirked.

"Nothing happened!" She exclaimed as the doors closed.

"That's none of my business." He said.

"Alright, but nothing happened, alright?" She said.

"Why do you suppose that man's name tag was upside down?" He asked, changing the subject. Harlee smiled as she realized what had happened.

"Almalexia's scent is still hanging in the air. Try and keep your hands to yourself, alright?" He teased, as Harlee elbowed him in the ribs. She scowled at him, for a brief moment, before her expression softened and she turned her head up to him.

"You do believe me, right?" She asked.

"Yes." He said as the doors opened to the penthouse suite. Harlee lead the way inside, Maxwell following close behind as the doors closed. As they walked into the room, Harlee began looking around the room, for any sign of the others. Finding nothing, she turned back around and walked to him.

"Either they've fallen asleep or they aren't here." She said. She opened the door to her bedroom. "Dahlia's not here, either." Maxwell turned his head to the empty closet.

"Their coats are not here." He said. "It appears you are alone. I will let you..." He turned away but Harlee jumped forward and grabbed his hand.

"Please stay. To be honest, I am not sure I want to be alone, tonight. I didn't think I would be so affected by the funeral but to be honest, with that and your story, I'm a mess. Please stay, have a drink with me?" She asked. Maxwell closed his eyes taking his hat off and sitting it on the desk. Brushing his hair out of his face, he turned to her.

"How about you take a hot shower, relax. I'll pour." He suggested. Harlee, who had been in her dress the entire day, through rainstorms, humidity and the sewers, realized just how great that sounded.

"Alright. Feel free to have a look about the suite. Through my room, there is a balcony with the absolute best view of the city." She said, pointing toward her bedroom.

"Then perhaps, I will wait for you there." He said as he moved into the kitchen, his boots tapping on the tile as he transitioned off from the carpet. Harlee watched as Maxwell grabbed two glasses from the cabinet and opened the doors on the bar.

Smiling, Harlee moved into her room, disrobed, draping her clothes across her bed as she grabbed her bathrobe and walked into the bathroom. Pushing the door behind her, she left it partially open. Turning on the hot water, she stared at herself in the mirror.

"What are you doing, Harlee?" She whispered to herself, as she tried to catch a sense of her conflicted thoughts and feelings. "Why did you invite him back, here?" She thought to herself for a moment and remembered the pain she saw in his eyes, as he told her his stories.

"That's why," She said aloud. "He's your friend and he's in pain. Just as you were." She nodded her head and dropping her robe to the floor, walked to the shower, pulled back the curtain and tested the water before stepping in.

Maxwell, eyed his many choices as he heard the bedroom door tap the doorframe but not shut. He turned his head, reactively, at the sound and saw the silhouette of the magnificent, blonde beauty, undressing. He hesitated to turn away but did so, out of respect. He reached out and picked up the bottle of "Wild Turkey," which he was accustomed with.

Setting the bottle beside the glasses, he looked back to the bedroom and saw a light from the bathroom but no Harlee. He walked toward the bedroom and gently wrapped on the door. After no answer came, he placed his hand on the handle.

May I come in?" He asked but again, there was no answer. He waited briefly and slowly pressed the door open. As he entered, he saw the bathroom door open and could hear the water running. Seeing Harlee's dress, shoes and lingerie, displayed upon the bed, lit Maxwell's predacious senses on fire, as he reached to knock on the door.

His fingers outstretched, he touched the door, causing it to sway open, slightly. Forcing his head away from the sight within, Maxwell clenched his fist, turned his body and walked back to the kitchen, placing his hands on the counter. He looked back to the bedroom door, which was now opened wide, Harlee's undergarments, clearly displayed, tempting him. Maxwell shook his head, as he looked at the bottle and glasses in front of him and left the room.

Eyes closed, Harlee reached out and grasping the dial on the shower wall, turned it until the water stopped. She took a deep breath and sighed, steam still rising as she continued to lean forward. Staring down at the water dripping off from her naked form, she smiled.

"It is purifying." She whispered to herself, feeling refreshed, both of body and spirit, though her mind was still plagued by thoughts ripe with remorse, uncertainty, curiosity, and conflicted desire.

"Maxwell?" Harlee poked her head out of the shower. "Maxwell, are you there?" She asked again, reaching blindly for a towel, while exiting the shower. She dried herself, before concealing her naked flesh within the robe and walked out into the bedroom. She turned her head and saw the bedroom door was opened wide. Looking about the room, she saw only her clothes.

"Maxwell?" She called out again as she walked out, poking her head out into the kitchen. "Maxwell, are you here?" She asked one last time before realizing he was not.

Confused, Harlee walked back into her bedroom and opening the door to her balcony, sat in one of the lounge chairs, putting her feet up on the chair beside her. She stared out, watching over the city, the wind gently kissing at her cheeks as she relaxed.

"I wasn't sure what you like?" Maxwell spoke, startling Harlee, as he sat the bottle, two glasses and a bucket of ice on the table. "I'm sorry." He spoke as he realized he had frightened her. Harlee, hand on her chest, smiled, shaking her head.

"It's alright. You just took me by surprise. I thought you had left."

"Had to get ice." He spoke. Harlee turned her head to the side and saw the bottle on the table.

"You really did come out of a western movie, didn't you?" She teased. Maxwell smiled.

"Would you prefer something else?" He asked pointing towards the kitchen. "I will grab you..."

"No, it's fine. Thank you." She said. Maxwell, nodding his head, placed two ice cubes in both of the glasses and opening the bottle of bourbon, poured into both, handing one to Harlee.

"Thank you." She said, gently taking a sip from the glass and felt as it tingled down her throat. She moved her feet out of Maxwell's way, allowing him to sit beside her.

"You're alright." He said as he leaned back in the chair, feet on the floor. Harlee placed her bare feet back across Maxwell's knees as they both admired the view.

"Did anyone ever tell you how Matthew and I met?" He asked, breaking the silence.

"No. I do wish to know, however." She answered. Maxwell took a sip before he began to tell his story.

"I was hired for a particularly nasty job and Almalexia couldn't help me. I usually traveled with a partner back then, if I had to travel far, so I traveled with another hunter, James. Another thing setting this job apart from the others is back then, it was not typical for different species of monster to work in tandem. The feeding gets too competitive you see.

The trouble here was, there is a chance any human being changed, can develop a rare alpha or omega trait. All this means, is that while most people who are sired, grow dependent upon their master, those with this trait do not.

James and I were asked to travel to this village, out in the middle of nowhere, up in some mountains. It seemed the locals had been running into some trouble with creatures feeding on their livestock. A few sheep, several cattle and some other animals, had been found, either drained of blood or shredded. A few of the townsfolk themselves, had been claimed but there were no witnesses to reveal what we might be hunting.

I suspected a Boggart or a sickly spriggan, perhaps, based upon the area. There was also a chance of cultist work, but with no other signs to go on, we dismissed the theory. What we found, however, was something entirely different.

Both being unfamiliar with the area, we hired a guide, who could help us track the creatures through the mountains. Unable to follow the typical signs of our prey; tracks, claw marks, blood, etcetera; we opted to begin a search of the local caves, in hopes of finding something. We searched for three days, up in the mountains, which were shrouded in clouds the entire time.

Finally, as evening approached on the third day, we found a cave, which looked promising. The entrance was rather cramped and so I opted to head in alone, with nothing but a torch and a hunting knife. Walking inside, I left the tracker and James outside, so I could investigate.

As I ventured into the cave, torch held out in front of me, I heard a number of large rocks collapsing over the cave mouth. I turned to see I was trapped inside and could not move the rocks from my position. Turns out my guide, was none other than a dastardly clever shapeshifter and what I was hunting, was no Boggart." Harlee sat on edge, hanging on Maxwell's every word.

"What was in the cave, Maxwell? What happened?" She asked anxiously.

"You know, it's no big deal. How about I just skip to the part where Matthew comes in?"

"No! Tell me what happened next!" She demanded.

"Oh, well, after I came upon him, I raised him as my own. What else is there to tell?" He said sarcastically.

"Maxwell!" Harlee yelled at him, a wide smile on her face from his teasing. "What was inside the cave?"

"Oh, that. You should have told me that's what you meant." His eyes were still closed but he grinned. "The cave wasn't all that deep and what I found inside, I had not prepared for. You see in regards to the alpha and omega traits, I explained earlier. Your alphas are the type to challenge the hierarchy of their group, in order to become the leader. Your omegas, on the other hand, are typically loners.

Now, inside the cave, lived an omega werewolf, which for some reason or another, had stricken an accord with this shapeshifter. There I was, lightly equipped, little to no room to maneuver and staring at the massive jaws of what must have been a wolf, older than myself.

I drew it out towards me, slowly making my way back towards the enclosed opening. The wolf followed me, its hulking shoulders barely managed to pass through the narrow tunnel without squeezing between the earthen walls. As he became more enclosed, I began thrusting at him with my torch. He fought back the best he could, though he could only bat at me, as I burned him repeatedly.

Eventually, the omega grew tired of my games and charged the gap. I had nowhere to go either. I tried to jump away as the wolf grabbed my right hip, and attempted to eat me. Pinned between the boulder and the wolf's jaws, I burrowed my torch into his eye socket. As the flame of my torch began to sizzle out, I started stabbing him in the head, repeatedly with my hunting knife. Finally, the wolf dropped and fell on top of me." Maxwell paused for a moment as Harlee asked.

"How did you get out with your injuries?"

"Well, I couldn't move, lost my torch and had this beast on top of me. I did the only thing I could, I fed. I fed on that tick bitten bastard until I was strong enough to escape. As his blood coursed through my system and his power became mine, I threw his corpse away. Next, with a great deal of effort, I managed to push the rocks from my path.

Outside, night was nearing its end but I could see clearly, I had been lured into a clever trap, on the night of a full moon. That shifter had arranged everything to perfection. He kept us lost in the mountains at the proper time of year and the proper altitude, to conceal the moon's phases. Then, on the night of the full moon, sprang his trap."

"It sounds as if he were a genius."

"No. If he were that, he would have ran far away, where even the grave worms couldn't find him. When I exited that cave and saw James' throat slashed, I got a good smell of the bastard. I quickly, cremated James and used the elder wolf's power, to track the shifter through the mountains and back to the village.

I'm not sure what he told the villagers but as I neared the town, I was met with an angry mob. They believed I was a demon, responsible for their troubles. I'll admit, they had me pegged as a creature of the dark but I had nothing to do with the village before arriving to help them. Needless to say, I was not in the mood to be prodded with pitchforks or burned."

"Did you kill them?"

"No...I wanted to. Instead, I proved to them what they already knew. Spread a little fear and some people have a tendency to back down. Luckily, I didn't have to go too far into the village, in order to find my treacherous friend."

"How did you prove your innocence?" Harlee asked.

"Well, after leaving the cave, I grabbed my pack, filled with the supplies I had brought for the hunt. As I said, I planned to catch Boggarts. Among the things we had brought, a chain linked net, made from silver was with us. As you might know, shapeshifters have a terrible aversion to silver, as do many creatures.

Once I tracked him down, it was a simple matter of throwing the net over him and watching him shriek in pain. As he howled, it became obvious he was not who he said he was. I left his fate to the townspeople, who promptly burned him alive."

"But then what of Matthew? Where does he come into this?" Harlee asked.

"He was offered to me, as an infant sacrifice." He stated bluntly.

"What!?" Harlee exclaimed.

"I told you, they thought I was a demon. They offered me the blood of a first born son, to keep me from destroying their village."

"Were you going to?"

"No...maybe...it crossed my mind, alright but that would have been bad for business. I explained that I didn't eat children and had no means to care for a child. That only made matters worse; however, as they began to believe I had bewitched the child. In the end, I traveled home with the babe and brought him to live with me."

"So that is how Matthew came to be your son." Harlee smiled as she nodded her head.

"I appreciate you telling me, thank you." She said, sipping again as Maxwell stared out.

"It's best you know more about me." He said. "Especially with what you're considering." Harlee rubbed her feet together as the wind picked up slightly. Maxwell placed his left hand on them and squeezed gently. She stopped to look at him, sighing gently, as he continued to stare out.

"What are you thinking about?" She asked him.

"I'm not sure when was the last time, I sat with someone. Just to talk."

"I know. It seems we are always in motion. It's peaceful, sitting here, talking with you." She spoke as she reached the bottom of her glass. Leaning forward, she sat her glass down and reached for the bottle.

"Please, allow me." Maxwell said, leaving his left hand in place as he sat down his own glass and refilled both glasses.

"Thanks."

"My pleasure." He said as they both leaned back.

"Tell me more about yourself." Harlee said. "Not about, the past, the mission, nothing like that. Tell me something about Maxwell?" Maxwell took another tilt from his glass, as he thought.

"Where would you like me to begin?" He asked.

"Anywhere. Do you have any hobbies? You know, besides killing things." They shared a smile.

"Before...this." He began. "I used to make things, with my hands."

"You mean like sculpting?" She asked, taking another swig and another reload.

"For starters," he said, setting the bottle down. "I also practiced some carpentry. I still enjoy reading." He mentioned.

"What do you read?" She asked him, as she began to feel the heat in her cheeks, the bourbon working its way through her system.

"I believe it is your turn." He asked. Harlee looked at him for a moment.

"Well, I was only four or five years old, when my sister and I were taken. I cannot say I really have any fond memories from before." She said and realizing she had, shot the contents of her glass. She made a scrunched face before setting her glass down and reaching for the bottle again.

"Should you slow down?" Maxwell asked softly.

"No. Someone has to drink it. You've barely had any." She said.

"I can't get drunk. It wouldn't matter how quickly I drank it."

"Really?" She asked. Maxwell nodded. "Wow that must come in handy." She said.

"It can, if I ever need information from someone. It's not all that great, however." He said.

"Yeah," she said. "I suppose if you ever wanted to forget something, you couldn't take the easy way."

"What about after we save your sister?" Maxwell asked. "What memories will you make then?" Harlee thought the question over, having never given it much thought.

"I suppose I will take Cilia far away from this place. Somewhere free, from all of this supernatural weirdness. Somewhere she and I can be safe." She said, taking another drink.

"I recommend somewhere by the sea. Somewhere remote, small. That will be your best chance at peace." He spoke in a solemn tone, aware he was convincing her to leave. They both continued to sip as she stared at him.

"You'll come with us, won't you?" She asked. Maxwell stared down at his lap.

"I have to remain here." He spoke. "I cannot stop until I have seen my objective through." Harlee frowned.

"Will you at least come to visit, once we are settled?" She asked.

"I would like that." He said.

"Promise me." She said.

"Pardon?" He asked.

"If you promise, then I know you will. You never break a promise, so promise me you'll come see me once I'm settled." Harlee stared at Maxwell, eyes wide and bright, brimming with hope. Maxwell sighed and downed his glass.

"I promise." He said. Harlee smiled with elation as he gently squeezed her feet. Harlee's legs squirmed a little, as she grew anxious, from the many thought streams running through her head.

"You know, Maxwell, I've been thinking." She said.

"A terrible idea, when you've been drinking." He mentioned.

"I know but I've been talking with Almalexia and the others, quite a bit. I have gotten to know them and through them, you."

"You should never take advice about me from Almalexia. That's almost as bad as the drunken reflections." He teased. Harlee placed her hand on Maxwell's thigh, gripping it tightly to catch his attention.

"I am serious. I have been learning a lot about you, from her and I..." She looked away as she blushed, slightly. "I don't want to just be another acquaintance, Maxwell. I want to be more than that, to you. I want to be one of your treasured memories but there is more.

I want to feel all those things, which I have denied myself. I am no angel but I have never felt the way Almalexia has. Felt a lover, pleasuring me so much, they drank away my soul. I want to feel you saturated into every fiber of my being, long after your warmth has left my bed." Harlee reached out, lowering her feet and leaned forward to kiss him.

Maxwell's eyes were transfixed on her. Her robe was slightly open, revealing much of what he desired. The half of his heart, which had long remained silent, begged for him to take her, then and there, while the pain of the many cracks, threatened to tear him apart. As Harlee loomed in closer, Maxwell stood and walked to the edge of the balcony.

"I cannot give you what you seek." He said as he placed his hands on the ledge and looked over it.

"Why?" She asked, rising from the chair, untying her robe and bearing herself to him. "Why won't you take me, as you would any other? Why won't you make me feel, the way you made the others feel? Am I not beautiful enough?" She asked in an alcohol infused state of anger, insecurity and envy. "Look at me, Maxwell. Am I not suitable for you to take, as you would Almalexia?"

Maxwell turned and stared at her, looking at every curve, every well-toned muscle, every detail, perfection. Maxwell walked up to her and as she embraced him, kissing on his neck, he began to pull her robe back over her naked form.

"It is not a question of you being desirable." He whispered to her as she stopped. "If I could, I would claim you in a fashion, which poisoned your immortal soul, leaving you unable to find satisfaction with another, ever again. I would infect your every dream, possess your every fantasy and then, in the end, when I am gone, there would be nothing left of you but emptiness and insatiable hunger.

No, I cannot claim you Harlee. Not because I do not desire you, but because there is more to you than object and beauty." He said as he sat her back down. "You deserve true happiness, while happiness is something I can never give you." He told her, kissing her on the forehead. Harlee pulled her knees up to her chest as she turned her head away from him.

"This is about Victoria again, isn't it?" She mumbled, her eyes closed.

"I would spare you the lesson, I learned long ago, if I could." He confirmed. Harlee was silent for a while before muttering under her breath.

"Had I met you first, could you have loved me, as you loved her?" Maxwell turned to face her and smiled as he realized she had already fallen asleep. Gently, Maxwell cradled her into his arms and carried her back to her bedroom. Laying her on the available side of the bed, he placed a sheet over her, tucked her hair behind her ear and kissed her on the cheek.

"You are more than a memory, Harlee. In aeternum te amabo." He whispered into her ear as he moved to the corner of the room and sat in silence.

Maxwell sat, watching over Harlee as she slept peacefully. Remembering her desire, not to be alone, he waited nearly three hours before he heard the elevator doors, ding. He could hear as Dahlia and John entered, their voices low.

"Thank you for a wonderful evening, John." Dahlia said. "Though, I feel ashamed. The point was for me to cheer you up."

"Don't worry, Dahlia. I had a great time as well. With Jules and Almalexia gone, Harlee with Maxwell, it was nice to just get out. Besides, I enjoy your company. You do not look at me as the others do."

"No?" Dahlia asked.

"No. Everyone else, still treats me as a child. You're different."

"Well, let's face facts. A past such as yours and mine, you cannot go back after that." They stopped for a minute as they noticed something.

"This is Maxwell's hat and coat." John said. Maxwell could hear his footsteps moving through the room. A moment later, a single beam of light traced across the floor of Harlee's bedroom.

"Harlee?" Dahlia whispered, poking her head in. Maxwell rose from the chair and finger pressed to his lips, walked into the light.

"Maxwell?" Dahlia whispered as the man approached and pointed to Harlee's sleeping form. Dahlia nodded and backing out of the door, allowed Maxwell to follow, closing the door behind him.

"Maxwell?" John spoke. "What are you doing here?" He asked.

"When I brought Harlee back, she invited me up to share a drink. When we got here, she asked me to stay, because she did not want to be alone."

"That's all?" Dahlia asked.

"She took a shower, while I went for ice. We had a few drinks, she fell asleep. I have been waiting for someone to come back, so she would not wake, alone. That is all."

"But nothing happened?" Dahlia asked.

"Nothing, other than what I just mentioned." He said as he walked to the closet, grabbing his hat and coat.

"Where are you going?" John asked.

"You two are here, now. There is no longer any reason for me to stay. I will return home and gather my thoughts. There will be much at stake." He said, adjusting his coat.

"Maxwell, home is a sewer, connected to some catacombs, filled with corpses and dead dreams. Stay here with us." Dahlia urged as Maxwell hit the call elevator button.

"That's why it suites me." He said as the elevator doors opened. "I will see you all, Sunday night." He said as the doors closed behind him.

Chapter 15 – Lie Still

Harlee awoke the following morning, her head screaming with malice at her. As she noticed the light coming into the room, she rolled, pulling the covers over her head. She groaned in misery for a moment as she heard her door open.

"Good morning, Harleequin." Dahlia teased as she entered the bedroom, carrying a tray full of eggs, toast, coffee, orange juice and bacon.

"Go away. Just let me die." Harlee groaned, making Dahlia smile.

"Not until you tell me every last piece of juicy gossip from last night." She said as she sat beside Harlee.

"Last night?" Harlee asked. "What day is it?"

"Saturday. Yesterday was the funeral. Last night, however, you and Maxwell...were alone." She reminded Harlee and waited for her to fill in the blanks. Harlee thought for a moment, then sprang upright and looked over to the balcony.

"Is he still here?" She asked, securing her robe. Dahlia shook her head.

"No, but he waited in here, watching over you, until John and I arrived. He said he did not want you to be alone, when you woke. Awfully thoughtful of him, I would say."

"Did he say anything else?"

"No. He said pretty much, you did not want to be alone, invited him over for a few drinks and then fell asleep. I was hoping you might be able to provide a few juicy details." Dahlia commented, still staring at Harlee. She continued to rack her bran for details but could not quite fill in the blanks.

"We were sitting on the balcony. He told me about Matthew, I told him about Cilia." The obvious finally struck her. "He was trying to convince me not to be the keeper." She thought aloud.

"But why would he do that?" Dahlia asked. Harlee tried to remember.

"I'm not sure but I don't really care. I'm going to go give him my answer." She said as she climbed out of bed and began dressing herself. Laying out her jeans and sliding on fresh panties, Harlee reached for a bra and shirt.

"You know, Maxwell seems to notice when you wear those dresses Matthew bought. Might be easier to capture his attention." She suggested Harlee stopped what she was doing as she considered Dahlia's proposal. Walking to the closet, Harlee grabbed a dress off from her rack and slid into it. Moving back to her bed, she pulled out her knee-highs, slid her feet into them and zipped up the sides.

As she stood back up, Dahlia began feeding her from off of the tray. She sipped her coffee and juice, in between bites, as she made her way to the restroom. A few minutes later, teeth and hair brushed, Harlee was tightening the strap on her leather jacket as Dahlia tossed her the car keys. Harlee hit the hotel lobby floor, passing Almalexia on her way out.

"Good afternoon, Harlee. You seem rushed." The succubus said as Harlee walked by.

"I have to give Maxwell my answer." She said as she kept walking. Almalexia tilted her head, curiously.

"I'll go with you." She said as she began to follow Harlee. "I must speak with Maxwell as well." She said.

"If you must." Harlee said as the two walked to the parking lot and climbed into the car.

"What is it with all of these people?" Harlee asked. Traffic was moving at a crawl as masses of people, flooded out into the streets.

"That is part of what I wished to speak with Maxwell about. We were so caught up with Father Matthew's death; we all missed the late announcement that the Feast will start tonight, opposed to tomorrow evening. For some reason, the forces controlling Sin City have decided to start early.

"Might it have something to do with that woman, who was with Auriel?"

"Maybe. I still find it strange Auriel is here and not just some lackey. She rarely shows herself in public and it's never good when she does."

"When was the last time?" Harlee asked.

"The last time was at the start of the last great human war. The time before that was The Fall." As the traffic began to move again, Harlee was speechless. By the time they reached the storage unit, Harlee managed to ask.

"What is Cilia doing, mixed up with someone so evil?" She asked.

"She is obviously under the effects of compulsion. The more important question is what does she have that is so valuable? There is not a shred of a chance she would keep a human near, which she was not feeding on. I'm not suggesting we kill your sister but whatever she knows, must be of the utmost importance to her plans." Harlee began to shake at the thought of how deeply woven, Cilia must be.

"All the same, Almalexia. If you hurt my sister..."

"Relax, Harlee. Maxwell and I have agreed to help you save your sister. We won't do anything to hurt her." Almalexia assured her as they reached the back alley manhole. Making their way down into the sewers, Harlee led the way to the gates.

"Maxwell!" Harlee called, rattling the locked gate. "Maxwell, are you there? It's me, Harlee. Almalexia is here too." She called, waiting for an answer. They only waited a few minutes before they heard Maxwell's voice from the darkness.

"My apologies. I was looking into the commotion outside." Maxwell spoke as he unlocked the gate. "May I assume the Feast has begun early?" He asked.

"That is exactly what has happened, Maxwell. What do you think Auriel is planning?" Almalexia asked.

"I haven't the faintest idea but this is also an opportunity for us. I need you to go back and gather everyone. The more chaotic it is out there, the easier it will be for us to remain unnoticed. I want for everyone, save Jules and myself, to join in tonight. The plan remains the same. We simply can get this over with a day early." Maxwell spoke as he walked through his altar room and into the armory.

"I will head back, then." Almalexia spoke as she turned to Harlee. "We'll come back for you. Everyone will love you in that outfit anyway." She held out her hand to Harlee, who relinquished the keys.

"Maxwell, I need to talk to you?" Harlee said as Almalexia left.

"What is there to talk about? You made your desires perfectly clear to me, last night. I wish to help you reunite with Cilia."

"I was drunk and confused, alright? I realize sober, I cannot simply walk away once Cilia is freed. However, if I stay here and help you, together she will be safe."

"You could, you know. Once Cilia is safe, the two of you could leave. Go far away from all of this madness."

"You and I both know that is bullshit!" Harlee raised her voice. "There is no place on earth, those creatures will not try to infect. By your side, is the safest place from those things, we could be."

"I thought Matthew was safe." Maxwell said. "I cannot predict every eventuality."

"I'm not asking you to. I'm asking you to let me help you."

"Harlee, you will never find happiness by my side."

"Then so be it! Don't you dare push me away!"

"You need to take Cilia..."

"SHUT UP!" Harlee yelled. "Just shut up! Quit pretending everything is fine! I am NOT leaving! I'm staying and helping you finish your mission! Final!" She continued growing more anxious and angry, her heart pounding. Maxwell didn't say anything. He continued to look away, equipping himself for the evening.

"Look at me, Maxwell." She said in a softer tone, as Maxwell tightened his quick draw holsters across his waist. "Look at me...please." Her tone softened further.

"I have one additional condition." He told her as he turned to face her. "In addition to those you already know." Her heart began to race as she swallowed hard.

"What is it?" She asked.

"When this is all said and done. Once your sister is safe and my affairs here are settled. You take Cilia, John, Almalexia, Dahlia and Jules, far away from here and never come back. I require you to escape this life with them. That is my extra condition."

"What about you? What will you do once we're gone?"

"Take the offer or leave it." Maxwell grumbled. Harlee agonized over her decision for a moment before reaching out her hand.

"Deal." She agreed as Maxwell looked at her hand.

"We have to exchange blood." He told her. Harlee jolted upright, thinking of Maxwell's fangs.

"Fine." She said boldly, undoing her jacket, dropping it to the ground, as she pulled down the strap on her dress, exposing her neck.

"Just be gentle, alright?" She asked as he smiled at her. "What? Go ahead and do it already." She demanded, a slight blush to her cheeks.

"Give me your hand." He told her as he placed her strap back. "I need to make a small incision on your hand and mine. You make your oath as we shake hands, transferring the blood. I promise you, I carry no diseases."

"You don't need to feed on me?" She asked.

"I'm not a vampire."

"You don't need to kiss me?"

"You're not making a contract with a demon."

"We don't even have to have sex?" She said jokingly.

"We're not summoning a demon."

"Just a handshake and a promise?" She asked in disbelief.

"Yeah. Humans are practical with their weirdness." He spoke as he pulled out his hunting knife and cut across his palm. Holding it out to her, Harlee watched as Maxwell's hand bled but began knitting itself back together. "That's it." He assured her.

"Alright." She said. "But you make the cut." She closed her eyes and held out her hand. She winced as she felt a sharp pinch and afterwards, felt Maxwell's hand gripping her own.

"State your oath." He told her.

"I, Harlee Castello, swear to defend your heart, as if it were the heart of my lover." She felt her palm grow hot and opened her eyes to see Maxwell's full of lament. Suddenly, Harlee felt a tightening in her chest and gripped her heart with her left hand, as she collapsed to her knees. Maxwell dipped down, catching her on his shoulder as she gasped, having grown short of breath.

"Don't panic, Harlee. I would never intentionally hurt you." She heard a softer tone to his voice as her forehead rested by his neck. She felt her heartbeat, radically changing pace as she continued to fight for air. As the heat in her hand dissipated, Harlee filled her lungs and attempted to slow her racing heart.

"What happened?" She asked as Maxwell lifted her from the floor and carried her to the workbench, where he rested her.

"You've become my keeper. Hearts that are connected protect one another. Your heart has just synchronized itself with mine." He told her. "And my heart will protect you, as you protect it." Harlee placed her hand back to her chest and felt the strong, steady pounding.

"Does that mean I am like you now?" She asked, a nervous tone in her voice.

"No. My heart will offer you a small amount of my power but that is all. Look at your hand." Harlee stared down at her palm and found it had already begun to heal. "You are still human, of that I can assure you."

"What now?" She asked.

"Now, we proceed with the plan."

"But what if Cilia really is compelled? How will I save her?" She asked. Maxwell sighed as he chose his words carefully.

"Harlee...your sister is not compelled."

"She has to be! Cilia would never work for their kind!"

"If she is not one of them, which I suspect she is not, then she is likely under the power of suggestion."

"Suggestion, compulsion, what's the difference?" She asked.

"With the power of compulsion, Cilia's mind, will, personality, all would be snuffed out and manipulated at her master's discretion. It is safe to assume your sister is too valuable to be stripped of her own mind. The most likely option is suggestion, which would work similar to Almalexia's toxin, without the sex fanaticism. She would merely feel as though she wanted to do anything Auriel told her. Cilia might believe she wants to help Auriel. Your presence alone may be enough to break Auriel's hold on her. With suggestion, you need to merely provide Cilia with something she wants more than helping her master."

"So it's simple then? Just walk in and ask her to leave?"

"And don't get caught." Maxwell suggested. Harlee nodded her head as she took everything Maxwell said to heart.

"Just be careful out there. What must be done is simple, but I would hardly call it easy." Maxwell said.

"I will. You're watching my back though, right?"

"Always." He spoke to her as he helped her down from the table. "The others will be here soon. You've better get going." He said to her. Harlee made her way back to the street level, where she awaited the others by the storage container.

She watched as troves of people, cheering excitedly walked by. She was approached by men and women both, who wished to "celebrate" with her, though she declined, on account of waiting for her friends. Half an hour passed by and she saw Maxwell's car pulling into the drive.

"Sorry for the wait." Dahlia spoke as she, Jules, John and Almalexia, exited the car. "Traffic is murder with all of these people."

"Is everyone ready?" Harlee asked. Everyone gathered nodded their heads.

"Be safe." Jules told her as she moved toward the back to meet Maxwell. Together, they joined into the larger group, making sure to keep an eye on one another as they walked downtown, towards the tallest building in all of Sin City. With so much going on and so many people to be wary of, they arrived before they had been given much chance to tire from the walk.

Harlee looked upon the massive campus ahead of them, the monstrous glass tower and the various other buildings surrounding. The crowd slowed as people began pouring through the gates. Harlee looked about, staying close to Dahlia as they passed through.

"Hey pretty girls, what brings you to the Feast this evening?" A friendly security guard asked as Harlee and Dahlia came upon the gates.

"They're with me." Almalexia chimed in, cutting between them.

"Oh my, sweet angel from heaven, Miss Almalexia, herself. V.I.P. passes for you three then."

"The boy, as well. If you please." She said, motioning back towards John.

"How unlike you, to bring a man with you." The guard said. Almalexia smiled.

"This one belongs to another, unfortunately but then again, the night Is young." She and the man exchanged an awkward laugh, as he also handed John a V.I.P. pass.

"What do we do with these?" Harlee asked.

"They should get us inside to the main event." Almalexia answered.

"Wasn't that a little easy?" She asked.

"I had the same thought myself. I expected, with Auriel here, security would have been stricter." Almalexia agreed.

"What does that mean?" Dahlia asked.

"Stick to the plan, stay together if possible and be ready to improvise." Almalexia suggested as they walked forward. Harlee stayed near to Dahlia as John began moving away, following another pack of werewolf thralls.

"Good luck, John." Dahlia called. John waved to them as he moved further away and out of sight.

"Let's head this way." Dahlia pointed to the first of the buildings they were to investigate. As they moved through the crowd, Dahlia and

Harlee could hear the sound of nightclub music. Pushing their way through the crowds, flashing their passes, they quickly moved to the front of the line.

"What the hell?" Dahlia said as they entered the room, lavish, bright lights, splashing against reflective panels and pools of water as hundreds of bodies danced, pressed tightly together. The strobing black lights above revealed the invisible body paint decorating those in the room.

Carefully, they moved through the room, careful to be undetected as they reached a potential access point. The music inside was blaring, disorienting their senses as they attempted to pass through the sea of people. Up above, Dahlia pointed to several hanging cages, groups of people, numbering from two to five, fornicating above the nightclub goers.

"This must be where they celebrate lust." Harlee suggested as they continued to push through the crowd. As they walked, various people, already in frenzy, grinded on them as they passed. Harlee could feel herself slowing, as her head fogged. Looking up at the lights, Harlee grew dizzy as the effect of the strobes and various colored lights, piercing through the veil of fog, seemingly slowed time.

"Dahlia, do you feel alright?" Harlee asked as Dahlia moved to the far wall. As she moved towards her friend, every passerby who brushed against her, set her every nerve on edge. Already, she could feel herself swooning.

"Dahlia, we have to get out of here." Harlee said. "There's something in the air, here. It's the same as Almalexia's toxin." She said as she passed a couple, who were kissing aggressively, placing their hands under one another's clothing. As Harlee passed, she was knocked into the couple, who incorporated her into their session.

Making contact with the first pair of lips she felt, Harlee grabbed the back of their owner's head and forced her tongue into their mouth. Her hands worked their way over her partner's body as she could feel a hand groping up her thigh. She felt as two fingers, penetrated her and she tipped her head back as she groaned with euphoric delight.

"Sorry, Harleequinn." Dahlia spoke as she wrenched against her friend, pulling Harlee from her blissful engagement.

"You're right. We have to get out of here." Harlee forced out, after catching her breath and forcing herself to think soberly. Dahlia nodded, red in the face as she herself struggled to resist. Harlee, after being drug from the center of the room several paces, began to awaken from the haze.

"Thank you." She said as she trembled slightly. "Remind me, to resolve certain urges, after this." She said to Dahlia as they cleared the tent and took in a deep breath, of normal, clean air.

"Don't worry, Harlee, we'll find the both of us a boy toy after this. Fuck me." She panted alongside Harlee as Almalexia approached them.

"Find anything?" She asked. Without looking up at the succubus, Harlee answered.

"Too much succubus toxin in there. If it weren't for Dahlia, I'd be trapped." Harlee said. Almalexia looked around before placing her hands on their backs.

"That's alright. I'll go in. John is already on site, looking for his mark. You two head to the fight ring." She said as she walked inside the nightclub, leaving Harlee and Dahlia to their own devices.

"Before we proceed, I need a drink." Dahlia said, as she walked over to the nearby tent. A moment later, she returned, two cups in her hands.

"Water." She said as she handed a glass to Harlee, who downed it in half a second. Dahlia stared at her, impressively as she sipped at her water before the two of them carried on.

"Alright. To the next stop." Harlee said as they approached the next building. As they grew closer, they noticed several canopies, with filled picnic benches of people, engorging themselves on various dishes. Harlee watched as one particular individual, vomited before proceeding to eat more.

"I understand now, Dahlia." Harlee said as she eyed the crowd. "Seven days of seven deadly sins, right? Everywhere we go here, there is going to be temptations. We will have to look beyond them but beyond that, I wonder if the nightclub's mist, wasn't the only object designed to trick our minds." As she said it, she could feel her stomach growling. Placing her hands on her stomach, she noticed Dahlia doing the same.

"The water." Harlee suggested. "It might have been drugged. Just ignore the hunger pains. We have to keep moving forward." She said as their stomachs growled angrily at them.

Not much further ahead, up the steps to the main building, Harlee saw Cilia. Her sister stood up above, surveying the area, as waves of people moved around her as a parting sea. Harlee ducked behind one of the food stands and observed her sister in between the gaps in the stands menus. Cilia glanced over the area once more, before moving on towards the building where Father Matthew had said the fighters' pit would be.

"Dahlia." Harlee said, turning to her friend, who was holding a pretzel, slice of pizza, drink and hotdog, juggling them in her hands as she took bites of each.

"Harlee. Can you help me? I can't get to my straw." She said, trying to reach the tip of the straw by craning her neck.

"Dahlia, take a few bites and get it together. Cilia just went inside the fighters' pit." She said as Dahlia glanced over in the direction she pointed. Nodding her head, Dahlia handed off some of her items to Harlee, who tossed them in the trash, to save herself from her own temptation.

As they walked towards the pit, they noticed several other attractions, dedicated to the other deadly sins. Turning to the left, just before the stairs, Harlee and Dahlia again flashed their passes, granting them access to the arena. Inside, men and women alike, fought in the ring below. They walked inside and noticed two fighters in the center, one, hands up in the air, the other, being carried out.

Harlee and Dahlia both made their way around the back of the last row, searching for any sign of Cilia. The fight announcer proclaimed the winner, followed immediately by introducing the next two contenders of the blood sport. Two more fighters walked into the ring, glaring at one another, everything to prove, as Harlee and Dahlia spread out further.

Harlee carefully crept through the crowded bodies, keeping an eye open for any trace of her sister. The two in the ring, lashed out at one another, gathering the attention of the crowd. Harlee glanced away for a moment, as the bodies jumped up in front of her.

Through a gap in the crowd, Harlee for a brief moment, made eye contact with her sister, who was across the ring. Cilia, upon noticing her sister, smiled wide. As the crowd continued to wave back and forth, Harlee lost sight of her and began pressing her way through the crowd.

She looked back to see where Dahlia had went. She could not make out the slightest sign of her friend, through the assembled thousands. With no sign of Dahlia, Harlee continued forward until a hand grabbed hers. Harlee turned her gaze and felt the strong embrace of her older sister.

"Harlee!? Is that really you?" Harlee looked into the brown eyes of her sister. Placing her free hand on her sister's shoulder, Harlee felt tears running in her eyes.

"It is. It's me Cilia, it's Harlee." She cried as she continued to pat her sister to ensure that she were real. Looking around, Harlee held tightly onto Cilia's hand.

"We have to get you out of here, Cilia. I have friends who can help us go somewhere safe." She said turning and trying to pull her sister away.

"My, my, dear Cilia. Who might this stunning young woman be?" Harlee heard the alluring, European accent of a sensual woman. Turning her head, she found the woman's body, matched her voice. The woman, Harlee knew as Auriel, stood behind Cilia, arms draped over her shoulders.

"This is my younger sister, Harlee. I have not seen her in a long time, Queen Auriel." Cilia said, pointing to Harlee. Harlee froze in fear as the queen of all vampires, turned her gaze upon her, eyes glowing red.

"Well then, Harlee. It is a pleasure to meet you. I do wish you would accompany me, back to my home away from home. I would love to hear more about you."

"Harlee!" Dahlia yelled as she tried to fight against the crowd, swarming out from the fighters' pit. Unable to combat the swelling tide, Dahlia was forcibly knocked backwards, as people shoved through her, unintelligibly. Pulling herself up onto one of the many tables, Dahlia tried to gain a vantage.

"HARLEE! WHERE ARE YOU!?" She screamed, hoping her voice could carry over the roar of the crowd. Tears began to swell in her eyes, the longer she looked. As the last of the patrons, walked from the tent, Dahlia ran towards the opening.

"We are sorry miss. This attraction is closed, for the evening. You will have to wait until tomorrow, should you wish to see more fights." One of the security officers told her as they barred her progress.

"My friend is still in there! Will you please let me grab her?" Dahlia urged. The two guards looked to one another and nodded.

"Come with me ma'am." The guard who had stopped her said, as he escorted her inside. Dahlia looked inside the arena and saw absolutely no one, save the janitorial crew remained.

"You must have just missed your friend in the crowd. It will be all right. You will just need to wait for her by the front gate." He urged her as Dahlia turned away from the tent, hands clapped on either side of her mouth.

"HARLEE!" She yelled as she made her way to the front gates. Dahlia waited, standing in front of the gates, for over an hour, waiting for any sign of Harlee.

"Dahlia, where is Harlee?" Dahlia turned her head to see, Jules, hood pulled over her head, having just passed through the gates wearing a general admissions pass.

"I don't know. We found Cilia and were separated. I searched everywhere but I cannot find her. I'm hoping if I wait here long enough, she'll show up." Dahlia spoke, keeping her eyes on the people walking out of the Feast. Jules kept her head down as she helped Dahlia look around. Before long, they spotted Almalexia and John, who approached them.

"Jules? What are you doing in here?" Almalexia asked.

"He sent me in. We saw Dahlia, who looked in trouble. I was sent to check on her." John began looking around as Almalexia listened to Jules.

"Where's Harlee?" He asked. Dahlia shook her head, pulling on her hair.

"She vanished."

"What happened?" Maxwell asked calmly once they had all reached the safety of the catacombs. He paced back and forth, between his various weapon racks and his workbench. Dahlia sat across the room with John, Jules and Almalexia.

"We went one at a time, searching through the different buildings which were on the blueprints. First, we went into the sex club and barely managed to escape with our wits. We began moving through the other sites on the map, in search of any leads. We were drugged, while near the gluttony zone and Harlee spotted Cilia, while I was attempting to grab some food.

We went in together, into the fighters' pit, following her and were separated. I waited outside for her but she never came out. I even went back in after everyone left but she wasn't there."

"You're sure Harlee did not come back out?" Maxwell asked.

"Positive. I stood outside of the tent, watching everyone who exited. There is no doubt Harlee would have seen me."

"Did you see, Cilia?" Maxwell asked.

"No." She answered. Maxwell continued to pace back and forth, without saying a word. After a long, anxious pause, John spoke.

"Maxwell? Are you..." He began as Maxwell grabbed the nearest rack and flung it across the hall, away from everyone else.

"FUCK!" He yelled as he grabbed another and threw that as well. "FUCK! FUCK! FUCK!" He continued to rage as he covered the entire hall with weapons. The lights above him began to flicker and fade as he continued to rage.

"Maxwell, calm down!" Almalexia yelled at him. "Do you really want to change now? With them here!" She motioned back to Dahlia, Jules and John. Maxwell stretched out his arms, clenching his fists tightly, as he tipped back his head and took a deep breath.

"I am sorry. Time's running out." He said as he took another deep breath and reassumed his smooth composure. "And you did not see her at all, today?" Everyone gathered, shook his or her heads. Maxwell closed his eyes for a moment, massaging their tips as he began pacing again.

"We need to infiltrate the main building. The rest of us have not been discovered, just Harlee. John, you have the best chance of success here. You cannot be compelled by Auriel. I want you to find a way inside from your district. You will not be as at risk. Take Dahlia with you. Almalexia, Jules..."

"You want us to take Dahlia and Harlee's place?" Almalexia asked, calmly. Maxwell nodded. Jules turned her attention to Maxwell.

"What will you do?"

"Don't worry about that. Each of us is going to go in tonight, wired. I will be monitoring all of your channels. Only alert if you spot Harlee, or one of your targets. Or if you need someone to back you up." He turned back towards his workbench and placing his palms down, leaned on it.

"How do you know John will be safe?" Almalexia asked.

"He is also my keeper. My heart protects the keepers from compulsion."

"So, Harlee?" Dahlia asked. "Is a prisoner?"

"It will not be so bad, as you might believe. Harlee can still be stricken with suggestion. Chances are, they will try to convince her she desires to be with them. Harlee is still there, unharmed, of that much we can be certain." Maxwell assured them.

"How do you know that?" Jules asked.

"Because Maxwell and Auriel have met before." Almalexia answered. "She will use Harlee to get to him. She knows the two are associated and understands Maxwell's code."

"You make me sound so simplistic." Maxwell grunted.

"Maxwell? You cannot allow Auriel to lure you into a trap." Almalexia said.

"Perhaps I intend to lure her into one of my own." He suggested as he thought matters through, a sinister smile on his face. "Listen, everyone. Our objective will be to find Harlee and get her out. Cilia as well, if possible. We know for a fact, Harlee will come with any one of us, regardless of whether or not she is under suggestion. The key is to make her remember why she wants to leave." He told them.

"Alright then." Jules spoke. "Should we all rest up and head back out tonight?" She asked.

"Go ahead, all of you." Maxwell said. "You all need a rest." He said as he began placing weapons on the workbench.

"Don't you think you should get some sleep, too?" Almalexia asked. Maxwell shook his head.

"It's an odd thing for an immortal to say but there's no time. I have preparations only I can make." He told her as she placed her hand on his back.

"Maxwell? We will get her back." She said. Maxwell smiled.

"Are you still jealous of her?"

"Extremely so." She told him as she hugged his back.

"Go get some rest, Lexi. I will be fine." He assured her as she patted him on the back once more, before turning and walking away. Once they were all gone, Maxwell raised his gaze to the cask, only twenty feet from him. Walking to it, he placed his hand on top of the box and stared at its archaic surface.

"Lie still." He whispered as he closed his eyes and considered what he must do.

Chapter 16 - Only In Your Dreams

Harlee awoke, sitting in a chair, at the far end of a thirty-foot banquet table. She looked around, seeing the empty crystal glasses and china plates, down the length of the table. She looked down and saw a red carpet, running the length of what appeared to be an elegant ballroom, straight out of a fairy tale.

Harlee placed her hands on the table and saw she wore black, silken gloves. Tracing the long sleeves up to her bare shoulders, she looked down and saw she wore a long flowing, red gown. The gown began as a choker and with two thin straps extending from it, flowed down her body, exposing nearly half of both breasts and fanning out, connecting to the back, just below her navel.

As she stood, she noticed the dress bore slits on either side, exposing both of her thighs, just below her groin. The gown extended all of the way to her feet, which were placed into tall, black, stiletto heels. Harlee noticed her toes were pedicured and painted blood red, to match her dress.

"Hello?" Harlee called out to the vast emptiness before her. She walked through the room, her heels clicking against the ballroom floor, echoed back to her. She neared the far end of the room, where a staircase rose up to meet a set of large double doors.

Harlee pushed them open and walked into the room beyond. The red carpet extended into the next room, at the end of which, sat Auriel on her raised throne. Several others stood beneath her platform, Cilia among them. Everyone wore renaissance era clothing. Taking notice of her entry, Auriel looked up and smiled at her.

"Ah, the princess awakes. How are you my dear?" She spoke, wide smile on her face, which was filled with deceptive kindness.

"I am not sure. Where am I? How did I get here?" Harlee asked, as she continued to look around, unable to put the details together.

"Why my dear, you are our most treasured guest." Auriel said as if hurt. "I do hope everything has been to your liking?" She asked as Harlee tried to remember. The blissful stream in her mind, convinced her, she was happy.

"My apologies, Queen Auriel, I remember now. Please forgive me." She said as she knelt into a deep curtsy.

"No harm done, my dear. I am just glad to hear you are enjoying yourself. We want to ensure our treasured guests enjoy themselves. How about you, Miss Cilia? Have you enjoyed your time here, thus far?" Cilia pressed her glasses back up against the bridge of her nose and smiled.

"It has been the greatest thrill of my life. If you would please excuse me, I wish to spend a moment with my little sister."

"But of course, my dear. Balthazar, dear. Might you escort these two fine ladies around? Nothing short of the royal treatment, for such distinguished guests, if you please." Balthazar stepped forward, clapped his hand to his chest and entered a deep, flamboyant bow.

"It would be my pleasure, ma'am." He spoke in his low toned voice, which made Harlee think of someone else she could not quite remember. Balthazar walked to Cilia and held out his arm to her. Cilia curtsied and accepted his arm as they walked in sync to Harlee.

"My lady." He said as he bowed and extended his other arm to Harlee.

"Kind sir." She curtsied and accepted as he led them out of the room.

"Has she revealed anything yet?" A commanding voice called down from above. Auriel looked up to the balcony above, to the woman dressed all in black, only her smile visible beneath her veil. Auriel knelt to the ground and bowed her head.

"She has not. It will not take long, however. She will soon reveal all of her secrets, I am certain." Auriel spoke, not once raising her level of sight.

"I do not want the girl harmed. I could care less about her connection to the other one but this one is special. She appears to be connected to Maxwell, and in that regard, she is most valuable."

"Do you wish me to search for him, Mother?" Auriel asked.

"There will be no need. Maxwell will come for her. When he does, everything else will be of little consequence. Do you remember your task, once he is in your possession?"

"Yes, Mother."

"Excellent. I will leave it in your hands, then."

"Forgive me but are you leaving, Mother?" Auriel asked.

"Shortly. There are other matters, which I wish to see to. This year's Feast already appears to be a success. It will be a shame to leave before its conclusion but I am afraid there are other pressing matters. Continue with the recruitment. My business can wait a few days, in order to help their...transition. I shall be sure to leave behind my gift, for your use. After, however, I must see to it Aurelius does not fall behind on his preparations."

"As you command, Mother. May all bow before your glory." Auriel spoke as the woman in black left.

"And as you can see over here, we have the gardens." Balthazar spoke as he walked, Cilia and Harlee both hanging onto an arm. "I must admit, this is one of my favorite places on the campus." He confided as they walked through the lush tropical garden. They walked through a hidden oasis, in the center of Sin City, complete with flowers of various size and color, with tall skyward reaching trees, which blocked out the morning sun.

"Sir Balthazar," Harlee asked. "Where is it, we have met before? I cannot help but feel I know you from somewhere." She asked as Cilia let go of Balthazar's arm and walked off to the side of the path. Walking out onto the larger, circular path, Balthazar grabbed Harlee's hand and began leading her through the steps of a waltz.

"Why, my dear. We have met before but only in your dreams. It was in there, which I called out to you before you arrived. Do you not remember?" He asked her as he twirled her gracefully and hand wrapped around her waist, slowly dipped her down. Harlee, hand on his chest, smelling of his sweet, masculine scent, stared into his large wild eyes.

"Yes. I do remember now." She smiled, continuing to dance with the man, as Cilia watched. As they finished, Balthazar brought Harlee close and bowed before her.

"Thank you for the dance, my lady. Would you care to continue the tour?" He asked.

"Indeed." Harlee said curtsying as she and Cilia began renewing their stroll. As they exited the gardens, Harlee came upon a pool of water and looked at her reflection. She smiled at how pretty she was and noticed as Balthazar approached beside her.

"You are quite beautiful, my lady." He spoke as he placed his hand on her shoulder. "An absolute vision, I would say." Harlee smiled but continued to watch in the distorted water as she remembered someone else. A man, wearing an all-black entourage, cowboy hat, old style vest and duster, appeared. Harlee stared at the man, trying to wonder who he was as a question left her lips.

"Had I met you first, would you have loved me, as you did her?" She asked the question without knowing why her heart pounded, agonizing over the missing pieces of her memory.

"I beg your pardon, my lady?" Balthazar asked. "I am afraid I did not hear you." Harlee turned from Balthazar to look back upon the man, who was gone.

"I am sorry, I must have been daydreaming." She said, smiling.

"Well, while in your presence, I often catch myself, much the same. Shall we?" He asked, holding out his arm.

"Umm, actually..." Harlee began. "Would it be alright, should I wish to walk by myself?"

"As you wish, my lady. Should you grow lost, simply ask any of the servants. They would be more than happy to guide you back to my side." He gently kissed the back of Harlee's hand as he walked away.

"Cilia?" Harlee asked, causing her sister to turn and stare at her.

"Yes, Harlee." Cilia asked. Harlee continued to stare in confusion at the world around her.

"Does something seem out of place, here? I cannot quite place it but it feels as though I am meant to be somewhere else." She said, unsure of the feeling she felt in the back of her mind.

"I do not know what you mean." Cilia said. "This is what we always dreamed of." Harlee smiled, nodding her head.

"Yes. You are right. Please forgive me. I am just confused."

"Take care, my sister. I will see you later." Cilia said as she walked away, taking Balthazar's arm and leaving Harlee behind. Harlee sat down at the water's edge, staring down at her reflection again as she thought. The fragmented remnants of memory escaping her grasp, Harlee looked back to the oasis around her. Rising from the water's surface, she continued her walk through the gardens, which led to a staircase. Placing her hand on the railing, Harlee followed the stairwell up, searching out the windows as she walked.

She passed the odd guard and servant, here and there, bowing her head to each as they passed. As she continued to climb higher, she kept her eyes facing out the windows. Eventually, she was high enough she could see over the tops of the buildings on the courtyard and noticed the city beyond them.

She stopped, turning her body and full attention to the outside world. She tilted her head to the side, feeling as though she were somewhere she did not belong. Again, her heart raced as incomprehensibly clouded thoughts swirled through her mind. She felt a single drop of water, land on her glove and dabbing her cheek, realized she had begun to cry.

"How did I get here?" She asked herself.

Later that evening, Harlee was escorted back to the dining hall, where Auriel, Balthazar and Cilia, awaited her. As she entered the hall, her senses were assaulted by the powerfully alluring smells of the evening's offerings. The servants beckoned her forward, onto the red carpet. Auriel, Balthazar and Cilia, all smiled to her as she entered.

"Ah, good evening, Harlee." Auriel said. "Did you find your walk about the grounds, to be enjoyable?"

"Quite, your highness, I thank you for your hospitality." She said curtsying. "If it is not asking, too much, might I be allowed to walk the grounds tomorrow?" Auriel eyed her suspiciously.

"Whatever do you mean, my dear? You are free to go anywhere within my palace."

"I know and I do appreciate that, however, I was wondering what might lie on the outside. I feel as though there is someone out there, waiting for me." She said as she stared at the south wall, as if peering through it.

"Tell me about this person who is awaiting you." Auriel said, leaning forward in her seat. Harlee tried desperately to remember, as glimpses of the man in the water, flashed before her eyes.

"He is difficult to recall, as if a dear friend, I had long forgotten. He is out there though, somewhere, I can feel him. He will be worried that I am gone, though as I recall, he and I argue frequently." She said, placing her hands to her heart as Cilia approached her.

"A sign that he is a dear friend. Try to remember, Harlee." She said. "Can you describe him to me?"

"His face?" Harlee spoke as Maxwell's smile stood still before her eyes. "His face..." She said again, as the stirring in the back of her mind spoke up, demanding her to stop. Harlee smiled and shook her head as she turned back to face Auriel.

"I am sorry, Queen Auriel. Please forgive me, my friend would not wish for me to reveal him." She said as Cilia and Balthazar both turned their heads to Auriel, who appeared just as perplexed as they did.

"What did you say?" Auriel asked sweetly, though her voice trembled slightly.

"My friend is quite dear to me. However, he is a rather private man. I am afraid he would not wish for me to reveal anything about him. Please forgive me." She bowed her head down again, before the puzzled queen of vampires.

"I see. I am afraid with circumstances as they are, it is dangerous to go outside. I must ask you be patient, a few days, is all." Auriel asked. Harlee smiled and curtsied.

"Thank you for hearing out my request." She said. Auriel smiled and bowed her head.

"Of course, now please. Eat, drink, enjoy yourself. Tomorrow, I wish to walk with you myself." Auriel spoke.

"I would be delighted, your highness." Harlee said as she was escorted to the table, where she enjoyed a night of fine dining, music and dancing. Once the hour grew late, Harlee was escorted up to her room by Cilia. The room was massive and flamboyant, drapes hung from the large, canopy covered bed.

"This room is incredible." Harlee said, as she twirled in a circle, taking in the entirety of the pure pink, princess styled room.

"Of course it is. This room was specifically decorated with you in my mind." Cilia spoke, adjusting her glasses. "Rest well, Harlee." Cilia said as she began to leave the room.

"Cilia?" Harlee began. Cilia stopped in the doorway, hand on the door handle.

"Yes?" Cilia asked.

"Would you like to leave this place with me?" Harlee asked. Cilia turned, walking back into the bedroom and looked at her sister.

"What do you mean?" She asked.

"You know just you, me, and my friends. Let us escape this place, go somewhere beautiful. The sea, we could go to the sea. We could be together again and see all of the things we never had a chance to. Won't that be great?" Harlee spoke, still high on elation as Cilia wrapped her hands around Harlee, hugging her. Hand against the back of Harlee's head, Cilia pet her sister's hair.

"More than anything." She answered. "That sounds grand, Harlee. Just you, me, and your friends. Let us all run away from this place and be together." Cilia pushed away, holding Harlee at arm's length. "Promise me you won't say anything though, alright?" She asked. Harlee nodded her head.

"Of course not. I do not want to offend Queen Auriel or Balthazar. They seem nice but I don't think my friends would trust them." Cilia kissed Harlee's forehead and started to walk away.

"Hey Cilia?" Harlee asked one more time.

"Yes, Harlee?"

"Do you remember that story you use to tell me, when I was little?" She asked. Cilia smiled wide, a small tear in her eye.

"In the great green room, there was a telephone and a red balloon." Cilia began as she walked across the room and sat beside Harlee on the bed, finishing the story. Cilia stayed with Harlee, holding her sister tightly most of the night, long after Harlee had fallen asleep.

"I love you, Harlee." Cilia said as she kissed her sister's forehead. Harlee smiled in her sleep and whispered a name, "Maxwell." Cilia eyed her curiously, stroking her hair a few minutes more, before she rose and left Harlee's room.

The following morning, Harlee awoke, alone. She rubbed her eyes as she rose from the bed and placed her feet on the floor. Looking around, she took in a deep breath and smiled as she exhaled. She looked over her shoulder to the far end of the room and saw a closed window. Walking over to it, she opened the window, took in a deep breath of the fresh air, and absorbed the sunshine.

She smiled to herself, at the dreams she had that night. She could remember her friends now, Dahlia, John, Jules, Almalexia, Matthew, and Maxwell. She had seen them, as if her heart had called out for her to remember. She also remembered she left her friends behind, in order to find her sister, who had been away for a long time.

She stared out over the bustling city and wondered when she would see her friends again. In the distance, Harlee was blinded, a bright flash of light striking her in the eyes. Shielding her vision, she stared out carefully as another burst of light struck her in the face. Confused by its meaning, Harlee walked back into her room at the sound of a knock on her door.

"Come in." She answered as the door opened and inside walked Cilia.

"Harlee, you should be getting ready. Queen Auriel wished to spend some time with you, today." Cilia spoke as Harlee remembered.

"Oh no, I am not too late, am I?" She asked. Cilia shook her head.

"Hop in the shower, quickly! I will lay out clothes and help you with your hair. Hurry, go!" Cilia urged as Harlee jumped up from the bed and checking to see where it was, ran to the bathroom in her room.

Inside, Harlee quickly turned on the shower as she disrobed. She let her hair down as she checked the water to make sure it was warm enough. Harlee stepped in and quickly began to wash every surface of her body. Sufficiently clean and scalded, Harlee jumped out of the shower and began drying herself with a towel as she walked out and saw Cilia.

"Hurry!" Cilia urged, showing Harlee the outfit she had readied for her. Blue gown, with silver shoes and gloves. The gown was cut much as the one from yesterday, although this one offered her a slight amount more modesty up top.

Cilia began brushing Harlee's hair out as Harlee sat in the chair and began dressing, the best she could. Once Harlee's hair had fallen flat, Cilia, placed a number of bobby pins in her mouth and began the process of drying and pinning her sister's hair. Harlee began buckling her shoes as Cilia put her hair into a bun and examined it.

"That will have to do. Now let's get you into your dress." She said as she began helping Harlee dress. After a brief few minutes, Cilia was zipping the back of Harlee's dress.

"Let us hurry. We do not want to keep her Highness waiting." She said, grabbing Harlee's hand and leading her down the stairwell. Harlee took special care to ensure that her ladies remained undercover as they stormed the stairs. Once they reached the ground floor, where she had first met Auriel, Harlee was surprised to see the woman, waiting for her, broad smile on her face.

"Good morning, dear." Auriel said, holding her hand out to Harlee. She wore a long dark emerald gown, which shifted color slightly in the light. Harlee and Cilia, both curtsied before Harlee accepted the queen's hand.

"It is a pleasure, to see you again, Queen Auriel." Harlee said. "What did you wish to show me today?" She asked as they walked, armed escorts lining the halls.

"You asked to see outside of my palace. While it is not safe to take you from the grounds, I can at least allow you accompany me, today." She smiled as she led both of the girls down a side hall. "Today, I have been asked to oversee the fights."

"It is such a brutal sport." Cilia spoke, adjusting her glasses. "I am not sure what people find so entertaining about such pointless barbarism." Cilia commented as she walked alongside them.

"My dear, Cilia. It is important for us to appeal to all interests and not just the ones, which we understand. Besides, it is important we test all of our candidates, in order to see which are the most worthy of our mission. We wouldn't want unfit individuals to be selected as guards or other important jobs, where physicality and the ability to fight, are important."

"And what of the other sins? Of what use, do those ruled by Gluttony serve?" Cilia asked.

"Well, let us just say everyone has their uses. Some of us will prove fit for some tasks where others, would simply be wasted. All will be revealed in time." Auriel said as they turned the corner and entered the tunnel leading to the fighters' pit.

Before them, thousands had gathered, to watch the fights taking place on the grounds. Two women, stood in the center of the arena, battling one another. With every blow, those spectating, bid on who they hoped the winner would be.

"See down there?" Auriel asked. "The people of this town have amassed to choose their champions, while over here," she motioned to a separate pool of people, sitting in a reserved, gated off section. "All of them down there, are bidding on which of the fighters, they desire, for their personal stock." Both Cilia and Harlee looked up at Auriel.

"Personal stock?" Harlee asked. Auriel turned and looked at the two of them, broad smile on her face.

"There is a new world order coming. Soon, this world will be saved from the mindlessness of human nature. For millennia, this world has suffered a great disease and I, along with many in my inner circle, have devised a solution to control this spreading illness.

With your sister's help, Harlee, we have begun constructing self-contained, self-sustained, eco safe environments. Within these settlements, our people will govern select populations and keep them from further damaging themselves or this planet. They will have access to clean water, food and shelter, in exchange for providing honest work and valuable resources."

"Resources such as what?" Harlee asked. It was Cilia, who turned to answer.

"There are many things, which humans might provide. The potential is limitless, when it comes to what could be achieved within these settlements." She said, as Harlee watched the conclusion of the fight. One woman stood, hands held high, while the other was assisted out of the ring. Harlee listened as the next fighter was announced and Auriel pointed to a man, who had been seated in the gated section.

"I would suspect that man, just won the bet on that young woman. A fine specimen indeed." Auriel laughed as the next two fighters, both men entered the ring. Harlee sat beside Auriel and Cilia, in the queen's private viewing box. As she watched the next fight, begin, she noticed a familiar face in the crowd, staring directly at her.

"Ah, it appears as though you have an admirer from the wolf pack, Harlee." Auriel cheered as she took note of the boy that was staring at her. Harlee, at once recognized John, as she tried to pretend she did not know him.

"I am not so certain he is staring at me so much as he is admiring you, your highness." She said as she sat back to watch the fight. She was not sure why, but the same voice, which had reminded her of her friends' existence, warned her now, not to reveal their identities.

"You do not know the boy?" Auriel asked.

"I may have run into him before, but there are so many people in this city, I am not sure." Harlee said, unsure of why she lied.

"Too bad. I might have offered him a seat if he had any manners. Not all of the dogs, know when to heel, when to pant, and when to obey. Obedience is a trait, many of the free range humans have yet to attain. It will not be long however, that particular issue will be resolved." Auriel said as she turned her attention back to the pit. The two men below were fighting fiercely. One was clearly to be the victor, however, his prey, using a variety of kicks and grappling techniques, continuously locked up his opponent's body, managing to prolong the fight.

Auriel eyed the underdog curiously and nodded her head. Harlee looked down, at a man who was watching their box. He turned around and began shouting to the man running the auction. Within a few minutes, the match was decided with one flying roundhouse to the face. As the expected victor fell to the ground, Auriel smiled at her intuitive decision. The man who had eyed Auriel now turned and bowed his head.

"Ah, good. My first prize of the day." She chimed as she waited for the next fight to begin.

"What will you do with the man, Queen Auriel?" Harlee asked.

"I already have quite the security detail but I believe this one would make a fine breeder, back on one of my ranches."

Ranches?" Harlee asked. "Do you mean to make him a horse breeder, your highness?" Auriel and Cilia both laughed at Harlee's ignorance. Still under the effects of Auriel's charm, Harlee smiled as they laughed at her.

"Oh no, my dear girl. I mean he will make an excellent breeder, for one of my human ranches. You see, the parents are not the real commodity. It is the children, which bear fruit and profits. Sure, the adults make excellent laborers and can produce a fair amount of blood but it is the children, who taste the sweetest and sell for the most.

That is a rather fine specimen, down there. The stock he produces will grow quite strong and taste heavenly. I will have to see if I can find an equally suitable female, to pair with him. Something strong, but without too many masculine qualities. I want any female stock produced, to maintain the fair, refined qualities of an elegant woman."

"What, exactly, are you looking for?" Harlee asked. "I might lend my eyes." Auriel thought for a moment, catching a glimpse at Harlee.

"Well, much the same as you and your sister, my dear. You two have come from fine stock indeed. Muscular, strong bodies, yet refined, elegant, beautiful to look at, much the same as a fine painting." She went on as the next fight began. Harlee watched on, the entirety of the time, feeling as though she were out of place. Shifting uncomfortably after the match's conclusion, she turned back to Auriel.

"I apologize, Queen Auriel. Might it be all right with you, if I head back? I am afraid this sort of thing is just not for me." Auriel and Cilia both stared at Harlee curiously.

"Harlee, I told Queen Auriel you might be interested in competing." Cilia told her as Harlee turned her attention to them.

"What?" Harlee asked.

"You have spent some time in this city, slaying the supernatural, in search of your sister. It seemed to me, you were a natural born fighter. I thought you would be excited." Auriel said. "That way, you could compete and earn your place. Should you win, I will let you and Cilia stay with me, forever, if you wish." Auriel suggested.

"Might I have a moment to think things over?" Harlee asked.

"Of course, my dear. Feel free to take your time. If you wish to return to the palace, any of my guards will see you safely returned. Please have your answer for me, tomorrow." Auriel requested as Harlee smiled.

"I will. Thank you for your understanding. Cilia, might you accompany me?" Harlee asked. "I was hoping we might have a moment to catch up. It has been nearly ten years." Cilia looked to Auriel, who nodded her head. Cilia rose to her feet, smile on her face.

"Well then, my dear, shall we?" Cilia said, holding her arm out to Harlee, who accepted it.

"My goodness, yes." She laughed and suddenly remembered she rarely did so. It came to her so suddenly, she zoned out for a moment.

"Only he has made me truly laugh." She heard the voice in her head whisper.

"Harlee, are you sure you're alright?" Cilia asked, gazing into her sister's eyes.

"Fine, sorry. I was just thinking about something. Let's be on our way." Harlee said as she took Cilia's arm and they walked back to the main building. As they walked away, Auriel stared at them from over her shoulder as her attendant approached her side.

"Do you wish for me to follow them, my Queen?" He asked her, head stooped low.

"That will not be necessary. They will not leave and once Maxwell is mine, I will have no further use for them." Auriel spoke as she turned her head back towards the pit.

"Harlee, what's the matter?" Cilia asked once they were back in Harlee's room.

"I am not sure, Cilia. I cannot help but feel as though Queen Auriel is not someone who I want to follow. I...I am not sure why I feel that way, but it is as though there is someone in my head, trying to warn me to get as far away from here as I possibly can. I want you to come with me Cilia."

"I know Auriel cannot be trusted, Harlee. I want, very much, to be free of this place myself. I will go with you." She said as Harlee's door was flung open and inside, walked a feminine form, wearing a hoodie jacket, the hood pulled down over her head. Eying the woman curiously, Harlee leaned forward.

"Dahlia?" Harlee asked as the woman closed the door behind her and removed the hood.

"Harlee, Cilia, great to see you both but we've got to move. I am not sure how long the others can keep everyone distracted. We need to move now." She said peeking outside of the door. Turning back, she saw Cilia and Harlee, still staring.

"Don't you want to go live by the sea?" Dahlia asked, snapping Harlee back.

"You're right. Come on, Cilia. It is time to go." She said, grabbing her sister's hand and moving beside Dahlia who was up against the door, holding her hand to her ear.

"Yes, Maxwell, I have it, over." Dahlia said as she continued listening.

"Maxwell's here?" Harlee asked as Dahlia held up one finger, signaling for her to wait.

"Now." Dahlia said as she drew her pistol and moved out the door to the right, taking the stairs. Dahlia kept low, watching ahead as Cilia and Harlee stayed close behind her. "Take off your shoes." She told them as she peeked over the railing. Without question, Harlee and Cilia both removed their stilettos as Dahlia waited for Maxwell to say the word.

"Go." Dahlia said as she vaulted over the rail, landing on the next floor, eight feet below. Harlee and Cilia, both athletic themselves, jumped as well and followed Dahlia towards the elevator.

As they stopped, Dahlia handed her gun to Harlee as she reached into her jacket for a pry bar. Harlee trained the weapon and switched between the two halls. Dahlia readied herself, putting the bar in place as she listened to her earpiece.

They could hear the elevator rising, steadily moving floor by floor. They listened as the elevator rose to their floor and continued moving upward. The moment the elevator passed, Dahlia hit the call elevator button and began pulling back against the doors.

"Help me." She said as the doors began to budge. Cilia moved and pressed against the doors, while Dahlia sat the bar down and pulled as well. As the elevator doors opened, Dahlia wedged her pry bar into the door, propping it open and unzipping her jacket, revealing three tethers and a small bomb, all of which, secured to her torso.

"Hold that elevator." She said as the elevator across the hall dinged. Harlee made certain the elevator was cleared and held it as Dahlia finished strapping her arsenal onto the cables.

"Lobby!" She yelled as she moved away from her contraption. Harlee quickly hit the lobby button, followed by the close doors button as Dahlia slid through. The elevator began to move as Dahlia took back her gun.

"Don't worry, ladies. We'll get you out of here." Dahlia said as she crouched down, waiting for the doors to open.

"How have you been?" Harlee asked, the dopamine high, having yet to wear off.

"Let's talk after we get out of here." Dahlia suggested. Moments later, the doors opened and Dahlia quickly shot the two guards awaiting them, in the heads.

"This way!" Dahlia called, leading them away from the other elevators. Harlee grabbed both guns from the guards and handed one to Cilia.

"You know how to use this?" She asked. Cilia nodded her head, cocking the gun. They followed Dahlia around a couple of corners and waited with her as she crouched down out of the way, behind some sculptures.

"Dahlia, what are we..?" Harlee whispered as Dahlia put a finger to her lips and shook her head. A moment after, Harlee flinched at the sound of an explosion overhead, followed by the groan of metal falling through a wind tunnel. Nearly two dozen armed security guards sprinted passed their hiding place as the main elevator crashed on the lobby floor.

"Now." Dahlia whispered as they ran towards the front, where the guards had just come from. Harlee, Dahlia and Cilia all rounded the corner and saw the front doors, unprotected. As they ran passed the tunnel, which led to the fighters' pit, Harlee was knocked to the ground by a blow to the back of the head. Harlee caught herself and saw as Dahlia stopped and turned.

"What the hell?" Was all Dahlia managed to say as she took five rounds to the chest and stomach.

"DAHLIA!" Harlee screamed, as she was splashed in the face by her friend's blood.

"Don't do anything stupid, Harlee." She heard Cilia say. "The two of us can still walk out of here."

"How could you do that to Dahlia?" Harlee cried as Cilia laughed.

"Are you kidding me?" Cilia said. "I have always hated that bitch." Harlee could hear as the security guards approached from behind.

"You may stand down." Cilia said. "I have the situation contained." She said.

"Why didn't you contain it upstairs? We have casualties because of you." One of the guards yelled back.

"Because I did not want to blow my cover, you dumbass. Had your men done their jobs, there would not have been any casualties. Do you have any idea how much harder it will be to get information from her, now?" Cilia yelled as Harlee, free from Auriel's suggestion, slowly reached for her gun.

"I would advise against that, dear sister. I will shoot you, too, if I have to."

"CRASH!" Everyone looked skyward as glass and gunfire hailed down upon them, while the lights flickered and dimmed. Guards began dropping to the floor all around as Maxwell landed in between Harlee and Cilia.

"Maxwell!?" Cilia yelled as she shot three rounds into his chest. Maxwell, face filled with anger, eyes gleaming with a twinkle of mayhem, calmly approached Cilia, and with little effort, disarmed the woman, before knocking her unconscious.

"Harlee, open this and take one out. Place it over Dahlia's heart." He said handing her a small silver box as more guards poured through the tunnel, Auriel and Balthazar among them.

"Hold your fire!" Auriel said, smiling as she walked. Harlee crawled to Dahlia's side as she opened the box.

"Maxwell, my old friend. It is such a pleasure to see you." Auriel said.

"Harlee, don't move and do everything as I say." Maxwell instructed. "Auriel! Allow me to tend to Dahlia, then let Harlee go!" He commanded, offsetting the tone of the room, as everyone observed his disadvantageous position.

"What reason would I have to do that?" Auriel asked. Maxwell's sinister smile, spread wide across his face, preluding his promise of death and carnage.

"How many years have we been trying to kill one another? One hundred?" He asked, the tone of his voice already lowering.

"Give or take.' Auriel replied. "I seem to remember us both coming close."

"How many of your men, do you suspect will survive, should I resist and begin feeding on them?"

"I would suspect none, knowing you, Maxwell. What is it you are getting at?"

"Simple. Allow me to perform my craft on Dahlia, saving her soul. Next, you will allow Harlee to leave, unharmed and unfollowed. When my people inform me she is safe, I will surrender myself to you. I know you've been dying to get closer to me." Maxwell said. Auriel contemplated the offer.

"Do I have your word?" She asked. Balthazar, stepped forward and looked at Auriel in disbelief.

"Your highness, forgive me but please tell me you are not considering his proposal. Is it not clear he only wants the woman out of harm's way, so he can engage us, without her being caught in the middle? I say we strike now and take them both." Balthazar yelled.

"I SAID STAND DOWN!" Auriel yelled with such force, her voice echoed back multiple times.

"Balthazar." She said in her usual tone. "I will forgive your insolence, this once, simply because you do not know Maxwell as I do. Do not have me mistaken however, when I say the next time you speak out of turn and try to compare your intellect to my own, I will cut out your tongue myself and personally deliver it to your master. Have I made myself clear?" She asked.

"As crystal, your highness." Balthazar spoke as he bowed.

"The thing about Maxwell, not many know, is he and his teacher both, believed honor was what separated them from us. Maxwell's word is worth more than gold. Maxwell, I accept your terms. Perform your ritual and the woman may go. My men will not move until we receive confirmation she is safe." Auriel said.

Maxwell approached Dahlia and Harlee, removing his hat and coat. He placed his hat on Harlee's head and wrapped his coat around her shoulders. Leaning down, he brought his mouth close enough to her ear, she could feel his breath on her neck.

"It is raining outside." He said. Harlee nodded her head as Maxwell stood back up and looked at Dahlia.

"I'm going to need you to fulfill that promise you made to me, Harlee." He told her as he knelt down beside Dahlia. "And ask your forgiveness, if I cannot fulfill my own." Harlee shook her head, tears still falling.

"I won't!" She yelled at him as he drew runes on and above Dahlia with his black chalk. "I won't leave you!" She yelled again. Ignoring Harlee, Maxwell smiled at Dahlia, brushing her cheek with the back of his hand.

"Hey there, Dahlia." He smiled at her. Dahlia had tears in her eyes, as she began losing color in her face and could barely breathe.

"I'm scared." Dahlia replied. "And I'm cold."

"It's alright, Dahlia. You will never have to worry about that. I'm going to take you somewhere nice and warm, where the sun always shines."

"That sounds nice." She said. "May I speak to Harlee?" Maxwell nodded.

"Take as much time as you need." He told her.

"Harleequinn?" Dahlia said weakly, reaching her trembling hand out towards her friend. Harlee shifted forward and grabbed Dahlia's hand.

"I'm here." She said.

"Please forgive yourself. Try to live, for both of us." Dahlia said. "Please, for me?"

"Anything you say, you beautiful bitch." Harlee joked, laughing uneasily as more tears fell from her eyes, splashing Dahlia, who smiled.

"Will you take care of the others for me?" She asked. "They're going to need someone to look after them without myself, Matthew or Maxwell around."

"I will." Harlee said, still crying.

"Good. I am ready, Maxwell. Don't think I've got much left." Dahlia said, tears in her eyes. Maxwell took in a deep breath and closed his eyes as he began to speak.

"I, the Sin Eater, Maxwell Grey, absolve you of your sins and take them in as my own. May you find rest in the kingdom of your Father." He said as he lifted the bread from Dahlia's chest. Dahlia gasped as a trail of ethereal black vapor, rose to be absorbed by the bread, which Maxwell consumed.

"Thank you," Dahlia sighed as she died. Harlee cried for her friend as Maxwell closed her eyes and kissed her on the forehead.

"She lived a hard life, though in comparison to most, she possessed a clean soul. May you find eternal piece, dearest Dahlia."

Maxwell whispered, reaching to Dahlia's ear and removed her earpiece, which he threw to Auriel. The vampire caught the earpiece and held it to her head.

"This is Maxwell, coms compromised, over."

"We read you, Maxwell. What are your orders, over?" A muffled voice answered.

"Dahlia is gone. I am sending Harlee out with her now. Have someone meet her at the front door, to evacuate. Wear your mask, over." There was a long pause before anyone answered.

"Copy."

"It's time for you to go, Harlee. Please hang onto these for me?" He said as he raised his right hand into the air and slowly reached into his vest pocket, removing the rosary and the blanket. Harlee stared up at him, eyes swollen and red. She reached out and gently cradled Maxwell's trinkets in her palms, before placing them into his coat pocket.

"I will, I promise." She said. "You remember your promise too, alright?"

"I won't forget it." He told her as he helped her place Dahlia's body onto her back. As Harlee began walking towards the front door, she turned her head back briefly.

"Don't you dare! Don't make a liar of yourself, Maxwell! Don't you dare break your promise!" She cried as the doors opened and two figures, one likely John, the other, probably Almalexia, helped Harlee and Dahlia escape.

"GO!" Maxwell yelled to them, as they stopped to stare at the thirty plus armed guards. "I SAID GO, DAMMIT! GET HER OUT OF HERE!" He yelled again. Eyes full of pain, Maxwell's comrades left him behind, shutting the door behind them.

"Tell me once they are clear." He spoke into his headset.

"I have eyes on them, Maxwell." Jules spoke, her voice still muffled. "They are clearing the grounds, now. They are all in the car, leaving now. Do you have any further orders?" She asked.

"Harlee already knows." He whispered. "Take care of her. I'm counting on you." He spoke as he pulled out his earpiece and slowly dropped to his knees.

"By my honor, Auriel. I am your prisoner." Maxwell said as Balthazar and thirty-five armed men bound his hands, taking him into custody.

Chapter 17 - I Will Protect You

"Harlee, calm down. We're going to figure this out, alright?" Jules spoke, tears pouring from her eyes. Across the room, Almalexia stared at the floor, lost in thought as John went through each and every weapon at their disposal, reloading each and every last clip, look of murder in his eyes.

"HOW CAN I CALM DOWN!?" She screamed at Jules. "CILIA, JUST...KILLED DAHLIA!" She spoke again as she began pulling her hair. "Oh, god..." She sobbed. "Maxwell...he stayed behind so I could escape. It's all my fault." She began to sink further into despair as Almalexia snapped.

"So then what are you going to do about it!?" She said pushing Harlee back, so their eyes met. "You said it yourself, it's your fault Dahlia is dead and Maxwell is captured. What are you going to do to rectify that?" Jules tried to interject.

"Alma, I don't really think that..."

"Let her speak for herself, Jules." Almalexia said. "She has done a fine job of speaking her mind, thus far." She spoke in a softer tone. Harlee thought for a moment.

"Maxwell made me promise, to leave with all of you. He wanted me to take everyone someplace safe, somewhere far away and to never come back." Harlee spoke.

"And is that what you intend? Do you intend to simply do as Maxwell says, promise or no?" Almalexia asked, her purpose slowly revealing itself. Harlee thought about the succubus' words.

"No." She said lightly.

"I'm sorry, Harlee. I did not quite hear you, beneath your self-loathing and defeatism. Would you mind repeating that again, once you've found your backbone?" Almalexia smiled as Harlee smirked at her.

"I said, NO, you bitch!" Almalexia laughed and gave Harlee a hug.

"I am sorry about Dahlia, but we need Harlee, right now. All of us do, Maxwell included." She said. Harlee nodded her head, remembering how Almalexia remained strong after Matthew's death.

"Right, I never told Maxwell how quickly I'd fulfill my promise. It cannot hurt to take a couple of extra days in between." She said.

"First, we see to Dahlia. Second, we figure out how to save Maxwell." Jules suggested. As everyone agreed, John stood.

"I have an idea, regarding Maxwell." He said.

"By all means, tell us." Almalexia said.

"The conclusion of the Feast is Sunday morning. Saturday night, will be a blood moon. Maxwell will be forced to change that night."

"We need to save him before he does and get him back here." Jules said. John shook his head.

"No. We wait for Saturday evening and break him out. Set him loose, he will target the supernatural over humans. So long as he can smell a vampire, werewolf or spirit infested pimple, he will continue to kill them indiscriminately." John explained, his suggestions invoking looks of horror, from everyone gathered.

"He will kill them all," John spoke, his anger threatening to come unhinged.

"What if he gets out of control?" Harlee asked.

"Now bear with me. What I am about to propose will be high risk but I think we should all infiltrate, Jules too."

"I'm down for that plan." Jules spoke.

"Now, I know there is little evidence it will work, but I believe if Harlee, were to bring Maxwell's heart with her, she could steer him." John said.

"WHAT!?" The room exclaimed.

"John! That's crazy!" Jules said. "All it would take is one stray bullet and both Maxwell and Harlee, would be dead."

"Not necessarily. You see Maxwell's heart is no average heart. The only true method to kill him, is with the dagger. Sure, if the heart is burnt to a crisp, destroyed on a molecular level, or something, he would die. Average objects however, do not seem to have much effect on it. Besides, all we need to concentrate on is keeping Harlee safe. The keepers are the ones, who can manipulate the heart." The room considered the suggestion as a whole.

"It is worth a try, I suppose. It isn't as if we have any other options." Harlee said. "I want to first tend to Dahlia's body. That is something I can do now, while we wait for the blood moon."

"In that regard, I recommend we cremate Dahlia, as we did Father Matthew. That way we won't have to worry about meeting her again, before the next life." John suggested.

"I think that's a sound idea." Harlee agreed. "But I want to have her ashes placed in an urn, for a time. She always wanted to be by the water. The ocean or sea. When there is time, I wish to go to the ocean and spread her ashes."

"That sounds like a fine idea." Almalexia said. "I'm sure Dahlia would appreciate that." As they spoke, Father Raz came down the stairs.

"I am sorry to interrupt and ever more so sorry we keep meeting under such circumstances, but we are prepared when you are." Father Raziel said.

"Thank you, Father. Sorry to keep calling you." Jules said. Father Raz sighed.

"That's the business, I'm afraid. There is always someone passing on before they ought to. I must say however, it grieves me to see so many of your friends, called home of late. I suspect that is why Maxwell decided to remain behind."

"I beg your pardon?" Harlee asked.

"I mean to say, I imagine Maxwell stayed behind, so as to keep anyone else from dying. I wish to tell all of you something, no other living soul knows about Maxwell." Everyone in the room stared at Father Raziel as he sat down.

"Do any of you know why Maxwell is here?" He asked.

"He's never said, only ever making reference to his mission." John said. "Only he has never told me what his mission is."

"I wouldn't expect him to. He never told Matthew either. Matthew had to learn it for himself, by gleaming the pages of a diary. You see, the thing Maxwell has failed to mention, is he has been tasked with hunting and slaying every last original."

"Tasked by who?" Almalexia asked. Father Raziel shook his head.

"Not even Matthew knew that answer, I'm afraid. Maxwell never revealed a name from what he saw."

"How many originals are left?" John asked.

"At least two." Harlee commented.

"Are you sure?" John asked. Harlee nodded.

"Auriel is the first of the vampires. Maxwell, himself told me. Auriel, however, threatened to cut out Balthazar's tongue and deliver it to his master. If Balthazar is the head of one of the elder clans, it would reason his master is either quite old or possibly, the original."

"I agree." Father Raziel said. "The other bit that puzzles me, however is why Maxwell opted to trade himself for you, when he was only a few feet from his objective."

"He told me he wanted everyone taken somewhere safe, far away from this place." She answered.

"Maxwell has lost people before. Why now is he so concerned about casualties?" Father Raziel asked.

"Maxwell has always cared deeply for his children." Almalexia said, "I would not have been surprised had he done the same for John or Jules." She said.

"Harlee, are you one of Maxwell's children?" Father Raziel asked.

"No. I have only known him for a little over a month." She answered. "But I am his keeper now." She said.

"You are?" He asked, smile on his face. "You've known him for a month and he entrusts you with safeguarding his one weakness." Father Raziel allowed the thought to permeate the room for a moment as all eyes turned to Harlee.

"John. How long did it take before you became a keeper?" Father Raziel asked. John thought for a moment.

"I have only been his keeper for two years."

"Seriously?" Harlee asked, realizing what Raziel was leaning towards.

"Harlee, do you know how many women, over the years, have been able to hear Maxwell's heart?" Almalexia bore a morose expression at Raziel's question.

"Several, I'm sure." Harlee stated. "It sounds as though plenty of men have."

"Three." Raziel said.

"Are you sure?" Harlee asked. "Jules can hear it as well."

"I counted Jules. The other two are you and..."

"Willow!" Almalexia growled. "I knew I didn't like that bitch for good reason." She continued.

"Yes, and Willow." Father Raziel confirmed.

"Who is Willow?" Jules asked.

"I've never heard of her either." John said.

"Willow was some half breed harpy, I didn't much care for."

"So all you actually mean to say is, Willow is a woman, who happens to know Maxwell?" Harlee said, smiling at Almalexia. The succubus returned the smile with a playful one of her own as Father Raz continued.

"Regardless, my point is, of the known three, who have heard the heart; you are the only one he has selected to become his keeper. Do you still believe everything is circumstance?" No one held an answer to Raziel's question. The only thing, which was made clear, was they would need to ask Maxwell, himself.

"Father Raziel." Harlee spoke, breaking the awkward silence.

"Yes?"

"When you came down, you said you were ready for us."

"I did."

"We wish to cremate Dahlia but disperse her ashes at a later time. Can you help us?" Harlee asked.

"Do you have an urn?" He asked. Harlee shook her head.

"I am afraid not, Father. You see, I haven't even washed the blood off yet." She said, holding out her hands.

"Oh my word, yes, of course. I should have known. Please forgive me." He said, shaking his head. "Yes, yes, we will begin shortly. Please, come this way, Harlee. Get yourself cleaned up." He said, as Harlee grabbed Maxwell's coat and hat, she followed Father Raziel up the stairs, away from everyone.

"Do you think she'll be alright?" John asked.

"It's going to take her awhile." Jules said. "I remember how I was when Kiefer died. I was not myself for months and my sister did not murder him. I cannot even begin to imagine what she is going through." She finished as Almalexia gently cleared her throat.

"I am not saying this to be callous, cruel or unkind in any way. The best thing we can do for now, is keep Harlee focused on saving Maxwell. Afterwards, there will be plenty of time to grieve, but for now, there is still someone we love in danger." Moving passed the others, Almalexia went upstairs as John and Jules remained.

"John, are you alright?" She asked, after staring at the expressionless boy for a moment.

"Yeah, I'm fine, why?" He answered gruffly. Jules continued to eye him.

"John, it's alright." She said. "I know Father Matthew and you were quite close and you cared for Dahlia. You have been so brave for everyone but it is just me here, now. If you need me, I'm here." She said as she opened her arms to him. John gripped his hands in his jacket pockets tightly as he stared at his feet.

After a few more seconds of silence, John rose from his seat, slowly dragging his feet towards Jules and buried his head into her upper chest. John wrapped his arms around Jules, squeezing her tightly as she cradled his head. Holding onto each other for a few minutes, they eventually released one another.

"Let's go join the others." Jules suggested.

"Alright." John said, following Jules up the stairs.

Harlee stood in the bathroom of the funeral home, washing Dahlia's blood from Maxwell's coat and her own body. Setting Maxwell's coat aside, she stared down at her arms and hands as she scrubbed them vigorously, hoping she might wash away the sensation, itself. As her hands came clean, she removed her dress and began splashing her face and chest. As she scrubbed her hair and scalp in the sink, there was a gentle knock at the door.

"Who is it?" Harlee asked, standing topless in the bathroom.

"It's Jules. I found some spare clothes of Maxwell's in the car. They look somewhat big but I thought they might be preferred over what you have. John says he'll give you his sweatshirt, so you can get out of that dress."

"I'm not covered." Harlee said. "You're alright, though." She said as she continued to scrub her hair. Jules entered the restroom and sat a pile of clothes on the counter.

"We're right outside, whenever you are ready." She said as she shut the door behind herself. A short few minutes later, Harlee walked out, wearing Maxwell's jeans, spare boots and John's hoodie, all of which were too big and yet too tight in particular areas.

"My, that's a new look for you." Almalexia teased as Harlee walked out.

"It'll do until we get back to the hotel." Harlee said. "Let's finish what we came here to do. Maxwell is waiting for us." She said coldly as she walked passed her friends. They followed close behind her as she walked to Father Raziel.

"We are ready." She told him.

"As you wish, please follow me." He said as he led them away to another room.

They all stood around Dahlia, who lay peacefully on the metal slide, leading into the furnace. Father Raziel prayed for Dahlia before he pressed the conveyor button. They all stood, watching, mourning as Dahlia slowly moved into the flames and the metal doors closed.

Later that evening, Harlee sat in her bathrobe, back at the hotel, Dahlia's urn beside her. John and Almalexia, who were both expected back at the Feast, returned and Jules had to return home, leaving Harlee alone. Turning on the television, Harlee began checking and cleaning her equipment. As if by design, she came upon the end of her and Dahlia's favorite movie.

"I hope you were the groom." She whispered to herself as she waited for Dahlia to deliver the rebutting line. Harlee smiled, even though Dahlia's voice never sounded off as she finished cleaning and reassembling her last weapon. Packing her things into her duffle bag, slid into her leather outfit and combat boots, Harlee picked up the hotel room phone.

"Hi, yes, I would like to call a cab." She said. "Yes, that is where I am. Ten minutes? No, that's great, thank you." She said as she hung up the phone, grabbed Maxwell's hat and coat, then left the room. Ten minutes later, Harlee stood outside, waiting as the cab pulled in. As the driver, a brunette woman her age, stepped out, Harlee opened her own door and climbed in. The driver eyed Harlee briefly, before climbing back in.

"Where are we headed tonight, ma'am? The Feast?" The driver asked.

"The House of Fallen Angels, if you please." Harlee asked.

"Are you sure you want to go there?" The woman asked. "That place is still closed down."

"That's alright." Harlee said. "Where I'm going isn't far."

"Alright then, if that's what you want." The driver said as she hit the fare button and shifting the car into gear, began driving. Harlee stared at the window while her mind drifted away with her thoughts. The driver attempted to speak with her on many occasions though Harlee was far from her reach.

"Miss! We're here!" The driver yelled again, startling Harlee.

"Oh, I'm sorry." She said, reaching into her bag.

"Don't worry about it." The driver said. "You seem as though you needed some help. Would you like me to walk with you? It's not safe out, tonight and we girls have got to look out for one another."

"Thank you but I will be alright." Harlee said, climbing out of the car and swinging her bag over her shoulder, shut the door. Harlee stared at the church, which was still surrounded by caution tape. She stared for several minutes, wrapping Maxwell's' coat around her tightly, as the evening chill sank in.

Turning from the cathedral, Harlee walked down towards the storage container, behind which, was one of the manholes Harlee could use to access the catacombs. Once she arrived, she carefully searched about, ensuring she had not been followed, before proceeding to climb down. She walked the familiar stretch by memory, arriving at the gate just as she pulled out Maxwell's keys and fumbled with the lock. Harlee opened the gate, locked it behind herself and traveled to Maxwell's sanctuary.

She sat down her duffle bag inside the altar room and unzipping it, pulled out Maxwell's hat. Placing it on her head, she walked to the altar, holding Maxwell's cask. Harlee gently placed her hand upon it and felt an immense surge of pain, flow from it.

"They're torturing you, aren't they?" She asked as she mustered her courage and placed both hands on the box. She felt the power of Maxwell's collected sins, coursing through her, burning her from the inside out, as she forced the clasps open, revealing the beating heart within.

While the pain subsided slightly, she removed her hands form the box and could see the heart's anxious rhythm, as it fought to preserve its master. Harlee could feel it, calling to her in pain, seeking comfort. She plunged her hands into the box, grimacing as the pain returned.

Scooping the heart from the chest, she held it securely in her palms, staring at it. It felt warm in her hands and seemingly cooed at her touch. Harlee stepped back and slid down the wall, laying her head on her bag as she outstretched her legs.

"I will protect you." She whispered to the heart as she pressed it up against her own. "I will keep you safe." She said as she curled up inside Maxwell's coat, tipped his hat over her eyes and continued to lay with the heart against her breast, as she fell asleep.

Chapter 18 – Start With the Liver

Good evening, Maxwell." Auriel said as she entered the cell. Her gown was black, though as it caught the light from different angles, the fabric turned to red. She approached Maxwell, who was hanging six inches from the ground, shackles around his ankles, wrists and throat. He remained silent and motionless, his head down, eyes closed as he hung, completely bereft of clothing save his boxer briefs.

"A fine specimen would you not agree, doctor?" Auriel said, turning to a tall, blonde haired woman, in a lab coat.

"Quite, Queen Auriel. Not only is the subject in superb, physical condition but it also continues to yield further quandaries to rouse my interests." The scientist spoke.

"I must admit, I've a few inquiries of my own." Auriel began as she placed her hand on Maxwell's bare chest and began slowly running it down his body. The doctor stared at Maxwell platonically as Auriel's fascinated eyes, flickered with hunger.

"So far, I have taken blood and tissue samples. Extracting saliva has proved itself to be a challenge."

"Yes, I heard about your last assistant." Auriel said. "We are obtaining a suitable replacement for you, now."

"It is of no consequence. I only hope the next, handles my research more carefully." She said. "Although, the event did produce yet another quandary, which..." The doctor trembled as she considered it. "Has me most excited to explore." She finished.

"I can tell." Auriel commented. "What did you discover?"

"To begin with, after we had taken the blood and tissue sample, my assistant proceeded to attempt taking the saliva sample. That was when the subject lurched forward, unexpectedly and tore out my assistant's throat. As I watched in awe, blood spraying in every direction, I noticed the subject's wounds, healed almost immediately upon ingestion of the flesh."

"He feeds on our kind, to heal himself." Auriel summarized.

"Not just that, shortly after, the subject gained an increase in strength, nearly breaking free from its chains. I must admit, the event left me in a rather...delicate state." She said. "Beyond that, however, we have found the subject has additional teeth, hidden beneath the gum line, which extend when necessary. There is also an oddity with the lower mandible, where utilizing a secondary set of mastoid muscles, offers a much larger bite radius."

"These extra teeth, you speak of. Are they resembling of our own fangs?"

"Not exactly, my queen. While our fangs are meant for piercing, his are meant for shear evisceration."

"Then they are comparable to a lycanthrope's." Auriel suggested.

"Based on what little data we have of their kind. I am suggesting the subject to have more in common with the Reavers."

"That's not possible!" Auriel declared. "Mother ordered those abominations, be wiped out over a millennia ago. Maxwell has not even been around for much more than a couple of centuries. Those creatures were too unpredictable, too unruly. They not only cannibalized but they fed on everything else as well." Auriel said.

"I am not disagreeing with you, your highness; however, the data does not lie and is suggesting the subject is both human and Reaver."

"Not to mention, the Sin Eater and more importantly, Grey's son." Auriel spoke. "One vessel, representing all four plains."

"Can you imagine the potential of this subject?" The doctor asked.

"Can you imagine the power?" Auriel spoke in admiration as she again placed both hands on his naked flesh.

"My queen, if I may, what does Mother demand we do with it?" Auriel pulled her hands from Maxwell's stone chiseled abdominals and backed away.

"When he wakes continue your experiments. Make me aware before you do, however. I wish to watch."

"Of course, my queen. You shall be notified the moment the subject is prepared."

"Excellent." Auriel said as she turned and left the cell. As the scientist returned to her clipboard, taking various notes as she paced around Maxwell, the elusive man slowly opened his eyes and smiled.

The following morning, Maxwell awoke to the feeling of a coarse sponge, scraping against his skin and his briefs, being pulled down near his ankles. Maxwell opened his eyes to see the scientist with a new assistant, this one a smaller brown-haired woman.

"Ma'am, this subject is rather...well..um" The young woman began.

"I know! I am honored to have such a perfect specimen, to experiment with." She said. The assistant looked back to Maxwell's naked body and shrugged at the missed message, as she moved to scrub Maxwell's other regions.

"Did they warn you about what happened to the last assistant, who got too close?" Maxwell asked, startling the two women.

"Ah, excellent. We can now begin. Would you please inform Queen Auriel, that the subject is awake?"

"Yes, doctor." The woman answered, dropping the sponge back into the bucket, peeled off her gloves and moved quickly to the door.

"How is the subject feeling this morning?" The blonde-haired woman asked.

"Doctor, please, call me Maxwell."

"I prefer to remain impersonal with my test subjects." She replied. "It helps to keep things uncomplicated."

"That's a shame, doc." Maxwell said. "You see, the trouble is, I'm a rather complicated man." He said as he smiled at her.

"I am unsure if you are making an attempt at flattery but I assure you, it will not work." The woman said. Maxwell looked over her for a moment as she adjusted her coat, making sure the creases aligned evenly across her shoulders. He smiled as he tilted his head to the side and began moving his lips, as if talking to himself.

"What is it?"

"Come closer, I do not wish to say it aloud." Maxwell said.

"I am not falling for that." The scientist replied.

"Then stay just beyond my reach but allow me to whisper in your ear." The doctor moved closer to Maxwell, extending her ear to him. "I was just admiring your flawless, mathematical symmetry." He whispered.

"What?" She replied, stumbling and catching herself on Maxwell's chest.

"It's alright. I promise not to hurt you. I must admit, other than Auriel, it has been a long time since I have encountered another pureblood, or fair ones, as they use to be called." The doctor pulled away, cheeks blushed and shook her head.

"I am not a pureblood. I was sired, about twenty years ago."

"Truly? You could easily pass for one. You see, in my youth they were called the fair ones, due to the fact from an anthropological standpoint, they were all physically flawless. Every curve, every line was perfectly designed, just as a masterfully carved diamond. You reminded me of them." The doctor's cheeks grew darker in shade as she stepped back further, though her hands never left Maxwell's chest.

"You mistook me as one of them?" She smiled. Maxwell smiled as well, shrugging the best he could.

"Do you wish to know another secret about me, doctor?" Maxwell asked. The doctor nodded her head as she leaned in closer again, to listen as Maxwell kissed her cheek. She backed away again, leaving his side this time, an offended look on her face, her hand covering the cheek Maxwell had kissed. The cell doors opened and in walked Auriel with the assistant.

"Ah." Auriel began. "How is our subject, this morning?" The doctor looked from Auriel to Maxwell and back.

"The subject, Maxwell, has just awoken. We will finish preparing him now and continue with our tests." She said, turning her eyes back to the man, who still bore his shameless smile.

"Good to hear." Auriel said. "If you do not mind, I will be overseeing your tests today."

"Not at all, your highness. Perhaps the subject will be more cooperative, in your presence." She said as Auriel moved to the desk and sat in one of the two chairs in the room.

"I wouldn't count on it, doc." Maxwell whispered to her as she drew close.

"Amelia." She whispered back. "My name is Amelia." Maxwell smiled as the doctor and her assistant, finished with the sponge. As they began to raise his briefs, Auriel raised her hand.

"That will not be necessary." She spoke. Amelia and her assistant nodded their heads, before resuming their torture. For hours, Maxwell was electrocuted, burned and stabbed, until he hung loosely from his chains. Each time, Amelia would cease, she took notes as Maxwell's wounds healed.

Auriel stepped forward, approaching Maxwell. Tracing her fingers across his lower back, over his hipbone and up his torso, she stood in front of him. Staring into his eyes, she smiled as she toyed with him.

"What is the matter, Maxwell? Are you tired?" She stabbed her nails into his chest and raking them down, left four trails of blood all the way down his torso, stopping at his pelvis. Maxwell merely stared back at her, making no reaction or notice of what she had done.

"The wounds are taking longer to heal." The assistant observed as the flesh slowly grew back this time. Amelia, curious, approached Maxwell and observed the reaction.

"What is the matter, Maxwell?" She asked with concern in her voice. "Why are you not regenerating as quickly?" She thought for a moment and staring at the man's body, realized the amount of nutrition it must take to maintain such physiology.

"You said he never lies, correct?" Amelia asked.

"Never." Auriel answered.

"Maxwell, is the reason you are not healing properly, because you have not fed, recently?" She asked.

"I would suspect so." He answered. Amelia turned her gaze back towards Auriel.

"Your highness, might we give him something? Food, blood, anything so we might proceed with our experiments?" Auriel thought the request over for a moment, before answering.

"If you feel fit to feed your lab rat, why not give him some of yours?" She suggested. Amelia swallowed hard, remembering what had happened to her previous assistant. She looked up at Maxwell, whose wounds were finally healing over. Amelia pulled her hair to the side, exposing her bare neck.

"Maxwell, do I have your word you will not harm me, should I offer you some of my blood?" Maxwell's eyes flicked to her curiously. His eyes locked onto hers, his piercing gaze filled with the promise of danger, as a wounded beast, which had not lost its wild luster.

"You have my word." He said after a long hesitation. Amelia stepped forward as Auriel and the assistant, both stared in anticipation at what was about to happen. Amelia placed her hands on Maxwell's shoulders and closing her eyes, slowly brought her neck to Maxwell's mouth.

Slowly, Maxwell's fangs extended as he gently placed them against Amelia's neck. The scientist twitched from the contact but soon found the embrace rather enjoyable. Closing her eyes, she allowed the sensation to flow through her, experiencing a vampire's ecstasy. She gripped his shoulders tightly as she felt her knees buckle.

Amelia's head lay against Maxwell's upper chest, listening to the inner workings of his body. As she rested on the man's chest, she could not help but notice that even though he possessed a pulse, his heart did not beat with a normal rhythm. Maxwell released her and she stumbled, catching herself around his waist. Her assistant ran to her side and helped her to her feet. Amelia looked up at Maxwell and saw his wounds had already healed.

"Intriguing." Auriel said as she watched. "Are you so compassionate to all of your victims, I wonder?"

"For you, Auriel, I would gladly tear out your throat." Maxwell assured her, smile on his face. "I give you my word." He said as Auriel smiled in amusement.

"Continue your experiments. I want a full report on his biology, recovery, every detail, no matter how simple it may seem." She said as she walked from the cell. Amelia slowly moved over to a chair and sitting in it, stared at Maxwell.

"Why not kill me?" She asked him.

"I can tell you are not evil." He said. "Call it what you may, but I can sense the sins of your once mortal soul and they are not enough for me to condemn you." He said.

"Is perhaps one of your abilities, as the Sin Eater, to sense the sins of those you meet?" She asked.

"Perhaps. More importantly, I gave you my word. That alone, was enough of a reason, to be gentle." He said. Amelia placed her hand over the wound in her neck, which partially drained of blood, had yet to heal.

"Why is your word so important to you?" She asked.

"It separates me from the rest of the monsters." He told her. "That and my choice to rise above the dominance of man. Each of us can choose, whether we live as the monsters from our childhood terrors or as those who reside among the humans, bound by certain oaths. This is my way. It is the way I preserve, in a world of darkness and pain." He answered.

Pulling out her clipboard, Amelia began jotting down notes. She made sure to include their discussion, minus his flirtation. Most importantly, she described the sensation she felt from Maxwell feeding on her. Noticing her prolonged absence, Maxwell spoke to her.

"Do you not have work to do?" He muttered.

"In a moment." She said. "Let's just say, I am more tired now than I had expected to be. Courtney, have you ever been fed upon?" Her assistant nodded her head nervously.

"Yes, ma'am. Are you going to feed on me, now?" She spoke, clearly afraid as she pulled her collar down. Amelia looked up at Maxwell and considered what he had said. Searching her feelings, Amelia attempted to remember how her life had been, before being turned.

"No dear. Please do not worry. I will not feed from you, without your permission. I wish to show the patient, we are not all as we are made." She smiled as she resumed jotting notes. Courtney relaxed as she looked at Maxwell.

"Are you alright?" She asked.

"You don't need to worry about me, either. I do not feed on humans." He told her. "Not so long as I can avoid it." He muttered to himself, under his breath, unsure of whether or not, his desire had ever been broken.

Amelia looked up from her notes and stared at Maxwell, whose head hung. She looked and saw Courtney was also studying the man, though she suspected her interest was less than scientific. Amelia looked up from her notes and eyed the man.

"Maxwell?" She asked. "Why is it so vital to you, to maintain the illusion of humanity?" Amelia asked.

"Do I have to answer?"

"I suppose not, though the distraction might prolong our next experiment." She suggested, holding up her long list of tasks.

"You're not going to pluck out my eyeballs, are you?" He asked.

"No, no eyeballs, but the queen has requested we test your healing capabilities on other tissues. She has asked, we perform surgery, start by damaging organs and even removing them to see if they can regenerate." Amelia said, smiling.

"Alright then, start with the liver." He grumbled.

"Maxwell! Give me something more than that!" Amelia and Courtney both eyed him, irritably. Maxwell sighed as he readied himself.

"I was human once." He said.

"You were?" Courtney asked.

"I was. I had a family, friends and a life."

"Is your family the reason you cling to your humanity?"

"Perhaps." He said. "It is an explanation, I had not considered."

"What do you believe?" Amelia asked.

"Another time. Can we proceed or may I rest?" He asked. Amelia turned in her chair, looking at the clock.

"Would you be willing to give us a saliva test, now that we've gotten to know one another better?" Maxwell thought to himself for a moment.

"Only if you're willing to do it." He said. Amelia thought for a moment before shrugging her shoulders and grabbing the swab and vial.

"I believe we have established trust." She said as she walked up to him. Grabbing a small stepladder, Amelia placed it in front of Maxwell and climbed up to the first step, placing her at eye level with him. Staring deep into his eyes, she pulled up the swab.

"Please open your mouth." She said. Maxwell opened his mouth, allowing Amelia to lightly swab the inside, before placing it into the container.

"Thank you." She said. "That was not so bad, was it?"

"Are the rest of your tests, as friendly?" Amelia walked over to her desk and picking up her clipboard, looked through her notes.

"Do you have anything in mind, Courtney?"

"When was his last physical?" She joked and immediately blushing, looked around the room before sipping from her coffee cup. Amelia grabbed a pair of latex gloves from her desk and began sliding them on.

"You cannot be serious?" Maxwell growled as Courtney looked to Amelia, dejectedly.

"No. I was joking. We can place some probes into your muscles and run some electro stimuli tests."

"Sure, why not? It might be fun, I suppose." Amelia nodded to Courtney, who began to ready the machine.

"I assure you, it will not hurt more than a little." Amelia said. The remainder of the day, Amelia and Courtney performed as many non-evasive treatments as possible, moving through their list. By evening, they called it a night but were soon to return, many grisly tasks awaiting them.

"Why have you not done as I asked!?" Auriel yelled the following morning, upon receiving Amelia's report. Amelia, who was knelt at the foot of stairs, leading to the throne, gently lifted her gaze to meet Auriel's.

"Your highness." She began, Courtney having not accompanied her. "Everything we have done was on the list of things you assigned us. We have merely gone about the path of least resistance, to gain a rapport with the subject."

"I did not ask you to build a relationship with Maxwell. I ordered you to learn all of his secrets."

"Yes, your majesty. It would seem many of the subject's secrets, are yet locked away in his mind. My professional opinion is he will be more cooperative, with only a small amount of manner." Amelia said as Auriel glared at her, from her throne.

"I see in your report, you were able to successfully obtain the saliva sample."

"Yes, your highness. The subject agreed to provide it, as a term to our mutual understanding."

"I see. Very well then, proceed with your work. I will be by to oversee your progress, myself. You are dismissed."

"Yes, your majesty. Thank you." Amelia said as she rose from her knees and walked back to Maxwell's cell. Once there, she showed her badge to the guard, who swiped his card in the door and opened it, allowing her to enter.

"Good morning, Maxwell?" Amelia said as she walked in to see he was already staring at her.

"Good morning, Amelia. I thought perhaps you had forgotten me and left me alone with your assistant." He joked. "She left as well. Test results came back, apparently."

"You would find for me, it is rather difficult to forget such a remarkable test subject. You are truly the find of a lifetime." She remarked as she moved to her workstation, setting down her clipboard, which contained a highlighted list of tasks for the day. Amelia turned back towards Maxwell and sighed.

"Her majesty, demands we begin with the live dissection. She wishes to know the extent of your healing prowess. I am to administer blood packets, to keep you alive." She said as she moved to her table of surgical tools, placing her hands upon it, her stomach churning.

"Maxwell, I do feel poorly about this." Amelia said as she prepared her surgical tools. "Please do not think less of Courtney and I. We do not have any other choice. If we disobey the queen, she will kill us both." She told him. "If you would allow it, I will give you something to numb the pain, morphine, sufentanil." She suggested.

"If you did, Auriel would be angrier." Maxwell sighed. "No, I think she wishes me to suffer."

"Please, Maxwell. I do not want to do this." She muttered, looking down at her feet.

"I do not blame either of you." He said. "I must warn you, if things go south, do not hesitate to run."

"What do you mean?" She asked.

"Has Auriel told you what she hopes to discover?" Maxwell asked.

"Not exactly, no."

"There is another side to me. One Auriel and only a few others have ever seen and lived."

"The Reaver half?" She guessed to which Maxwell nodded.

"Auriel is hoping to discover what causes it to come out." He said. "If you happen to find something, don't hesitate, run."

"I must admit, Maxwell. You seem to have me rather conflicted between the two halves of my own nature." She told him. "The scientist in me finds you absolutely fascinating, mixed with the vampire's detachment; I simply wish I could dissect you."

"But..." Maxwell said hopefully.

"But you have managed to appeal to the human within me, and I now find myself conflicted." As they stood, talking to one another, Courtney entered the room, bruises on her face, arms and legs, extremely shaken as she walked in, carrying several folders. Amelia and Maxwell turned their gaze on the frightened woman as Auriel entered the room behind her.

"I have the test results, ma'am." Courtney said, tears in her eyes, her voice trembling.

"Thank you, are you alright?" Amelia asked, accepting the documents as Auriel walked up to Maxwell.

"You forcibly fed on her, didn't you?" Maxwell asked.

"I was feeling peckish, so I thought I might grab a snack. What happened is her own fault for resisting." She said as Courtney, still quivering moved away, holding her injured arm and trying to hide her bruised face. "I was preparing to tear out her throat and drain her for the insult but then I noticed the files she had dropped and my day became much more exciting." She said as Amelia's eyes grew wide, while looking over the data.

"Maxwell, your blood changes shape, consistency and make up, rendering you immune to the venoms we administered two nights ago." Amelia said. "There is only one creature I know, which can do such a thing."

"A shifter." Auriel commented. "And a powerful one at that. Tell me Maxwell, where is it you found the time to snack on such a rare creature? We know based upon recent events you metabolize the blood you drink within twenty-four hours. This leads me to a theory of my own." Auriel said, her face only inches away from Maxwell's.

"Tell me, Maxwell. When you killed the original shifter, Caines, all of those years ago, did you happen to feed on him?" She asked, sinister smile on her face.

"What are you suggesting, your highness?" Amelia asked.

"What I am saying, is when Maxwell feeds on a lower creature, such as yourself or your assistant here, he rapidly burns off the blood. In the case of an original, such as myself and perhaps one of the old bloodlines, the effect seems to bind itself to him. Tell me Maxwell, if I were to allow you to feed from me now, what new power would you gain?"

"It wouldn't matter if I ventured a guess." He answered.

"And why is that?" She asked leaning closer.

"Because the day I feed from you, is the day I rip out your heart and eat it!" He growled convincingly at her, as he pulled against the neck shackle as hard as he could. The tip of his nose nearly touching hers, Auriel smiled, but remained unfazed.

"Well now, what a shame. Amelia was just telling me how mannerly you have become of late. I suppose I will have to do something about that attitude of yours." She spoke as she forced her hand, through Maxwell's left oblique, causing him to groan in pain, saliva seething through his clenched teeth.

"Queen Auriel!" Amelia moved towards her. "Please don't kill him." She said. Auriel laughed as she pulled her hand out, one of Maxwell's kidneys in her hand. Maxwell coughed and wheezed as Auriel reached out with her filled and bloody hand.

"Bring the table." She spoke as Amelia moved the table in closer. As she reached Auriel, the vampire queen plopped Maxwell's kidney on the table and grabbed a retractor, using it to hold Maxwell's wound open.

"Have I ever told you, Maxwell, I once spent quite some time, studying the human body?"

"I...hadn't...figured you...the intellectual." Maxwell continued with his typical snarky humor as he groaned in pain. Auriel smiled at his insult as she continued to peek around inside his wound, which continued to bleed.

"Doctor, administer a blood pack." Auriel ordered as she continued to dig around inside Maxwell's open wound. Courtney stood in horror as Amelia, using her supernatural agility, quickly fetched the blood pack. Holding it up to him, Maxwell turned his head away from it.

"Maxwell, you need to feed." Amelia told him.

"I would rather die." He said grabbing the pack in his teeth and wrenching his head, threw it away. Auriel stood, stabbing her fingernails into other parts of Maxwell's body, leaving behind several stab wounds.

"So you refuse to feed? You think your rebellion will make me stop? You think it makes you better in some way? Human, come here." Auriel commanded. Courtney slowly approached. As she grew near, she bowed her head.

"Yes, my queen." She said. "How may I serve you?" She still shook visibly in the queen's presence.

"Offer yourself to Maxwell." She commanded. Courtney looked up at Auriel.

"But my queen, I am already so depleted and drained of blood." She whimpered. Without warning, Auriel quickly jerked Courtney upright, dislocating the woman's arm as she bit into her neck. Courtney cried in pain as Auriel forced her against Maxwell's face. Maxwell lurched back the best he could as Auriel laughed.

"What's the matter, Maxwell? Don't enjoy the taste of human?" She laughed as she turned to Amelia.

"Feed on him." She demanded as she herself, tossed Courtney aside and bit into his chest. Maxwell groaned as Amelia reluctantly approached.

"Please, your majesty, allow me to tend to my assistant." Amelia asked as Auriel stared at her, eyes glowing red.

"I command you to feed on Maxwell!" Auriel growled in her dark tone, seizing control of Amelia's body. She walked towards Maxwell, emptied of her own will. She approached Maxwell from behind and kneeling down, wrapped her arms around his waist and sank her fangs into his right hip. As the first taste of Maxwell's rich blood, touched her tongue, an entirely new world of sensation flooded Amelia's brain, overwhelming her. As her captive persona was forcibly released from Auriel's compulsion, she backed her head away, though driven by personal desire, maintained her grip on his waist.

"Why have you stopped?" Auriel asked as she looked at Maxwell's blood. Staring up at Maxwell, she rolled his head from side to side.

"What is it, which gives you such intoxicating flavor?" She mused as she allowed his head to drop. "Amelia, take care of things here." Auriel said, leaving the room. Amelia immediately moved to Courtney's side and made sure to help her stop the bleeding.

"Stay here." She said, moving away from her and turning to Maxwell. "Your wounds!" She exclaimed as a black substance, seethed from his wounds. Amelia quickly eyed the wound to his side and saw the blackness had flooded the entire area. The lights in the lab, began to flicker and fade, as Maxwell opened his eyes, which had begun to change color.

"The organ will grow back. Please move the instrument." He groaned as the black fog, began to pour from his body and Amelia saw his skin begin to churn. Amelia quickly removed the retractor and watched as the fog, formed around the hole, resealing it. Blinking his eyes several times, they slowly reverted back to their regular color.

"What are you, Maxwell?" Amelia asked, fascinated by the man.

"Your...assistant?" He groaned weakly, his face still covered in her blood. "I didn't?"

"No, that was the queen. She will live." Amelia said. "Maxwell, do you need to..." She unhooked the top two buttons of her blouse and slid the collar of her shirt away. "Do you want to feed on me?" She asked, pulling the shirt lower, exposing the top of her chest. She pulled out a handkerchief and wiped the blood from Maxwell's face, locking eyes with him as she neared. She stepped up, bringing the nape of her neck to his lips.

"Go on." She said. "I don't mind so long as it's you. I trust you." Maxwell closed his eyes, opened his mouth and sank in his fangs. Amelia closed her eyes and moaned excitedly as she felt the bite on her flesh. She tightly gripped Maxwell's hips and pressed her body tightly against his. She fully embraced the ecstasy she felt, her knees buckling as she felt him drink her away.

Maxwell released her and Amelia slowly made her way down Maxwell's body. Stumbling backwards, she made her way to her chair and sat. Courtney, staring between Maxwell and Amelia laughed exhaustedly.

"You can feed on me, too. That was hot." She said as Amelia nodded her head. Maxwell, still hanging from the chains, spoke.

"Tomorrow evening, you two need to run as far from me as you possibly can." He mumbled.

"What happens tomorrow, night?" Courtney asked. Maxwell averted his eyes, ashamed and not wanting to answer.

"Maxwell?" Amelia began, "It's the Reaver, isn't it?" Maxwell lowered his gaze as he gripped his fists tightly.

"Tomorrow night...The 'other' me will be freed. Not even these chains will stop me, and I will kill everything, which gets in my way."

Chapter 19 – It Is Time

Harlee sat in the car, staring towards the largest building in Sin City where the Feast was being held. John and Jules had gone in ahead of the others, communicating through the earpieces Maxwell had given them. Almalexia sat in the front, behind the wheel. Harlee held her hand over the left side of her chest, where Maxwell's heart had been secured.

"We are going to save him." Almalexia spoke, looking to Harlee through the rear view mirror. Harlee nodded her head as John's voice came on.

"We've both made it through the gates. Security is tight, to say the least." He said.

"I am walking up the west side, now." Jules said. "There is a long line of people, waiting to get inside the nightclub."

"Avoid the nightclub," Harlee warned. "It's a trap."

"Alright." Jules answered curiously.

"Almalexia." John said.

"I am here, John."

"There are not nearly as many people here tonight. I thought the last night was supposed to feature the main event?"

"It is, John. The chosen thralls will likely have been taken somewhere Auriel and Balthazar can initiate them, where no one would notice." The coms went quiet for a moment as Harlee continued to stare at the tower, the moon rising behind it.

"They are on top of the skyscraper." Harlee said. Almalexia turned to look at Harlee, who had leaned forward in her seat, to better stare.

"That makes the most sense." John spoke.

"Agreed." Jules said. Almalexia thought for a moment as she contemplated their next move.

"All of the guards on the ground will be the youngest of the wolves or hired humans. All of the elders will be at the ceremony. I say we find a weak point, exploit it and move in. John, any ideas?" Almalexia asked.

"If we enter on my side, I can get us close enough to take one of the guards down. We won't have much time but it might be enough to get us in." He said. "I will lose my cover but if we don't think of anything else, we might lose our chance to save Maxwell."

"Alma, if you do this, you place your entire coven at risk." Jules warned. "You can sit this one out." Almalexia gripped the steering wheel tightly, causing it to groan.

"I know but I have no choice." She said. "I only hope wearing a mask will be enough." Her body visibly tense. Harlee could feel Maxwell's heart pulse aggressively in her jacket. Even Almalexia sensed it, turning her head to stare at Harlee curiously. Again, the heart pounded against

Harlee's own, the reason growing clear as she looked up to Almalexia and saw the blood moon rising above the tower.

"It is time." Harlee said. Almalexia turned and seeing the moon, stepped out of the car.

"We move according to plan. John, wait for us to enter. If everyone is distracted upstairs, then Harlee will be free to roam. With our V.I.P. passes, we should easily grow close. John, Jules, wait for us by the entrance to the tower. We will be there shortly." Almalexia said as Harlee opened her door and followed behind.

"Alma, do you think you could attract multiple guards together?"

"I do. For what purpose?"

"We are going to be met with some heavy resistance and none of us has a weapon. It would help if someone could gain us an edge." Jules suggested.

"Done. I will lure them somewhere, we will be less noticeable. We are nearing the gates now. Let us know what you come up with." Almalexia said as she and Harlee reached the gates.

"Passes please?" The guard spoke as both women flashed their passes, smiles on their faces. The guard looked over them and nodding his head, motioned for them to pass through the metal detector. Passing through, they continued toward the back of the courtyard as Jules broke the silence.

"Alright, I have eyes on four guards, on the east side by the slave pits."

"We are on our way." Almalexia said as she and Harlee moved with purpose, through the grounds, passing a number of sinners, doing just that, in unhindered excess. They quickly made their way to the slave pits, where they saw John and Jules, waiting for them, watching the commotion.

"Stay out of the way." Almalexia spoke. "Jules, come with me. You and I are going to lure them towards the pit. John, Harlee, help us ambush them. Lock them up. John, I want you to take their clothes and make it look as though nothing has happened."

"Understood." John and Harlee said as Jules and Almalexia walked away.

"This way." John said, grabbing Harlee's hand and leading her away towards the tent. They watched from a distance as Almalexia and Jules flirted with the men, Almalexia, likely dousing them all with her pheromones as they spoke. After a moment, one of the guards pointed towards the tent, Harlee and John were hiding in. Without incident, all four men began acting strangely and followed the two women as they approached.

"Get behind something." John said as he and Harlee both moved behind various supply containers.

"Oh, baby, I hope you two are ready for a rough night." One of the men spoke as Almalexia was forced up against a crate.

"Hey, who says you get first grabs." One of the men complained, grabbing onto his friend who was already kissing on Jules' neck.

"Boys." Jules interrupted. "Who said anything about taking turns? We are all professionals here. You're good at pointing your gun but I aim to prove I'm better at firing it." She said reaching out and grabbing hold of the other man's groin. The one kissing her, continued.

"Dirty freak." Harlee whispered to herself as she watched. Taking the hint, the fourth man in the group, began assisting with Almalexia's clothes. As Almalexia was forced harder against the crates, she caught a glimpse of Harlee's hiding place and winked. Harlee, seeing all four weapons, out of someone's hand, moved into position and saw John opposite of her, ready to strike.

Quickly, they pounced on their prey, striking one opponent each, in the back of the head, knocking them unconscious as Almalexia and Jules, incapacitated the other two. Harlee smiled, as she felt her adrenaline begin to flow but also felt as Almalexia's toxin, hit her. She stumbled slightly, bumping into John, whom she noticed had also been affected, from where her hand accidentally landed. They both felt their hearts race as Almalexia and Jules shook them out of it.

"Now, you two, this is not the time." Jules said as she shook John, who stared at her, dreamily. Almalexia approached, slapping the both of them.

"Sorry about that." She said. "But we don't have time. John get dressed, we have to go." John and Harlee nodded their heads as John quickly began to undress. As Harlee and Almalexia, drug the bodies away, Jules stopped and smiled at John as he stripped. He stared at her and Almalexia grabbing the last guard, nudged Jules as she passed her.

"I will slap you, too." She said as they each picked up a weapon before looking outside carefully and moved towards the entrance of the building. John, who had dressed quickly, was straightening his tie as he followed them.

"If there's trouble, I will be right behind you." He told them as they moved inside. Harlee placed her hand over Maxwell's heart, which had begun pounding more strongly than before, causing her to wear down.

"Are you alright?" Jules asked.

"Keep moving." Harlee said. "Maxwell is in distress."

"It is likely what we are about to encounter is no longer Maxwell." Almalexia warned. "Remember, he will attack the supernatural before he attacks humans."

"But what about you?" Jules asked. Almalexia sighed as she secured her ski mask.

"He is fast. Maybe faster than I am, in that state. I have no way to be sure but if Matthew is to be believed, Maxwell's mind will be overblown and the beast will be stupid. This will give me a decent advantage. No one is going to shoot me over a massive, ravenous monster, chasing me." She smiled confidently as they moved on, keeping low to stay out of sight.

"Harlee, where do you suspect they have taken him?" Jules asked. Harlee thought briefly and pointed towards the far east wall.

"There is a stairwell, leading down, that way. I would bet they have him underground, where he would be easier to contain." They all ducked down as they heard a man scream in terror. Several more armed guards approached as an average height, brown-haired woman, wearing a purple blouse, grey skirt and high heels, ran to meet the guards.

"You cannot approach the subject! If he feeds on one of you, he will only grow stronger. The chains are barely containing him as it is! Once those break, we can only hope to reinforce the door!" Almalexia and Jules both turned to Harlee.

"Good guess," they spoke in unison as they silently followed the pack of guards, who left the brown-haired woman behind. As she stood, watching the men run off towards the far east side, Almalexia crept behind her and placing her hand over her mouth, dragged her behind cover.

Harlee placed her gun to the woman's chest, whose eyes were streaming tears as she looked at them in terror. As Harlee leaned closer, the woman's eyes looked more surprised as she began to mumble into Almalexia's hand. Harlee placed one finger to her lips, before using the same finger, to signal a blade sliding across her throat. The woman nodded and Almalexia released her mouth.

"Harlee?" The woman asked, her voice barely a whisper.

"How do you know my name?" Harlee asked. The woman looked around carefully before answering, a smile on her face.

"Maxwell told me about you. He said he stayed behind for a fierce woman, with blonde hair and eyes, nearly as bright and blue as his. Said he told her to run far away but she never listens to him."

"How do you know Maxwell?" Jules asked. The woman's eyes grew sad.

"I was captured during the second night of the Feast. I have been working with Doctor Amelia, experimenting on Maxwell." The woman was cut short as Almalexia grabbed her throat.

"Easy, Alma. She said she was forced." Jules said, prompting Almalexia to let go. The woman rubbed her throat for a moment before continuing.

"My name is Courtney. Doctor Amelia is still down below, trying to keep the guards from attacking Maxwell. I am so glad you came. We were hoping someone would come to save him. That poor man," She said, shaking her head, tears in her eyes. "That poor, beautiful man."

"Classic Maxwell." Almalexia rolled her eyes, shaking her head. "Captured prisoner, charms his captors."

"Maybe you could take a lesson from him." Harlee smiled. Almalexia smirked as she turned back to Courtney.

"You need to get out of here." She told her.

"What are you all going to do?" Courtney asked.

"We're going to break Maxwell out and kill some bad guys." Harlee said as Jules continued to look out. Courtney nodded her head and pulled a key card from her blouse pocket.

"This will get you in the elevators and open the door to Maxwell's cell, over there." She pointed to the east wall, only thirty feet away. "Good luck. Please save Doctor Amelia, as well. She is one of the good ones." Courtney said as she looked carefully, before running towards the exit.

"Let's go!" Almalexia said, turning her head and running to the elevator. She inserted the card and pressed the down button as Harlee and Jules worked to catch her. The elevator doors opened and all three of the girls, climbed in as Almalexia inserted the key again. The doors closed without her pressing another button and they each readied their weapons, as the elevator moved down.

As soon as the doors opened, Harlee, Almalexia and Jules, braced themselves against the sides as they peeked out. Beyond, they could hear the yells of the security guards, just down the hall. There was a tall blonde woman, who could only be Doctor Amelia, standing in front of four men, who were holding the doors shut as several others, inside, tried to escape.

From a distance, Harlee could see the room beyond the door, had filled with steam, the hands beating on the glass barely visible. She saw brief, horrific glimpses beyond, something large, wailing about as others attacked it. One of the men, holding the door shut, vomited as he bore witness to something within.

Harlee, Jules and Almalexia, stepped out of the elevator, running towards Amelia as they fired at the men in front of the door. Amelia dropped to the ground as the guards turned their heads to receive the gunfire. Two dropped but the other two, moved too quickly to be human. Dodging the majority of the fire, they pulled their own weapons as the blonde stood and charged them, herself.

"I hope you're here for Maxwell!" She yelled as she took the men by surprise, slashing the first man's throat with her scalpel and biting the second as Harlee shot him.

"Are you Doctor Amelia?" Jules asked as they approached.

"I am." Amelia responded, wiping the blood from her face with a handkerchief.

"We ran into Courtney. She asked us to get you out of here." Jules continued as Amelia looked at Harlee and smiled.

"Harlee." She said placing her hands on Harlee's shoulders.

"Yes?" Harlee answered.

"I am glad you came. Maxwell was hoping you wouldn't but...what does he know." She smiled, hugging Harlee and looking to Jules and Almalexia.

"Do you need my help?" Amelia asked.

"No. Get out of here." Harlee said. Amelia nodded her head and left, taking the elevator up. As the three remaining approached the door, they saw no one attempted to escape the room. Blood was smeared on the window, barely any light beyond it. As they stared inside the room, they felt a heavy thud against the side of the door, followed by an enraged scream.

"He's already loose!" Almalexia said as several more heavily equipped guards, too many to count in the blink of an eye, ran up on them, weapons trained.

"Don't move!" One of the riot gear armored men yelled as Jules, Harlee and Almalexia stared at each other.

"Drop your weapons and put your hands where I can see them!" The man yelled again as Harlee slowly struck the I.D. badge through the door scanner.

"Fuck me," she said. "This is going to be one hell of a night." The light on the door turned green and she, Almalexia and Jules, all jumped from the door, hitting the ground and tucking in as the door flew open and the guards opened fire.

Chapter 20 - Irrevocably Changed

John could hear the barrage of gunfire both in his earpiece and then again as an echo from down below. He ran inside, the compound, following several other armed guards who ran passed. As John followed them inside, he heard the elevator doors on the eastern wall open, a tall blonde haired woman running out.

"Doctor Amelia, is the subject secured?"

"There are some men downstairs now, trying to keep him contained." Amelia answered. "I was told to evacuate."

"Alright ma'am, you're clear." He told her as she proceeded towards the exit. John stared at her bloody lab coat and wondered what sort of trouble he had landed in. Following the guards to the elevator, John climbed in with four other men. As the doors opened to the floor below, they walked out into a bloodbath.

Bullet casings lie all over the floor, tiny boats floating in pools of blood. They could hear screams coming from behind the elevator as they stepped out, weapons trained. John stood behind the armored guards and was gently tapped on the shoulder.

"We need to go back up." John heard Harlee whispering into his ear. John, observing the gruesome scene before him, walked backwards, returning inside the elevator. He could hear the screams of the men he had accompanied as Almalexia and Jules followed him. As John pressed the close doors button, he caught a good look at the three, blood soaked women.

"Are you all okay?" He asked worriedly.

"Jules took a round in the arm." Harlee began.

"Just a graze, dammit." Jules argued.

"We have all taken some spills and some shrapnel but nothing serious." Harlee finished as they heard something outside of the elevator doors.

"What was that?" John asked as a loud thud boomed from beneath the ascending elevator followed by the two toned, bestial roar, Harlee and John remembered from all too recently. They could hear as something latched onto the bottom of the elevator and again heard Maxwell's roar.

"The moment these doors open, we split up. Jules, Harlee, you two run for the elevator. John, you...AH!" Almalexia shrieked as a bladed arm, pierced through the metal floor, stabbing through her right thigh. As the succubus collapsed to the ground, Harlee pulled her aside as she stumbled, the bladed limb piercing through the floor, again.

The arm pierced through the floor, several more times, as everyone attempted to move out of the way, narrowly dodging each strike. The elevator doors opened and the four of them poured out, as Maxwell roared angrily from below, tearing through the metal.

"Jules, Almalexia! Run to the next elevator! John and I are the Keepers! We will slow him down!" Harlee yelled, her hand over her left breast.

"Be careful." Jules said as she aided Almalexia across the room, while John and Harlee stood their ground. They watched eagerly as Maxwell continued tearing through the metal flooring. First, they saw, as his arms broke through, followed by his body. He called out angrily again as he rose to his feet and with eyes void of all humanity, stared at his prey, with a deranged smile that revealed his many extra teeth. Harlee and John both trained their weapons as Jules and Almalexia neared the elevator.

The lights continued to flicker and fade as Maxwell charged forward, His two additional limbs, trailing behind him, ripping the floor as he cackled in his hellish voice. His claws and fangs both ready to strike, as Harlee and John opened fire, using short bursts of bullet spray, to slow him.

"DON'T LOOK BACK! KEEP RUNNING!" Harlee screamed over the sound of gunfire and Maxwell's bone chilling laugh. As the first of the bullets hit their mark, Maxwell stumbled only slightly as he laughed again. His head turned sideways as he continued smiling at Harlee and John, his black and red, vertical slits for eyes only worsening the paralyzing fear, they both felt.

Lunging forwards, Maxwell raised both limbs, slashing at Harlee and John, while throwing shards of tile up into the air. Using their slightly enhanced bodies, Harlee and John avoided the first attack, shielding themselves as the shards of tile peppered them. Maxwell's feet hit the ground a few paces from Harlee, before Harlee landed. Reaching out with his hand, Maxwell attempted to grab onto Harlee. Rotating her weight around Maxwell's wrist, Harlee moved her body as a gymnast, redirecting her momentum and throwing herself out of reach.

As she slid on her back, she looked back and fired three more bursts into Maxwell, who shielded himself and slashed at John, who had managed to stab into his arm. Harlee pushed herself off from the ground, while in motion and began running around, mirroring John. John ducked beneath another swipe, shooting at Maxwell who dodged. As the elevator doors, sounded off and opened, he averted his gaze towards Almalexia and Jules and opening his mouth, to its fullest, roared.

"WE'LL MEET YOU ON THE ROOF!" Harlee screamed as Maxwell charged forward, heading straight for Almalexia.

"I DON'T THINK SO!" John yelled, grabbing onto Maxwell's leg, shooting him in his bare knee. Maxwell yelled in pain and kicked John in the chest with his uninjured leg as the wounds on the other, healed almost instantly.

"JOHN!" Harlee, Jules and Almalexia screamed as the boy flew across the room and landed in a heap on the floor. As Maxwell barreled forward, Harlee, thinking on her feet, unzipped her jacket and squeezed Maxwell's heart.

The creature groaned, horrifically as it toppled over. The noise emitted was more horrible than a knife scraping across glass. Harlee winced from the sound, as she continued squeezing the heart. As the elevator closed, Harlee relaxed, the effects weakening her as well.

The moment she released her grip however, she was swept off from her feet as Maxwell's flailing limbs slapped her sideways as they had with John. Harlee slid across the ground, instinctively shielding the heart as she struck a support column painfully. The force from the blow, arched her back as she wrapped around it. A spray of stomach bile escaped her mouth, as all of her strength was stricken from her, and her lungs nearly collapsed.

She could hear Maxwell tearing apart the elevator doors and turned her head to confirm it. Placing her now bloodied hands beneath her, she slowly pressed off from the ground. Droplets of blood, pattered the tile below her and she recognized the nausea and dizziness, associated with head trauma. Pressing her body against the pillar, she witnessed Maxwell, wrenching open the doors and begin climbing up the shaft.

"JOHN!" Harlee groaned as she dragged her battered body across the floor, seeing John, only a few yards away. She could hear him groan and thanked God he was still alive. As she reached him, she could feel Maxwell's heart, pound in her chest, as she felt a flood of strength coursing through her. Harlee looked down at her hands, which had slowly begun to heal and she remembered what Maxwell had told her.

"My heart shall protect you, as you shall protect my heart." She whispered as she rolled John over. She could see where he was badly wounded but even he had begun to recover.

"On your feet!" She yelled at him. John's eyes flickered as he opened them and slowly rose to a seated position.

"ALMALEXIA! JULES!" He yelled, pressing himself from the floor, as Harlee did the same.

"We are going to have to catch up to them." Harlee said, looking at the only other elevator, which had been destroyed during her initial escape.

"I suppose we are taking the stairs then." John said, turning his head towards the long, spiraling stairwell. Several armed men, still scrambled up above, trying to evacuate people, while sorting out the chaos.

"Suppose so." Harlee said as they ran towards them, grabbing fresh clips and weapons from the dead guards. Making their way up the stairs, they readied themselves for war.

"ALMA! HE IS RIGHT BELOW US!" Jules yelled as one of the bladed limbs pierced through the floor, barely missing Jules, who had perched herself up on the railing beside Almalexia.

"I KNOW THAT! YOU DON'T NEED TO YELL AT ME!" She yelled back as the limb was pulled away and Maxwell's eye, came into view. He roared at them as he began reaching up again, trying to grab onto one of the two as Jules opened fire at his arm.

Maxwell pulled his arm away, screaming in anger as one of his bladed limbs, punched another hole into the floor. Almalexia looked up as they neared the thirtieth floor, knowing they would never make it to the fiftieth, let alone the top, before Maxwell claimed them. Quickly, her eyes glimpsed the trapdoor in the elevator's ceiling and she pointed it out to Jules.

"We need to climb on top. Maxwell will keep trying to tear through. Once he does, we drop the elevator." She said as Jules nodded her head.

Jules stood, being sure to keep an eye on the floor as Maxwell moved from place to place, peering at them hungrily. Jules allowed her gun to hang from its strap as she pressed up against the door, pressing it open as Maxwell seized her ankle and wrenched her down to the floor.

"ALMA! HELP ME!" She screamed as she rolled away from his claws and blades, as they pierced through the floor, one after the other. Jules cried out some more, feeling her flesh peel away as Maxwell grazed her arms and legs. Almalexia pointed her gun and began unloading it into the floor, until she heard Maxwell scream once more.

"UP!" She cried as Jules, without further command, launched herself onto the rail and kicking off from it, pulled herself up on top of the elevator. Almalexia fired, until her gun emptied. Maxwell reached out with both hands and began peeling the metal away as Almalexia kicked painfully out, pressing a number of the buttons on the panel as Jules, grabbed her hand and pulled her out of harm's way.

The elevator stopped as Almalexia and Jules grabbed onto the service ladder. Jules quickly pointed her gun and fired at the elevator cables as Maxwell's arms reached out through the trapdoor. As his face rose above the opened panel, he reached out with his limbs. The cable snapped, releasing the elevator. Maxwell fell along with the metal deathtrap, screaming in rage the entire way down.

"Do you think that will stop him?" Jules groaned.

"Not likely." Almalexia said. "He will jump off before it hits the ground. Come on let's go." She said as she pulled against Jules, who groaned but did not budge.

"Jules?" Almalexia asked as Jules smiled at her, pulling her hand away from a large bloody gash in her side.

"JULES! HOLY SHIT, NOT YOU!" Almalexia cried as she lowered herself to stare at it.

"Looks as though I'm not going to keep up." Jules moaned, as her head bobbed slightly. Below them, they heard the massive sound of the elevator hitting the ground floor, ricocheting up to them.

"BULLSHIT!" Almalexia yelled after the noise dissipated, while looking to the elevator doors. "Don't move!" She commanded as she carefully moved towards the doors, ignoring the pain in her leg, which had barely begun to heal. Almalexia, supporting herself in the tiny frame, hit the door switch for the elevator, causing the doors to open.

"Jules, carefully come over to me. I am getting you out of here, if it kills me." She declared as she held out her hand. Jules stared at her. Smiling, she slowly made her way towards her. Grabbing onto her hand, Almalexia stared her in the eyes.

"Jump to me." She said. Jules immediately looked straight down.

"Stop being a baby. I am much stronger than anyone from the movies you've seen. Now jump!" She ordered again. Jules, closed her eyes as she pressed off with what little strength she had remaining. Almalexia, pulled against Jules' arm, pulling her through the gap, where she tumbled onto her, causing her injured leg to give out.

Rising to her feet, Almalexia made quick work, to drag Jules around the corner, where she pulled her inside one of the many empty rooms. In the silence, Almalexia could hear, voices coming from her earpiece, which was hanging down by her torn shirt collar. Jules, propping herself against Almalexia's chest, grabbed the earpiece and placed it into her ear.

"Harlee, it's Jules." She whispered into the earpiece.

"Oh, thank God. Is Almalexia with you?" She asked.

"We're both here. I am not sure what floor we are on but we are somewhere between thirty and forty. Harlee, I don' think we are going to make it to the top." She groaned as Almalexia, took the earpiece from her.

"What do you mean? JULES!?" Harlee responded as Almalexia placed the earpiece back into her own ear.

"Disregard that. Jules will be fine." Her voice trembled as she tried to convince herself. "Maxwell wounded her in the gut. It's bad but I am going to apply first aid now." She said, removing her jacket and gently resting Jules' head down upon it. As Almalexia began unzipping Jules' jacket, Harlee spoke again.

"Almalexia! I need you to figure out where you are. John and I are on our way!" Harlee yelled, the sound of gunfire in the background. "We will make it to you! Just hang on!" Harlee continued as Almalexia tore off one of her sleeves. Examining Jules' wound, she gently placed it over Jules' wound, and began tying it down.

"Keep pressure on it." Almalexia ordered as she stood. "You will be alright, so long as I can lead everyone away."

"Are you leaving me behind?" Jules asked.

"Maxwell is after me, not you." She said. "If I don't lead him away, he will kill us both. Harlee and John are on their way. I will make sure they find you." She said as she kissed Jules on the forehead before running out into the hallway. "Alma here. Jules is in the last room on the left, looks to be...the thirty fourth floor." Almalexia said as she froze in place.

She could hear sounds from the elevator chute. As she watched, bearing witness to Maxwell's bladed limbs, piercing through the doors. As the powerful arms pulled the doors apart, she saw Maxwell's eyes and face, smiling at her. Almalexia waited for Maxwell to begin chasing her, before speeding down the hall, leading him away.

"Make sure you get to her!" Almalexia yelled, in part from her concern for Jules, and another, from sheer terror.

Maxwell shrieked gleefully as he charged after Almalexia, shredding the floor and walls as he ran. Almalexia ran as fast as she could, hopping every other step, compensating for her injured leg. She could hear the sound of Maxwell's jaws working, ready to consume her flesh. She dodged sideways, into one of the many darkened rooms. Slamming into the edges of the doorframe, Maxwell broke through and began flipping furniture, in search of her.

Almalexia, crawling on all fours, moved through the office cubicles, as Maxwell continued to flail and rage. She saw lights, approaching from the far side of the room and quickly dropping to her stomach, rolled across the floor, hiding from sight. The guards running passed her, noticed Maxwell and opened fire, their automatic weapons, providing adequate light for Almalexia to move about.

Army crawling through the room, Almalexia shielded herself as a trail of bullets, tore through the floor inches from her. Rolling out of the way, she held out her hands, in defense of office furniture, which was being thrown freely through the air. As more lights appeared in the distance, she saw a lopped head, roll towards her as she heard the sound of Maxwell chewing on bones.

Her guts churned, at the sound and pushing away from the head, placed her back to the wall of the outside row. As the fresh batch of lights passed by, she moved from the cubicles, to the opposite doorway. The sound of gunfire and screams, drowned out any noise she made, allowing her a chance at escape as Maxwell redecorated the office.

As limbs and fluids, splashed across the desks and cubicles, Almalexia rose and ran. Her leg, rapidly healing, she was able to cover ground quickly, before she heard Maxwell's shriek. Barely turning her head, she saw as the beast threw aside the corpse it had been feeding on and began chasing her. Bounding across the furniture, he cleared the room in a matter of seconds and slashed at her.

Almalexia dove, feeling as strands of her hair, were cut. Tumbling forward, she kicked off from the ground again, dashing through the doorway, the stairwell in sight. Maxwell flipped a couch after her as he renewed his pursuit.

As Maxwell lunged, Almalexia threw herself sideways, up the first few stairs. Almalexia using all four limbs, propelled herself to her feet as Maxwell slid passed. Almalexia rounded the stairs to the next floor, as armed guards approached from down the hall. Removing her ski mask, before they noticed, Almalexia yelled out to them, pointing behind her.

"There is a beast, trying to kill me!" She yelled as the men ran passed her and seeing Maxwell, opened fire. Almalexia continued to flee up the stairs as she heard the screams of the dying, below. Almalexia heard the sounds of Maxwell's gleeful shriek and knew he was back on her scent. As Almalexia rounded the next corner, she noticed a large group of men and women, wearing tactical clothing, armed for war, aiming at her.

"FIRE!" The brown haired, brown eyed, glasses wearing woman, dressed in business attire at the center of the pack, yelled. Almalexia stopped, vaulting over the divider and ran up the next set of stairs as Maxwell caught the bullet spray in the torso. The Reaver averted his eyes from Almalexia, in favor of the gunmen. Almalexia avoided the incoming fire, by climbing to the top of the stairs and hid around the corner, halfway up to the next floor. From her new vantage, Almalexia watched the scene while avoiding stray fire.

Maxwell charged toward the gunmen, shielding his face as he raged. As Maxwell neared, one man stepped forward, launching a net from his weapon, ensnaring Maxwell and tripping him. Clearing to either side, the group allowed Maxwell to fall beside them as he slid through the glass barrier. As he tumbled over the side, another man, using a concrete nail gun, drove three nails through the netting. Maxwell's fall stopped suddenly as he dangled over the edge of the balcony, suspended by the net.

"Kill the other one." The glasses wearing woman spoke, gesturing towards Almalexia. "Where your masks. She is a succubus." The woman spoke, adjusting her glasses. Almalexia took flight again as she pressed her hand to her ear.

"Maxwell has been captured." She said.

"We see them." Harlee answered. "The one in charge is Cilia."

"Your sister?" Almalexia said, stopping for a moment.

"Keep going. John and I will be to Jules soon. We are going to...OH SHIT! Almalexia run! Maxwell is loose!" Harlee said as Almalexia heard Cilia call back.

"He's stronger than we anticipated. Try again!" She demanded as her men returned to try and capture him again. Peeking over the railing of the floor above, Almalexia saw as Harlee and John, fried at Cilia's men. They dodged back as Cilia, shaking her head grabbed the rifle from one of her men and kneeling down, launched a grenade towards the source of the fire. Almalexia could hear John and Harlee yell, just before the grenade burst.

"JOHN ! HARLEE! ARE YOU ARLIGHT!?" Almalexia yelled. From where she now hid from the approaching gunmen, Almalexia could not see what had become of her allies. For a time, all she could hear was radio chatter, Cilia and her men yelling, accompanied by the fury of their weapons. She tried to peer over the edge once more, repeating her question.

"We are alright, barely." John groaned. "She hit us good, but we will recover."

"Watch yourself, Almalexia." Harlee moaned out. "I cannot imagine Auriel is going to let that pass, without sending in reinforcements. Be safe." She said as the smoke cleared, allowing Almalexia to see, Harlee and John, dashing up the opposite stairwell, partially hunched over, nearing the thirty fourth floor. Cilia's men had returned their attention to Maxwell, paying no notice to the two ascending the stairs.

Almalexia saw as Maxwell rose above the ledge, spearing one of Cilia's men in the shoulder as he did so. The man, without missing a beat, stabbed into Maxwell with a blade as he pushed himself up and over the Reaver's back. Maxwell tipped sideways as two more of Cilia's men, threw themselves on him, void of any regard for their lives, while Cilia watched.

Almalexia moved to aid her friend, only stopping at the sound of the psychotic laughter. Moving back slightly, she saw as all three men, were thrown back over the side as Maxwell charged, barreling into the others, knocking Cilia to the side. The woman grabbed a pistol from her side and began firing at Maxwell as he continued to engage with her soldiers.

Her inhuman soldiers did their utmost to oppose the man, dodging his attacks and teaming up to fight off his powerful limbs. They showed signs of neither fatigue, pain nor fear as they relentlessly attacked Maxwell, with their bare hands. Maxwell reached out with his stabbing limbs, slashing at Cilia as he contended with the other men.

Almalexia, having nearly recovered from her stab wound to the thigh, vaulted down to the floor below, landing just beside one of the many carbines, lying on the floor. Grabbing it, she pointed it towards the others, pulling the trigger. At the last second, the man she had fired at dipped backwards, avoiding the bullet.

Almalexia stared in astonishment as she fired again, to the same result. One of the men, flipping over one of Maxwell's limbs, threw a blade in midflight towards Almalexia. Almalexia moved out of the way as Cilia, ejected her clip and reached for another. Seizing her opportunity, Almalexia aimed and fired at Cilia's chest.

A spatter of blood shot through the air, as one of the men, moved his body, between Almalexia and Cilia, taking the bullet in the shoulder, defending her. Almalexia, smiled as she opened fire, forcing the man to grab onto Cilia, taking several rounds in the body as he ran away.

One of Maxwell's attackers, disengaged as she charged towards Almalexia. The succubus stood her ground as the woman, jumped, kicking both feet at her. Almalexia avoided both kicks and narrowly blocked a punch to the throat as the woman engaged with superhuman strength and speed. As they fought, exchanging blows which the other deflected and returned, Maxwell managed to grip onto one of his three attackers and threw one over the edge of balcony. As the man plummeted, thirty plus stories below, Maxwell began lashing out at the remaining two, still smiling.

Almalexia dipped down, avoiding a kick to the head as she spun and swiped, knocking the legs out from beneath her opponent. As she advanced, the woman sprung her body up and quickly flung both arms forward, multiple times. Seeing the blades the woman had released, Almalexia avoided a few but took another two into her right shoulder and left hip.

The woman sprang up, kicking at Almalexia's outstretched arms. Clearing the gap between them as she landed, the woman wrapped her hands around the succubus' shoulders and began striking at her with her knees. Almalexia fought as ably as she might with her wounds and quickly, ripped one of the blades from her hip and used it to block her opponent's attacks.

With no pain reflex, the woman continued to strike out, each time, inflicting a fresh wound onto her arms and legs. Launching herself up into the air, she took a blade into the inner thigh, as she landed on Almalexia's shoulders. Twisting her thighs and dropping her body weight, she flipped Almalexia, while removing the blade from her shoulder. Almalexia landed painfully onto her back as the woman jumped towards her, aiming for her face.

Outstretching her feet, Almalexia caught the woman in the chest, twisted sideways, grabbing the knife from her attacker's thigh and stabbed the woman through the face. As her attacker's body twitched, the muscles firing off by instinct while the brain died, Almalexia witnessed Maxwell grasping his final attacker. With a malevolently joyous laugh, the Reaver ripped the arms and legs from its opponent, spraying every nearby surface with blood.

Dropping half of his victim, Maxwell slowly turned his gaze towards Almalexia and smiled. Pulling her knife from the woman's face, Almalexia backed away slowly, her peripherals on the staircase. Maxwell dropped the remainder of his bloody toy, the man still alive, made no sound as Maxwell stepped onto him, walking towards Almalexia. Slowly, he approached, smile wide, black and red eyes fixated on her. Almalexia attempted to think her way through the situation, as Maxwell lunged.

"BOOM!" Was all Almalexia heard, as Maxwell was sent sideways, something powerfully concussive, having just hit him in the side of the head. Turning her gaze, Almalexia saw Harlee, holding a military rifle, perched below as John, carrying Jules, descended.

"Thank you, Harlee." Almalexia said as she turned and fled up the stairs.

"I'll meet you upstairs." She said, running as well.

"Cilia is on her way down." Almalexia said as she heard Maxwell roaring with anger, likely on the pursuit again.

"I know." Harlee said. Almalexia moved to the next level as she saw Maxwell below her, coming up the stairs.

"Go after her." Almalexia advised as she ran to the next floor.

"We don't have time for that now." Harlee said. "DUCK!" She yelled. Almalexia saw that she was aiming her rifle and Almalexia dropped down as Maxwell lunged into the air. She could hear as Harlee's rifle fired several times, striking Maxwell in the face and chest. The moment he stumbled back, Almalexia bolted, running towards Harlee who was moving up to the floor she was on.

Maxwell rose to his feet and charged as Almalexia met Harlee at the stairwell. Together, the two proceeded up the stairs as Maxwell ran across the floor to follow. Harlee quickly opened the duffle bag, which was strapped over her shoulder as she ran.

"Where did you find that?" Almalexia asked.

"On one of the bodies downstairs!" She yelled as she pulled from it, a grenade belt and pulling the pin, tossed the entire belt onto the steps as they ran. Maxwell screeched angrily as he was hit by the blast.

"Don't look back!" Harlee yelled as they continued to run, the sound of howling not far above them.

"Sounds as though Auriel and Balthazar, are sending friends." Almalexia said as they continued running.

"Let's duck aside." Harlee whispered. "They are after Maxwell but they won't hesitate to kill us too." She said as they stepped into one of the many vacant rooms in the building and hid. They did not wait long, before they heard both Maxwell below and the wolves outside their room.

They both covered their mouths, concealing their labored breathing from the beasts, who had begun sniffing them out. Maxwell roared from below, immediately gaining the attention of the wolves. As they bounded passed, Harlee counted three of the beasts. Waiting until they heard the sounds of engagement, Harlee and Almalexia ran from their hiding place, nearing the completion of their climb.

As they reached the final floor, they ran towards the far end of the floor, finding the staircase leading towards the rooftop. They searched below, seeing Maxwell and the werewolves fighting. Harlee and Almalexia took a deep breath, eying one another. Harlee ejected her clip and counted her bullets as she reached into her bag, handing Almalexia a pistol and three extra clips.

"Are you ready?" Harlee asked. Almalexia looked over her freshly healed wounds and cracking her neck, nodded her head. Reaching out for the door latch, they carefully opened the door and slowly snuck toward cover as they heard Auriel, addressing nearly fifty people.

"Tonight, each of you shall ascend beyond the mortal coil. You shall each be irrevocably changed, improved with strength, vitality and abilities, you have never dared to conceive. Choose wisely. Shall you join the ranks of the noble houses and become Vampyr, or join the hunt, alongside your fellow clansmen, the Lycanthropes? Each shall grant you opportunities far beyond any you might see as you are, as we transition to our rightful place as masters of this world." Auriel spoke, to a cheering crowd, each eager to join the ranks of the immortals.

Harlee and Almalexia both carefully peeked out as all eyes were upon Auriel and Balthazar. As everyone formed into two lines, Auriel, using a sanctimonious blade, slashed her hand, which began bleeding into a large goblet. Taking a small glass vial, filled with red fluid, from the altar beside her, she poured it into the offering cup of an ancient statue, which rested behind her. Harlee stared at the statue, which looked to be a fierce, yet motherly woman, draped in dark clothing, a veil over her eyes.

Auriel bowed before the statue, before turning back to the congregation, and holding up her goblet. To those who approached her, she offered them a drink to immortal life as Balthazar transformed into his lycanthrope form. To those who knelt before him, he offered his cursed bite under the power of the blood moon.

After each received their blessing, from either source, the men and women gathered, cut their hands, offering a few drops of blood to the statues offering bowl, before dropping to their knees, giving their prayers to the statue of the woman, whom neither Harlee nor Almalexia recognized. As people began doubling over in pain, their chosen gift having activated, Auriel stood, hands open wide, smiling.

"Excellent. Our time is upon us. Soon we shall rule all which walks the four planes." She smiled as everyone turned his or her attention toward the sound of a loud crash. Harlee and Almalexia shielded themselves as glass rained down over everyone. Harlee looked through the gap in her hands and saw, standing on the support beams of what was once the skylight, Maxwell, head reared, roaring wildly as he smiled.

Chapter 21 - Wash Away Their Sins, Wash Away Their Pain

Immediately upon reaching the rooftop, Maxwell's eyes darted about, eying the plethora of supernatural creatures around him. Every last guard, protecting Balthazar and Auriel, charged in unison, those who could, changing to their lycanthrope form. Maxwell jumped, charging forward to meet his opponents head on as Harlee and Almalexia stared at one another.

"GO!" They yelled to each other over the chaos and rising above their cover, opened fire onto the gathered crowd.

"KILL THEM!" Auriel shrieked as her agents, breaking off from Maxwell, charged, avoiding the gunfire, making their way towards the two women, who were attempting to take down as many as possible.

Not far from them, Maxwell, tore into the masses of creatures attacking him, slashing wildly about, blood spewing in every conceivable direction. Almalexia, having ran out of ammunition, drew up her knife and grabbing a night stick from Harlee's bag, engaged the approaching threats, hand to hand.

The smell of smoke and gunpowder permeated the air, creating a thick fog, ripe with the stench of death. Through the mayhem, Harlee could see the hunter's moon, shining down on them, as droplets of rain fell. As the water splashed down, it washed away some of the blood, which had already accumulated on Harlee's face.

Harlee continued to lay out covering fire for Almalexia, who was fighting off multiple adversaries. They continued their panicked attack as Maxwell continued to eviscerate and feed upon his adversaries. The rain only intensified as they battled, watered down blood, now leaked its way into Harlee's clothes and shoes, coating her.

Balthazar approached, towering over everyone else, pushing his way through the crowd, nearing Maxwell. The Reaver looked up at him, tearing a throat free with his teeth as he dropped another corpse and lunged. Balthazar charged, the two powerful creatures colliding in air, knocking several bodies in every direction.

Watered down crimson, splashed over everything as people fell to the rooftop. Harlee ejected and exchanged another clip, cocked her rifle and began firing again. Almalexia downed another opponent and narrowly avoided the bodies of Maxwell and Balthazar as they rolled about, saturating one another in the thick sanguine.

They both ceased their rolling, Balthazar looming over Maxwell, fangs bared as he slashed across the man's body with his large claws. Blood coated the massive werewolf's fur, Maxwell's hair dyed red. Maxwell retaliated, thrusting out towards the wolf's body, with his sharp limbs. Retaining his intelligence, Balthazar defended his body well, while attempting to continue his relentless assault.

Harlee could feel Maxwell's heart pounding against her chest and knew Maxwell was growing weaker. She quickly turned her attention to the two and shot a round, striking Balthazar in the skull, the bullet wound too shallow to do any real damage. The moment's distraction, however, as the beast looked to her, proved sufficient for Maxwell, to strike him in the jaw, knocking him backwards as their battle continued.

"HARLEE! BEHIND YOU!" Almalexia yelled as she was forced to the ground. Harlee turned her attention, just in time to see Cilia, standing behind her, gun pointed to Harlee's head.

"Look at what you've done, Harlee." Cilia said, gesturing out to the chaos and countless bodies surrounding them. "Blood, you have spilt, is literally raining down upon everything below this roof. It is flowing, as a river down upon this city and at its center, is you." Cilia said as Harlee looked around, watching as Almalexia fought back to her feet, Maxwell bit into Balthazar's chest and Auriel slowly approached through the aisle way her followers opened.

"I did not sew this." Harlee yelled back. "You are also standing at the epicenter of all this and I came to rescue you!" She screamed as Cilia adjusted her glasses, smiling.

"Had you never considered that I am already saved?" She asked. Harlee's eyes opened wide as she was overwhelmed with confusion. "I was working to create something beautiful." She spoke. "And though you cannot stop the storm which shall wipe this city clean, you have proven yourself too much an annoyance to allow to live. I had expected better from you, sister." Cilia spoke as she pulled the trigger.

"HARLEE!" Almalexia yelled as Harlee closed her eyes. Five more rounds fired, which Harlee heard over the roar of the chaos. Harlee opened her eyes and saw Maxwell, in Reaver state, standing in front of her. Lowering his head slightly, Maxwell raged at Cilia as he charged forward. Cilia, quickly jumped to the side as Maxwell slid towards her and was only spared his wrath as Balthazar pounced him from behind, impaling him through the back.

Harlee, seized her moment and charging Cilia, kneed her sister in the stomach as Maxwell wrestled with Balthazar. As Cilia stumbled backwards, Harlee downward punched the kneeling woman in the face and kicked her gun far from reach. Cilia attempted to recover as Harlee kicked her again in the ribs, angrily, blotting out all other distractions as she released her pent frustrations.

"YOU BITCH!" Harlee screamed as she struck her sister again, knocking her to her stomach. Cilia laughed as Harlee continued to strike her, all while Almalexia dealt with her overwhelming numbers and Auriel joined Balthazar.

"Doesn't it feel good?" Cilia asked, rising to her feet as Harlee relented. "Violence without purpose, is pointless, but when channeled properly, plotted, and executed, wrath can be such a beautiful sin, can it not? I tell you, sister. I have been set free. I have found purpose and fallen in love with violence incarnate. Soon, my lover, shall be born again into this world and there is no one, who can impede his resurrection. Not even the late Father Matthew." Harlee stared at Cilia, who smiled wide.

"IT WAS YOU!?" She asked. Cilia only continued to smile as Harlee was knocked to the ground by Cilia's brutish guard, striking her from behind. As Harlee collapsed, both Cilia and her bodyguard fled from the chaotic scene.

"AAAHHHH!" Harlee screamed, a combination of enraged and agonized as she absorbed the revelation. Rising back to her feet, Harlee lashed out at the first person she could lay hands upon. Striking them several times in the body and head, Harlee silenced their efforts in the brawl and moved to another. She worked her way through multiple adversaries as she saw Maxwell bat Balthazar away as Auriel struck him. Stabbing her hand through Maxwell's chest, she forced him to stare eye to eye with her.

"Why Mother desires anything from you, eludes me." She spoke, shaking her head at the creature as Harlee kicked up a weapon, catching it, aimed and fired. Auriel tipped her head to the side as Maxwell lunged forward and seizing the side of Auriel's shoulder in his powerful jaws, wrenched near the entirety of her deltoid from the bone. Auriel cried out in pain, as her arm dropped uselessly to her side and she jumped away from Maxwell.

No sooner had Maxwell swallowed the chunk of flesh, pain seared through Harlee's chest as Maxwell's heart screamed to her. Maxwell and Harlee both, doubled over as Almalexia scooped Harlee into her arms, carrying her away from harm. Maxwell dropped to his knees, the Reaver's eyes filled with pain and regret as it reared its head and shrieked terribly.

Balthazar quickly reverted back to his human form as he grabbed hold of a thrall and dragging the screaming person toward Auriel, crunched the young man's neck and handed him off to the queen. Auriel fed indiscriminately, from the boy, not leaving a single drop behind as she eyed Balthazar.

"Resolve things here. I am returning to Mother's side." She ordered and walked away as Balthazar bowed. No sooner had she made the stairs, did Balthazar turn his gaze back towards Maxwell and reassume his true form. Harlee saw through blurred vision, Maxwell, in human form, rising to his feet, wearing nothing but his boxer briefs. As Balthazar charged him, Maxwell quickly reacted and jumped to the side.

Balthazar narrowly missed Maxwell but tore through several of his own. The wolf tried to turn and stumbled on the narrow path as Maxwell lifted a knife from the ground. Several remaining thralls engaged Maxwell, who used a series of quick strikes with the blade and bit into one.

He fed from it, regaining some of his strength as Balthazar attempted to lash out at everything in his way. Maxwell ran up on the elder wolf and jumped. As he slipped overtop of Balthazar's arm, he stabbed Balthazar in his eye, blood splashing his already crimson painted body.

As the lycanthrope cried out in pain, Maxwell stared at Harlee and Almalexia. He looked down, bereft of words severe enough, to express his remorse. Shaking his head, he knelt and grabbed a broken piece of pipe. Holding his makeshift weapons, Maxwell cut down several more attackers. Almalexia defended Harlee as she recovered and Balthazar jumped at Maxwell.

Maxwell, jumped back, avoiding the fistful of claws and began quickly slicing at Balthazar's shins, wrists and chest. The wolf growled at him in frustration as the last few remaining thralls, found value in their lives and fled. Alone, Balthazar bellowed as he charged at Maxwell, jaws opened wide.

Maxwell attempted to jump wide but was ensnared in the werewolf's grip, its claws digging into his torso. Maxwell stabbed the wolf repeatedly, in the hand as he was lifted up to its mouth. Almalexia and Harlee, both ran to help him as Maxwell, flicking the pipe in his off hand, stabbed upward, impaling the beast through the roof of its mouth.

Balthazar stumbled backwards, crying in pain as he attempted to remove the pipe. Maxwell, wasting no time, charged the beast, stabbing him several times in the chest. As he raked the blade horizontally, he plunged his hands inside the freshly carved gash, arms fully submerged in the creature's chest. From behind, Harlee and Almalexia could only see as Balthazar's outstretched limbs grew limp and he fell forward, dead.

"MAXWELL!" They both screamed, against the sounds of the storm and torrential rain. Harlee, slid through the bloody rain and wrapped her arms around Maxwell, who was kneeling on the ground, head in the air, panting heavily. As Harlee held onto his waist, tears in her eyes, Almalexia stayed her distance, observing as Maxwell opened his arms to the rain.

"Please, lord God, I, your servant, ask of thee." Maxwell began, his chest and entire body, reeling with exhaustion. "I ask of thee now, in the name of your children and your son. Wash away their sins, wash away their pain. Wash it all away, as blood in the rain." Maxwell muttered as Harlee placed her head against his chest, still cradling his heart against her own.

Exhausted from his ordeal, Maxwell dropped against Harlee's grip on him. Gently, she wrapped her arms around him as Almalexia, removing her jacket, placed it over Maxwell's shoulders. He listlessly turned his head toward Harlee's ear and whispered.

"I thought I told you to leave." He said.

"And you thought I would listen?" She asked. Almalexia hovered over them, protectively, and placed her hands on Maxwell and Harlee's shoulders.

"We should head back. I am curious to find out what became of John and Jules." Almalexia suggested. Maxwell and Harlee both nodded, as the two women helped Maxwell to his feet and draping his arms over their shoulders, supported him.

Chapter 22 – Your Pain Is Your Salvation

Once back in the car, Harlee carefully placed Maxwell's heart back into the cask. Being sure to seal it tightly, while in Maxwell's presence, she tucked the cask away. Almalexia drove, dropping Maxwell and Harlee at the hotel before leaving to check on John and Jules. Cloaked in a shared blanket, they made their way to the penthouse suite, both looking solemn. The clerk at the front desk waved to them nervously as they entered, before returning to his monitor. Upon exiting the elevators, Harlee kicked off her boots, and then removed her pants and vest.

"I am going to take a shower." They both mumbled in unison. Dropping the blanket on the tile, Harlee and Maxwell both moved through the suite, Harlee to her bedroom, Maxwell, the kitchen. Immediately upon reaching the door, Harlee turned her head to see Maxwell's bare back, as he grabbed a bottle of bourbon from the cabinet, while leaning over the counter top for support.

"Would you care to join me?" Harlee asked. "I could go for a drink and the shower in here is bigger." She mentioned, gesturing towards the bathroom. Maxwell turned to face her, eying the bourbon.

Without a word, he grabbed two glasses and followed Harlee into the bedroom. Harlee moved into the bathroom, turning on the water in the shower. Undershirt and panties, already covered in bodily fluids, Harlee climbed into the shower. She placed her back to the wall, allowing the water to wash her clothing and flesh as Maxwell stepped in.

"Care for a drink?" He said, offering her a glass, already filled. Harlee smiled at him as she scoffed.

"After the night I had." She said, grabbing the bottle from Maxwell and took a long draw from it. Maxwell smiled as he climbed in, wearing his briefs and sat beside her. Maxwell closed his eyes, as he tipped his head backwards, allowing the steaming rain to rinse his hair. Harlee stared at him and his chiseled body.

"Drink?" She asked, nudging him with the bottle. He opened his right eye slightly, seeing enough to accept the bottle from her and took a draw from it, himself. Handing it back to her, he continued to sit quietly, his eyes closed.

"Jules will be alright, Maxwell." Harlee said. "Her wounds were not life threatening." She tried to reassure him but felt she failed to do so. Maxwell nodded his head, though he did not look at her.

"John and Almalexia are both alright, as well. Auriel may have escaped but with Balthazar gone, things will be safer, for now."

"What about you?" Maxwell asked, just above a whisper.

"What about me?" Harlee asked, turning the butt of the bottle skywards.

"Are you going to be alright?" He asked her, genuine concern in his voice. Harlee finally allowed her thoughts to sink in, as her depression returned.

"I don't know." She spoke from a broken heart, voice drenched in despair. "I never imagined Cilia would betray me and now Dahlia." She guzzled from the bottle again as she continued to think in deeper layers. Maxwell gently placed his arm around her shoulders, holding her close to him. Harlee entered his embrace openly, placing her head on his chest as she pondered.

"Focus on what you can affect." He told her. "Allow what has happened, to mold you, but do not let it poison you. Focus on the things, which you can change. Otherwise, the weight of the world will crush you, in time." He whispered.

"What of you?" She asked. He smiled, as he took a long pause.

"I will remain." He told her. "That is the only guarantee I have, and the only comfort I can offer." He said as he stood and began washing his body.

"Would you like for me to get out?" He asked, bar of soap in his hand. Harlee shook her head.

"Would you like some privacy?" She asked him. Slowly, Maxwell dropped his briefs and began washing his body. Harlee averted her eyes, only briefly as she snuck several prolonged glances at the man's rippling body and supernatural gifts. Her cheeks growing hot, Harlee turned away again as Maxwell finished and gently massaged her scalp.

"May I?" He asked her, bottle of shampoo in his hand. Harlee stood and turned her back to him as he began washing her hair, his fingers gently digging into her scalp, offering tremendous relief. Harlee closed her eyes and placed her hands over her heart as she fell into the sensation of his hands upon her, caring for her. He placed his hands beneath her chin, cupping the nape of her neck as he gently tipped her head backwards. The water poured down the back of Harlee's head and ran down her back as Maxwell, rinsed her hair, tenderly pulling on it at times.

"Thank you." She told him as he finished.

"Thank you...for not listening." He said as he stepped out of the shower and wrapping a towel around his waist, took the half-drained bottle from Harlee and left the bathroom. Harlee watched as he walked away and stripping off her clothes, thoroughly washed herself. Turning off the water, Harlee stepped out, securing her bathrobe as she walked out into the bedroom and saw Maxwell, sitting on the balcony, in the rain.

She watched him for a moment, as he sat. Not moving, not drinking, simply sitting in the rain, his head to the sky. Harlee walked to the balcony door, hesitant to go out. She could feel her heart, thundering in her chest, daring her to take the step. Harlee slid open the door and was instantly doused in the rain.

"It's purifying, isn't it?" Maxwell asked her, as he had before.

"You told me once before, your pain is your salvation." She raised her voice, to be heard over the rain.

"I did." He answered, not taking his eyes from the sky.

"And that, at times, when the pain is too much. It is alright to numb it, for a time."

"Until you find the strength to go on." He finished.

"The only problem with that is I don't know how to numb it. All I feel, is this ache where my heart once resided. A hole, where all I loved was torn away."

"You will find a way and you will endure." He muttered again.

"How do you do it?" She asked him, her heart racing faster than ever.

"How do I what?" He asked her.

"How do you numb the pain? And find your strength again?" She asked. Maxwell thought for a moment and raised the bottle.

"A stiff drink can allow a temporary mend." He suggested. "In small amounts, give you a chance to sort your thoughts." Harlee shook her head.

"That isn't what I asked. How do YOU numb that much pain? I have felt the pain in your heart, Maxwell. How can anyone ever hope to numb that much?"

"How do I dull the pain?" He repeated her question to himself, as he turned his head, his moonlight blue eyes, staring through hers, into something so deep as the well of her soul. Harlee eyed Maxwell curiously, her body quivered beneath his gaze as his eyes perceived every last inch of her body.

Harlee's eyes, locked on Maxwell's, she wrenched herself forward, pulled by the invisible strings of a skilled puppeteer, and slowly climbed into his lap as she locked lips with his. Maxwell embraced her, grabbing onto her glutes as he squeezed tightly, returning the embrace of her lips. Harlee grabbed onto the back of his head, digging her fingertips into his skull as he ripped open her bathrobe.

As Harlee's firm, full breasts, trembled from the force, Maxwell stood, helping Harley's clothing to the floor. She dipped back her head as he began kissing on the nape of her neck and slammed her against the outer wall of the balcony. Harlee groaned, as he continued to kiss her, suckling her breast as she reached down, throwing his towel away.

They paused momentarily, to stare at one another, both shocked at what they were doing. The moment soon passed and the two, resumed their carnal activities as both released the entirety, of their pent up feelings. Harlee dug her heels into Maxwell's lower back, as her thighs attempted to crush him, within their grasp.

Maxwell gently twisted Harlee upside down, as he burrowed his face into her upturned pelvis. Harlee cried out with excitement as she felt herself, dousing Maxwell, in a spray of ejaculate fluid. Maxwell paid no mind, as he continued to feast upon her, without relent.

Harlee, with no hope of escape, opened her eyes long enough to notice his throbbing member and latched onto it, with her mouth. As she began to suck upon it, as if she would drown without its gifts, she was forced harder against the wall as Maxwell thrusted against her face.

Harlee, accepting all he had to offer, gripped onto his waist tightly as she unleashed wave upon wave of excrement into his accepting mouth. His tongue, provided a cavalcade of tantric convulsions, which ran the entirety of her body, until she felt he were soon to unbind her eternal spirit.

Harlee worked the entirety of Maxwell's physicality, hands working all that her mouth could not as the man's musculature tensed and he groaned. Gently stroking with one hand, that which was not being swallowed whole, Harlee rapidly increased her efforts, in correspondence to his muscles' contractions. Graciously, she accepted him as he released in her mouth as she into his.

Flipping her back over, Maxwell pinned her against the glass door, smearing her breasts and vagina against it as he entered her from behind. Harlee cried out in bliss as she felt the man, pressing her diaphragm with every thrust. Working with him, Harlee propped herself against the frame of the door, leveraging her body and tilting her pelvis back, allowing her to press back against him.

Eyes closed, every last inch of her body tingling, Harlee breathed against the glass, panting as she worked the penetrating force behind her, hard as she could. As the glass fogged over completely, she finally felt a surge of release, powerful enough to cause her knees to buckle. As the strength left her legs, Maxwell caught her in his arms and pulling out, swept her off from her feet and carried her into the bedroom.

Laying her back down on the bed, Maxwell spread her legs as far as her athletic body allowed and bruising her glutes with the severity of his grip, penetrated her again. Arching his back, he ensured the entire length of his supernatural gifts, explored Harlee in a way, which robbed her of all other senses.

She moaned, as she had never done before, her hands gripping onto anything they could find as her body balanced on the fulcrum of Maxwell's grasp. He continued to ravage her body. She screamed out with each successive orgasm, until her grip failed her and she remained no more than a willing passenger on the Maxwell experience.

She could feel sweat coating her entire body and felt as his, dripped onto her naked form from the extended session. Harlee thanked each and every last deity she could think of, for the man's endurance as she fought hard, to find her second wind. She tasted salt, as every pore in her body, grew overly saturated, with the essence of their impassioned, rage-filled sex.

Harlee's heart fluttered as she felt her life flitting away, her entire being quaked as she released one last orgasm, feeling as Maxwell filled her from within. Maxwell released her, both of them falling to the bed, Maxwell's shaggy chest against her bare torso. They both breathed heavily as Maxwell kissed her sweetly, while petting her hair. Harlee returned with her own affection, rubbing the small of his back.

As he pulled out of her, she filled her lungs at last, though as he had once promised, she felt his essence, continuing to consume her. He lay down beside her as she snuggled into him, too exhausted to rise from the bed. She felt, as her heart slowly changed pace, while listening to the beating in his chest. Her breathing leveled out and she closed her eyes, exhaustion quickly claiming her.

Harlee lay in her bed, gently woken from Maxwell's stirring. She looked up and saw him sitting at the foot of the bed, staring out the window. She slowly rose to a seated position, tucking the sheet beneath her arms, covering herself as she sat, watching him.

"Did I wake you?" He asked without turning to face her.

"It is alright. You couldn't sleep?" She asked him.

"I did for a short while. Please, go back to sleep." Maxwell suggested. Harlee smiled, dropping the blanket.

"Aren't you going to tuck me in?" She said, a naughty smile on her face. Maxwell returned her smile as he slowly crawled towards her on all fours. Harlee tensed as she wriggled her body into position, preparing to be devoured once more. Maxwell's skin slid across hers as she felt his hot breath on her chest and neck. Slowly, his lips pioneered the course to hers, her thighs around his waist, ready to accept him.

"BOOM!" Harlee and Maxwell both turned to face the window, as the room grew bright. In the distance, they saw as flames arose from the Tri Corps Headquarters building. The wind picked up aggressively as several more explosions, sounded off. Harlee and Maxwell both leapt from the bed, searching for clothes. Maxwell ran from the room, to borrow some of John's. As Harlee began sliding on her panties, she stood, hearing the elevator doors ring.

"GET DOWN!" She heard Maxwell yell, as the sound of assault rifle fire permeated the air. Harlee dropped to the floor as holes punched through the walls. Crawling on her stomach, she neared the edge of the bed and grabbing her undershirt, covered her torso. Maxwell cautiously moved back into the room, and ducked down beside her, quickly checking her over to ensure she was unharmed.

"Stay down." Maxwell whispered in her ear, as he pressed his body down on top of hers. Gently, Maxwell placed a pistol beside Harlee, which she accepted.

"What is going on?" She asked.

"It appears as though my family has come home." He said. "The Grey Brides have made their move." He said as he slithered off from her.

"What do you propose?" She asked.

"Wait for my signal." He said as she felt him passing over her feet. She watched as Maxwell, still down on all fours, slowly opened the door and peered into the darkness. She saw lights, beaming across the room as men searched for them. Maxwell looked up and shot to the ceiling. As she saw him, crawling away, she could hear the radio chatter on the shoulder of the one of the men.

"Alpha, have you engaged the target?" A woman's voice sounded off.

"Yes, we have confirmed Maxwell's presence. What are your orders?" A man replied as Maxwell exited the bedroom, continuing to crawl across the ceiling, Harlee losing sight of him.

"Finish the mission." Was all the woman said as the radio chatter, cut out. Harlee slowly army crawled towards the door, gun pointed. She noticed at once, as the lights turned to the ceiling and the guns opened fire. There were no screams, no signs of panic, only highly trained, military efficiency as the men engaged Maxwell. Using the sound of the muzzles to cover her movements, Harlee moved into the doorway and trained her gun at the back of one of the passing men.

"We have him held back. Find the woman, kill her." One of the men spoke as Harlee rolled back against the side of the wall, adjacent to the door, gun trained. The man gently kicked against the door, pressing it open as his light began unveiling the room. Harlee held her breath as she anticipated what was about to happen.

The moment the man peered around the corner, Harlee fired three rounds at the underside of his chin. As the man toppled backwards, Harlee rolled away as bullets began spraying into her bedroom. Staying low to the ground, Harlee managed to lie at the dead man's side and trained his gun back through the wall, towards the bullets' source.

As Harlee opened fire, she heard men shuffling aside, their frantically waving lights, confirming it. Harlee emptied the clip and grabbing another from the man's hip, ejected the magazine, while loading another. She ducked down behind the body as she was met with return fire. Harlee, being much smaller than her downed adversary, remained concealed as she felt a number of bullets striking the corpse.

"GRAH!" She heard the bestial roar of Maxwell as she saw him leap through the darkness, sinking his fangs into the throat of one of the men as he forced his meal to aim and fire upon his comrades. The remaining three soldiers, did their best to move out of the way as Harlee added to the firefight. Flanked, one of the men dropped before he could find cover as the other two, managed to dodge many of the bullets, avoiding any fatal wounds.

Ducking behind the furniture, the two men continued firing, in an attempt to tag either of their targets. Maxwell quickly ran out of bullets as he tossed the drained body towards its comrades and charged. Both men opened fire as Harlee reloaded, Maxwell taking several hits in the process. Harlee jumped up, catching the attention of both men. She fired as Maxwell pounced.

Harlee's target dropped, blood spraying out the back of its skull as Maxwell tackled the other. Harlee, rising to her bare feet, shuffled through the bullet casings and plaster as she walked up on Maxwell. Maxwell stood over top of the convulsing man, feeding on him ravenously as she watched bullet holes in Maxwell's back, seal over.

Harlee stepped backward as blood spurted out at her. As Maxwell finished with his first, he moved toward the second and bit into him. Harlee moved to say something but hesitated as Maxwell continued.

"Maxwell? Are you still, you?" She asked nervously, pointing the gun. Maxwell stopped and turned his blood soaked face towards her as his eyes flashed back to normal.

"I am sorry, I am still here." He said, confused. "I am not sure what came over me. I just felt, so hungry." He ripped off a piece of the man's clothing and wiped his face clean. Harlee stared down in horror at the ravaged bodies.

"Alpha, the strike on the others was unsuccessful. What is your status?" The radio chatter came back. Harlee crouched down, carefully tiptoeing around the blood as she grabbed the radio.

"Who is this?" She asked. No response came as another loud explosion, sounded off in the distance.

"Get dressed." Maxwell said as he moved into John's bedroom. Harlee stood and ran to her room, to finish dressing herself.

A short few minutes later, Maxwell and Harlee, fully dressed, took up the weapons of their fallen foes and called the elevator. Maxwell grabbed his hat and coat on his way out, as Harlee zipped one of Dahlia's old jackets. The doors closed, leaving the destroyed room, behind. As they rode down, Harlee whispered to Maxwell.

"The other attack, do you think it was John, Jules, and Almalexia."

"They said they were unsuccessful. I trust they handled themselves." Maxwell spoke back as the elevator doors opened. As they stepped out, Harlee moved over to the desk, the clerk lie face down, dead. She quickly scanned the lobby. Several other bodies lie strewn as Maxwell walked towards the door. Harlee followed him, looking back at the wanton destruction ahead of her.

Several buildings were ablaze, mobs of people, worked together in an attempt to put them out. Harlee turned her head at the sound of a parked car, exploding. She searched carefully for any signs of what had caused the warzone.

"Up there!" Maxwell growled as he wrapped his arm around Harlee's waist and jumped. Harlee held on tightly as he latched onto the railing of the fire escape and jumping again, landed atop the building. Just ahead of them, several forms, clad entirely in black, tactical gear turned and fled.

Harlee aimed her weapon and fired as Maxwell charged. Both figures dropped, slid as the bullets sailed passed and jumped, launching themselves from the building top. Rolling as their feet touched the ground, they continued to run as Maxwell leapt after them, leaving Harlee behind.

Holding no intentions of staying out of the fight, Harlee charged, knowing Maxwell's gift to her had offered her some physical enhancements. Arms fully propelling her body, Harlee's feet touched the edge of the landing and she pressed off, launching herself into the air. As her feet struck the roof, she stumbled out of surprise but continued to run.

She carefully trained her rifle and aiming low, fired two three round bursts. One target, jumped, while the other who slid again, took three rounds in the back. As the injured member slowly rose, Maxwell caught up to him and shattered his legs. The soldier attempted to draw his weapon as Harlee kicked it out of his hand. Drawing a blade, the soldier slashed at Harlee, who with little effort, disarmed him again.

"Who are you working for!?" She yelled, pointing the gun at the soldier's head. Without a moment's hesitation, he drew a second blade and before Harlee had time to react, drove it through the side of his own head.

"SHIT!" She yelled as she looked up at Maxwell, who had leapt to another set of buildings and was still pursing the others. Harlee jumped the next clearing and ran after Maxwell.

"Stop him!" A woman yelled, as she and her remaining men, ran in separate directions. As she jumped to the next rooftop, her men turned and trained their guns on Maxwell. As they opened fire, Maxwell launched himself in the air and Harlee dodged behind cover.

She whipped around the corner and returned fire as she saw John and Almalexia running from the right flank, firing on the enemy as Maxwell propelled himself passed, still in pursuit of the woman. Harlee sprinted forward, using John and Almalexia's distraction to pick off one of the men. She dropped to the ground, sliding behind cover beside them.

"Follow Maxwell!" Almalexia said as she sprang forward with supernatural speed, moving in on the enemy, drawing their fire.

"Go Harlee! I'll cover you!" John said as he trained his rifle. Harlee nodded her head as she readied herself in a four-point stance.

"GO!" John called as he jumped out and began firing on the enemy, Almalexia attacking them from the front as Harlee sprang. Charging the ledge, she propelled herself over the gap and continued sprinting as she crossed the next roof and cleared the next jump, in pursuit of Maxwell. She could see him, up above, on the next roof, engaged in combat with the woman.

Ignoring the ladder, Harlee jumped up onto the building's electrical box, three step jumped and using her upper body, launched herself up above and joined Maxwell. Maxwell dipped to the side, avoiding a blade as he spun and kicked. The woman blocked his kick and threw her knife as she stepped back. Maxwell, catching the blade, threw it back. Narrowly avoiding the blade, the woman rolled backwards as Harlee slammed into her.

As the two women, tumbled, the masked woman, kicked off from Harlee. Harlee, reaching out, latched onto the woman's mask, as she was forced backwards. Maxwell descended from the air, attempting to strike the woman, who through a series of agile movements, launched herself backwards, back turned.

Harlee continued after the woman, as Maxwell jumped in front of her, arms wide. As Harlee moved from behind Maxwell's back, she saw several more armed men, weapons trained on them, standing beside the blonde haired woman. The woman, slowly turned to face them, wide, beautiful smile on her face. Maxwell tensed, his whole body shook as she stared at him, eyes flashing with obvious delight.

"Oh Maxwell, it is so good to see you, after so many years. You look well. I am glad to see the years have been kind to you. If you will excuse me, however, I have work to do. There is a resurrection to consider." She said as she turned and walked away.

"WAIT!" Maxwell yelled, stepping forward as a burst of rounds, fired at his feet. Moving backwards, he continued to shield Harlee as she tried to see around him.

"Goodbye, Maxwell. I will be sure to send you an invitation to the party." The woman spoke as she and her men disappeared from sight. As they vanished, another explosion sounded off from the ledge they had stood on. Maxwell turned, placing his body over Harlee as she shielded herself.

As the explosion cleared, Maxwell turned and launched himself up above. Harlee, looking up ran after Maxwell. Climbing up to the ledge, Harlee jumped up onto the next building and saw Maxwell standing. She walked up to him, as he continued to stand, staring out at the city, no sign of those he pursued, to be found.

"Maxwell?" Harlee began. "Maxwell, are you alright?" She asked him, noticing the tuft of blanket and the rosary, in his hand.

"Victoria?" Maxwell whispered into the night, as all around him, his city burned, ash falling from the sky, instead of rain.

Made in the USA
Lexington, KY
15 May 2017